"Frimmer sews together this unsettling family drama with both surgical precision and an abiding sense of love. Her medical fiction will strongly appeal to fans of Grey's Anatomy and Kimmery Martin." — **Sandra Block** author of *What Happened That Night*

"Heather Frimmer's gripping novel pulled me in from the first page. *Better to Trust* is a nuanced exploration of secrets, identity, and family. Told with equal parts insight and intrigue, the story reminds us that we never know what those closest to us may be carrying inside. This compelling blend of medicine and mystery will keep readers turning pages to the end." — **Saumya Dave**, author of *What A Happy Family*

"Heather Frimmer's latest novel, *Better to Trust*, is an unforgettable story in which lives are literally at stake. Whether facing a critical operation, the potential destruction of an esteemed career or the conjunction of marriage with unresolved sexuality, a triumph of voices emerges—entangled yet somehow harmonic as a symphony. Frimmer's richly hewn and deeply connected characters draw you in and stay with you long after the book is closed." — **Maureen Joyce Connolly**, author of *Little Lovely Things*

"Tense, insightful and full of heart, Heather Frimmer's *Better to Trust* tackles complex themes of opioid addiction, sexuality, medical ethics and family ties. Populated with intriguing, multidimensional characters, it will keep you engrossed until the end." — **Daniela Petrova**, author of *Her Daughter's Mother*

"Heather Frimmer's second novel, *Better to Trust*, plunges readers into the lives of three connected characters: Alison, a woman dealing with a debilitating brain condition and questioning her sexuality, Grant, Alison's neurosurgeon, who is secretly addicted to prescription pills, and Sadie, Grant's troubled teenage daughter. I was immediately drawn in by Alison as she navigates her road to recovery after brain surgery. Each step in her struggle felt earned and real—I couldn't help but root for her. At the same time, she must face her crumbling marriage and grapple with her evolving sexual identity. Her story is further complicated by Grant's and Sadie's narratives, and the ways they intersect. Frimmer has written an emotional page-turner that fans of women's fiction will not be able to put down." — **Sarahlyn Bruck**, author of *Daytime Drama* and *Designer You*

"*Better to Trust* is a multi-faceted, captivating, unputdownable story. Frimmer weaves a narrative rich with insight into the issues plaguing modern teens and couples. Using her medical knowledge, Frimmer shines a light on the complex world of medical ethics, allowing the intensely intriguing plot to ignite." — **Galia Gichon**, author of *The Accidental Suffragist*

BETTER
TO
TRUST

BETTER
TO
TRUST

a novel

HEATHER FRIMMER

Wyatt-MacKenzie Publishing
DEADWOOD, OREGON

Better to Trust

Heather Frimmer

ISBN: 978-1-954332-03-4
Library of Congress Control Number: 2021936451

Wyatt-MacKenzie Publishing
DEADWOOD, OREGON

www.WyattMacKenzie.com

To my family
With all my love and gratitude

*Better to trust the man who is frequently in error
than the one who is never in doubt.*

ERIC SEVAREID

CHAPTER ONE

Alison

June 3, 2019

ALISON LEANED HER BODY WEIGHT on the walker, using all her strength to slide the damn thing forward with her left hand. Grunting with the effort, she advanced her left leg and dragged the dead weight of her right leg behind her.

"Good job." Svetlana pointed down the long corridor. "Soon we'll make it to the end." Alison found it odd that Svetlana used the word "we" all the time. She was trying to make it seem like they were in this thing together, on the same team working towards a common goal, but she wasn't the invalid, Alison was.

She stopped to breathe. The end of the hallway was only a few hundred feet away, but it seemed like miles, every step a slow torture. She'd made some progress since she'd transferred to Spaulding Rehab Center from the hospital two weeks ago, if dragging herself from her room to the next could be considered progress.

"Let's go." Svetlana slid the walker forward. "We can do this. We're not done yet for today."

"Okay," Alison managed. She was a woman of few words these days. Her thoughts flowed fine, but the connection between her brain and her mouth was tenuous. She'd never even heard of aphasia before this whole thing happened. When she first heard the word, she'd pictured ambrosia, that sickeningly sweet fruit salad great aunt Frieda used to bring to family functions, but the more she learned about aphasia the more it became clear that the similarity ended with the sound of the words. Aphasia was not pink or fluffy or sweet.

"I'm really proud of you. We've been putting in the effort and it shows." Svetlana said, as if doing two hours of physical therapy a day had been Alison's choice. There was a time when doing a two-hour work-out at the gym was one of her greatest joys, when running a faster mile or setting a new personal bench press record gave her a sense of accomplishment, the natural high lingering long after she arrived home. Now, she dreaded these therapy sessions, knowing the effort it would take to move just a few feet.

"Al...alright," Alison stammered. She would like to tell Svetlana that some days she'd rather give up before they'd even started, but this was the best she could do. Since learning about her condition, she had become a self-made expert on aphasia. Trapped with her thoughts, she'd spent hours on her iPad reading books and research papers, personal memoirs from people who've had strokes or bleeds or tumors and lived to tell their stories, articles from speech and occupational therapists about how to rehabilitate after these devastating events. The YouTube videos of patients with aphasia were horrible to watch, but she couldn't make herself look away.

She felt thankful she didn't have the fluent type of aphasia. Those unfortunate souls spouted endless streams of gibberish. They seemed to know exactly what they wanted to say, but the words changed on the trip from their brains to their mouths, the train tracks crisscrossing over each other so that the messages come out mangled and unintelligible. The rails in Alison's brain, on the other hand, were straight but severely damaged. Occasionally, a train finished the journey: "okay" and "alright" had the greatest chance of reaching their destination; but many of them crashed and burned. No matter how hard she tried, she couldn't make the words come out.

"I have an idea," Svetlana said, stopping at a row of chairs along the wall. "We're going to learn how to stand up from a chair."

"Nnnnn ... now?" Alison wondered why Svetlana introduced new challenges near the end of their sessions when Alison already felt depleted.

Svetlana helped Alison maneuver the walker in front of a chair and motioned for her to take a seat. "Yes, now. This skill will come in handy, especially once you get home."

Alison collapsed into the chair and exhaled, grateful for the brief respite. She considered telling Svetlana she wasn't up for any new tricks right now, but she knew the woman wouldn't take no for an answer. When Grant had said Svetlana was the best physical therapist in town, he must have known she would be a good fit: tough, aggressive, and no nonsense. "No" wasn't in her vocabulary.

Svetlana lined the walker up in front of Alison and took a seat next to her. "Okay, we're going to lean forward, hold onto the walker and bend your knees," she said, demonstrating the posture.

Alison tried to maneuver her body into that position, but it didn't feel right. Before her surgery, her body had always done exactly what she'd asked, but now, even the simplest things were a struggle.

"Lean more and bend deeper." Svetlana adjusted Alison's arms and legs with her hands. "Now we're going to put weight on the walker and press up through the bottom of our feet."

Though Alison could picture what Svetlana described, making her body follow suit was another story. She leaned forward and pressed as hard as she could through her left arm and the bottom of her feet, trying to engage her quads. Her legs burned and fought against her. She gave one last push and suddenly she was almost there. When she was nearly standing, Alison began teetering to the left. Instead of keeping her eyes up as Svetlana always instructed, she looked down at the floor, trying to regain her balance.

"Amazing job," Svetlana said, taking hold of Alison's left arm and guiding her back to the chair.

"Fe ... fell." Alison managed.

"You didn't fall," Svetlana held her hand out for a fist bump. "You stood up. It's not going to be perfect the first time. We'll work more on this tomorrow."

As Alison's hand met Svetlana's, she felt relieved that the session was almost over, but also proud of her determination and accomplishment. She'd harnessed the power within her and almost stood without help, something she'd never thought possible. It had taken all the effort she could muster, but she'd put her mind to it and done the work.

The floor clerk stopped next to them. "Mrs. Jacobs has a visitor," she said.

"She's not supposed to have guests during therapy," Svetlana said. Alison wondered who it could be. Her husband, Michael, always visited right after work, so he wasn't due for at least a half hour.

"She said it's important."

Svetlana helped Alison up and guided the walker into a turn. "Okay. Give us a few minutes."

With lots of lifting and shimmying, Svetlana settled Alison back into bed. She propped Alison's right leg onto a pillow and raised the back of the bed to a comfortable angle. After Svetlana left, Alison heard Cynthia's voice in the hall, making small talk with the clerk about the recent early summer heat wave. Leave it to her sister to talk to anyone—the cashier at Whole Foods, her massage therapist, the exterminator—anyone willing to lavish her with attention. Alison wondered why Cynthia was here today. She hadn't bothered visiting since well before Alison was transferred here.

"Hello," Cynthia came in and planted a kiss on Alison's cheek. "It's so good to see you." She looked like she'd been crying, her eyelids pink and puffy. Probably overreacting to something or other. Classic Cynthia, Alison thought. Alison was the one in rehab, not Cynthia. Grant had operated on Alison's brain, not Cynthia's, so if anyone had a reason to cry, it was her, not her histrionic sister.

"Been a ... while," Alison managed.

"I know." Cynthia took a seat. "We've had a lot going on at home. Trying to get everything sorted out. There's been so much going on. I don't even know where to start."

"Where ... where?"

"Sadie? I left her home to do homework. Maybe she'll come next time."

"No." Alison would have loved to see her fifteen-year-old niece, but that wasn't what she'd been trying to ask. She was wondering why Grant hadn't come today. It was a Monday, so he must be at work, but he'd been coming with Cynthia whenever he could.

"We've had some changes in the family that I want to fill you in on. And I'd rather you hear about it from me than finding out some other way." Cynthia's voice sounded shaky.

"I ... don't."

"I know it sounds vague, but I promise I'll tell you everything. I'm just not sure the best way to say it without making you upset."

All this talking in circles meant Cynthia was hiding something. Maybe her news would explain why Grant hadn't come with her. Could he be sick? So many of their friends had received unexpected diagnoses—cancer, multiple sclerosis, heart disease—but Grant seemed so strong, somehow above the fray. Alison prayed that Sadie was alright. She couldn't bear it if something bad was going on with her.

"Okay," Cynthia continued, "I should just tell you. We're always honest with each other. I don't know why this is so hard for me."

"What?" Alison widened her eyes, trying to tell Cynthia to come out with it already. She could handle whatever her sister had to say.

"There was an article," Cynthia took a deep breath, "in the Newton Reporter ... it's about Grant."

An article about Grant didn't seem like earth-shattering news. He was always being written up for something or other related to his job, but the look on Cynthia's face told Alison this article was different.

"I didn't know anything was wrong," Cynthia went on. "I thought he had everything under control."

Alison had no idea what Cynthia was talking about, but she could tell by the pitch of Cynthia's voice and the terrified look on her face that whatever was going on was a big deal.

"I can't imagine what this could do to his career." Cynthia covered her face with her hands.

"What ...?" Alison had no clue what was going on.

"Please, Alison. I need this to stay between us," Cynthia pleaded. "For the sake of Grant's career, I need you to lay low."

Alison's husband, Michael, entered the room holding a newspaper. "Alison, you have to see this," he said, stopping short when he noticed Cynthia at the bedside.

"What is this all about?" Michael asked, holding the paper in the air. "Did Grant do something wrong?"

Cynthia stood up. "I can explain. It isn't how it looks. He's a good surgeon."

"Does this have anything to do with what happened to Alison?" Michael waved the newspaper at Cynthia. Alison wished he would hand it to her so she could figure out what they were talking about. She needed to see the article for herself.

Cynthia sat back down and started sobbing. "I feel like our family is falling apart."

Michael slapped the newspaper onto the bed. "I don't understand what you're saying. Is there more you're not telling us?"

Alison had never seen him so worked up before. She picked up the paper with her left hand and scanned the headlines on the front page, one of them jumping out at her. She read the first few sentences.

LOCAL NEUROSURGEON SLAMMED WITH LAWSUIT
By Julia Barker

Renowned neurosurgeon, Grant Kaplan, 44, of Newton was formally served with a lawsuit on January 23rd of this year. The plaintiff, Jeffrey Stone, 35, of nearby Lincoln, has completely lost hearing in his left ear since he underwent surgery last year for an acoustic neuroma, a benign brain tumor. The two parties are currently in the discovery phase of the case.

"It's all too much," Cynthia sobbed. "I don't know what to say, how to make things right."

Alison's stomach clenched. She didn't know the full story, but she could tell this was no run of the mill legal suit. There was something Cynthia wasn't sharing and she couldn't help wondering if it had to something do with her surgery.

"I hate to say it, but something seems rotten in Denmark," Michael said.

Cynthia wailed and tried to approach Michael for a hug.

"I think we need some time," Michael stepped back. "I suggest you leave us alone for now."

CHAPTER TWO

Grant

February 5, 2019
Four Months Earlier

GRANT FASTENED THE TITANIUM COVERS over the three burr-holes he had drilled in the skull and pulled the scalp flap back into place. The patient had tripped on the curb while walking his dog, landing headfirst on the cement. He relished the sound of the pneumatic drill as it tunneled through the bone, the sharp pop as the scalpel pierced the dura, and the familiar smell of bone dust in the air, the brain slowly returning to its rightful place against the inner table of the skull. These patients usually awoke from anesthesia feeling much more themselves, their neurologic exams noticeably improved, and their families appreciative of his skill and talent. It was a mindless procedure, but it was nice to have a quick win once in a while. Most of his surgeries, aneurysm clippings and AVM resections, were much more complicated and lasted several hours. It often took days or even weeks to see any improvements, if the patients were so lucky. Even though he was one of the nation's experts on the treatment of vascular malformations, he had to psych himself up before scrubbing in for those cases.

As Grant finished stapling the scalp flap together, he noticed the incision looked swollen, like something was pushing up from underneath. Damn it. With today's packed schedule, he couldn't afford to waste any time. He quickly removed the staples, hoping the nurses wouldn't notice the speed bump. Draining the small collection of blood with a suction catheter, he hummed along with the Charlie Parker saxophone riff coming through the speakers to assure the staff everything was on track. When the bleeder stopped, Grant replaced the staple line and returned the stapler to the instrument tray.

"One down. How many more to go?" He looked over at Wendy, his favorite surgical nurse and right-hand woman. With her bleached blond hair and prominent crow's feet from her two-pack-a-day smoking habit, her look was less than classy, but no one kept an OR running like she did. Though she was nearing retirement, Grant hoped Wendy would stick around for at least a few more years. He had no patience for anything less than exemplary competence and efficiency. In fact, he had filed with the OR director a list of staff members he found acceptable, and only those on the list were allowed to step foot inside his sacred temple.

Wendy checked her schedule. "Craniectomy for a massive MCA stroke. We'll be ready to go within a half hour, Dr. Kaplan."

He pulled off his surgical gown and gloves. "Let's keep moving. I can't afford any delays today."

Grant stepped out for a breather and Vikram Chawla, his preferred anesthesiologist, followed behind. They had trained together during their residencies and had both stayed on here when they graduated. Over time, they'd come to learn each other's habits and eccentricities. Grant didn't need to explain to Vik how he wanted his patients anesthetized, and Vik knew Grant wouldn't tolerate small talk or unnecessary chatter. No blathering about headlines or baseball scores during his operations.

In the hallway, Vik grabbed a paper cup from the top of the water cooler. "How about a drink?"

"With the way my schedule looks today, I could use something stronger," Grant said. "I swear Wendy's trying to kill me."

Vik filled his cup. "It's her job. Keep the OR humming. The quicker the turnover, the better for the bottom line."

"I wouldn't have it any other way. You know that."

"Sometimes it might be nice to have a few minutes to decompress." Vik walked over to the floor-to-ceiling window overlooking the Charles River. "Maybe take a walk outside."

Grant stepped up to the window and looked down at the trees along the river, the bare branches coated with ice. "No sunlight for us."

"Going anywhere for February break?" Vik asked.

"Not this year," Grant said. "Too many surgeries."

"Meera booked a trip to some resort in Mexico. I told her as long as there's no boats."

"Not even the kind where you can see fish through the bottom?" Grant said. "The twins would love it."

"No way. Just thinking about that makes me nauseous. Puking over the railing isn't my idea of a vacation."

"Remember the time you lost your lunch on the booze cruise before you'd even had a drink?" Grant asked.

"The memory is burned in my brain forever."

Grant pulled his Claritin bottle out of his pocket and slid one into his mouth. He didn't normally need it midday, but with today's line-up, he'd make an exception. Some days he needed a little extra push to reach the finish line.

"Allergies still bothering you?" Vik eyed the bottle. "In February?"

Grant nodded and put it back into his pocket.

"Maybe you should take the family somewhere, too," Vik said. "It's good to take a breather from this place once in a while."

"I don't know if I can spend that much time with Sadie. Her teen drama is over the top these days."

"That bad?" Vik asked.

"She's a bit Jekyll and Hyde," Grant said. "One minute she's my sweet little girl, and the next she's the devil incarnate."

"I'm not looking forward to the teenage years." Vik tossed his cup into the garbage can next to the water cooler. "The twins want to be with me all the time. It's exhausting, but not bad for the old ego."

"Enjoy it while it lasts," Grant said. "Sadie spends every minute with her friends."

"How's high school going?"

"Not sure," Grant said. "She doesn't really share much. When we ask her what she did in school, she always says 'nothing'."

"This is when kids start to experiment with things."

"Like what?"

"Smoking, sex, smack," Vik chuckled. "So many selections

available to teenagers these days."

"Sadie would never do anything like that," Grant said.

"Just make sure you keep an eye on her." Vik flipped through a magazine someone had left on the window ledge. "Seriously? You made the list again?"

"What?"

Vik held up the copy of *Boston Magazine* and pointed to the page. "It's getting a little ridiculous."

Grant shrugged. "I can't help being the best."

"They don't even have a section for anesthesiologists. It's like we're not even doctors."

"But you still pull in the big bucks."

"Good point," Vik said. "I may not get the accolades, but I'll be able to pay for college."

Wendy poked her head into the hall. "Doctors, the next case is teed up."

Before going back into the OR, Grant's cell phone buzzed in his pocket. He pulled it out, saw Michael's name and pressed ignore. His brother-in-law was probably calling to drone on about the Red Sox spring training. Grant was a lifelong fan, but Michael's passion for the team bordered on obsession. Grant would call him back on his way home when he had nothing better to do than listen to monologues about batting averages and stolen base percentages.

"Wendy, what would I do without you to keep me in line?" he called from the sink, as he scrubbed up for the next case.

"You'd be nowhere without me, Dr. Kaplan," she said.

Grant slipped his arms into the surgical gown she held open for him and waited for her to tie it around his waist. "Okay, team," he said, stepping up to the operating table. "Let's crack this one open before it's too late."

❀

After he finished the last surgery, Grant went to the locker room. He loved the feel of a hot shower after a long day in the OR, the way the water washed the burnt smell of bone dust from his hair and the dried sweat from his body, leaving him invigorated and ready to face the rest of his day. Despite the scalp bleed as he'd closed, the subdural drainage had been the highlight of the day. The other patients he'd operated on were pretty much gorked. He never said that derogatory term out loud, but that didn't stop him from thinking it. If those patients regained any neurologic function it would be nothing short of a miracle. As he rinsed the shampoo from his hair, his recent malpractice case flashed through mind. Lawsuits weren't uncommon in neurosurgery, but it was still an annoyance he didn't have time for in his busy life. He hoped his lawyer would settle it soon and make it go away. He shut off the water and wrapped a towel around his waist.

It always felt so refreshing to put on street clothes after a day in the OR. Sitting down on the bench, he looked at his phone to see he'd missed three more calls from Michael with two voicemails, and two missed calls from Cynthia. He decided to call Michael back first to find out what could be so important. It had to be something more than baseball.

"Where have you been?" Michael asked.

"I was scrubbed in."

"Alison's in the hospital. Wellesley Community. She passed out at school and came in by ambulance."

"Jesus. What happened?"

"I'm not sure yet. They're still running tests."

"Did she vasovagal?"

"What the fuck does that mean?" Michael said.

"Sorry." Grant often used medical terms without realizing.

"She passed out," Michael continued, "And it's all so confusing, and we needed you. We *need* you, I mean."

"What did the tests show? Did they do a CT or MRI?"

"I don't know. It looked like a donut."

"Okay and did they give you results?" Grant hoped they had done a CTA and an MRI, but he knew it wasn't likely at that podunk hospital.

"They said she's bleeding into her head and they're not sure why. I don't know how this happened. She's so healthy."

"Shit," Grant said. He gathered his keys and wallet, and slammed his locker. "I'm heading to the garage right now. Is Cynthia with you?"

"Yeah, she's sitting right here."

"Okay. Tell her I'll be there in twenty-five minutes."

As he ran down the stairs and into the hospital garage, Grant thought about what could have caused the bleed. The most common cause of spontaneous intracranial hemorrhage was hypertension, but Alison definitely didn't have high blood pressure. She was a vegetarian and a fitness fanatic, an early adopter of all the newest exercise crazes. Lately, she'd been obsessed with some new surfboard class at her health club. That left more ominous reasons—tumor or aneurysm or some other congenital vascular malformation— none of which spelled good news.

He drove out of the garage, took a few quick turns through the narrow cobblestone streets, before speeding onto Storrow Drive to the Mass Pike. He accelerated and merged into an opening in the left lane, ignoring the honking and raised middle finger of the driver behind him as he considered his next steps. First of all, Alison should be transferred to his hospital as soon as possible. A community hospital was no place for anything more serious than constipation or Strep throat.

He used the voice recognition in his car to call Calvin Shin, one of his partners at Downtown Neurosurgical Associates, and the one he respected most. Cal was the only other neurosurgeon who consistently made it onto the *Boston Magazine* list every year.

"Hello?"

"Hey, Cal," Grant said. "I have a bit of a situation."

"What's up, bud?"

"Cynthia's sister had a spontaneous brain hemorrhage a few hours ago. She's in the ER at Wellesley Community. From what I can tell, the staff is sitting with their thumbs up their asses."

"Alison? Shit—that sounds like their MO. What can I do?"

"She needs a real work-up," Grant said. "They haven't even done a CTA yet."

"We need to get her over to the mecca," Cal said.

"My thought exactly," Grant said. "Do you think I can transfer her to your service?"

"Whatever you need, bud," Cal said. "I can come in tonight and get things going once she arrives."

Grant turned the car into the hospital garage and parked in

the first open spot. "Thanks, Cal. I'll keep you posted." As he hung up, gratitude surged through him. He was so lucky to have friends like Cal and Vik by his side no matter what.

❀

Grant entered the ER and followed a nurse through the automatic doors. If he checked in at the desk in the waiting room, the high school dropout at the window would make him fill out every line of the stick-on name badge, and he needed to get in there as soon as possible.

Walking down the ER corridor, he passed an elderly man repeatedly moaning, "Can I get some help over here?", an obese woman whose oxygen mask was sliding off the side of her face, and a teenage boy lying on a gurney in a pair of red underwear. Finally, he saw Alison in one of the last patient rooms and she waved at him to come in. Doing a quick inventory, he noticed her pink skin and symmetrical smile. He felt relieved to see her looking healthy, alert, and neurologically intact. It must be a small bleed, he thought with relief.

Cynthia sat on the chair next to the bed, holding Alison's hand.

His wife stood up when Grant walked in. "What took you so long?"

Grant could tell by the tone of her voice she was stressed. She had always been protective of her little sister and was probably feeling out of her element here. He gave Cynthia a peck on the cheek before leaning down to hug Alison.

"I came as fast as I could," he said. "Where's Michael?"

"He went to grab something for us to eat," Cynthia said. "I think he couldn't stand all the waiting."

"How are you feeling?" he asked Alison.

"I've been better. It's like my head is being squeezed in a vice."

"You passed out at school?"

"Yeah. I don't really know what happened. One minute I was fine and the next thing I knew, I woke up in an ambulance."

"It sounds like you were out pretty good. Were you doing anything strenuous when you passed out? Exercising or something?"

"No," Alison said quickly. "Nothing out of the ordinary."

"Has the doctor been in to talk to you yet?"

"We saw a PA," Cynthia said, "but we're waiting for the neurosurgeon to see her."

"They probably don't have someone in-house. Did the PA say what the scan showed?"

"She said I have a bleed in my brain," Alison said. "That I may need to stay overnight."

"That's it? How big is the bleed? Did she say anything about mass effect or midline shift?"

"Grant, quit it with the doctor speak," Cynthia said. "Alison is anxious enough as it is."

"I'm just trying to gather the necessary—"

Before he could finish his thought, a doctor in a white coat strode into the room. Grant knew right away by his straight posture and confident gait that this had to be the neurosurgeon. No weak egos in my specialty, he thought.

The man walked past him and stopped at the side of the stretcher with his back to Grant. "I'm the neurosurgeon on call," he said to Alison. "I understand you passed out at work."

"Yes," Alison said. "I don't remember much."

He asked Alison to squeeze his fingers with both hands, and then instructed her to lift her legs off the table while he pushed down on them. Grant watched him perform a perfunctory neurologic exam.

"Are you going to grace us with an introduction?" Grant asked. At this point he didn't care if he sounded rude. This guy wasn't even close to good enough to take care of Alison. He had to figure out a way to get her out of here, and quick.

"I'm Dr. Howie," the doctor said, turning around to shake Grant's hand.

Grant recognized the crooked smirk. "Seth?" Seth Howie had graduated near the bottom of Grant's medical school class at Tufts. He had matched in family medicine and only managed to switch to neurosurgery when a resident at a program somewhere in the corn belt had a sudden psychotic break. Grant and his friends used to call him "Howie will he graduate" behind his back.

"You escaped Kansas," Grant said.

14

Seth smiled. "Iowa. I was counting the days. What are you doing here, Grant?"

"Alison is my sister-in-law. So, what can you tell me, Seth?" Grant wanted to gather all the information so he could ship her out. He didn't want her here to begin with, and the fact that Howie was on the case only increased his sense of urgency.

"Alison suffered a spontaneous parenchymal hemorrhage in her left frontal lobe, of uncertain etiology," Seth said. "We're trying to sort out the differential diagnosis."

"What does that mean?" Alison asked.

"Sorry," Seth said. "We need to do a few more tests to figure out why you're bleeding into your brain."

"Are there any deficits?" Grant asked.

"A little weakness in her right hand," Seth said. "Other than that, she's neurologically intact." Mastering the neurologic exam took years of practice, and Grant knew he couldn't trust Seth's results. He itched to do the exam himself, but that would have to wait until Alison was on his turf.

"I don't feel so intact," Alison said. "I can't even remember what happened. And the whole school must have seen me being carted away. It's all so strange."

"I'm going to take care of everything," Grant said. "Seth, I'm requesting a transfer. Calvin Shin will be accepting her to his service."

"This is something we can deal with here," Seth said. "There's no need—"

"Need or no need, that's what I want, and you're going to make it happen."

CHAPTER THREE

Sadie

February 5, 2019

"WE HAVE TO TAKE OUR SHOES OFF in the entryway," Sadie said, opening the front door of her house and leading Piper inside.

"Nice digs," Piper said without acknowledging Sadie's comment. The soles of her black boots made a clomping noise on the wood floor. She ran her finger along the top of the table along the wall and then picked up Sadie's mom's favorite abstract sculpture.

"No," Sadie said, taking it from Piper and placing it back on the display stand. "My mom doesn't like it when I touch things."

"I'm just admiring. That looks expensive."

"I guess." Her mother loved to spend money, but since they had just met, Sadie didn't feel comfortable discussing that with Piper. Walking over to the wall to take off her boots, she hoped Piper would follow suit. She couldn't bring herself to ask her again.

She took off her new fitted leather jacket and hung it on the bannister. At the beginning of the school year, Sadie had gotten a new wardrobe. The transition to high school was the perfect time to reinvent herself, to stop being the boring girl and stand out a little. Tired of plain t-shirts and jeans and tennis sneakers, she'd picked out a pair of lace-up boots, black jeans with rips in the knees and a few black and gray tops. She'd even dyed her hair black and started wearing thick mascara and black eye-liner. Learning how to put on the eye-liner proved much harder than she'd expected. The women in the YouTube videos made it look effortless, but Sadie ended up with rings around her eyes and had to keep wiping it off and starting over.

When her mom first saw her hair, she'd pursed her lips and looked away. Later, Sadie had heard her parents talking about it in their bedroom.

"What's gotten into her?" her mother said.

"It's just hair," her father said. "It'll grow back."

"I just don't want people to get the wrong impression of her. I want her to make friends and be happy."

"We have to give her a little leeway. She's growing up."

"Sometimes I feel like maybe we're giving her too much rope."

"Leave her alone, Cyn. She's fine."

Annoyed with her mom's judgy tone, Sadie also knew they both loved her and wanted the best for her.

Now, Sadie walked toward the kitchen. "Should we figure out our project? I'll get some snacks."

"We have plenty of time," Piper said. "Relax a little."

The proposal for their project was due a week from Thursday. When Mrs. Marrone had said they needed to choose partners for their weather forecasting assignment, Sadie had felt her stomach drop. As everyone chatted and paired up, she dreaded being the only person left without a partner, but then Piper had turned around and asked her to pair up. Sadie was so relieved, she hadn't stopped to wonder why Piper had noticed her all of a sudden. For the first half of the school year, Piper hadn't seemed to know she existed.

"Where's your mom?" Piper asked now.

"Not home," Sadie said. "She's at the hospital with my aunt."

Sadie was used to coming home to an empty house, but today it seemed even quieter, their voices echoing off the hardwood floors and ceilings.

"What happened?"

"I'm not sure." Her mother had sent a cryptic text around lunchtime, saying that Aunt Alison had been taken to the hospital, but she was fine and no need to worry. Sadie wished her mother would accept that she wasn't a baby anymore, that she could handle whatever was going on. Her aunt was the healthiest person she knew. She had been known to run a half marathon and get on the treadmill later the same say. It was surely a false alarm.

"You're lucky your mom gives you space," Piper said. "My mother is always in my business. She's constantly telling me she's there if I need to talk and blah, blah, blah. It's so fucking annoying."

Sadie forced a laugh. "Yeah, so annoying,"

Sadie actually thought it sounded wonderful to have a mother who showed interest in her life, but she would never admit that to Piper. Her mother didn't work, but she always seemed to be busy anyway, her days full with volunteering fundraiser committees, coffee with friends, Weight Watchers meetings, anything other than spending time with her daughter. When people asked her mom if she worked, she told them she was an attorney-turned-homemaker, and Sadie would bite her lip. Her legal career had ended a few years after law school and how could she claim to be a homemaker if she was barely ever home?

"She wants to have the sex talk with me every fucking day," Piper said. "As if I don't know everything already."

"Really?" Sadie wanted to ask what exactly she knew about sex and whether any of that knowledge was first hand. Sadie hadn't even been kissed. She had known Piper could teach her a few things.

Piper had told her she'd just moved to town from Brooklyn, but some of the girls from the ice rink said she had been in their classes at the other middle school, that she was a pathological liar and not to be trusted. Sadie suspected Piper didn't always tell the whole truth, but did anyone? Her parents left out important stuff all the time. Her other friends loved to exaggerate what they did on their vacations. She knew for a fact Caroline hadn't gone to Cape Cod with Jason Thorne as Caroline had implied. Their families just happened to be vacationing at the same beach resort, the photo on Caroline's phone cropping out Caroline's little sister and Jason's mom. How was that any different?

"I probably know more than my mom does," Piper said. "I don't think she's gotten any since my father left."

"When was that?" Sadie couldn't imagine talking about her mom like that.

"Five years ago."

"Wow."

Piper started climbing the stairs.

"Where are you going?" Sadie asked. As she watched Piper climb the stairs with her boots on, she couldn't help thinking about the dirt stains she'd have to scrub away later so her mother wouldn't know.

"Your parents won't be home for a while. It's a good time to do a little exploring."

"Exploring?"

"Scavenger hunt. It's one of my favorite games."

Sadie followed Piper up the stairs. "I'm not sure that's such a good idea. My mom's a bit of a control freak. She knows exactly where she keeps stuff and she'll notice—"

"Don't worry," Piper said. "I do it all the time."

Though she had never been here before, Piper seemed to know which room was which without asking. She made a beeline to the medicine cabinet in the master bathroom. Grabbing a few bottles from the shelf, she turned them around to scrutinize the labels. "Advil, boring. Pepcid, boring. Tylenol, boring." She examined every bottle while Sadie stood in agony, wishing the torture would end. She couldn't imagine how angry her mother would be if she caught them snooping around in her room.

Piper took a bottle of Claritin off the shelf and shook the contents. "So far, your parents are a disappointment," she said. "Where's the good stuff? There's got to be something."

Sadie grabbed the bottle from Piper and placed it back on the shelf. "Are you crazy? My parents will kill me if they come home."

"People always say that, but what would they really do?" Piper closed the cabinet and walked over to the dresser.

"Let's go figure out our project," Sadie said. "We have Oreos." She felt stupid the second she said it. Cookies weren't going to entice Piper, but it was the first thing that came to her mind.

"Are you for real?" Piper opened the middle drawer of the dresser. "The hunt's not over." She reached underneath a pile of folded shirts and took out a flat rectangular box.

"Rainbow loom?" she said. "Is this yours?"

Sadie felt her cheeks turn red. "No, I mean, it used to be, but now it's my mom's." After the craze ended, Sadie's mom had become addicted to making bracelets on the loom. She said it calmed her nerves.

"Your mother uses it? I thought my mom was the lamest of them all, but this moves your mom into first place." She put the box back where she'd found it and closed the drawer.

"The underwear drawer is the most common place to hide valuables," Piper said, opening the top drawer.

"This is a bad idea. My mom will definitely notice if anything is missing."

"Don't worry." Piper stretched a purple thong between her thumbs. "I just like seeing what's here." She snapped the thong back into the drawer. Reaching her hand to the back of the drawer, she found an envelope and pulled out a wad of fifty-dollar bills.

"She likes to keep cash around, just in case," Sadie said. She always wondered why her mom kept all that money in her drawer. Maybe it was a symptom of her anxiety, like she was paranoid that the banks would fail and they would need stockpiles of cash to buy food and gas.

"For what?"

"I don't know. Emergencies, okay?" Sadie felt her heart speed up. "Can you put it away now?"

"She won't notice if we each take a few." Piper took some bills out of the envelope, pocketed a few, and handed some to Sadie, who grabbed the envelope and stashed it back in place before Piper could take any more money. Sadie stuffed the bills in the pocket of her sweatshirt. She'd have to remember to return them before her mom came home.

"Not bad so far," Piper said. "But there's got to be more."

Piper walked over to her father's nightstand, opened a drawer, and took out an old copy of Playboy magazine. "This is so old school." She waved the magazine at Sadie. "Doesn't your dad know he can use his phone?"

"Put it away!" Sadie didn't want to think about what her father did while looking at the pictures. "I could get in trouble."

"I could get in trouble," Piper mimicked. She threw the magazine back and rummaged around. "I thought he would have something juicier. My brother said this one doesn't even show anything."

"We have some good snacks downstairs," Sadie said. "My mom has a secret junk food addiction." Back on that again. She couldn't think of any other way to lure Piper out of her parents' room.

Piper reached her hand to the back of the drawer. "Wait a minute, I think I've struck gold." She held an orange pill bottle up in the air. "Ahhhhhhh," she sang, as if holding up the holy grail.

"Not a good idea," Sadie said. "My father might be taking those for something."

Piper read the label on the bottle. "Who's Robert Ward?" Piper asked.

Sadie shrugged. She had no idea who that was and she didn't care. She just wanted Piper to put the bottle back and get out of here.

"Part of the label's missing, so we'll have to inspect," Piper said.

"No," Sadie said. "I really don't think..."

Piper opened the safety cap and emptied a few pills into her hand. One side of the pill had the number 40 and the other was etched with the letters OC.

"Jackpot," Piper said. "If my brother is good for anything, it's teaching me what pills look like."

"What do you think it is?"

"I don't think, I *know*," Piper said. "It's Oxy." She returned the pills to the bottle, replaced the cap, and put the bottle in her pocket. "Now, let's go have those Oreos."

CHAPTER FOUR

Alison

August 23, 2019

"MRS. JACOBS, IT'S TIME FOR LUNCH." Rhea entered the bedroom without knocking. In the five months since her surgery, Alison had learned that being an invalid meant an end to privacy. "I've made your favorite soup."

Chewing a sandwich or a piece of steak was now impossible, so Alison's diet consisted solely of soft foods. Rhea had been working as her home health aide since she'd arrived home from Spaulding last month, so she knew Campbell's tomato was one of the few foods Alison could force down her throat, but calling it a favorite was a bit of a stretch.

Alison raised her left hand as a sign of thanks, the right side of her body still quite weak. Svetlana said she would continue to gain strength, but the progress had been so slow that sometimes Alison wondered why she continued therapy at all.

Rhea rolled the tray table in front of Alison's chair and adjusted the height. She insisted Alison transfer from the bed to the chair first thing every morning: to work the core, she said. Alison remembered a time when working the core meant planks and crunches and push-ups, and now simply moving from the bed to a chair was strenuous exercise. She used to be so active, and now she barely moved. Alison ran her left hand over the left side of her head. Her hair had finally grown in to about six inches. For several months, there was only peach fuzz over the scalp incision, but now, her hair looked almost normal. She wouldn't be gracing the cover of *Vogue* anytime soon, but at least children didn't point at her anymore on the rare occasion she left the house, asking their parents what had happened to that woman. There was still a bony ridge where the two cut edges of skull weren't quite flush, an imperfection that would be with her forever.

"It's nice and warm," Rhea said, holding the spoon up to Alison's mouth.

She swallowed the spoonful and Rhea wiped the dribble from the right side of her mouth with a napkin. A few months back, Alison had made her way to the linen cabinet and pulled out the napkins she and Michael had bought on their honeymoon in Portugal, the blue and white geometric patterns on the fabric paying homage to the signature tiles lining the buildings of Lisbon. Using cloth napkins would be better than filling landfills with paper ones. At first, she'd been embarrassed that a stranger had to help her eat, walk, and even use the toilet, but now she was used to it. Even though Rhea had only been with her a few weeks, the intimacy of her job made it seem like so much longer.

"Good," Alison said. Since she'd returned home, Cynthia had been calling a few times a week. Alison refused her calls and Rhea got the picture, blocking Cynthia's advances like a mama bear protecting her young cub. The last thing Alison needed was to listen to Cynthia's histrionics and sobbing. Dwelling on Cynthia's drama would only hamper her recovery.

"Uh, I ..." Alison was trying to say, "Thank You," to express how grateful she felt to have Rhea by her side supporting her in so many ways, both physical and emotional. Though Rhea was paid nicely, this was no easy assignment. There was a lot of heavy lifting and Alison wasn't exactly scintillating company.

"I, um ..." Something that used to be so easy was now the most difficult thing in the world.

Rhea zipped her gray hoodie sweatshirt over her pink scrub outfit and smiled, her long black hair in a ponytail draping down her back. Alison wondered if she ever let her hair down, and how she combed out all the tangles.

"You ... nice," Alison said. It's wasn't even close to eloquent, but it was the best she could manage.

"My prayers at church have been working." Rhea wiped Alison's mouth again. "You're speaking so much better."

She was right. Alison had made significant progress, getting stronger and finding new words every week. On a good day, she could even string one or two words together. Okay and alright now felt like old friends.

"Alright," Alison said.

Despite this progress, she couldn't help thinking Rhea's prayer skills could use some work. The results, though significant, seemed underwhelming, but she wasn't in any position to judge. Michael would find some overused cliché to fit the situation like, "Don't look a gift horse in the mouth," or "Beggars can't be choosers." His constant use of trite phrases had been kind of cute when they were first dating, but after more than ten years of marriage, it had gotten old.

Rhea fed her the last spoonful of soup, wiping the errant drips with a clean corner of the napkin.

"There's more healing to come," she said. "You're not even close to the end of your journey."

Alison reached her left hand to grasp Rhea's.

"I've got more prayers in me yet, Mrs. Jacobs," Rhea said. "How about a nice nap after lunch? Rest helps with recovery."

❀

Sometimes in that blurry moment of transition from sleep, Alison forgot she wasn't the same person she used to be. Her dreams hadn't changed, even though everything else in her life had come to a screeching halt. She often dreamt about Becca, just like she used to, and when she was unconscious, her brain in that pleasant dusky anonymity of sleep, she was herself again. She could walk, feed herself, and most importantly, talk. She shared her thoughts eloquently, blissfully free of the struggle of transporting words between her brain and her mouth.

In today's dream, Becca walked down the school hallway past the main office, wearing the yellow sundress that accentuated her breasts. Alison watched her from above as she walked from her classroom to the cafeteria to the teacher's lounge. It was their school, and yet everything looked different, the hallways recognizable but the colors more vibrant, grays and browns turned to bright oranges and greens. Becca stopped to curb the prepubescent antics of Greg Foster, the undisputed class clown, and he obeyed without argument. Alison marveled at the expert way she managed student behavior, just like she did in real life, making it look easy. Alison would have gone toe to toe with Greg, and she undoubtedly would have gotten frustrated and sent him to Principal Weaver. At only twenty-nine, Becca was a better teacher than Alison had ever been.

"Did you have a nice nap?" Rhea's voice snapped her awake. "Nate will be here any minute."

She helped Alison swing her legs over the side of the bed, placed the walker in front of her, and watched as Alison slowly maneuvered over to the chair.

"He's taking the bus here today," she said.

"Alright..." Alison said.

"Nate just tried out for the school play," Rhea said. "I'm sure he'll have a lot to say about that." There was no doubt. Rhea's ten-year-old son talked about anything and everything. Sometimes, Alison wondered how his little brain wasn't deprived of oxygen.

"Hi, Mrs. Jacobs!"

Nate bounded into the room, dropped his backpack on the floor, and sat in the chair next to hers. He brushed his hair off his forehead and smiled. "You're never going to believe what happened today. I had the best day ever. You know I was trying out for The Lion King, right? Well, auditions were today, and we had to sing a song and read some lines—"

Sometimes she wondered if her speech therapist had given Nate an assignment to sit by her side and talk. Supposedly, listening to people speak helped the brain cells reconnect with each other, reminding the sections of the brain involved in speech to come back from their extended sabbatical. At first, Alison found Nate's diarrhea of the mouth irritating, but now it had become part of her day, distracting her from her depressing thoughts. She also liked hearing about what was going on at her school, even if she had to get it from the perspective of a fifth-grader.

"Nate, slow down," Rhea said. "Mrs. Jacobs will follow better if you speak a little more slowly."

Alison wished she could tell Rhea that she still understood everything perfectly. It was forming words that posed the problem.

"It," she said. "It okay." She was thrilled "okay" was back to stay. She'd missed that word so much.

"So, I got up on stage and I was so nervous and my heart was beating so fast. Mrs. Logan smiled and told me I was going to do great. Then I sang 'Hakuna Matata' and she loved it. Cooper just sang 'Happy Birthday' but I wanted her to be able to picture me in the role, to really imagine me as Timon."

"Ni ... nice." She'd seen Nate in the school hallways, of course; he was one of those magnetic kids who never went unnoticed, with his mane of wild hair and expressive face, but he'd never been her student. Now Nate had become Alison's lifeline to her old self, her connection to the person she'd been before her life fell apart. She'd taken medical leave for the last few months of the year, hoping her disabilities were only temporary, but now that the new school year was starting, it was becoming clear she may never teach again. She expected small improvements, a few new words or increased strength on her right side, but she couldn't imagine standing in front of a classroom for seven hours a day. Retired at thirty-eight.

Rhea put her arm around Nate. "That's wonderful, Honey. I knew you could do it."

Watching Rhea with Nate made Alison think about what she was missing. She had always wanted to be a mother, and Michael was desperate to be a father. After a year of trying, Alison started reading about infertility online, about timing sex to the right time in her cycle, and ovulation test strips and sperm-friendly lubricants. After those efforts failed, they turned to a specialist and eventually went through three rounds of in-vitro fertilization, all for nothing. Now it was too late. That ship had sailed, as Michael would have said. She would never be a mother now.

Nate bent over and unzipped his backpack. "I can't wait until she posts the cast list on Friday afternoon."

"Patience, my love," Rhea said. "It's a virtue."

"What?"

"Nothing. Why don't you get a start on your homework? It's your weekend with your father. He'll be here in an hour."

※

After Nate's father picked him up, Rhea went to the kitchen to make dinner, leaving Alison alone with her thoughts. These days, her thoughts didn't make great company. The longer she was alone, the more negative they became. She kept asking herself why this had happened to her, and never came up with any good answers. Now, she picked up her phone and opened the article from the Newton Reporter, again. She'd read it countless times, but for some reason she kept coming back to it. She skimmed until she came to the section with the quotes. When she reached the part about Grant, her heart sped up. No matter how many times she returned to it, the article still evoked a visceral reaction. Maybe if she kept rereading it, she would uncover the information she felt she was missing. She took a breath, her eyes moving down the screen.

"He knew full well about the risks of the surgery," Dr. Kaplan said. The doctor refused to give any further comment. Multiple attempts to contact the doctor for more information have been declined.

It had been two months since she'd first read this article and so much was still unclear. Had Grant done something wrong? Did this lawsuit have anything to do with the results of her surgery? She'd thought Grant was an excellent surgeon, but this case made her wonder if she'd been mistaken. Cynthia's reaction to the malpractice case seemed overly dramatic. Was there something she wasn't divulging? Alison scrolled further down.

The plaintiff had this to say about the outcome of his surgery. "This should have been a straightforward operation," Stone said. "Dr. Kaplan has devastated me. My hearing loss affects not only my daily life, but also my livelihood as a violinist with the Boston Philharmonic. It took countless hours of practice to make it to this level. I never thought I'd lose my career like this." Stone and his family are suing for medical bills, lost wages, and pain and suffering.

Had it really been a straightforward surgery? Had Grant made an error or was the unfortunate result merely bad luck, a rare complication? The more times she read the article, the more the questions multiplied.

Michael came into the room and leaned down to kiss her on the cheek. When he saw what she was reading, his eyes narrowed in anger. "Not again. This isn't healthy for you. It's not going to do you any good to keep rehashing this over and over."

"But ..." She wanted to tell Michael that she needed answers, that maybe pushing Grant and Cynthia away was increasing her anxiety rather than alleviating it.

"Why are you so obsessed with this?" he asked. "Do you think there's more to the story?"

"Not ... not sure," she said.

"I'm not either, but I'm not willing to give him a pass. You'll likely be dealing with issues for the rest of your life. He can't just walk away from this scot-free. He has to own up to his mistakes just like anyone else. Being a surgeon doesn't make him a god."

"I ..." she stammered. Michael seemed so sure that Grant was at fault, but he didn't have any more information that she did. He'd jumped to conclusions, assuming that Grant had been responsible for Alison's complications. Alison wasn't so sure, but she didn't know how to fill in the gaps. For now, she'd have to lie low and hope more information came to light.

CHAPTER FIVE

Alison

August 26, 2019

THE LATE AFTERNOON SUNLIGHT peeked through the blinds, awakening Alison from her nap. She couldn't remember the details of today's dream, but she had a vague sense it had been about Becca again, a feeling of warmth enveloping her whole body. Pushing herself up to a seated position and propping the pillows behind her back, she grabbed her phone from the nightstand and looked back through the emails Becca had sent while Alison was in the hospital. They were all heartbreaking, but the last one always made her cry.

From: IrishBecca@yahoo.com
June 11th, 2019, 6:15 PM
To: aljacobs12@gmail.com

Alison,

As you can tell from all of my previous emails, the past months have been excruciating for me. I've tried to call a lot, but most of the time, they won't tell me anything. Something about a stupid privacy policy. If another nurse quotes that fucking policy, I might lose my shit. Priscilla said you're now at Spaulding. She said Michael called her to fill her in. It was weird that I had to hear this from our principal, but I'm desperate to get news any way I can. The last time I visited you in the hospital, Michael thanked me for coming and then he said I didn't have to come so often. He clearly didn't want me there.

Maybe he somehow sensed our connection. I figured I'd take a short break so he doesn't get too suspicious.

Knowing you're out of the hospital makes me breathe a little easier. I can't stop worrying about you. You're going to get better. I know you will. All I want to do is hold your hand and help you through this. I need to be there for you. Being apart like this isn't healthy for either of us. I don't know how much longer I can take it. One of these days, I'm just going to show up again. I don't care who sees me. Enough is enough.

Always,

Becca

Alison wiped tears from her cheeks. Becca's suffering was palpable, and Alison couldn't imagine how much more she'd have to endure if she stayed. Becca deserved so much more than that. Alison's phone vibrated with a text from Becca, as if she knew Alison was thinking of her.

"What's happening, sexy?"

Becca never failed to make Alison smile, but the one time she'd visited her at home about two weeks ago, introducing herself to Rhea as a colleague from work—true but not nearly the whole story—had been strange and awkward. Being in the same room with Becca and not being able to talk to her, to tell her how she felt, to reach out and run her fingers over the freckles on her arm was beyond painful.

On one hand, Alison wanted to ignore the text to make it easier for Becca to move on with her life, but her fingers itched to reply. She used her left hand to scroll through the emojis and chose the red kiss mark, pausing a second before pressing send. Not able to type words, she could at least communicate in this rudimentary way. From what she'd learned, some aphasics could read, others could write, and the lucky few were able to do both to varying degrees. She'd watched a YouTube video about a Princeton classics professor who had relearned how to write academic papers but still couldn't order a hamburger and French fries.

"I miss you," Becca said.

None of the emojis really said, "I miss you, too." The closest she could get was the thumbs up sign. She would have to remember to download more than just the basic ones that came with the phone.

"Who are you texting?" Michael came in without knocking. It was his bedroom, too, but somehow Alison expected him to knock. When she had first come home, she'd slept in a rented hospital bed for a few weeks and Michael had given her space. Even after she no longer needed the hospital bed, he never returned from the guest room. Their marriage had been unhealthy long before the vessel burst in her brain, but now, she didn't know how they would ever come to terms with it.

Alison shook her head and threw the phone on the coffee table.

"It was someone," he said.

She shrugged her shoulders and looked out the window, the afternoon light giving way to evening.

"Alison, you never text me. I'd be happy to communicate with you any way you want. Text, Morse code, carrier pigeon. I don't care, as long as you let me in."

She couldn't bring herself to look at him.

"When life gives you lemons, you make lemonade, dammit. The Alison I know wouldn't give up like this."

"Alright," she said.

Damn. Things were far from all right, and Michael knew it. He knew their relationship, their lives, and probably their future was far from all right. She wouldn't blame him if he'd found another woman. It's a human trait to crave contact with other people, to long for the warmth of someone else's hand on yours, the feeling of soft fingertips on your inner thigh or along the underside of your breast. If he had made eye contact with a woman during his daily commute on the train, if he approached her and did that thing where he looks away when he gets uncomfortable, if he got her cell number and then called her later in a moment of loneliness, Alison would understand.

"Nothing seems right, Alison." He crossed the room and sat down on the bed facing her chair. "I feel like I've lost you, and you're sitting right in front of me. Maybe if I sleep in here again, things would improve."

She shook her head. The last thing she wanted was to have him beside her, snoring and farting in his sleep. She needed to focus on her recovery without any added distractions.

"You won't even give it a chance?" he asked. "We have to do something to get our relationship back on track. We can't kick the can down the road forever."

Alison shrugged.

"You've given up? Is that what you're saying?"

"Okay," she said.

"No, not okay. I'm glad you found that word, but it's not very useful right now. When are you going to recover 'crap,' and 'shit,' and 'fuck,' because I feel like you'd get a lot more use out of those."

Alison was keenly aware of how messed up this whole situation was. She was the one living as an invalid, left with only memories of the normal person she used to be, and the faint glimmer of hope that one day she'd be able to do half the things she used to take for granted. But maybe she shouldn't shut him out like this. He'd been by her side through this whole fiasco, so maybe he deserved one more shot.

She reached out her left hand out to take his. "I ... I know."

His mouth turned up into a tentative smile. "I have no doubt you're in there. You're the same person you've always been."

He didn't know who she really was. She wasn't proud of some of the choices she'd made. You would think a near-death experience might make her think twice, maybe cause her to take a close look at her bad decisions and start fresh.

"I think it's time for me to move back in here," he said. "I can't live the rest of my life in the guest room. I want to sleep next to my wife."

Her phone buzzed. She pulled back her hand back and they both reached for the phone. Alison got there first, her left hand as nimble as ever.

Michael raised his eyebrows.

She held the phone up so Michael couldn't see the screen.

It was a text from Becca. "I want to spread your legs and ...."

She coughed and tucked the phone into the side of her chair.

"What does it say?" he asked.

Alison shook her head and buried the phone farther down next to the cushion.

"Fuck, Alison," Michael said. "You have to stop shutting me out."

"Okay," she said.

Michael groaned in frustration and stood up. He had nothing more to say.

CHAPTER SIX

Grant

February 6, 2019

GRANT ADDED TWO SCOOPS of chocolate protein powder to the blender and topped it off with a few Adderall tablets, his morning pills. He secured the lid and pressed the button on the blender. He had started having a protein shake for breakfast a few years ago, and now it had become part of his routine, the whir of the blender at 6 AM a familiar sound in the Kaplan house. Adding just a few to his shake made the day go much more smoothly, his focus razor sharp, distractions and annoyances so much easier to tolerate. The benefits outweighed the guilt, the hollow feeling in the pit of his stomach dissipating as the thick, sweet liquid slid down his esophagus.

Cynthia came into the kitchen wearing her well-worn gray sweatpants and oversized Brandeis sweatshirt, which dated back to their college days. Her mouth started moving, but he couldn't hear her over the whir of the blender. When he raised a finger in the air to tell her to wait a minute, she gave him a dirty look. He stopped the blender and poured his shake into the portable plastic cup with the hospital logo printed on it.

"I didn't sleep at all last night," she said. "I couldn't stop thinking about Alison lying in a hospital bed."

He took his first sip and felt an immediate boost in his mood. The medication hadn't yet reached his bloodstream, so it had to be the placebo effect, but if it helped him tolerate Cynthia, he'd take it.

"Do you think she's going to be okay?" she asked.

"I don't think, I know. Calvin's the best of the best."

"I just don't understand," Cynthia said. "We just talked on Sunday night. It was a totally normal conversation."

"That's the way brain bleeds happen. It's not a gradual thing. You're fine, and then all of a sudden, you're not. Welcome to my world."

"It's so scary. I don't know how you deal with this all the time."

"Don't worry. He put his shake down and wrapped his arms around her. He realized he hadn't hugged her fully, more than a sidearm or a lean as he pecked her on the cheek, in a very long time. It felt surprisingly good to be close to her. "She's on my turf now, and I'm going to watch over her. I promise."

Now he could feel the Adderall fine tuning the frequency of his senses. A few years ago, during a routine visit with his primary care doctor, Adam Silver, Grant had mentioned that he was having trouble staying focused during surgery, and Adam had written him a prescription without any questions. No self-respecting top doctor needed pills to keep them on their game, so Grant hadn't intended to fill the prescription. But a few weeks later on a hellish day after one of his residents found a cerebrospinal fluid leak he'd missed and he spaced out during a conversation with Wendy, he'd reconsidered. Since then, Grant had become a bit loose with the recommended dose of one pill in the morning, taking several throughout the course of the day to keep his adrenaline pumping. It made him feel more alive: the blue color of the surgical drape was brighter, the beeping sound of the anesthesia machine in perfect rhythm with the movement of his hands, his surgical drill sharper and more precise. On the unfortunate days when he reached the bottom of the bottle without calling for a refill, everything seemed dull and sluggish, like a video playing in agonizingly slow motion.

Releasing Cynthia, he reached for his shake and took another large sip. The downside of the Adderall was that he needed a little help coming down after the work day ended, but it was nothing a few tabs of Oxy couldn't handle. He usually took one or two during his commute home and was ready to deal with Cynthia's nagging and Sadie's mood swings by the time he pulled into the driveway.

"When's your protein shake obsession going to end?" Cynthia

stepped away, putting distance between them again. "Haven't you heard about the real food movement?"

"Can we skip this today, Cynthia? It works for me." So much for closeness, he thought. He didn't know why she felt the constant need to criticize his food choices, but he decided to let it go today. If he wanted to be nasty, he could insinuate that her diet could use some tweaking too—she could afford to lose more than a few pounds— but he didn't want to attack her.

"Dr. Otis says you should have at least five superfoods every day," she said.

"I seem to remember you mentioning that before." He'd never understood her obsession with Dr. Otis. The celebrity doctor was a narcissistic, money-hungry quack. When his reality show had aired a few years ago, Cynthia had forced Grant to sit and watch with her. That asshole strutted around the hospital with a self-congratulatory look on his face telling patients that he had saved their lives and that if they'd gone anywhere else, they surely would have died. Every time Grant cursed at the TV, Cynthia shushed him without taking her eyes from the screen.

She listed, "Blueberries, sweet potatoes, asparagus, kale, almonds—"

"I've got it," Grant said. He didn't ask her if the Doritos she kept hidden in the drawer under the oven qualified as a superfood. He knew she took the bag out late at night and though she tried to bury the empty bag at the bottom of the garbage bin, the chemical ranch smell always permeated the kitchen in the morning.

"When are you going to get over that jerk?" he asked. "He also recommends all kinds of other bullshit." Grant could feel his speech speeding up, one of the effects of the pills. A pressure buildup at the back of his brain forced the words out faster and with more emphasis. "I mean, raspberry açai supplements for weight loss?" He knew he should stop talking, but he couldn't let it go. "Close your mouth and you'll lose weight. It's not fucking rocket science."

"What are you saying?"

"I'm saying that if you just stop eating, you won't be so fat." He knew he'd gone too far, but he couldn't help it.

"What the hell, Grant? My sister bled into her brain, and

you're on my case to lose weight?" She tugged her sweatshirt down over her behind. "Your timing is impeccable."

"I was using you in the general sense, not you specifically. You know I love you just the way you are." He said, trying to dial back his comments.

"It certainly sounded like you were referring to me." Tears gathered in the corners of her eyes.

"I apologize," he said.

"Not so fast," she said. "Your apology doesn't erase the nasty things you just said."

"I wasn't trying to be mean. It just came out."

"Maybe you should think before you speak."

"Forgive me," Grant said. "Everyone's stressed. When I go in today, I'm going to check on Alison and make sure Calvin's got her work-up going."

"I need to know what's happening," she said. "She must be scared out of her mind."

He gave her a quick kiss, grabbed his shake and his keys from the counter. "I'll keep you posted."

⚛

When Grant arrived at the neurology floor, he immediately checked the board. Alison had been assigned to the room the staff referred to as "the penthouse," a large corner room with panoramic views of the Charles River and the Boston Museum of Science. This was the room he reserved whenever he operated on VIPs, but he didn't think it would ease Alison's mind to know that the King of Jordan had once stayed in that room after Grant successfully repaired a ruptured brain aneurysm.

He sat down at the nurses' station next to the floor clerk and opened the electronic medical record. The nurses buzzed around the floor taking vitals, dispensing meds, and finishing charts in time for the morning change of shift. When the food service cart rolled by, the smell of bacon traveled straight to his olfactory cortex, waking up his brain cells. He typed Alison's name in and scrolled down past the results—blood work, chest x-ray, a consultation from one of the neurologists—until he found the report from her brain MRI. He held his breath while the report opened, then scanned down to the impression section.

"Large arteriovenous malformation involving the left frontal and parietal lobes, measuring 5.1 x 4.5 x 6.2 cm, with large cortical draining veins and arterial supply predominately from the middle cerebral artery."

He clicked on the icon to bring up the images. The pictures looked even worse than the report sounded, the collection of tangled vessels occupying a large part of the left side of Alison's brain and displacing the normal brain tissue to the right. He saw the small hemorrhage that had brought her in to the emergency room, but that was the least of her problems. At any moment, one of those abnormal vessels could rupture and cause a massive bleed, pushing her brainstem down out of her skull and killing her instantly.

"Oh, fuck," he said. He wasn't surprised, but he'd been hoping they would get lucky, that the bleed would be from a small aneurysm or a benign tumor, not from an AVM the size of a fucking golf ball. He knew first-hand how tricky this condition could be to deal with, how quickly things could go south even in the most skilled hands. He stood up and started pacing back and forth.

Kendra, the floor clerk, looked up from her computer. "Dr. Kaplan, watch your language."

"Not today, Kendra. Alison Jacobs is my sister-in-law."

"The nice lady in the penthouse? She seems okay. We chatted when she came in last night."

"She's okay now," he said. "But she's got a huge AVM. It's not an easy one to fix." He sat back down at the computer and double checked the name on the top of the image to confirm this was indeed her scan. Her name shined back at him from the top of the screen.

"Damn it," he said, his legs oscillating uncontrollably.

"Are you okay, Dr. Kaplan? You seem on edge this morning."

"It's a crappy situation, Kendra. I don't want to be in the middle of this. A six-centimeter AVM in an eloquent part of her left hemisphere."

"That doesn't sound good," she said.

"It's not good, and I know Dr. Shin isn't going to feel comfortable dealing with it." Cal was an excellent general neurosurgeon, but Grant knew from years of working together that this case would be too complex for him, the kind he would usually pass off to Grant without a second thought.

Kendra took a sip of her coffee and turned back to the computer screen. "I'll leave you doctors to sort that out," she said.

When Grant entered Alison's room, Cal was at her bedside explaining the results, and Michael stood on her other side. Grant clapped Cal on the back and came around the bed to kiss Alison on the cheek.

"Blondie." Grant sat down at the foot of the bed. He'd been calling her this since Thanksgiving weekend in his senior year of college when he'd gone home to meet Cynthia's family, the sounds of "Sunday Girl" and "Heart of Glass" drifting through her bedroom door. "This is the lengths you'll go to get out of work?" he said.

Alison smiled. She seemed relieved to see him.

"I'm in the middle of explaining what's going on," Cal said. "Would you like to take over?"

"Continue, by all means," Grant said.

"I was explaining that an AVM is not a tumor, but more a tangle of arteries and veins that's not supposed to be there."

"If it's not a tumor, then why is it such a big deal?" Alison asked.

"It forms a mass that can push on important parts of your brain," Cal said. "Also, the walls of the vessels are thin, so they can rupture and bleed without warning."

"That's what happened yesterday?"

"Exactly. Luckily, the bleed you had was a small one. Like a warning bell. Otherwise, you might never have known about this until it was too late."

"I don't feel so lucky," she said.

Grant agreed that the word didn't seem to fit. A ticking time bomb in the part of the brain that controlled movement of the right side of her body seemed particularly unlucky to him, especially since he wasn't even sure of the best way to treat it. He'd handled his fair share of challenging cases over the years, and the results had not always been good. He still had nightmares about Mrs. Altimari, the little Italian lady who had stroked out while he was attempting to coil her aneurysm, and the look on her son's face when Grant said there was nothing else to do, that hospice was the logical next step.

"I guess it's the way you look at it," Cal said.

"I live a healthy lifestyle," she said. "I don't smoke or do drugs, and I work out almost every day."

"Unfortunately, this can happen to anyone, at any time, regardless of how well you take care of yourself," Cal said.

"Working out can actually cause an AVM to bleed," Grant said.

"Oh," Alison said. "So, what do we do now?"

"To be perfectly honest, I'm not sure," Cal said, looking over at Grant.

"You're not sure?" Michael said. "There must be treatment options." Grant could tell by Michael's silence until now that he was feeling overwhelmed with the situation.

Cal didn't respond, his eyes still on Grant.

"It's not a straightforward case," Grant said. "The size and location of the AVM poses a challenge. Now that the bleeding has stopped, we have time to talk about different possibilities."

"This isn't my area of expertise," Cal said. "If you were anyone else, I would be transferring you to Grant's service. I'm going to do some research and figure out the best place to send you for further management. I think there's a guy at Cleveland Clinic."

"This is one of the best hospitals in the country," Michael said. "Why would we want to go to Ohio? There's no place better than here."

"You're right," Cal said. "But the only person in Boston I would trust with my family member happens to be your brother-in-law."

"He's also the best person for the job," Michael said.

"It's a tricky situation," Cal said. "He certainly could lose his objectivity if he chose to treat Alison. It's not looked upon favorably."

"Dr. Richman in Cleveland is really good," Grant said. "He gives all the talks at the national conferences. I'll get you an appointment with him."

CHAPTER SEVEN

Alison

August 27, 2019

SITTING ON THE EXAM TABLE in the physical therapy office the following day, Alison was surrounded by the same sad collection of people who were always here. Jared, the college kid on the rowing machine in the corner, had torn his ACL during a soccer match and was working to regain flexibility and get back on the roster. The elderly lady doing tricep extensions in the corner had suffered a small stroke a few months ago. Alison tried not to watch Thomas, the middle-aged man with early onset Parkinson's disease, but his prominent tremor, shuffling walk, and flat facial expression drew her focus every time. Looking at him made Alison wonder if she evoked the same sense of pity in others.

Svetlana finished with her last client and walked over to Alison. "What are we up for today?" she asked.

Alison wanted to give an honest answer. Nothing. Nada. The big goose egg. That's what she was up for. She would have preferred to lie in bed feeling sorry for herself, wallowing in misery and counting all of the things she'd planned to do with her life that would never come to pass. Alison had thought she would be so much better off five months after surgery. At the beginning, she had tried to maintain a positive attitude. She knew she had a long way to go, but she was determined to get there, little by little. As the weeks and months wore on with such slow progress, maintaining mental strength proved difficult.

"No time for laziness," Svetlana said. Sometimes Svetlana exhausted Alison to the point that she wished her dead, but her persistence had made Alison stronger, far from perfect, but definitely moving in the right direction.

"Okay," Alison said. To get through the hour of torture, she told herself it was basically the same thing as physical training at the gym. She had loved those sessions, looked forward to the way her muscles would burn after fifteen reps with heavy weight, the exhilaration of finishing a set of sprints, the way her trainer would yell at her to keep going and she would, the adrenaline shooting straight to her brain. Alison used to push through the pain, telling herself it was for her own good, but now, her motivation was lacking. At the gym, she saw results, her muscles more defined, her body leaner and stronger, but here it was so much more difficult to see the effects.

Svetlana took off her sweatshirt so she was just wearing a tank top and athletic shorts. Alison would swear the woman was ninety-nine percent muscle. Maybe she'd been a wrestler or a rugby player back in high school.

"Too ... too," Alison wanted to ask Svetlana if she was too hot, but her mouth wouldn't form the word. She knew exactly how "hot" felt—the feeling of lying on the chaise on her deck in the summer sun—but she still couldn't say it.

"Getting ready to work," Svetlana said, moving the walker off to the side.

Supporting Alison under the arms, Svetlana used her weight to help her stand. "Today we start with a cane. No more walker for you." She placed a cane in Alison's left hand. It wasn't a wooden cane like you would see in a Broadway show, or one of those with flowery designs elderly women used around town, but more of a no-frills practical cane. The black rubber handle looked like a bicycle handlebar and four prongs at the base created wide contact with the ground. Even though switching from a walker to a cane was a move in the right direction, having to use this kind of cane made Alison's stomach burn, an obvious reminder of how far she still had to go.

"This one is good for safety." Svetlana pushed the cane from side to side, demonstrating how difficult it was to topple. "Very stable."

Alison grabbed the handle and held on for dear life. It felt strange to stand without the walker. The room seemed so much bigger than it had a few minutes ago, almost vast, the distance to the floor enormous. She imagined what it would feel like to fall, her shoulder hitting the ground with a loud thud, the pain shooting from her arm up to her neck. She'd become so accustomed to the secure feeling of the metal frame of the walker around her, keeping her safe, but also holding her captive, creating a barrier between her and the world.

"You must learn the technique," Svetlana said. "It's different than with a walker. You use the cane in your good hand to support your weak leg." She grabbed an extra cane from a rack along the wall and demonstrated, planting the cane at the same time as one leg and then bringing the other leg forward while the cane swung back.

"See how the cane follows the natural motion of my arm? It shouldn't feel awkward."

Easy for her to say. She had full use of her arms and legs; since Alison's surgery, even the simplest tasks felt awkward. Things she used to do without a second thought—cutting food with a fork and knife, typing an email on the computer, blow drying her hair—were now impossible.

"Try a few steps," Svetlana said. "We can do this."

Alison wasn't sure why Svetlana placed so much confidence in her. Yes, she'd shown up for all her appointments, mostly because Rhea insisted on it, but she hadn't done anything particularly brave or impressive or inspiring. Maybe this was her moment to shine.

Stretching her left arm forward, she anchored the base of the cane on the floor, but when she tried to advance her right leg, it refused to follow her command. With a lot of effort and writhing and grunting, she managed to drag it around, her toes dragging on the wood floor. Taking a step with her left leg proved easier, but then she had to start the whole cycle over again. She took a few more uncoordinated steps, each step so arduous, she wondered how Svetlana found the patience to watch this horrendous spectacle.

"Good job," she said. "Don't be afraid to put some weight on the cane. Really use it."

"Alright." Alison took a moment to breathe and gather her

strength. One of the photographs on the opposite wall caught her eye, a woman wearing a numbered bib crossing the red finish tape, her arms raised above her head in triumph. She didn't look like Becca—her dark hair was straight and her skin had an olive tone—but something in her expression still brought her to mind. Maybe it was the look of supreme determination behind her beaming smile, the same expression Becca got during a tough workout.

"You ready to keep going?" Svetlana asked.

No, not really, Alison thought, but she didn't want to disappoint Svetlana. After a few more steps, her quadriceps muscles started to burn, like when she used to do barbell squats, but there was no accompanying sense of satisfaction. She stopped for another breather and looked again at the photograph. She couldn't fathom the sense of personal victory that woman must feel at finishing the grueling race. Alison's marathon had just begun. There were at least twenty more miles left to run and she was already totally spent. Maybe it was her eyes that reminded her of Becca. They had the same mischievous glint that Becca use to get when they were planning a quick rendezvous in the staff lounge.

Her breathing slowed, but suddenly she felt light-headed, the walls further away, the line where the walls met the ceiling strangely wavy, the photographs on the wall off kilter. The bright colors in the photo blurred and swirled into a muddy brown, and she felt the warmth rush from her head, a sudden nausea.

"Are you okay?" The look on Svetlana's face heightened Alison's anxiety. She stepped behind Alison and helped her over to the exam table, using a towel to dry her neck and chest.

Another therapist came over. "What happened?"

"She was doing great," Svetlana eased her down and placed two pillows under her legs. "It must have been too much all at once."

"I'll get an ice pack and some juice," the other woman said.

When she left, Alison looked up at Svetlana and lost it, the sobs escaping in ugly bursts and gasps. The tears ran down the sides of her face onto the exam table, wetting the neck of her shirt. The more she tried to reign in the tears, the more they flowed. Even with all of the ups and downs, this was the first time she'd cried since her surgery.

Svetlana patted Alison's face with the towel. "What happened?"

"I ..." Alison wanted to be a good patient and prove herself, but it was too much, too soon. She was embarrassed that taking a few steps was so excruciating while Jared over on the rowing machine would be scoring goals again within a few months. People used to have trouble keeping up with her in spin class, and now she couldn't walk across a room without taking multiple breaks.

"It's okay. Just rest for now," Svetlana said.

The other therapist returned and placed an ice pack on Alison's forehead. The chill centered her, calming her queasiness.

"Her color's coming back," she said, moving the ice pack from her head to the back of her neck."

"Should I give your husband a call?" Svetlana asked.

Alison shook her head. If Svetlana called Michael at work, he'd show up all annoyed and distracted, the last thing she needed right now. Really, she wished Becca could be here encouraging her with her sweet smile. She'd know just the right thing to say to make Alison stop feeling sorry for myself, to make the glass seem half full rather than half empty.

"You'll tough this one out alone?" Svetlana said.

"Alright."

"That doesn't sound so good," the other therapist said.

"That's as good as she gets," Svetlana said. "She doesn't say much. Are you ready to sit up?"

They put their hands on her back and helped her up. Once she was sitting, Alison again noticed the woman in the photograph, still beaming, so proud of making it through the race. Becca was with her in spirit, encouraging her to dust herself off and keep going.

Svetlana looked at her. "Don't let this get you down." She brought her fist to meet Alison's.

The other woman handed her a can of orange juice and Alison tried to take a sip without dribbling. The juice tasted more sour than sweet, but she swallowed it, losing only a few drops out of the corner of her mouth.

Svetlana dried her chin. "We'll try this again another day."

❀

When Alison arrived home from physical therapy, all she wanted to do was take a nap, but Rhea insisted she stay awake until after lunch. After Rhea arranged the pillows behind her back and elevated her right leg on the ottoman, she went to make lunch.

Alison picked up her phone and looked through her Facebook feed. Remy Abelson, her college roommate, had posted photos from her trip to Machu Picchu: thirty-seven shots of her with her husband, two awkward tween boys, and a younger girl smiling among the ruins, jagged mountains rising up in the background. In the years after college, they used to speak every few months, catching each other up, but each time Remy announced another pregnancy, Alison found it more difficult to hide her jealousy. "Evan just looks at me funny and I get pregnant," Remy would say, and Alison would force a laugh. How could she say something so blatantly insensitive? Why was getting pregnant so easy for her and impossible for Alison? As the years went on, they spoke less frequently, and since the surgery, not at all.

On Cynthia's page, there was a photo of Sadie beaming at her eighth-grade graduation, one arm around Alison and one around Cynthia. The pure joy on their faces reminded Alison how much she missed them both. She missed laughing and having fun with Sadie: listening to her stories from school, watching silly TV shows, and taking trips to the mall. And as much as Cynthia sometimes got on her nerves, Alison missed their weekly phone calls and holiday get-togethers. She wanted to believe they'd get past this and be sisters again, but she wasn't sure it was possible.

Becca's profile picture was one Alison had snapped after a workout, her face flushed and her eyes sparkling, looking straight at the camera. Alison's breath caught. She felt guilty thinking about Becca when Michael had been so attentive through this whole thing. It felt reassuring to know he was in her corner, but at the same time his constant attention could be suffocating at times. She longed to see Becca, to touch Becca, but then she would see Michael trying so hard to help her get better, and she'd be overwhelmed with guilt again. She went back to the newsfeed and scrolled down past a photo of a friend from graduate school sitting in the stands at the U.S. Open and one of Michael's co-workers beaming in front of the Hamilton marquis.

The phone rang and Rhea came in a moment later.

"It's your friend, Becca. She said it's important."

Becca knew Alison wouldn't answer her cell phone. Usually, Rhea said she was resting or eating lunch when Becca called, somehow sensing how difficult it was for Alison to speak with her. This time, Becca must have been persistent.

Rhea handed her the phone.

"Hi, Alison," Becca said. Her voice was raspy, like she'd been at a concert singing at the top of her lungs. Maybe it was always that way and Alison had forgotten, but it sounded incredible. "How are you?"

"Alright." To say Alison missed Becca would be an extreme understatement. It was as if a vital piece of her had been amputated that day she'd passed out at school. As the paramedics loaded her into the ambulance, strapping her to the stretcher and turning on the flashing lights, they left behind the Alison Jacobs who felt loved and desired and connected to another human being. Not a day went by when she didn't long to hear Becca's voice, to see her familiar smile, to collect her auburn curls in her hands.

"School is not the same without you," Becca said. "Last year I kept telling myself it was temporary, but now with a new school year starting, it's just so weird that you're not here. It's surreal to be setting up *your* classroom. You should be the one doing this." There was a slight lisp when she said "school" and "classroom," the air passing through the gap in her front teeth.

"Okay, I ..." Alison wanted to say it was even more strange for her, sitting at home doing nothing while her old colleagues geared up for a new school year, like she had stepped off an amusement park ride and it kept right on going without her.

"I put up all of your posters and decorations so it will feel like your class when you come back." Everyone was deluding themselves with all this talk about her coming back. She couldn't walk or talk, so teaching a classroom of fifth graders seemed out of the question. "It's looking good."

When everything happened, Becca had been working at school for nearly a full school year, covering Marisol Estrada's second grade class during her maternity leave, and then when Alison went on medical leave, Becca was reassigned to her classroom. At her first weekly staff meeting a year ago, Alison noticed her broad smile while she shook hands and introduced herself to the other teachers and staff. For a few weeks, they only saw each other in passing, occasionally making small talk over lunch in the teacher's lounge, until they discovered a common interest. They were both obsessed with working out, so they made a date to meet at the gym after school once a week, which soon turned into nearly every day.

"How's your physical therapy going?" Becca asked. "I can't stop thinking about you."

"Yes." She wanted to say that Becca was always on her mind as well. She couldn't stop herself from comparing Becca and Michael, imagining how Becca would react differently than Michael. Her marriage had always been predictable and she'd loved that in the beginning. It was comfortable to always know what Michael would say. But from the first day she met Becca, she'd felt a connection that kept her on her toes and never stopped surprising her. It was exciting.

They spent the first few months side by side on the treadmills or elliptical machines, sharing the details of their lives while pushing each other to go longer and harder. A few weeks in, they began sharing more intimate details of their lives. Alison spoke about her struggles with infertility—the drugs and procedures and monthly heartbreak—and Becca shared that she'd come out as a lesbian when she was a sophomore in high school. Before this, Alison had appreciated female beauty in a detached way, like admiring a painting behind protective museum glass, but after Becca's revelation, something changed. Alison started watching Becca as she exercised, noticing the way her calf muscles undulated as she ran, the way her hair bounced on her back, the way the sweat collected on her upper lip. She found herself imagining what her breasts looked like under her sports bra, how kissing her would be different than kissing a man, whether her pubic hair was natural or waxed. The harder she tried to push these thoughts away, the more they flooded her mind. Sometimes Becca caught her watching and smiled, like she could read Alison's thoughts. She'd never been attracted to a woman in this way before. There were a few brief flickers of guilt about Michael, but mostly she was consumed by thoughts about Becca. Maybe because she was attracted to a woman instead of a man, it didn't feel like cheating, more like an experiment.

"I know it's hard for you to see me," Becca said now. "But that doesn't erase how we feel."

She made it seem like their relationship could endure anything, like Alison's disabilities were just a small pothole rather than a massive sinkhole. She wanted to tell Becca that seeing her now was too painful, that watching her gather her curls at the back of her neck made Alison long to turn back the clock and erase the events of the past few months.

"Alison," she said. "I love you, and that feeling isn't going away no matter how many of my phone calls you decline."

They became more than friends right after Christmas break. Becca had gone home to visit her family in Texas, and during those excruciating eleven days, Alison thought about her all the time: while watching a movie with Michael, while lighting the Hanukah candles with Sadie, while watching the ball drop with Grant and Cynthia. That day, after their first workout post-vacation, Becca suggested they use the showers. She took Alison's hand and pulled her into one of the stalls. Before she closed the curtain behind them, Alison looked around the locker room to make sure no one saw them go in together. As her heart raced, her mind filled with a mixture of terror and excitement.

Alison watched Becca take off her clothes and step in, shocked to finally have answers to some of the questions she'd been obsessing about for months. Becca's naked body was more beautiful than she had imagined, her belly curving smoothly up to her meet her waist, her breasts small and round, her nipples firm and pink.

"Are you going to join me?" Becca asked. Alison couldn't believe this was actually happening. Even though she'd been fantasizing about this, turning it into reality was a whole different story. Was she really ready for this? What about Michael? She had never been unfaithful to him. Would being with a woman even be considered an affair?

Becca stood with her eyes closed, letting the water saturate her hair and run down over her chest, and then she opened her eyes and looked at Alison, the look on her face saying everything Alison needed to hear. Pushing thoughts of Michael out of her head, Alison stripped off her gym clothes and crossed the threshold into another life. Becca put her arms around her, tickling her back with her fingernails. Alison ran her hand along the smooth skin of Becca's shoulder and then dared to cup her breast in her hand, running her thumb over her nipple. Moaning, Becca pulled her closer so her pelvis pressed against Alison's thigh. Michael had never turned her on like this. Not even close.

"I've been waiting for this day," Becca whispered.

"Me, too." Alison guided Becca's face to hers for their first kiss. Her lips were soft and full, nothing like Michael's thin lips and Alison knew right away that kissing a woman was nothing like kissing a man, and when Becca put her fingers inside her, Alison knew her life would never be the same again. A small part of her couldn't believe this was really happening, and a much bigger part of her knew nothing could be more right.

"Did you hear me?" Becca asked now. "I said I love you."

"I ..." Since she had awakened in the hospital, she'd thought about Becca all the time: as the nurses checked her blood pressure and rewrapped the bandages on her head, she wondered what Becca was doing. When she couldn't sleep, she remembered lounging on Becca's bed and talking about teaching, and what books they were reading and which countries topped their travel bucket list. Had she finished that Kate Atkinson novel she was reading? Would she take someone else to that B&B in a castle in Ireland they'd been fantasizing about? And when Michael told a corny joke and Nate cracked up, Alison wanted to cry because she missed laughing with Becca so much. But despite her constant thoughts about Becca, she wasn't sure if it was love. Lust, undoubtedly, but whether it was truly love, she wasn't quite sure.

"I know your feelings haven't changed," Becca said. "I'm coming to visit tomorrow, and I won't take no for an answer."

"Wait ..." Alison wanted to tell Becca not to waste her time trying to recreate what they'd had. She missed the passion between them, but she didn't know if it would be the same after the surgery. Was there a better match out there for Becca? Someone who didn't drool when they ate and could fully participate in life without physical limitations? She couldn't imagine going back to the gym with Becca now. And what about Michael? Before the surgery, Becca had been hinting about divorce and Alison wasn't blind to the flaws in their marriage, but he had been standing by her side through all of the challenges of recovery. She wasn't at all attracted to him anymore, but she had to believe his loyalty was worth something.

Struggling to see past her disabilities to the future, Alison wanted to do what was best for all three of them, if there even was such a thing. Should she stay with the husband who provided for her but bored her to tears, or run off with the lover she craved? If she believed the articles in women's magazines, intimacy was the driving force of a marriage and sex with Michael was lackluster at best; but was what she felt for Becca enough? She wasn't sure. But Becca had made her intentions clear and as the line went dead, Alison could do nothing about it.

CHAPTER EIGHT

Grant

February 19, 2019

GRANT JABBED THE POWER BUTTON on the blender for the third time, but nothing happened. Switching the plug to the other outlet didn't work either, the powder sitting on top of the milk, the two pills suspended halfway down. He thought of using the shaker bottle that had come in the package with the protein powder, but when Sadie came downstairs, he lost his train of thought.

"Dad, I missed the bus," she said. "Can you drive me to school?"

He was already running late for office hours, but with Cynthia at an early Pilates class, he had no choice.

"Get ready quick," he said. "I'm running late."

Putting the blender jar in the sink, he grabbed his bag and phone from the kitchen table. He'd take his pills when he got to work. Sadie jammed her feet into her boots and followed him out the door.

After he dropped Sadie at school, Grant sped out of the parking lot, ignoring the aggressive hand motions from a traffic agent in an orange vest. He made it to the Mass Pike in record time, but as soon as the highway came into view, he saw the snarl of traffic. He made a quick call to Wendy to fill her in.

"Get here as soon as you can. There are important patients on the schedule today," she said.

He wasn't sure what she meant, but he was too focused on merging onto the highway to ask any questions. As he sat in traffic, his thoughts turned to Alison and Michael. They had flown out to Ohio last week for a consultation, and the guy out there, Wally

Richman, had suggested a plan for treatment. From the note Alison had emailed to him, it looked similar to what Grant would have recommended—surgery followed by stereotactic radiation—but it would require a several-week stay in Cleveland. Alison could probably take a leave of absence from school, but he wasn't sure Michael's accounting firm would spell him during tax season.

As Grant finally reached his exit, his stomach started to churn. He wasn't sure if it was thinking about Alison's dilemma or skipping his morning shake that was causing the queasiness—maybe a combination of the two. He tried to grab his bag from the backseat to take out his Adderall, but he couldn't reach it and watch the road at the same time.

When he got to the office, Grant hurried through the crowded office waiting room, saying a quick good morning to Wendy and the new front desk girl, Laura, as he passed the check-in desk. He was the only surgeon in the office today, so he knew all of these people were waiting to see him. He much preferred being in the operating room to seeing patients in the office, but consultations were a necessary evil. No consults, no surgeries. Anesthetized patients didn't complain or babble on about their bowel movements or bring in pushy family members who asked a zillion stupid questions; more importantly, in the OR, he could fix their problems with his drill and his scalpel. In the office, all he could do was talk.

Throwing his work bag down onto the desk, he reached into the side pocket where he kept the bottle, finding only a few tissues and some loose change. His heart sped up while he checked every pocket and then emptied out the contents of the bag onto the desk, sifting through old issues of The Journal of Interventional Neurosurgery, napkins, and keys. Where the fuck was it? He always put it in the same place so that he could make his shake in the morning and start the day right. He must have left it on the kitchen counter when he was messing with the blender. A bead of sweat trickled down the side of his face as he opened the bottom drawer in his desk. He took out a few bottles, turning them over in his hand to read the labels. Vicodin, Neurontin, Percocet. No Adderall.

This wasn't good. He couldn't leave with a waiting room full of patients, so he tried to put it out of his mind. Before he had started taking the pills, he'd muddled through somehow and that's what he would do today. He pulled up his schedule on his computer and scanned down the page. The first patient on the schedule was Scott Ainsley, a curator at the Museum of Fine Arts. Grant had resected his brain meningioma last week. Scott had been at work when he'd noticed changes in his vision, the paintings suddenly blurry. Grant felt an overwhelming sense of fatigue as he put on his white coat, forcing one arm in and then the other. He wouldn't let the pills rule his life, he told himself as he walked down the hall.

He knocked on the exam room door and entered. Scott was sitting on the exam table with his wife, Patricia, in the chair next to him. Grant extended his hand.

"Scott, how are you?"

"Feeling so much better," Scott said, returning the handshake.

"How's your vision?" Grant knew he sounded more curt than usual. On most days, he liked to chat with his patients, make a little small talk before launching into questions about symptoms, but today he was in no mood.

"Totally back to normal. I can't thank you enough."

"Any weakness in your hands?" Grant took both of Scott's hands and told him to squeeze as hard as he could.

Scott followed the command. "I'm feeling strong. Do you notice any difference?"

"Very slight," Grant said. "You're looking good."

"Can I go back to work? I can't wait to see my Cézannes and Monets again."

"What?" Grant had lost himself for a minute, his mind drifting back to the pills. He didn't remember leaving them on the kitchen counter. Maybe they were still buried in the bottom of his bag. He'd have to check again before his next appointment.

"Scott asked if he can go back to the museum," Patricia said.

"Museum, right." If he had left the pills on the kitchen counter, there was a good chance Cynthia would find them. Damn it all. He didn't want to have to explain to her why he was still taking them all these years later.

"Is he well enough to go back to work?" Patricia asked again.

Grant tried to focus on the conversation. He had no idea what Patricia had asked, so he waited for one of them to give him another clue. To buy some time, he walked over to the sink, took a paper towel from the dispenser and used it wipe the sweat from his face.

"Are you feeling okay, Dr. Kaplan?" Scott asked.

"Fine," he said. "Just a busy day."

"So, he can go back?"

"Trish, give him a minute," Scott said.

"It's a simple question," she said.

Grant leaned against the counter and took a deep breath. If he could focus on their voices for a few minutes, he could give them the answers they were looking for and get the hell out of this room.

"Yes," he managed. "I think you're ready."

Scott smiled. "Thank you so much for everything. It might be an everyday thing for you, but you made a really difficult time a lot easier."

"It was nothing," Grant said. "And how's your pain?"

"Essentially nonexistent at this point," Scott said. "I took a few of the pills you prescribed for the first two days after surgery, but I haven't needed anything more than Tylenol since then. Who knew that having your skull cracked open would hurt less than a pulled muscle?"

"Did you bring your pills with you?" Grant always asked his patients to bring their pill bottles in, ostensibly so he could see how many they had used and to make sure they weren't taking any medications that might have interactions.

"We did." Patricia reached into her purse and pulled out two bottles of pills. "Scott would have forgotten, like he does everything else. You couldn't fix his memory while you were in there?"

Grant looked at the labels, trying to ignore the pounding in his head. The label on the first bottle said Crestor. Before this event, Scott had been perfectly healthy, so he'd only been taking this medication for mildly elevated cholesterol. The other was Oxycontin, the pain reliever Grant usually prescribed for post-operative pain.

Grant held up the bottle of Oxycontin. "You don't need these anymore?"

"I haven't taken it in five days."

"I'm so pleased with your recovery," Grant said. "I'll dispose of them for you. We have a program for that."

"Those have some serious street value." Scott laughed.

"That's why we dispose of them safely," Grant put the pill bottle in the pocket of his white coat. He didn't need to take Oxy right now, but he could certainly add them to his stash for after-work use.

⚘

Grant stood in the hallway, talking a moment to lean against the wall and gather himself. He only had one new consult left to see before lunch, but he was having trouble ignoring the incessant pounding in his head, as if one of his surgical drills was twisting through his brain matter, trying to burrow its way out. As his head throbbed, he couldn't help thinking about the pending lawsuit. With a tumor sitting right next to the auditory nerve, hearing loss was a known complication of that surgery, but Grant couldn't stop ruminating about it. He wished the case were settled already. The rhythmic pounding had now spread to his temples. After he got through this next appointment, he'd try to get a refill of his meds at the hospital pharmacy during the lunch break. A brief thought of quitting cold turkey crossed his mind, but he pushed it away. With everything going on with Alison, now was not a good time to make major changes.

"Dr. Kaplan." Wendy said, walking toward him. "I need to speak with you for a minute." Her voice sounded strange, the words coming out in slow motion.

"Later," he said, waving her away. Whatever she wanted to talk about would have to wait.

"But Doctor ..."

He grabbed the chart from the slot outside the door. "Hello, I'm Dr. Kaplan," he said as he entered the room.

"Grant, I've known you for over twenty years. Your name is one thing I do know in this whole mess." Grant looked up from

56

the chart to see Alison sitting on the exam table, Michael standing by her side.

"What the hell are you doing here?" He put the chart down on the counter. She looked like the picture of health, her blond hair framing her face and cheeks glowing.

"We thought we'd do this the right way," Michael said.

"Do what the right way?"

"A consultation," Michael said. "An official opinion."

"From me? I'm not sure that's a good idea."

"We went to Cleveland to see that Dr. Richman," Michael said. "Not so rich in personality. What an asshole, and a godforsaken city to boot. We couldn't get out of there fast enough."

"It was a nightmare," Alison said. "He's supposed to be this world class expert and he just came across as a jerk."

"I've never met him in person," Grant said, "but I've seen him speak at conferences. He's very well respected."

"He gave us that treatment plan I sent you, but he also said we could just watch it." Alison's eyes started to well up. "He said the risks of surgery are very high because of the size and location of the tumor. He didn't seem to be in favor of surgery."

"It's not exactly a tumor," Grant said. "It's more like—"

"What kind of expert says there's nothing they can do?" Michael said.

"He also said I need to take it easy," Alison said. "No caffeine, no exercise, no sex."

"It's bullshit," Michael said. "There has to be something to do other than sit here and wait for it to bleed."

"I can't do that," Alison said. "I can't just sit and wait. The anxiety will drive me crazy."

"I'm not going to sugarcoat this," Grant said. "This is not an easy case. But there are some possible treatments."

"Like what?" Alison asked.

"Do you want me to go into the details?"

"Yes," she said. "I know this is awkward, but we need to hear what the options are, other than sitting and waiting for doomsday."

Grant couldn't believe he was having this conversation with his sister-in-law. He thought back to medical school ethics course,

Professor Farr saying if you couldn't be impartial, then let someone else treat the patient. He had also said things like, "The physician's personal feelings may unduly affect his medical judgment" and "when family members are the patient, the physician may fail to perform the more intimate parts of the physical examination."

"What do you think?" Michael asked.

Grant's thoughts continued to swirl. When he'd first started practicing, he'd seen his neighbor, Hallie Vitek, who'd had a pituitary adenoma pressing on her optic chiasm. Though Grant knew he could perform a flawless surgery, Professor Farr's words echoed in his head while he evaluated her visual acuity and tracked her eye movements. On the off chance she had a complication, that would have caused a neighborhood scandal. It pained him to do it, but he'd decided to pass her off to Cal.

"Grant, we need your opinion," Alison said. "Dr. Richman may think we should do nothing, but he doesn't know me. You do."

"Well, I would recommend a combination of treatments, similar to what Dr. Richman outlined," he said, pulling himself together. He had to at least pretend to be a professional. "Debulking surgery followed by stereotactic radiotherapy."

"What does that mean?" Michael asked.

"Your AVM is too large to be treated with one modality," Grant said. "We'd have to get a little bit creative."

"Do you think it will work?" Alison asked.

"I'm not sure. But, since watch and wait isn't something you're willing to live with, it's worth a shot."

"It's going to have to work," Michael said. "There aren't any other options. Plus, being closer to home would be better." Grant understood the subtext. Staying in Boston would allow Michael to sneak over to the office and continue preparing tax returns.

"I didn't mean the treatment," Alison said, looking at Grant. "I meant you as my doctor."

Grant wasn't sure how to answer. He shook his head once and watched Alison's face fall. "I have to look into it. With you being family, there may be a conflict of interest."

"I understand the recommendations, but that doesn't apply

here, right?" Alison said, her forehead lined with worry. "Better to trust someone I've known half my life than some random stranger. You're my best hope. I need you to do this for me."

He wasn't one to shy away from a challenge, especially one this critical, and it was clear Alison and Michael wanted him to agree. He remembered receiving some sort of statement about treating family members in the envelope with his license renewal last month. He'd have to find that in the pile on his desk and look it over later.

CHAPTER NINE

Alison

August 28, 2019

SITTING ON THE BACK DECK the day after Becca's call, the late summer sun warmed Alison's skin. Even in late August she already noticed the days getting shorter, the humidity less intense. The hydrangea plants along the edge of the deck were still in bloom, their silky purple petals splayed open to the sky. She adjusted her sunglasses and looked up at the passing clouds. After being trapped inside for so long, she'd forgotten how nice it felt to breathe fresh air.

"It's nice out," Nate said. "How come we don't always sit out here?"

"It's hard for Mrs. Jacobs to sit in these chairs," Rhea said, pulling a pair of jeans from the laundry basket on the patio table. "But a short time is fine, right?"

"Alright," Alison said, wiping a trickle of drool from the corner of her mouth. The breeze lifted her hair and cooled the back of her neck, a reminder that small things could still bring her pleasure. She'd been able to walk to the chair with only the cane for support, a victory she longed to share with Becca. Alison's mind kept turning back to what Becca had said on the phone yesterday, that she would visit today, no matter what. Alison wasn't sure what Becca expected from the visit, whether the future Becca envisioned was based in reality or purely fantasy.

"Nate, why don't you tell Mrs. Jacobs about your part," Rhea said, placing the folded jeans in the pile. "She's been waiting to hear."

Nate looked up from his homework. "Oh my gosh, it's amazing. Mrs. Logan said she was going to post the cast list on Friday afternoon, but she put it up early and everyone was crowding around the board and I couldn't see the list and then finally I got to the front and oh my gosh." Nate bounced in his chair.

"He's a bit excited," Rhea said.

"Cooper got Simba which is great because he can really sing even though he only sang Happy Birthday for the auditions, and Elise Cohen got Pumba which makes sense cause she's a lot taller than me and—"

"Nate, you're keeping Mrs. Jacobs in suspense."

Alison couldn't tell Rhea that she couldn't focus on Nate's monologue, that whatever suspense she thought he was creating was lost on her. Her mind was tuned to the Becca channel. She couldn't stop thinking about whether Becca would show up, and if it would be awkward and what they would say to each other.

"Drumroll, please ... I got Timon!" Nate stood up, puts his arms out and did his best jazz hands. "Which is totally amazing and I'll have to work on my comic timing to get it right. They say comedy is the hardest to master." While Nate went on about how he was ready to rise to the challenge, Alison prayed that Becca wouldn't visit during dinnertime. Having Becca watch her eat would be mortifying.

"I'm not sure Mrs. Jacobs knows who your character is. Maybe you should explain a bit."

He grinned. There was nothing Nate liked more than explaining.

"Okay. M ... M ... More," she managed.

"So, he's the meerkat. The cute funny one. Mrs. Logan says we should get ready to ham it up." He rolled his eyes and did another set of jazz hands. "She said we might get to improv a little bit. That means make stuff up."

He pulled a skirt from the pile of folded laundry and held it in front of him, swinging his hips from side to side. "What do you want me to do, dress in drag and do the hula?" he said in a funny voice.

"Is that one of your lines?" Rhea asked.

"Yeah, I have to start memorizing. I've never had to remember so many before."

The latch on the fence door clinked and Alison's heart jumped.

Becca walked across the backyard, her hair bouncing as she climbed the stairs up to the deck. Makeup free and wearing her workout clothes—leggings and a form-fitting t-shirt—she'd never looked more beautiful.

"Look who's here," Rhea said. "What a nice surprise."

"Ms. Corrie, what are you doing here?" Nate asked. "It's like that time when I saw Mr. Harrison in Market Basket. He had tons of junk food in his cart. Cheetos, Chips Ahoy, Ben and Jerry's. It was so weird."

Becca laughed and tousled Nate's hair.

"Teachers are people too, Nate," Rhea said.

"No worries," Becca said. "I remember feeling the same way when I was a kid. There was nothing more humiliating than seeing a teacher in public. Hello, my dear," Becca bent down to kiss Alison's cheek. Alison felt an embarrassing rush between her legs, something she hadn't felt in a long while. It felt good to know she could still get turned on, but it was also a depressing reminder that the chemistry between them was as strong as ever.

Becca sat down. "You look great." People felt the need to tell Alison how great she looked when she knew she looked like crap. She used to look great. She used to be fit and toned, turning heads when she walked down Beacon Street, even though forty wasn't far off. Now, she looked old and haggard, twenty pounds lighter despite the Ensure shakes Rhea tried to force on her, and most of that weight was muscle. Her face was emaciated, her cheeks concave, and dark circles rimmed her eyes.

"She does, doesn't she?" Rhea said. "My prayers are being answered."

"How's the physical therapy going? Still working hard?"

"Yeah..." She lifted the cane in the air.

"You two haven't visited in a while," Rhea said. "We'll give you some time to yourselves. Nate, let's go get a snack inside."

"But Mom, I was just getting to the part when Timon meets Simba. My star moment. Ms. Corrie would want to hear about it, too."

"There'll be plenty of time to share more later. And you should save some surprises for the actual show." Rhea opened the sliding door and motioned for Nate to follow her.

Nate picked up his backpack and followed his mother inside.

"I'll tell Mr. Harrison you send your regards," Becca said as they left.

"So, how are you?" Becca said.

"Alright." In truth, she was lonely. Her life seemed meaningless without work, and the kids, and most of all, without Becca. Alison wished she could tell Becca that with words, not only with her eyes.

Becca leaned forward so they were almost touching. "I've missed you more than I can say. When you stopped taking my calls, I told myself you needed your space, that you were still grieving and I needed to let you go through the process, but I can't do this anymore," she said, her eyes glassy.

"Okay. I ... I ..." Alison was trying to say that not an hour went by when she didn't think of her, picturing her muscular calves, her gap-toothed smile, the look of tranquility on her face after sex. Alison loved when Becca got aroused, the way she would clench her muscles and hold her breath as she neared climax, but she relished that peaceful moment afterwards even more.

"I miss your body next to mine," Becca said. "But really, I miss talking to you and sharing everything. I didn't fully realize what we had until it was gone. I took you for granted. It was torture for me when I couldn't see you in the hospital. You can't cut me off again."

"I ... sorry," Alison's heart beat harder at Becca's confession. She missed their closeness, too, but she could barely speak simple words so sharing seemed impossible. One of these days, Becca would wake up from her fantasy and realize that hitching herself to this broken-down wagon was a horrible mistake. She was young and beautiful and could find someone else in a split second.

Becca wiped her eyes and took her phone out of her bag. "Look," she said, holding up a photo of one of the Irish castles they'd talked about visiting. "It's still there, waiting for us."

Alison shook her head, picked up her phone and scrolled to the Tinder app they'd downloaded together one afternoon as a joke. She showed Becca the screen and raised her eyebrows in question. Find someone else, she wanted to tell her. Someone who isn't broken.

"I've looked," she said. "Anything to get you out of my head, but everything comes back to you, Alison. Other women can't compare."

"Miss," she managed. She did miss her, desperately, even though she was sitting right here on her deck. Moments in the past few months she'd longed to share with Becca—a small victory at physical therapy, a silly joke from Nate, a news brief on CNN— come crashing to her mind.

"I know you do," she said. "I understand why you've been trying to push me away, but I won't let you do it. Your condition doesn't erase our connection."

"I ..."

"Remember how scared you were before your surgery? When we were together that afternoon at my place after you got your diagnosis? I swore to you that day that I would be there for you no matter what. We knew it would be hard and we'd have to figure it out. Michael ... your family, school. It's been harder than I thought, but I'm still by your side. Remember you were worried you might never wake up? Well, you did. You did wake up and you're still here. It's time to make the most of the life you've been given." Becca sat back in her chair, a look of exhaustion on her face.

In theory, Alison knew she was right. She couldn't spend the rest of her life feeling sorry for herself. She needed to focus on the future rather than dwelling on the past, but knowing that and doing it were two different things.

The breeze picked up and a paper nearly blew off the table. Becca caught it and anchored the math worksheet under a Citronella candle.

"I can't get away from Singapore math, even outside work," Becca said.

Alison covered her smile with her napkin, hoping Becca wouldn't notice she was wiping drool at the same time.

"We're good together, Alison. We like the same things, we laugh at the same stupid jokes, we even read the same books. When's the last time Michael read a book that didn't have to do with the Red Sox or accounting theory?"

She was right. Michael and Alison had never had much in common other than a comfort with each other, a shared desire to have children, and being Jewish. Ten years in, the attraction had faded, the children weren't coming, and religion seemed irrelevant, since the whole point of marrying a Jewish man was so the kids would be raised Jewish. The light had faded from their marriage long ago, but now leaving seemed so complicated. She literally couldn't walk out the door.

"How are things with Michael?" she asked.

Alison shrugged her shoulders.

"You don't have to feel guilty," she said. "He's not the right person for you and that's okay. Divorce happens all the time."

Alison knew this was true, but Becca saying it didn't sit right with her. Becca had never been married, so she had no idea how hard it was to make this decision. "Alright," she said. It was the best she could do.

"No, it's not," Becca said. "You deserve to be happy just like anyone else."

She reached out to hold Alison's hand. Alison raised her eyes to the house and saw Rhea carrying the laundry basket across the living room. Her heart sped up, from Becca's touch but also because Rhea and Nate were right on the other side of the sliding door.

"I ..." Alison was not sure what to say. Part of her wanted to agree that their promises still stood even though she was now an invalid, but the more rational part understood that everything had changed.

Becca trailed her fingers along the back of Alison's hand. "I know," Becca said. "You don't even need to say anything. I can see it in your eyes."

Alison wondered what Becca thought she was seeing in her eyes since she didn't feel sure about anything. Becca leaned forward and brought her face within inches of Alison's. Her breath smelled like the spearmint gum she used to pop into her mouth after quickies in the faculty bathroom during their half-hour lunch break. She put her hand on Alison's cheek. Just as their lips touched, the sliding door opened.

Nate bounded onto the deck and stopped short. Becca pulled back and slid her chair away from the table. The brief moment of peace that had settled over Alison at the touch of Becca's lips instantly evaporated.

"I just came to get my math homework," he said. "Were you kissing?"

Of all people to walk in at that moment, Nate would be her last choice. His diarrhea of the mouth could explode at any minute, blurting out their secret in gym class, or in the middle of play practice, or to Rhea at home.

"I was just whispering something to Mrs. Jacobs," Becca said. "Not a big deal."

"Is it a secret?" he asked. "I'm a really good secret keeper. Even ask my mom."

"I'll bet you are," Becca said.

"So, what's the secret?"

"It's between us," Becca held her index finger over her lips.

"It really looked like you were kissing," Nate said. "What would Mr. Jacobs think about that?"

"Mrs. Jacobs and I are very good friends," Becca said. "Sometimes friends kiss when they haven't seen each other in a long time."

"Like that?" he asked.

"Yes," Becca nodded. "Now maybe you should go finish your math homework. You wouldn't want to get an incomplete."

"Fine," Nate walked over and grabbed his math worksheet from the table. "I'll go work on my fractions."

"Well, that was a close call," Becca said once Nate was back inside. "Let's hope he keeps his mouth shut."

"I ... hope," Alison said.

"Alison ..." Becca's voice trailed off, but Alison knew what she was about to say. "I want there to be a day when it doesn't matter if Nate or anyone else walks in on us. I know we had only started talking about your marriage before everything happened and maybe it's not appropriate to bring it up now. But I love you. And I miss you like crazy. My feelings haven't changed. I'm here for you always, no matter what."

As Becca talked, Alison wondered what would have happened

if Michael had walked in instead of Nate. In that case, maybe he would have been the one to call it quits on their failing marriage, letting her off the hook and giving her one less thing to worry about.

CHAPTER TEN

Sadie

February 23, 2019

"WHEN WILL YOU BE HOME?" Sadie's mom asked, turning the car in the direction of the train station.

"I don't know," Sadie said. "Maybe eight or nine."

She pulled her flowery skirt down to cover her knees, part of an outfit her parents had given her for eighth-grade graduation, wrapped in tissue paper in a white box with a pink ribbon. She had opened the gift at her party with everyone watching, and smiled politely, knowing she would never wear the skirt in public. As soon as she got to the station, she would put on the short black one she had bought at the mall with her babysitting money. Her mom let her get away with a lot, but clothing was one battle she always fought. She wouldn't let Sadie leave the house in short skirts or crop tops, and if she wore leggings, she always insisted her shirt cover her behind. Sadie found it strange that she was so strict about this one thing when she let so many others slide.

"Text me when you're on the train and I'll come pick you up."

"That's okay," Sadie said. "Piper's parents will drive me home."

When Sadie had asked her mom if she and Piper could go downtown today, she told her they would be walking the Freedom Trail as part of an assignment for American history class, and then meeting Piper's parents for dinner at Faneuil Hall. Her mom had agreed immediately, without asking questions. Piper's mom was single and Sadie wasn't even taking American history, so her mom had failed, or passed, the test, depending how you looked at it.

"You have a lot going on," Sadie added.

"What do you mean?"

"You know, everything with Aunt Alison."

Sadie didn't understand exactly what was wrong with her aunt—something about bleeding in her brain—but she knew everyone was on edge. Her father was usually the one who calmed people down and said that everyone was making a big deal out of nothing, and even he seemed anxious.

"Who told you about that?"

"I heard you and Dad arguing about it last night." Sadie had been headed downstairs to get some ice cream, but she'd stopped when she heard the tone of her parents' voices.

"I can't believe they just showed up in my office unannounced," her father said. "It was a fucking ambush."

The only other time Sadie had heard that word was in social studies last year when Mr. Tryniski had used it to describe the surprise attack on Pearl Harbor. How could that have anything to do with Aunt Alison and her father?

"Don't be so dramatic," her mom had said. "It wasn't an ambush. They're just trying to find the best person to take care of her, and you're the best in the country."

"There are lots of good surgeons," her father said. "They should have gone with the guy in Ohio."

"This is the not the time to be humble, Grant. You know this is your area of expertise. I need you to do the right thing here."

"I don't know what the right thing is, Cynthia," Grant said. "The ethics are tricky. I looked up the AMA statement when I got home. It recommends against treating family members unless it's an emergency."

"This *is* an emergency. You said yourself that she could bleed again at any time. My sister is in trouble and you're the one who can help her. I know she can be a lot to deal with sometimes, but she's still my sister, and I can't lose her."

Sadie heard her mom's voice crack, the way it always did when she was about to cry, and she felt her own eyes burn. She was upset because her mom was crying, and because her aunt was in trouble, but most of all because she was being shut out of the conversation. No one was telling her what was going on, like she was still a little kid.

Sadie loved her only aunt so much, sometimes getting along better with her than she did with her mother. She felt like she could say anything to Aunt Alison, share what she was really thinking without fear of judgment. With her mother, she always felt on guard, like she needed to filter everything first. Every six months or so, Alison would pick Sadie up and take her shopping at the fancy mall in Chestnut Hill, often buying Sadie a cute top or a bracelet or a bottle of the fancy shower gel her mother said was too expensive. Afterwards, while they shared a tortilla salad for lunch, Aunt Alison always made Sadie promise not to show her mother the gifts. It was their secret.

Her mom stopped the car in front of the station and turned to look at Sadie. "I'm sorry you had to hear that," she said. "That argument was between me and your father."

"Is she going to be okay?"

"I don't want you to worry. The adults will figure it out."

"I'm not a baby anymore," Sadie said. When she was younger, she used to think her parents treated her too much like an adult—talking about politics at the dinner table, using anatomically correct names for body parts, bringing her along to cocktail parties—but now that she was a teenager, they were doing the opposite.

"You have enough stress in your life with all your schoolwork and skating." Sadie hadn't mentioned to her mom that she would be missing her required Saturday practice at the rink today. She would make up a story, tell Coach Volkov she'd been in the bathroom with diarrhea all day, using graphic detail to avoid questions.

"I'm almost an adult," Sadie said. "You can start treating me like one."

"Almost, but not quite," her mom said. "I'll make sure to share what you need to know. Now go learn about Paul Revere."

Her mom opened her purse and took several twenties out of her wallet. "Just in case," she said.

Sadie took the money, opened the car door and slammed it behind her. When she didn't see Piper on the platform, she found a seat on a bench. At times like this, she wished she had a sibling so someone else understood what she was up against. Opening her backpack, she pulled out her black skirt and sat down on a bench to put it on under her longer skirt. Once she had it over her hips, she slipped off the flowery skirt and stuffed it into the bag.

When she looked up, Piper was walking in her direction, her hair now bright pink instead of the usual black.

Sadie stood up. "When did you do that?" Sadie asked, pointing to Piper's hair.

"Last night," Piper said. "I needed a change. The black was getting depressing."

Disappointment flooded through Sadie. She had been looking forward to walking around Boston like twins with their raven black hair and thick eye liner, and now everyone would be looking at Piper's hair while Sadie faded into the crowd.

"It looks cool," Sadie said.

"Cool? We have to work on your vocabulary."

The condescending tone was one of the things Sadie didn't like about Piper, but she accepted it because otherwise they got along well. Hanging out with her was so much more exciting than spending time with the skater girls, which usually involved watching a movie or stupid TV and talking about, but not eating, food. Sadie used to be best friends with Emma, one of the most talented skaters at the rink, but now that Emma was being groomed to try out for the Olympic team, she didn't have much time to hang out.

"What should I say?"

"Lit, sic, snatched," Piper said. "Cool is out. You probably got that from your parents."

Sadie knew that was true. Her parents used that word all the time. Until recently, she had spent so much time with them, as all only children do, that she couldn't help talking like her mother.

"Got it," Sadie said. "Your hair looks sic."

Piper ran her hand over her hair. "Thanks."

The train pulled into the station, making a screeching noise as it came to a stop.

Piper got on first and chose two seats along the window facing into the compartment. As the train pulled out of the station, Sadie watched the familiar stone station building disappear into the distance, remembering how she and her mom used to take this train to go to the Boston Ballet every January. This year, Sadie had talked her way out of it, telling her mom they'd already seen all the ballets and it was getting boring. The truth was she didn't really enjoy sitting next to her mom for hours at a time. She couldn't shake the feeling that her mom wanted to be somewhere else, that they were only going so her mom could post a picture of them together on Facebook with the caption "mommy daughter day," not because she actually wanted to spend time together.

"So where are we going?" Sadie asked.

"Wouldn't you like to know." Piper pulled a metal water bottle out of her bag and offered it to Sadie. "Have a few sips. I've already gotten started."

"I'm not thirsty," Sadie said.

"Yes, you are." Piper took off the top and handed the bottle to Sadie.

Sadie took a sip and coughed. "What is this?"

"Vanilla vodka," Piper said. "My mom never uses the liquor cabinet. Good, right?"

"Yeah," It actually tasted like rubbing alcohol mixed with vanilla extract, but Sadie pretended to like it. "So, where are we headed?"

"I have plans, but first I'm messing with this guy." Piper nodded toward an older guy sitting across the train. He had to be at least thirty, and he was wearing a V-neck T-shirt that showed his thick chest hair. He looked over at them and winked.

Sadie felt her cheeks flush.

"He's hot," Piper said.

"Gross," Sadie whispered. "What's with the chest hair? Put that away."

"I don't mind a little sleaze." Piper blew a kiss back at him. "It's hard to find in Newton."

Sadie elbowed Piper. "Are you crazy? He could be a psychopath."

Sadie took her phone out of her purse and opened up her Instagram. As she scrolled down, she saw a picture Piper had posted of the train guy pursing his lips. The caption said "Train Hottie." How had Piper taken a picture and posted it without Sadie noticing?

"Really?" Sadie held up her phone. "This is too much." Despite her mother's voice playing in her head, Sadie kind of enjoyed the slight danger of this flirtation, the way her heart raced as the guy's eyes met hers.

"Don't worry, we're getting off at the next stop."

"Where are we going?"

"You'll see." The train stopped at the Kenmore station. Piper grabbed Sadie by the hand and pulled her out the door, dipping her top off her shoulder as a farewell to the train guy.

"That was crazy," Sadie said as they climbed the steps to the street.

"If that's crazy, you've got to start living a little."

"Point taken."

"What rock have you been hiding under?"

"I've been at the rink. The skater girls are rule followers. But that doesn't mean I don't know how to have fun."

"Oh yeah?" Piper said. "You can prove that to me today."

❀

Commonwealth Avenue was full of college students, families with kids in strollers, and couples holding hands, all enjoying the unseasonably warm winter day. Piper walked with purpose, her easy confidence making Sadie excited for their day. She didn't know what Piper had planned, but she knew for certain it wasn't the Freedom Trail. Every time Piper handed her the water bottle, Sadie felt obliged to take a small sip. The longer they walked, the dizzier she felt, her thoughts swimming around in her head like goldfish in a bowl. It was disorienting, but somehow exhilarating at the same time.

"Where are we going?" Sadie asked.

Piper opened a glass door and Sadie followed her through into a shopping area. It seemed like a normal mall, the sides of the hall lined with some of the same stores they had in Chestnut Hill.

"Shopping?" Sadie couldn't imagine they'd come all the way downtown to try on clothes and buy makeup.

"Better than shopping," Piper said, stopping at a kiosk that said Skywalk on the front.

When Piper asked for two tickets, her voice sounded so smooth and sure, unlike when Sadie spoke to adults, stumbling her way through what she was trying to say. The ticket woman pointed them towards an elevator and they piled in with a large family and a group of Asian tourists with selfie sticks. Sadie hoped none of them would smell the vodka on her breath.

"Is this an observation deck?" Sadie asked. "I've never been up here."

"Never? Haven't you lived here your whole life?"

"Not here. Newton."

"It's the same thing. You suburban girls think you're so much better than everyone," she said with a bite. And Piper lived in Newton, too. Why was she pretending they weren't from the same place?

The elevator dinged and the attendant herded everyone into a window-lined room, binocular viewers spaced evenly along the edges of the room. Piper quickly claimed one of the viewers, inserting two quarters into the slot.

"Take a look," she said turning the viewer to face toward the Back Bay and the river. "This way is the best."

At first, Sadie could only look with one eye and then the other, but after a few seconds, she got the hang of it. From this high up, the river looked so shiny it almost seemed fake, like the one Emma had made for her science fair diorama a few years ago. She recognized the salt shakers on the bridge across the river, the one close to where her dad worked. On the streets below, cars passed in complete silence, the lack of traffic noise strangely surreal.

"This is really cool," Sadie said, wanting to take back the word the second she said it. "I mean, sic. It's totally sic."

They spent a few more minutes exploring the observatory checking out the views from all sides: the famous red and white Citgo sign, the bright green turf of Fenway park, the mirrored surface of the Hancock tower. When Sadie pressed her face to the glass, it felt like she was flying above the city, like being in an airplane, but better; no distracting engine noise, no flight attendants bumping her elbows with the drink cart, no barriers between her and the sky.

"This is amazing," Sadie said, her breath fogging up the glass.

"Yeah," Piper said. "One of my favorite spots."

Sadie looked over at Piper and smiled, relieved when she smiled back. What would the other girls at school say about them going downtown together? They might never admit it, but Sadie knew they would be jealous of her and wish they were here instead.

"Let's go soon," Piper said. "We have a lot of stuff to do."

They spent a few more minutes before making their way back down in the elevator and outside.

"What's next?" Sadie asked, wondering what else Piper had planned. As they walked, the sky became more overcast, the afternoon sun now barely peeking through the clouds. Sadie zipped her jacket to keep out the chill.

"You'll see." Just past Fenway Park, Piper turned onto a side street Sadie had never been down before.

"What's on this street?" Sadie walked as fast as she could to keep up with Piper.

"They make memories here," Piper said. "Indelible ones."

Piper stopped at a storefront and pulled open the door. "My brother said this place is the best."

A sign over the door read, "Inked." Inside, the walls were covered from floor to ceiling with designs for tattoos, small and large, simple and intricate, and everything in between.

"What the hell?" Sadie whispered. She hesitated once she stepped inside, her stomach starting to churn from drinking the vodka on an empty stomach.

"Why are we here?" She'd seen people with tattoos before—that senior girl with the eyebrow piercing and the sleeve of flowers, the mechanic who fixed her father's car, even Aunt Alison had a small heart on her ankle—but she had certainly never been to a tattoo parlor.

"Why do you think?"

If Piper wanted to get a tattoo, that was her choice. Maybe Piper wanted Sadie there for moral support, to hold her hand through the pain. Sadie felt honored that Piper had chosen her.

An extra-large man with a nose ring and barely any virgin skin stood behind the counter. "Can I help you ladies?"

"Yes." Piper stepped up the counter. The man towered at least a foot over her. "We'd both like to get inked today."

"No way," Sadie said.

"Why did you think we came in here?"

"I thought it was for you."

"I'm not doing it alone. If I get one, you get one."

"I can't do that. My mom would kill me." Every time her mom saw someone with a tattoo, she never failed to mention that people with tattoos weren't allowed to be buried in a Jewish cemetery. Sadie didn't care where she was buried, but the permanence of it felt scary.

"Why don't you stop worrying about your mommy and live a little," Piper said.

She hated how Piper said mean things just to make her feel inferior, like she always had to keep Sadie a few rungs below her.

"Why did you think we came in here, Sadie?" Piper said. "To window shop?"

"I don't know. You didn't give me time to think anything. I need to prepare for something like this."

The nose ring guy looked annoyed. "I like a good catfight, but we have a lot of appointments today. Getting inked," he said, making quotations with his fingers, "is not to be taken lightly."

Sadie turned the laminated pages of the book to a section with sports designs—soccer balls, football helmets, ballet slippers.

"We need a few minutes," Piper said. "Right, Sadie?"

"I've got a guy coming in for a long session," he said. "Why don't you ladies come back when you've had time to think this through?"

"What's he getting?" Piper asked.

"A tiger covering his whole back. The teeth are my favorite part," he said. "If you girls are stalling, I'll go set up."

"No, Sadie will go first," Piper pushed Sadie forward so firmly that the counter dug into her chest. "I'm still deciding." Piper walked over to the side wall and pretended to be enthralled by the display of astronomical designs—Saturn encircled by its ring, shooting stars, and phases of the moon.

"I'm not sure yet," Sadie said, looking down at a book of designs on the counter to avoid making eye contact with the large man.

"It's time to make a statement, Sadie Kaplan," Piper said over her shoulder. "Now or never."

Sadie could tell by the tone of Piper's voice that if she didn't do this, their friendship would be over before it had really begun. Suddenly Piper seemed larger than life and Sadie felt small. The nose ring guy tapped his fingers on the counter. Sadie pictured walking down the hall at school on Monday, the other girls gasping at her tattoo, Piper by her side. For once, she'd be the one with the exciting weekend story and she wouldn't have to exaggerate.

"Okay," Sadie said firmly, pointing to a design in the book. "I'll get this one."

CHAPTER ELEVEN

Alison

September 6, 2019

OVER A WEEK SINCE BECCA'S VISIT, Alison was strangely excited to be taking a trip to the craft store of all places, anything to get her out of the house and away from her circular thoughts. As they got out of the car, she insisted on walking on her own. With practice, she'd gotten much smoother with the cane, more accustomed to moving her body in rhythm with it. When they reached the curb, Rhea held her right arm to help her step up. Nate opened the door and Alison leaned and thumped her way through.

Nate had come off the bus all excited about a new social studies assignment: pick a country and research the culture, food, and dress. For his masterpiece, he needed a piece of green poster board, construction paper, and markers.

"What made you choose Ireland?" Rhea asked as they walked down the first aisle.

"I wanted to pick a country I'd heard of. Cooper chose Bhutan and that sounds more like a piece of furniture than a country, and I also wanted to choose one that had some interesting stuff to research. Canada or Mexico are too boring since we hear about them all the time."

"I'm sure there's a lot you could learn about those countries, too," Rhea said. "Don't be such a big shot."

"I remembered Ms. Corrie told me her family was from Ireland," Nate said. "So that was an easy choice."

"Okay," Alison said. Since Nate had walked in on them last week, he'd been talking about Becca non-stop—Ms. Corrie this, and Ms. Corrie that. It was probably just a harmless crush, but

Alison couldn't help wondering if it was a sign of something more ominous. Maybe talking about her was his way of processing what he'd seen. She hoped he hadn't mentioned anything to Rhea. It was mortifying enough that Alison needed her help with showering and using the toilet. She didn't need Rhea involved in her relationships as well.

"What kinds of things will you put on your poster?" Rhea asked. "Do you have any ideas?"

"Of course, I do," he said. Nate never ran short on ideas. "For foods, I want to find pictures of Irish stew, potatoes, and of course, Guinness."

"How do you know about Guinness?"

"I'm in the world, Mom." He rolled his eyes and kept walking.

Because even a small incline or irregularity could trip Alison up, she looked down as they walked to the next aisle. As they did, she noticed a pair of silver Birkenstocks and a familiar birthmark on the calf. It was Cynthia, Sadie standing behind her, her hair back to its normal brown color. As Alison tried to turn around, her right leg caught on Nate's sneaker and she started to fall. Rhea grabbed her arm before she completely lost her balance.

"Alison, are you okay?" Cynthia rushed down the aisle and took her other arm.

"I'm fine." She did her best to right herself. She hadn't seen Cynthia for months, since she'd come to visit her at the rehab place. Alison didn't have patience for her hysterics right now, or ever for that matter.

"I didn't know you were going to, I mean I wouldn't have come if I ..." Cynthia released Alison's arm and fumbled with the buttons on her shirt. "I'm not trying to stalk you or anything."

Alison wasn't ready to see her again, not even remotely ready to deal with the rift in their relationship and the horrible missteps that had brought them to this point. This would be the perfect moment for Nate to start chattering again about his ideas for the school project.

Alison looked down at the basket Cynthia was holding, full of an assortment of bands for her Rainbow Loom. She never wore her creations, but she spent hours on YouTube learning how to weave ever more complex patterns, claiming it kept her from going to the fridge when she was bored.

"Still?" Alison asked, motioning her chin toward the basket.

"I know," she said. "It's the only thing that helps with my anxiety. I have a law degree and I spend hours braiding rubber bands."

"I love those bracelets," Rhea said.

"Really?" Cynthia said. "Sadie won't wear them anymore."

"Not a chance," Sadie said.

"I will." Nate raised his hand. "As long as the colors aren't too girly."

"What are you shopping for today?" Cynthia asked.

"Nate has a class project about Ireland, so we're here for supplies," Rhea said.

"Ireland's beautiful," Cynthia said.

"Ms. Corrie is Irish," Nate said. "A lot of the boys at school think she's pretty, and sometimes we make bets on who she'll pick to do cleanup duty after lunch. I don't mind clearing tables with her."

"Really?" Rhea said. "You don't seem to like cleaning up around the house."

"Yeah, and some of the sixth-grade boys made a bet about which one of them could get her to kiss them first. It doesn't have to be on the lips. It can be on the cheek or something, but I think Dylan Hoenig will win. He's the sneakiest." Alison closed her eyes and hoped that Rhea would change the subject. All this discussion about Becca and kissing was making her nervous.

"That's quite a bet," Cynthia said. "She's the friend who visited you in the hospital, right?"

"I guess it doesn't matter who wins. I can just ask Mrs. Jacobs. I know two girls can like each other and get married and everything, if they want. I mean Elise Cohen has two moms, the fat one had her and the skinny one had her little brother."

Holding her breath, Alison prayed Cynthia wouldn't pick up on his quick comment.

"Nathaniel," Rhea scolded. "Be appropriate."

Cynthia's face didn't seem to register anything. She seemed to have missed Nate's revelation.

"Nathaniel," Rhea said, "let's go collect the rest of your supplies and leave Mrs. Jacobs to talk with her sister." Alison watched them disappear into the next aisle, wishing they would have stayed. Even Nate's babbling would be better than dealing with her sister.

"Wow," Cynthia said. "He really seems to be keen on your friend Becca."

Alison looked at the shelf, feigning interest in a paper mâché kit.

"How are you?" Cynthia asked. "It's been a long time."

She shrugged. Cynthia was acting like she was unaware of why they were estranged, as if it had nothing to do with her.

"A lot has happened since we last saw each other," Cynthia said. "I think about you every day, Alison, about how things could have turned out differently between us."

Alison refused to look at her. She blamed her sister for their estrangement, but she still felt the loss of their relationship acutely. Cynthia knew her better than anyone else, and she missed their closeness, being able to pick up the phone and just chat or ask her opinion on the news or goings on at school or even on whether to buy a pair of earrings. She missed being together for birthdays and holidays. She missed having a sister.

"I am not my husband," Cynthia said. "He messed up in ways that are bigger than I could have imagined, but I can't rewind and correct what happened. I can't erase the past or make myself more observant than I was. When I think about all the signs I didn't see, I want to slap myself."

Sadie stared at the floor, seemingly embarrassed by her mother's emotional outburst.

What signs was she referring to? Alison didn't know what Cynthia was talking about, but she knew it didn't sound good.

"I don't even know where to begin," Cynthia said. "There's so much to catch you up on."

"I ..." Alison wished she could ask questions, but at the same time she wasn't sure she wanted to hear the answers.

When Cynthia stepped forward to give her a hug, Alison held her cane out to stop her from coming any closer. Cynthia's face fell and she started to scrunch up her eyes. She was about to cry, the same martyr act she'd relied on since their mother died in a car accident when Alison was eight, the car careening on black ice into a ravine. Only four years older, Cynthia had been forced to step up. Their father could barely get himself to work and back, so Cynthia had no choice but to take care of her little sister. She had to wake Alison up in the morning, help her pick out her clothes, and cook dinner which mostly consisted of pasta with sauce from a jar. Cynthia rarely did it with grace, turning every task into a martyred act without embracing the responsibility.

"Maybe we could talk sometime," Cynthia said, her eyes welling with tears. "Just you and me."

"Enough," Alison said. She'd always hated this silly act, and she certainly couldn't stomach it right now.

Cynthia started to sniffle.

"It's okay, Mom," Sadie said.

"Enough," Alison said again. "It your ..." She wanted to say that her act wasn't going to work this time, that she needed more time to heal and figure things out.

"Fault, your fault," Alison stammered, her fingers twitching on her cane.

"How could you say that?" She wiped her nose with her wrist. "I've always looked out for you and this is the thanks I get?"

"No." Alison banged her cane on the floor. With a ticking time-bomb in her head, she hadn't been thinking straight. Cynthia was supposed to steer her in the right direction and she had failed.

The noise of her cane hitting the floor jarred Cynthia. Her face froze and then twisted with anger. "You act like you're completely innocent in all this, but you're not," Cynthia hissed, a spray of spit spewing from her mouth. "You decided to let Grant do your surgery. I didn't tie you down or handcuff you to the operating table. That was your decision, Alison. And now that it went south, you blame me. This is just like you. Always acting like you're better than everyone else. Well, this whole thing sucks. For everyone involved. And this time, you can't claim to be perfect. Because you're not."

Cynthia turned around and was out the door before Alison could respond. An employee in a green apron looked over to see what the commotion was about. Sadie came to Alison's side and placed a hand on her back.

"I'm sorry," she said. "My mom's having a hard time with all of this."

"I ... know."

"She misses you a lot. And I miss you, too. They never let me visit." Alison figured that was the case, but it seemed unnecessarily cruel to punish a child just because the adults couldn't find a way to reconcile.

"I've decided that's stupid," Sadie said. "Just because you two are fighting doesn't mean I can't see you. I'll figure out a way to get to your house."

As Alison watched her go, she realized how far she'd fallen. Not only was she an invalid, but a fifth-grader had nearly outed her and her only sister had just spewed poisonous venom at her in public. And to make matters worse, her teenage niece was the most mature of them all.

CHAPTER TWELVE

Grant

February 25, 2019

"THIS LOOKS DELICIOUS," Grant said, helping himself to a piece of meatloaf and a spoonful of mashed potatoes. This weekly Monday night menu had lost its appeal long ago, but he didn't feel like arguing about food right now. Things had been tense between Cynthia and him since Alison had shown up last week for a consultation. One false move could set her off.

"It's the same thing we always have," Sadie said.

"I don't know what I would do without Whole Foods," Cynthia said. "It's a life saver."

When Cynthia had decided to leave the law, Grant had imagined she would be at home cooking and taking care of the house. He would walk in the door after a long day at work to the smell of homemade pasta sauce bubbling on the stove, Cynthia tossing a salad in the wooden bowl they'd picked up in Montepulciano on their honeymoon. In reality, they ate a lot of prepared takeout and Cynthia hired a cleaning girl to come once a week. He wasn't sure what Cynthia did with her time, but taking care of her family didn't seem to be her top priority.

He took a bite of mashed potatoes and washed it down with a sip of red wine. "Yeah, maybe someone would have to cook," he said, the dig too tempting to pass up.

"Do we have to do this today?" Cynthia said.

"Mom has a lot going on," Sadie said. "She's on the committee for the fall fundraiser at the synagogue again."

"Again?" Grant remembered last year's mind-numbing conversations about the tablecloths, centerpieces, and invitations like it was yesterday.

"Yes, again," Cynthia said. "They invited me back, if you can believe it."

"Mazel Tov." He would need something more than red wine to make it through this dinner. Reaching into his pocket, he found the paper envelope he'd stashed there earlier. He had taken some of the Oxycontin tablets from his office drawer and put them in an envelope so he could access them easily without having to take out a bottle and unscrew the cap. He slid two pills into his hand, and then pretended to cough so he could sneak them in his mouth.

"Enough," Sadie said. "Why are you two always on each other's cases?"

Grant washed the pills down with a sip of wine. "I'm sorry," he said. "I think we're all feeling a little stressed right now."

"About Aunt Alison?"

"Yes," Cynthia said. "She needs your father's help."

"You know about it?" Grant said.

"I heard you and Mom arguing," Sadie said.

"Discussing," Cynthia said. "We both want to do the right thing for my sister, don't we?"

"You keep saying that, but the right thing is not so clear to me," Grant said.

"It is to me."

"Well, it's not *your* medical license on the line."

"Don't get on your high horse with me," Cynthia said. "She's my sister and she's waiting for an answer."

"Have you talked to Aunt Alison about this?" Sadie asked her mom.

"She called yesterday. She feels weird about the situation, but she's on board with it."

"On board with what?" Sadie asked.

"With seeing your father as a patient. Alison knows he will give her the best chance."

"There are other choices," Grant said.

"If she were anyone else, you would have started treatment already."

"I don't want to fight about this." Grant leaned back in his chair, relishing the feeling of relaxation as the Oxy travelled across his blood brain barrier. "I just think it's not a straightforward decision and we shouldn't take it lightly."

"What happens if you decide not to treat her?" Sadie asked. "Will she die?"

"I hope not," Grant said. "But she has a tricky problem. Even my cowboy colleagues don't want to touch her with a ten-foot pole."

"She could die?" Sadie asked again.

"All of us could die at any moment," Grant said. "There are no guarantees in life."

"Don't feed us that bullshit, Grant," Cynthia said. "We all know that Alison's best chance is with you, so this conversation is over."

Grant gave Cynthia a pointed look. "To be continued," he said.

A whimpering sound came from Sadie's side of the table, and when Grant looked back at her, there were tears streaming down her cheeks.

"I can't lose her." Sadie gulped for breath and pulled her hair into a bun, securing it with a rubber band from her pocket. "Not right now."

"Oh, sweetie, Aunt Alison won't die," Cynthia said. "Not if your father has anything to say about it."

As Sadie dried her eyes with a napkin, Grant notice black marks on the back of her neck. Had one of her friends drawn something on her with marker? The skin around the marks was red and angry. Maybe the Oxy was making him see things, but when he squeezed his eyes shut and opened them again, it was still there.

"I hope you can convince him to do this, Mom," Sadie said through her tears. She turned to Grant. "You need to do this, Dad."

Grant grabbed hold of Sadie's chin and turned her face away so he could inspect her neck. It was a figure skate etched in black, the laces tied in a neat bow, the toe-pick ragged and sharp.

"What the fuck is this?"

Sadie pulled her hair back out of the bun to cover up the evidence. "I forgot about it, with everything going on."

"You forgot you were trying to hide it from us?"

"What?" Cynthia said. She got up from her seat and came around the table to see what they were talking about. When she lifted Sadie's hair and saw the tattoo, she licked her index finger and tried to rub it away.

Sadie scrunched up her face. "Mom, really?"

"Sadie Jane Kaplan, haven't we taught you better than this?" She looked at her finger and then continued rubbing. "When did you get this?"

"I don't know."

"Don't give me that," Cynthia said. "Was this what you did in Boston on Saturday?"

"Piper really wanted me to get one," Sadie admitted.

"And you just went along with it?" Grant couldn't believe this.

"Between this, and your new clothes, and that awful girl, I don't know what's going on with you lately," Cynthia said.

"That's offensive, Mom. Piper is my best friend."

Giving up on her effort to erase the tattoo, Cynthia groaned and started gathering the plates from the table, her motions rushed and jerky. "She's not the kind of friend you need," Cynthia said, making more noise than necessary stacking the plates.

"This is so unlike you," Grant said. Sometimes he felt like he was watching his daughter disappear a little more every day. How long would it be until he couldn't find the old Sadie anymore? He could still remember the feel of her tiny hand in his when they took hikes together on Sunday mornings at Nahanton Park while Cynthia slept. Full of questions, Sadie never gave him a moment of peace. What kind of bird is that? Why do the leaves fall off the trees? Where do the squirrels sleep at night? Now, he was lucky if she talked to him at all.

"I'm a teenager. I'm supposed to experiment."

"This experiment is permanent," Grant said firmly. "Do you know how much it costs to remove them? Ed Kerrick makes a mint specializing in just that."

"So, it's not permanent," Sadie said with a snarky tone. She had never spoken to him like this before. Maybe it was all Piper's influence. He hadn't met the girl yet, but he didn't like the sound of her.

"You know what I mean, Sadie." He narrowed his eyes. "Don't contradict me."

"Well, the experimentation ends here and now," Cynthia crashed the plates into the sink. "As of today, you're grounded for a month."

Sadie stormed up the stairs and slammed her bedroom door with a bang.

⚛

Grant excused himself to the bedroom. He swallowed another pill, then sat down on the side of the bed and put his head in his hands. He punched himself in the thigh, first lightly, and then several more times with more force. The pain felt strangely satisfying, a reminder that he was human and alive. In quiet moments like this, he felt ashamed that he had to rely on pills to get through his days, that they'd become such an integral part of his life, but he didn't linger too long in that feeling. Everyone had points of weakness, soft spots and defects they never allowed anyone else to see, and if this was his, so be it. Grant was a loyal husband, a good father, and an excellent surgeon. So what if he took medicine to keep him at his best?

He couldn't believe his little girl had gotten a tattoo. Grant wasn't sure what was going on with her. Was she trying to prove something to them or was this just normal adolescent exploration? He wished she'd chosen a less permanent way to declare her independence. He couldn't help thinking about the boy with the tattoo. Five years ago, Grant had been paged to the emergency room for a head trauma. A seventeen-year-old boy had been riding on the back of his older brother's motorcycle without a helmet and was thrown from the bike at high speed. He was awake and alert when the medics wheeled him in, constantly asking if his brother was okay. Grant had noticed the music note tattoo behind his left ear as he inspected the boy's head for bruising and lacerations, making him wonder about his connection to music. Maybe he played the trumpet or the sax, or maybe he was a piano virtuoso. As the minutes passed, the boy became more confused and stopped responding to questions. His CT scan showed a skull fracture with a huge epidural hematoma that needed to be evacuated immediately. Though Grant rushed him to the OR and removed as much of the blood as he could, it was too late. The boy hadn't been much older than Sadie was now.

After that day, Grant couldn't stop thinking about that kid, the fear in his eyes, the smoothness of his skin, the way he had asked about his brother. But the thing that really haunted him was the sound his mother made when she heard the news, a painful keening he would never forget. That sound recurred is his dreams, startling him awake in the middle of the night, his pajamas drenched in sweat. Weeks later, in the middle of an operation, he found his mind turning back to that day and wondering whether he could have done anything differently, whether he had missed that the boy's pupils were unequal or his reflexes asymmetric, whether he could have gotten him up to the operating room any faster or used a different surgical technique. He couldn't imagine the devastation the boy's parents felt when they heard their son was gone before his life had really begun, his music silenced well before his time. Though he'd lost patients before, this one stayed with him in a different way. This one was his fault.

The pills had definitely helped him move on, but he wasn't really addicted. He could stop at any time. Grant punched his leg a few more times, the sharp pain in his quadriceps centering him and calming him down.

"What are you doing?" Cynthia walked into the bedroom and closed the door behind her.

"Cramp. Too much lifting at the gym." Grant couldn't remember the last time he'd been to the gym.

"What the hell is happening with Sadie? As far as I'm concerned, I think we should lock her in her bedroom and throw away the key."

"Don't you need a parent's permission to get a tattoo?" he said. "When did she get it?"

"It must have been Saturday when she went downtown to

walk the Freedom Trail."

"The Freedom Trail my ass. She's declaring her freedom loud and clear."

Cynthia shot him a look.

Grant could feel the blood surging to his head, his face heating up. "How did you let this happen?" he said, before he could stop himself. "You quit your job to be a stay-at-home mother. As far as I know, that entails keeping track of the kid."

"I don't know what your problem is all of sudden. Now you're blaming me for Sadie's bad choice?"

"I'm just saying that maybe this could have been prevented if you didn't spend all your time volunteering for other things, letting our kid run wild."

"I'm doing my best," Cynthia said. "I spend plenty of time with her, more than she would like."

"It seems to me that you spend more time at synagogue fundraisers, lunching with the ladies, and Weight Watchers meetings. How are those meetings working for you by the way?"

"Fuck you, Grant."

"Is that an offer?"

Cynthia reached into her pocket and pulled out the bottle of Adderall Grant must have left on the counter last week ago. After looking everywhere for it when he got home from work, he'd given up and called Adam's office for a new prescription. "Is everything okay?" she asked, her tone softening. "I thought these were a temporary thing." She reached out to touch his arm.

"It was," he said, brushing her hand away.

"It's been years. I had no idea you were still taking them," she said.

"It really helps me focus, tunes my brain to the right frequency. It's not a big deal."

"Something tells me the hospital might not agree with you," she said. "Remember what happened to Alvin Cassidy?" A few years ago, one of the anesthesiologists had been suspended from the medical staff. Rumor had it he had been injecting himself with the pre-filled Fentanyl syringes from the narcotics cabinet, even going so far as to place a PICC line into a vein in his ankle for easy access. No one on staff knew where he was now, and when anyone talked about him, it was always with a head shake or proclamation like, "What a shame. He was such a good doctor."

"Are you threatening me?" Grant asked.

Cynthia threw him the bottle. The plastic bottle felt smooth and familiar in this palm. "No, I'm just saying it's time for you to stop this nonsense. You don't need these pills. Especially with a lawsuit hanging over your head."

"Don't worry about it, Cyn," he said, tucking the bottle into his pocket. "I have everything under control."

CHAPTER THIRTEEN

Sadie

March 14, 2019

AFTER ALISON LOCKED THE CAR, they walked to pay the parking fee at the machine. With Alison's surgery scheduled for the next morning, Sadie had assumed their annual back to school shopping trip would be cancelled, but her aunt had insisted they keep the date.

"Let's start on the second floor and make our way downstairs," Sadie said. She had this weird routine at the mall—she had to walk by every store. If she missed even one, she felt like her mission was incomplete.

"Just like your mother," Alison said. "A methodical planner."

"I'm nothing like her," Sadie said emphatically. "She's much more anal than I am."

"My sister does like things her way," Alison said.

Sadie stopped in front of her favorite bath store. "Let's go in," she said.

"We usually save this one for last."

"I'm allowed to change things up a little." Sadie wanted to prove she was more flexible than her mother.

A wave of fragrance hit Sadie as they entered the store: rose and almond and lavender, the combination of smells overwhelming. Bath bombs and handmade soaps in an array of rainbow colors were stacked on shelves against the walls and on tables throughout the store.

"We did a lot of damage here last year," Alison said.

"Why do you think I wanted to come in?" Sadie grabbed a basket.

They wandered around the store, Sadie piling soaps and shampoos and bath bombs into her basket. She squirted a sample of hand cream into her palm, holding out her hand for Alison to smell. It smelled like sugar cookies.

"Yum, right?" Sadie said, holding up a bottle of shampoo. "I'm going to get some more of this, too. It makes my hair feel so soft."

"Fair-trade, honey," Alison said, looking at the label. "Your mom may even approve."

Sadie laughed and put the shampoo in her basket. "It depends what phase she's in at the moment. But she still wouldn't buy it for me."

Alison picked up two bottles of nail polish, one black and one bright pink. "Would she buy these?"

"No way." Sadie took the pink one, opening it and using the brush to test the color on her pinky. "I like this one." She put the bottle in the basket. When Sadie looked up, she noticed something had changed on her aunt's face.

"What is it?" she asked.

"I'm thinking about tomorrow," Alison said. "The shampoo made me think—"

"About your hair?"

"Your dad said they have to shave the side of my head for the surgery." Alison ran her hand through her hair.

Sadie gave Alison's hand a quick squeeze. "They have to shave it to keep things sterile. That's what dad says. But it grows back really quick."

"I know. I guess the whole thing is a little scary."

"My dad will take good care of you," Sadie said. "He's one of the best neurosurgeons in the country." Sadie had heard her mom say that so many times it was almost meaningless, but she didn't know what else to say. It felt strange being the one to offer comfort and advice to her aunt rather than the other way around.

"I know everything will be fine," Alison said. "I just can't help thinking about what could go wrong."

"It's been a little tense in our house in the last few weeks," Sadie said, immediately sorry that she'd let that information slip.

"What do you mean?"

"It's nothing. I don't want to make you more nervous than you already are."

"Now you have to tell me."

"Um, okay, but don't tell my mother I said anything."

"You know your secrets are always safe with me," Alison said.

"They've been arguing about your treatment," Sadie said. "Me and Mom had to push Dad to take you on as a patient. Dad said something about ethics and not treating family members unless there was no other choice. Mom insisted only the best was good enough for her sister."

"Cynthia said that?" Aunt Alison seemed surprised.

Sadie nodded.

Alison leaned forward, hanging on Sadie's every word. "And then what happened?"

"My dad caved."

"Your mom strong-armed him? Sounds like my sister."

"Exactly," Sadie said. "It's her way or the highway. That's what Uncle Michael would say, right?"

"Something like that. Are they still arguing about it?"

"I think they've both come to terms with the situation." Sadie could tell this discussion was making her aunt anxious. Lifting her hair to reveal the back of her neck, she knew exactly how to change the topic of conversation. "Look what I got."

"Wow, when did you do this?" Alison reached up to run her fingers along the outline of the ice skate.

"A few weeks ago. When Mom and Dad found out, I was supposed to be grounded, but then I think they forgot. My mom didn't tell you?"

Alison shook her head.

"Do you like it?" Sadie prayed her aunt would approve. Since getting the tattoo last month, she'd had more than a few second thoughts. At the time, an ice skate had seemed like the perfect design to choose—a symbol of her dedication and perseverance, of her single-minded determination to excel—but the more she thought about it, the more it seemed like a mistake. Emma had a shot to make it to the Olympic team, and Sadie would be left with early morning practices in the freezing rink and lame routines at the Bay State Games, a handful of bored parents watching from the stands.

"I love the way the laces curl over each other. It's lovely." Alison reached her arm around Sadie and pulled her in for hug. "Just like you." In Alison's embrace, Sadie felt tears prick her eyes, but she continued smiling, like a rain shower on a sunny day.

Alison kissed Sadie's cheek and then took the basket of bath goodies from her.

"Wait a minute." Sadie went to the wall and grabbed a few of the sunshine bath bombs she knew her aunt loved.

"Are we done here?" Alison asked. "Because I'm ready for a big tortilla salad. I can't eat anything after lunch, so we have to make this meal count."

Following Alison to the counter, Sadie reached into her pocket for the money her mother had thrust at her as she'd walked out the door. Today, her mom's money would come in handy. Hopefully the small present would help her aunt relax and take her mind off her upcoming surgery.

CHAPTER FOURTEEN

Alison

September 10, 2019

A FEW EVENINGS AFTER THE CRAFT STORE RUN-IN, Alison was thinking about her argument with Cynthia, about her sister's selfishness and ridiculous sense of entitlement, when Michael walked into the bedroom carrying his alarm clock and favorite pillow.

"It's time," he said, placing the pillow on his side of the bed and the alarm clock on the nightstand. "I'm not asking permission to sleep next to my wife. I was waiting for you to ask me, but since that's not happening, I made an executive decision."

Alison kept her eyes on her phone. Maybe if she ignored him, he'd give up and go away.

"How's Nate?" Becca texted. "Keeping his mouth zipped?"

Choosing the blushing face emoji, Alison tried to tell her he'd almost outed them a few days ago.

"Did he tell Rhea?" Becca texted.

"No." She was now able to type two and three letter words. Maybe speech therapy was actually doing something.

"Maybe it's time to let people know," Becca said.

"Can you put your phone away and listen for once?" Michael said.

She tucked her phone into the side of the chair. She hadn't thought he was serious when he'd suggested moving back to the bedroom a few weeks ago. She felt her muscles stiffen with anxiety, unsure how to respond to his sudden move.

"It's time for us to reconnect," he said.

Their wedding portrait caught her eye, a fixture over the bed that she rarely noticed anymore. Looking at it now brought her back to that late September afternoon, the sunlight glinting off the dark blue water of Boston Harbor and the way Michael smiled at her with his whole face as they exchanged vows. No one had ever looked at her that way before. One of the reasons she'd married him was that he was so in love with her. It had felt good to be doted on, to be the center of someone else's universe, but that feeling wasn't enough for her anymore.

"No ... not yet," she stammered. She tried to stand up from the chair using the strength of her left leg, but she couldn't make it happen. Her left side had been getting a lot stronger to compensate for her right, but she still wasn't able to stand without assistance.

Michael reached out to help and she accepted his hand without thought. His grip felt steady and firm, just like he was. In the past, his steadiness and clockwork predictability had made her feel safe and secure. When they first met, he'd already signed on with a big accounting firm with a six-figure salary, bonuses, and eventual partnership. With Michael, Alison knew she would never have to worry about paying the bills. There would always be money for groceries, gym memberships, a home in a nice neighborhood. No matter what was going on in the world, people always needed help with their taxes.

After he pulled her up, Michael put his hands on her shoulders. "I know we have a lot to work on. I'm willing to do whatever it takes to make things right between us."

"I ...don't." She attempted to say she wasn't ready for this, that sleeping in the same bed wouldn't make things better between them. The proximity may even exacerbate their problems, his warm breath on her neck and arm flung across her body making her to feel trapped and claustrophobic.

"We'll be like the Sox battling back from behind to win the pennant. If they can do it, so can we," he said, a self-satisfied smile on his face.

His baseball analogy didn't fit. There were no relief pitchers, no coaches, no rookies to pull up from the minors. It was just Alison and Michael and they were no longer a good team. No amount of coaching or strategizing could change that. She kept thinking about a conversation they'd had right after coming home from the fertility clinic that last time. As soon as she looked at the ultrasound screen—the little gray blob in her uterus sickeningly still, no faint flickering of the heartbeat—she knew this time would be the same as all the others. She felt the familiar crushing disappointment, but also an unexpected sense of relief. A baby had been their goal for so long that she hadn't stopped to think about whether it was still something she wanted or whether she was just going through the motions. Maybe if they stopped trying, they could reclaim their lives.

She was silent all the way home in the car and Michael gave her some space, but over dinner, he insisted on talking about it.

"You can't let this get you down," he said. "So many couples have been through the same thing and eventually, it works. I have to believe it will happen for us, too."

She had pushed her food around the plate.

"There's no reason why we won't get lucky," he said. "Your eggs are healthy and my sperm count is good. We just have to keep trying."

She couldn't stomach any more discussion about oocytes and fallopian tubes and sperm motility. Getting pregnant had been the sole focus of their marriage for the past four years, and she had nothing to show for it other than feelings of loneliness, inadequacy, and frustration. Getting pregnant was all they ever talked about anymore, the only thing they had in common. They never talked about funny things that happened at work or the binge-worthy new shows on Netflix or interesting articles from *The Boston Globe*. Maybe a baby would have created a new ground to stand on, a fresh start, but with each failed cycle, that hope faded away.

"I think it might be time to give up," she said. "I don't think I can take any more disappointment."

"How can you say that? I've never known you to give up on anything."

"Well, this might be the thing that breaks me. I can't do this anymore."

Michael wouldn't let her give up. He wanted to keep trying and look at other options like adoption and surrogacy. Failure was not something he was willing to accept.

Now, Michael walked to the nightstand and plugged in his alarm clock. "We have so much history. Isn't that worth something?"

Alison considered the word. History was a thing of the past, irrelevant, obsolete. Michael hadn't done anything wrong. He was the same man who'd stood by her side through all the in-vitro cycles: the man who given her the hormone shots in her butt to increase egg production, who'd squeezed her hand to take her mind off the pain as the catheter passed through her cervix, and whose shoulder absorbed her tears when only one line showed up on the stick; but she was no longer the same woman.

He came back over to her, placed his left arm around her lower back and swept her into a dance turn. "Remember our first dance?" he asked. "You still look just as gorgeous as you did that day."

"Right." He couldn't really mean that. She'd come a long way since the surgery, but she was far from gorgeous.

"Triple step, triple step, rock step," he said with a poor attempt at a Russian accent. "I'll never forget. Those Russian dance teachers burned it into my brain." Alison's mind remembered the steps, but her body wouldn't follow along. She allowed Michael to take her in his strong arms, turning her in circles as he said the steps out loud.

He started singing "It Had to Be You," the song from their first dance, and continued to move her around the room. His singing always made her smile. The notes weren't perfect, but he sang with joy and an uncharacteristic sense of abandon. He flopped onto the bench seat at the foot of the bed, pulling her down onto his lap.

"We've made so many good memories, Alison," he said, wrapping his arms around her. "This is just another challenge we'll get through."

"Not sure," she said.

Michael helped her stand and assisted her into bed. He then undressed down to his boxer shorts, his belly hanging over the elastic waistband. Never one to carry any extra weight, this year had changed everything.

"Past." Alison wasn't sure what she meant. Was she trying to tell Michael that she agreed with him, that they might still have a life together or was she trying to say that their marriage was a thing of the past, a buried artifact not worth excavating?

"It's time to work on our future," he said. "Like they always say, marriage takes work. It's not always going to be a cakewalk."

Alison didn't know what more to say. The silence stretched out between them.

"You know I've been hearing things around town," Michael said. "At racquetball the other night, Andy Samuel said something about a surgeon who's taken a leave of absence because of drug use. Do you think that could be Grant?"

"No ... no way." Alison's first instinct was to defend her brother-in-law. She couldn't imagine this horrific rumor to be true.

"There might be something to it," Michael said. "I think we should try to dig deeper, don't you? We deserve to know the truth."

Alison pulled the covers up to her neck, wishing she could hide underneath them for the next few months. This whole thing was so overwhelming in so many ways.

"Alison, are you even listening to me? Alison?"

He gave up waiting for her response and turned onto his side. His broad back was covered with brown hairs, growing thicker with each passing year. "Goodnight," he said. "We'll talk more about this tomorrow."

She closed her eyes. With everything they'd shared, she would always love Michael, but she wasn't sure she wanted to be married to him anymore, especially now that he was making allegations about her family. The questions she'd been asking herself came rushing back into her head. Her attraction to Becca was undeniable, so much stronger than any she'd ever felt for Michael. But was sex enough? Was what she had with Becca worth forsaking her commitment to Michael? Her relationship with Becca had made her question everything. Michael had never been the right man for her, but maybe no man would ever be. She thought about Becca's suggestion that they tell people about their relationship, share the news on their terms rather than waiting for others to jump to conclusions. With her mind swirling with thoughts, she was suddenly so tired. The constant back and forth was exhausting, and Michael's insinuations had made it even worse. She closed her eyes, hoping to have some answers in the morning.

❀

The next afternoon, Alison sat in the living room waiting for Sadie to arrive. She'd texted in the morning asking if she could come after school. Alison was glad for the spur of the moment plan because advanced notice would have worsened her anxiety. She was scared Sadie would see her as weak, that she would realize how much Alison depended on Rhea to navigate the world, that her disability would completely change their relationship. The doorbell rang and Rhea went to answer it.

"Well, hello," Rhea said. "It's nice to see you again."

"Hi." Sadie stepped inside, her hands clasped in front of her.

Alison stayed seated. She didn't want Sadie to see her limping or using the cane. When she smiled, she hoped Sadie wouldn't notice the right side of her mouth drooping.

"Can I hug you?" Sadie asked.

"Okay," Alison said. People seemed to think that being disabled made her fragile, that hugging her would somehow worsen the damage.

Sadie came over and leaned down to hug her, before taking a seat on the couch.

Rhea excused herself to the kitchen.

"It's so strange to see you," Sadie said. "It's been forever."

"I ... know."

"That wasn't my choice," she said. "My mother basically forbade me from coming over. Every time I ask, she has another reason. At first, she said she wanted to give you time to heal, and then she started saying that things were complicated and having contact could make it worse. Whatever that means. My parents have been really weird lately."

"Alright," Alison said. She couldn't even imagine the level of tension in their house. "Your ... mom?" Alison stumbled, trying to ask whether Cynthia knew about this visit.

"She thinks I'm at mock trial practice," she said. "I'll have to

Uber home in a little bit. They've been really strict with me since everything happened. To keep me away from bad influences, they say."

"Who?"

"They never say, but I know they mean Piper," Sadie said. "The girl who made me get the tattoo."

Getting a tattoo seemed like a pretty innocent teenage dalliance, not a major transgression. There had to be more to the story that Alison hadn't pieced together yet.

"Ddddd ... your Dad?" Even though Grant had drastically changed the course of Alison's life, she still wanted to know he was okay.

"It's been rough," Sadie said. "They're both really hard to be around. So moody and irritable. I never know what's going to set them off. I'm just trying to keep my head down and get through the day."

"Alright ... I ..." Alison attempted to tell Sadie that she understood how hard that must be, that she would always be there for her in spirit, even if she couldn't put that sentiment into words.

"I guess I didn't realize how much I really depended on you until you disappeared from my life," Sadie said. "My family is falling apart and I don't know how to fix it. Friends are one thing, but family is another."

Sometimes this girl was shockingly smart, internalizing things adults took their whole lives to figure out. Alison had ached for Sadie, too, thinking about her often: the funny things she said, her cute smile, her unconditional love.

"Miss you ... too," Alison stammered. Sadie's face lit up. Despite the ridiculous mess their family was in, Sadie seemed happy to be here. Her smile made Alison want to stop wallowing in misery, feeling sorry for herself and perseverating about all of the things she could no longer do. There were still so many things she could do, and she had her whole life ahead of her to do them.

"I know I'm supposed to depend on myself," Sadie said. "but sometimes it's just hard to do it alone. Sometimes I just need someone to lean on. Mom and Dad are constantly fighting now. Mom keeps saying she doesn't trust Dad anymore." Alison's mind drifted to Becca. Was Becca her found family, the person she turned to for comfort and support? Was Becca the one she could trust to have her back no matter the situation?

"It's just ... everything with my Dad ..." Sadie began crying, her shoulders heaving with each sob.

"Okay." Alison took Sadie's hand. She was so proud of the incredible young woman Sadie had become, so strong and smart and amazing. Even with the difficulties in their family, she was doing her best to keep her head up. She inspired Alison to be a better person. Alison wished she could tell Sadie to trust in herself and her boundless abilities, that she should find her inner strength, the warrior within. With these thoughts, she realized she should heed her own advice, if not for herself, then for her niece. Sadie needed her. She didn't care if Alison walked with a cane, had trouble finding words, and dribbled when she drank. Sadie loved Alison just the way she was.

CHAPTER FIFTEEN

Grant

March 15, 2019

GRANT HELD HIS ID CARD up to the reader and entered the pre-operative area. Early morning was the busiest time here, with all the staff hustling to get patients ready for the first surgeries of the day. As he looked around for Alison, he found the background noise of the nurses chattering and monitors beeping more irritating than usual, like an annoying fly buzzing next to his ear. He had decided to take another Adderall to make sure he was extra sharp. He could deal with the annoyance if it improved his concentration. This was not going to be an easy case, and he couldn't afford to fuck it up.

"Well, good morning," he said when he found Alison on the other side of the room, Michael standing next to the stretcher. "How are you feeling?"

"My body feels fine," she said, "but my mind, not so great. I think I've been doing too much Googling."

"I told her to stop, but she wouldn't listen," Michael said.

"Never a good thing," Grant said. "Didn't I warn you to stay away from the computer?"

"I can't stop thinking about the odds. If only one in a hundred thousand people get AVMs each year, how did I get so lucky? You know I'm not religious, but I can't help thinking that someone up there is trying to tell me something."

"Alison, stop with the philosophical nonsense," Michael said. "Sometimes the toast just lands jelly side down."

Grant patted Michael on the back. Usually he found Michael's incessant use of pat phrases annoying, but today he was thankful to have Michael on his side.

"He's right," Grant said. "Sometimes things just happen. And now is not the time to wax poetic about why." Grant pressed his hand to the side of his neck to try to slow his carotid pulse.

"The number of people who have disabilities after surgery is so much higher than I thought," Alison said.

"What do you mean?" Grant asked.

"I got sucked in to a message board. Some woman kept talking about how her husband lost all his short-term memory and another one's permanently in a wheelchair."

"That's not going to happen," Grant said. "I'm very good at what I do. Which website were you on?"

"AVM survivors' network or something like that."

"She was obsessing about whether she'll ever be allowed to exercise," Michael said. "I had to take away her computer."

"We'll talk about all those things later," Grant said.

"But what if I end up on the wrong side of the percentages?" Alison said. "Someone has to. There are people behind those numbers."

"I could go through the chances of getting every complication," Grant said, "but that isn't going to make you feel any better. Right now, the best thing to do is focus on the surgery and recovery." The room felt stuffy all of a sudden. He hoped he'd said enough to get her off this topic. He couldn't take any more talk about complications and message boards.

"Okay," Alison said. Grant could hear by the pitch of her voice that she was trying not to cry. If he didn't change the topic, he'd never get her under anesthesia.

"Did Vik come to see you yet?" Grant asked.

Alison nodded. "He asked me all sorts of questions and looked in my mouth. Something about making sure it would be safe."

"Great, then all we need to do is get the consent signed and we're good to go."

Grant grabbed her chart from the nurses' station and opened up to the informed consent page as he walked back to the bedside.

"So, this is when I tell you about the procedure you're having, the alternatives and the possible risks. I think we've been through all this already. You know this isn't a straightforward surgery and there's always a risk of bleeding, infection, and a small risk of stroke. Having said that, I got my reputation for a reason. My patients do exceedingly well."

Over the years, he'd shortened the informed consent discussion considerably. Some may think he sounded conceited when he bragged about his skills, but for the most part, his confidence put his patients at ease. In this case, a lot of what he was saying was an act. Alison's AVM was so large and in such a difficult location that he wasn't at all sure she was going to do well, but he had to pretend. Usually he felt a sense of ease while the patients signed consent, a feeling that he could handle anything that came his way, but today felt different. Today, the pep talk was more for him than for her. He would have to do his best to forget who his patient was and hope his years of training and experience served him well.

Grant cleared his throat and handed Alison the clipboard. "I just need your John Hancock right here," he said, pointing at the line for her to sign.

"How will we know if the surgery was a success?" she asked.

"I'll know how much I was able to resect, but we'll keep you sedated for most of the day. Give your brain time to rest before we take out the breathing tube. We'll also carefully monitor your vital signs to make sure there aren't any fluctuations."

"Okay, I think I've heard enough," Alison said while she signed her name on the line. "Any more talk and I'm going to rip up this form and walk out of here." A small part of Grant hoped she would do exactly that. Maybe he'd agreed to take on her case too easily. He should have encouraged them to get another opinion after they wrote off the guy at the Cleveland Clinic.

"Let's do this," Michael said.

Grant took the clipboard back and patted Alison's leg. "I'm going to take good care of you." He could still feel his heart rate racing and now there was a whooshing sound in his ears that he'd never noticed before. As he was placing the chart back on the rack at the nurses' station, he heard Michael calling his name from across the room.

"Grant, are we doing the right thing here?" Michael asked.

"We don't want to have any regrets," Alison added.

"Absolutely," Grant said, walking away toward the OR entrance. "You're in good hands." He held his ID up to the card reader and entered through the double doors.

☸

When Grant reached his usual room, everyone was busy preparing for the case. The scrub nurse counted instruments on the sterile tray, while Wendy reviewed the schedule on the computer, and Vik programmed the anesthesia machine.

"Dr. Kaplan, we'll be ready to start in ten minutes," Wendy said.

"I have a stellar team," Grant said, doing his best to seem relaxed. "What would I do without all of you?"

When he went to the hallway to grab a cup of water, Vik followed him. Grant filled his cup from the cooler and drank it down in three big gulps.

"I wanted to check in with you," Vik said.

"What do you mean?"

"See how you're feeling about this whole thing. This is a big deal."

"You mean the fact that my sister-in-law has an AVM the size of Texas?"

"I meant your decision to perform the operation," Vik said. "It's not too late to change your mind you know."

"I can't do that. I'm the best person to do this. How could I forgive myself if I sent her away and she had a bad outcome? I really have no choice."

"There's always a choice," Vik said.

"What are you saying, Vik? That I should call it off?"

"Not necessarily. I just want to make sure you've considered all the possibilities. What if you go ahead and she still doesn't do well? Have you considered that?"

"I can't think that way. Right now, I just need to stay focused and get her through the surgery."

"I hear you," Vik said. "You know I've always got your back."

One of the transporters wheeled Alison past them and she

gave them both a nervous smile. As the gurney rolled through the OR doors, Grant and Vik both followed behind.

"Don't worry," Grant said. "I have everything under control."

Though Grant understood Vik was only trying to look out for him, the last thing Grant needed today were doubts. He did his best to put the conversation out of his mind so he could focus on performing the most flawless surgery of his career.

※

After Wendy got Alison situated on the table, Grant walked to the sink in the hall. Before starting his scrub, he placed two fingers on his neck to check his pulse. It still felt a bit fast, but now that things were moving in the right direction he had calmed down a bit.

He set the timer next to the sink for five minutes, and turned on the water with the foot pedal. Wetting a sterile scrub brush, he cleaned under his nails and then squirted soap into his hands, rubbing his hands together and spreading the lather all of the way up to his elbows. The scrub sink was the closest Grant got to a house of worship, using this time to center himself and clear his mind. He worked through the surgery step by step in his mind, envisioning the entire thing from the first incision to the closing staples. At the end, he took a moment to hope that Alison would come through the surgery intact and healthy. Some might call this a prayer, but since Grant didn't subscribe to religion, he would never put that label on it. Today he almost wished that he did have faith, but he had to believe that even an atheist surgeon deserved a little divine attention in this extraordinary situation.

As he rinsed the soap off his hands and forearms, he pictured the water washing his sins down the drain. He lifted his foot off the pedal, pushed open the OR door with his back and stepped into the embrace of his blue sterile gown and gloves. Wendy tied his mask behind his neck and fit his plastic goggles over his eyes.

Vik had already administered sedatives through Alison's IV and intubated her. With her arms strapped to the arm boards at shoulder height in a T shape, she looked like the angels Sadie used to make in the backyard on a snow day.

"Okay team, let's do this. It's definitely a Getz and Gilberto kind of day," he said to Wendy. She gave him the side eye as she turned on the music, knowing full well this album was reserved for only the toughest of cases. Hopefully, the bossa nova music would keep him positive and focused for today's crucial operation.

A blue sheet extended upwards from Alison's upper lip, separating his surgical field from the rest of her body. When he stepped to his side of the sheet, he saw that his chief resident, Matt, had already shaved the left side of Alison's head and positioned her in the headrest and skull clamp for cranial stabilization. When Grant looked down, he noticed a pile of blond hair on the floor.

The lights over the operating table seemed much brighter today. Grant wasn't sure if that was because they had just replaced the old fluorescent bulbs with LED lights or whether it was an effect of the Adderall. When he tried to focus, he noticed his heart rate now felt irregular, the beats either too close together or too far apart. He couldn't take his pulse in his neck because he couldn't touch anything but the sterile field, so he took a few deep breaths to try to break the unsettling rhythm.

"You okay?" Vik gave him a look of concern over the curtain.

"We're all ready to go," Matt said.

"I'm fine," Grant said. He asked for a scalpel and made the first incision along Alison's left temple and then over and behind her ear, trying to camouflage the incision in her hairline so that no one would ever notice the scar.

"Time of first incision is 7:04 AM," Wendy said as she typed that information into the electronic chart. "On-time start Dr. Kaplan."

"Close enough." After he pulled the scalp flap over the top of her head, he passed the bone saw to Matt. Though Grant had done this more times than he cared to count, he couldn't bring himself to cut Alison's skull. When Matt rested the blade on top of the shiny bone, and turned on the switch, the whirring noise began. Grant knew this was the same noise he'd heard during every craniotomy, but this time it sounded different: louder, higher pitched and much more irritating. When the noise shot straight to his auditory cortex and jangled his brain cells, he wanted to plug his ears with his fingers to make it stop. The familiar burnt smell of bone dust filled the air. It usually didn't bother him, but today he could feel it coating his nostrils and mouth, making him queasy. Swallowing his saliva, he willed the nausea to go away so he could concentrate on the surgery. Finally, Matt finished cutting through the skull and removed a segment of the parietal bone to expose the dura.

"Good job, Matt," Grant said. Every time he spoke, or even just exhaled, he felt the heat collecting under his mask. He wondered how he ever managed to breathe in this thing without suffocating. The room felt like it was at least eighty-five degrees, sweat dampening his scrub cap. "I'll take over from here." Maybe if he was operating, he'd be able to clear his mind of diversions: the heat and the noise and his irregular heartbeat.

Usually Grant would need to peel back the dura before he got a sense of what he was dealing with, but now he could see the reddish discoloration of the parietal lobe even through the thick, white membrane. The dura pulsated with each beep of the anesthesia machine. Grant asked for a scalpel and sliced through the dura, taking special care not to nick the AVM or the brain tissue, and then folded it back on itself to expose the surgical field.

"Wow," Matt said. "That's a whopper."

Grant had decided not to tell Matt about his relationship to Alison. The chief resident was known for following the rules at all costs and making sure all the more junior residents did the same. The situation was already complicated enough without getting into a conversation with his subordinate about the ethics of taking on his sister-in-law as a patient. As the attending, Grant could pull rank and shut the conversation down, but he would rather not have to play that card.

"It sure is," Grant said. The malformation looked even bigger and angrier than it had on the MRI scan. The bright red arteries and maroon veins crisscrossed over each other in haphazard ways, forming tangles and gangly knots. It reminded Grant of the puzzles Sadie used to do on the airplane, the ones where she had to keep her eyes on one squiggly line as it meandered over others, tracing the same line to the finish without straying off course. He tried to track the path of a dilated vein as it intersected several arteries until it disappeared deep in the brain tissue, and then when he tried to track another one, he started getting light-headed. This wasn't going be an easy case. He wasn't sure how much of the malformation he would be able to resect without causing serious deficits.

"How are we going to approach this?" Matt asked. The heat inside Grant's mask now felt stifling, and his breathing was shallow and rapid. No matter how many times he breathed, he couldn't force air down into his lungs. The edge of his scrub hat was sopping wet and he could feel the sweat trickling down the side of his face and threatening to drip into the surgical field. "The Girl from Ipanema," which Grant usually found uniquely beautiful, now sounded haunting and ominous. Something was very wrong.

"She's holding stable over here." Vik tried to make eye contact with Grant.

"Thanks." Grant avoided looking up, afraid that Vik would be onto him the instant their eyes met.

"Is everything on track, Dr. Kaplan?" Wendy reached around from behind him to dab his forehead with a towel.

"Yeah, all good." When Grant asked for the forceps and tried to lift the delicate arachnoid membrane from the surface of the parietal lobe, his fingers began to tingle. No matter how he adjusted, he couldn't maintain a confident grip on the instrument. As his heart threatened to pound through his sternum, he knew he had to get out of this room before he passed out on the operating room floor.

"I need to step out," he mumbled as he walked toward the door, his feet moving in slow motion.

"Dr. Kaplan?" Wendy followed him into the hall.

"I need a minute," he said. "Tell Matt to keep going."

Grant ripped off his gown and gloves and dumped them in the hall trashcan before staggering to the locker room. He sat down on the bench and bent over so his head hung below his knees, trying to get his breathing under control and his heart rate back down. Peeling off his scrub cap, he grabbed a towel from the pile on the bench and dried the sweat from his hair.

What was wrong with him? He'd had his fair share of challenging cases, but nothing like this had ever happened before. He had to get back in there before everyone started to get worried. Matt was an excellent chief resident, but not good enough to handle this case on his own. He sat up and took a few deep breaths.

Grant stood up, opened his locker, and reached into the pocket of his pants. He found the yellow envelope and tipped a few Oxy tablets into his mouth. He had never taken it at work before, usually reserving the opioid to help him come down at the end of the day, but today was not a typical day. He had to do something to calm himself down and this was the only way he knew how. Stretching his legs onto the wooden bench, he decided to lay down for just a few seconds until the medicine took effect.

When he opened his eyes, he felt much better. The tingling in his fingertips had subsided and his heart rate had returned to normal. The Oxy must have done the trick. He walked back to the sink outside his OR and scrubbed up again, realizing immediately by the look of fear in Wendy's eyes that something had gone seriously wrong while he'd been out. In his absence, the perfect order of his OR had fallen apart: the music had stopped, the cardiac monitor galloped, and the staff were all yelling. Blood-soaked gauze pads covered one of the steel Mayo stands. The clock on the wall read 8:37. He couldn't have been gone for half an hour.

"We called you over the PA several times, Dr. Kaplan," Wendy said. What the hell was she talking about? He hadn't heard any overhead pages. How long had he been in the locker room?

Once his gown was tied, Grant retook his position at Alison's head.

"What the fuck, Matt?" he said.

"Dr. Kaplan, I don't know how this happened." Matt's breathing was ragged and panicky. "I can't stop the bleeding."

When Grant looked down at the surgical field, he couldn't see anything through the sea of blood. This was his worst nightmare. In the month since Alison and Michael had shown up in his office, he had run through the steps of this operation over and over in his head, but he had never allowed himself to imagine that things would go this wrong, that he would be standing where he was right now. He now pictured Alison confined to a wheel-chair, her once toned body slack and pudgy, and the horrified look on Cynthia's face when he told her what had happened. He tried to regroup before his thoughts pulled him under.

"Matt, I'll take over from here," Grant said. "I think Dr. Shin needs an assistant in the next room." Cal already had an assigned resident, but if Grant was going to get this operation back on track, he needed to remove all unnecessary distractions. He tried to suction away the blood, but the more he sucked out, the more seemed to accumulate. He couldn't see what the hell was going on. Grabbing the Bovie device from the scrub nurse, he began cauterizing all of the possible bleeders.

"I'm sorry, Dr. Kaplan." Matt stepped back. "I did my best."

"Put on the Herbie Hancock, Wendy," Grant said. He needed some funkier jazz to center his energy and bring everyone's focus back to the task at hand. As the synthesizer sounds of "Chameleon," filled the room, the staff began bobbing their heads in rhythm with the beat. It was that kind of song. He looked back down at Alison's brain and took a deep breath. Let's do this, he thought.

The bleeding had slowed down and Grant could now get a sense of what was happening. It looked like Matt had nicked one of the dilated veins in the AVM. Venous bleeding was not usually this brisk, but because these veins were in direct communication with arteries, they were under higher pressure. Grant bovied the vein and then used a suture to close the hole, temporary fixes until he could resect as much of the AVM as possible. Now that the energy in the room had come back down to normal, Grant felt a lot better. He settled into his ergonomic chair, allowed Wendy to adjust his magnifying goggles over his eyes, and let the sounds of Herbie Hancock put him in the zone.

CHAPTER SIXTEEN

Alison

September 17, 2019

"WHEN ARE YOU GOING TO TELL HIM?" Becca texted.

Alison checked to make sure the bathroom door remained closed.

"Don't know" she typed.

Michael had been back in the bedroom for only a week, but it felt like ages. Every time he woke Alison with his snoring or pulled the covers to his side or flung his arm at her chest, her thoughts turned to Becca. She'd never seen Becca sleep, but she imagined her as the portrait of peace, her lips parted, the muscles of her face relaxed, her breathing soft and even. Becca should be the one sleeping beside her instead of Michael.

She longed to tell him this wasn't working, but every time she had almost gathered the nerve, it dissipated. She didn't want to hurt him.

Michael opened the bathroom door, wearing a towel around his waist, his love handles pooching over the top. Who'd came up with that stupid name anyway? There's nothing she wanted to hold onto less.

While he brushed his teeth with his electric toothbrush, she wished she could tell him to keep his personal hygiene in the bathroom. His wandering tooth brushing had always irritated her.

"Want to go for breakfast at the diner?" He finished brushing and returned the toothbrush to the bathroom.

Michael knew she avoided going out because she still drooled and struggled to eat with her right hand. She hated when people stared. Michael insisted no one was looking, but she knew all eyes were fixed on the invalid with oatmeal on her chin.

Alison shook her head. The past two weekends had been a drag because Rhea only worked weekdays. Michael used to make meals and help her eat, but otherwise, he would leave her alone. Now that he was back in their bed, he'd been annoyingly attentive, suggesting they go out and do things together, even following her to the bathroom. He saw this move as a sign of hope, while Alison was afraid it was the beginning of the end.

"You don't want to go there?" he said. "I thought you liked their oatmeal. We can go anywhere you want."

"No," she said, surprised by the strength of her reaction. A few days ago, she would have gone along with it, powerless to speak her mind. But today, she didn't want to go with him to the diner. She didn't want to go anywhere with Michael.

He threw his towel on the floor and lay down naked on the bed next to her. "I could work up a sweat before I take a shower," he said. "How about a trip to Funkytown?" He leaned over to kiss the side of her neck. Funkytown had been his euphemism for sex since they'd seen it used on some show they'd watched together years ago. He loved having a secret code word so they could talk about having sex without anyone knowing. She'd found it funny at first, but the term had lost its luster long ago.

"I ... don't ..." She wanted to say she wasn't at all interested in sex with him right now, and she wasn't sure she ever would be.

"Come on, Alison. It's been forever. I'm not sure how much longer I can take." It had been a long time. A month ago, she'd let him sleep in the bedroom for one night. When he turned on the Playboy channel and wrapped her left hand around his penis, she decided to go along with it, the only time they'd been close to intimate since her surgery.

Michael sat up and straddled her chest, bringing his penis to her mouth. If she did what he wanted, he would finish soon enough and then maybe leave her alone. When she started licking him, he took that as an invitation to plunge himself deeper into her mouth, and she started gagging. And then, she smelled it, the recognizable smell of Michael's genitals when he hadn't yet showered, a sour, yeasty odor. Gagging and breathing in that smell, she knew she wouldn't be able to do it, that she couldn't do this anymore.

She pushed him off and turned onto her side, trying to catch her breath. Tears came to her eyes as she reached for her phone on the nightstand. When Becca asked her earlier when she would tell Michael, she hadn't known the answer, but now she did.

She picked up her phone and tapped the emoji button, scrolling through until she found the one with a tear coming out of one eye. She turned the phone so Michael could see.

"I'm sorry," he said, covering himself with the sheet. "I know this is difficult for you."

"Enough," she said, throwing the phone down on the bed.

"You're frustrated. When you get better, things will improve between us, too. I know it."

What? He thought this was about not being able to perform? About her feeling inadequate in the bedroom?

"All of your effort is paying off. I can see the improvements with physical and speech therapy. You may not notice, but I see it."

"No." The blood seemed to surge through her arms and legs as suddenly she knew. All the questions that had been filling her mind for months, since before her surgery, disappeared. She knew the answers, or at least enough to take the first step. She had to make him stop talking. With a grunt, she picked up her phone again. She used her left arm to help her sit up and took a breath. This was a crucial conversation so she needed to make sure her meaning came through crystal clear. She typed the letter D and then stopped. She wasn't sure what came next. She picked an E and then a V. Was the next letter an O or a U? She chose the O and then RS.

The word, DEVORS, shone at her from the phone screen.

"What are you spelling?" Michael asked.

She wasn't completely ready for this conversation, but at the same time, this moment was long overdue. When she turned the phone to face Michael, his face fell and the finality of what she'd done hit her. Alison's eyes filled with tears. She felt guilty causing him pain, but she also felt lighter than she had in months. She knew it was the right decision.

"What do you mean?" he said. "I know we have stuff to work on, but I never thought it would come to this." He pointed to their wedding photo. "You're just going to throw us away, after everything we've been through? We can get through this, Alison. I know we can."

"I'm sorry," she said. She finagled herself out of bed and limped to the door with her cane. She needed some space to breathe and she had to text the news to Becca. Now that she'd broken free, she couldn't wait another minute to see her.

"Alison? Where are you going?"

Alison reached the doorway and stepped through.

"You can't just walk out on this conversation," Michael said. "We're not done discussing this." Something about what he said struck her as funny and she started giggling. What had just happened could hardly be called a discussion since most of her communication happened through texts, but she'd gotten her point across. There was no turning back now.

※

Michael called Alison's name down the hallway, his voice fading the farther she walked. No matter how many times she and Becca had talked about it, no matter how often she'd imagined how the conversation would go, she never thought she'd get up the nerve to do it. The whole thing seemed like one of her crazy dreams, but with each step she took, the more reality set in. She wiped tears from her face with her shirt.

When they were newly married, Alison never would have envisioned their marriage ending. Whenever she heard about couples divorcing—family friends, parents from Sadie's preschool, former professors—she always wondered what they'd done wrong. Maybe they hadn't taken the time to nurture their marriages, underestimating how much work it took to keep a relationship healthy. She and Michael knew better than to become a statistic. When she looked back on that younger Alison, full of innocence and naivety and false bravado, she now saw the error in her thinking. That Alison hadn't considered that sometimes things didn't go as planned, that sometimes people were forced to face situations they would never have imagined, and those things changed who they were and how they saw the world. When bad things happened to good people, those good people were forever changed. If she'd never had the surgery, she might have stayed married to Michael.

As she reached the front door, she relied less on the cane, her right leg able to bear more weight. Whether her perception was a true reflection of her physical strength or purely mental, she didn't know and frankly, didn't care. It felt amazing to walk on her own two feet.

She walked down the ramp Michael had installed while she was in the ICU, stopping at the bottom to catch her breath. She took her phone from her pocket and found Becca's name.

"See you," she typed. As she waited for a response, Michael's footsteps echoed inside the house.

The ellipsis popped up on the screen.

"What?" Becca responded.

"Need see you," Alison typed.

"At the gym." Alison pictured the way Becca looked when she worked out on the elliptical, the way her biceps muscles tensed and relaxed, beads of sweat collecting on her upper lip. "Should I come now?"

"Now." Alison texted. "Did it."

Michael opened the front door and stormed down the ramp. "You can't just walk away like that, Alison. Seriously? It's like our marriage doesn't mean anything to you."

"No," she said. To Michael it might seem like she had taken the decision lightly, but her mind was quiet for the first time in what felt like forever.

"What do you mean, no?" he said. "We have to talk about this."

"No." She wanted to tell him that the conversation was over. It felt so good to be finally free, as if she'd been wearing one of those weight belts from the gym, and she'd finally figured out how to release the clasp and let it drop to the floor.

"No isn't good enough." He reached out to take her hand and then took it back, his eyes making contact with hers for a split second before he shifted his gaze to the house across the street.

"I've stood by your side for this whole year. I've paid for Rhea and put up with her son. And this is the thanks you give me. Really fucking appreciative." Michael was moving past shock into anger: his voice louder, his tone more clipped, and she couldn't remember the last time she'd heard him swear.

Even if her speech were normal, nothing she could say would make this moment better for him. She appreciated everything he'd done for her. It couldn't have been easy to live with a wife who couldn't walk, talk or even feed herself. Plenty of men would have distanced themselves or even walked away. Painful silence stretched between them as she waited for Becca to arrive.

"Where is this coming from?" he asked in a quiet voice.

Out of the corner of her eye, Alison saw a flash of lime green, Becca's Volkswagen turning onto the street. With this timing, maybe she could avoid the question. Becca stopped the car in front of their driveway, got out and walked around to Alison's side. Her tank top was darker under her arms and in the small of her back from her workout.

"Alison, you can't run away from me. Let's talk about this."

"Go," she said to Becca, pointing to her car.

"Are you sure?" Becca asked. She looked to Michael and back to me.

"Yes," Alison said.

"Is this for real?" he said.

Even if Alison could talk, she couldn't possibly answer that question in any rational way, but somehow it all made perfect sense. Maybe not to Michael, but to her. Becca took Alison's hand and helped her into the car.

CHAPTER SEVENTEEN

Sadie

March 15, 2019

SADIE PULLED OPEN THE DOOR to the rink and adjusted her skate bag on her shoulder. As much as she sometimes hated practice, the cold air and the familiar smell, a combination of hockey player sweat and rubber floor mat, comforted her today. Exhausted from staying up most of the night thinking about how Aunt Alison's surgery would go, she was glad to have practice to distract her from her thoughts. Everyone said her father was excellent at his job, but Sadie couldn't help thinking there was still a chance that something could go wrong, that Alison's problem would be too complicated to fix.

"I'm so glad we don't have school today," Emma said, following Sadie through the door. "We need to get ready for the Bay State Games."

Sadie nodded and continued to the locker room. She was having trouble focusing on what Emma was saying. "Yeah, why don't we have school again?"

"Teacher development day," Emma said. "I already told you that in the car."

"Right." Sadie didn't remember hearing that, but she had probably been lost in her thoughts.

"We need a lot more practice on the precision line routine." Emma followed Sadie into the locker room. "The intersection and the interlocking circles are still really rough."

Sadie put her bag on the bench and took out her skates, practice dress, and leg warmers. The other girls were arriving, too, chatting while they got ready for practice. "That's why we're here,

Emma. Are we playing 'state the obvious'?"

"No need to be nasty." Emma pulled on her tights and her dress. "I'm just starting to get nervous. Our pairs routine needs work, too."

Sadie didn't respond. She and Emma had been competing together in pairs for five years, but she still felt her face flush every time they stepped onto the ice holding hands. It wasn't her fault there were so few boys in competitive ice skating, but that didn't make performing a pairs routine with another girl any less embarrassing. Sadie didn't feel like talking about it, especially today.

"What's up with you?" Emma asked. "Are you worried about your aunt?"

"No," Sadie said. "Just leave me alone, okay?"

"I'm sure she'll be fine. Your parents will call with an update as soon as they know."

"Dad said the operation could take up to eight hours." She didn't want to tell Emma how worried she really was, like she might jinx it and make things worse. She would have to stay busy to keep her mind from going in circles.

"Are you still hanging out with Piper?" Emma asked.

"Sometimes."

"She is such a liar. You can't believe anything she says."

They finished dressing and sat down on the bench to lace up their skates. "I like her," Sadie said.

"You don't even know who she really is."

"What do you mean?"

"That girl's secrets have secrets," Emma said. "Caroline went to her house in seventh grade. Did she tell you?"

"No." Sadie finished tying her skates and stood up to make sure they were tight enough. "And I don't want to know."

"Her mother's in prison, Sadie. Not exactly ideal friend material."

"That's not true. She said her mom's always on her case."

"Maybe in her weekly phone calls, but other than that—"

"Enough, Emma. I can't deal with you today." What Emma was saying couldn't be true. Every time they'd hung out, Piper had made such a big deal about what a nag her mom was and how lucky Sadie was that her mom gave her space. It must have been the result of the school gossip mill, the story becoming more distorted as it got passed along. Or maybe Emma was trying to sabotage her friendship with Piper.

"Whatever." Emma walked toward the rink. Sadie grabbed her water bottle from her locker and took a sip, blinking away tears. If Coach Volkov saw her cry, she would get angry and say something like, "Champions never show their emotions" or "Nancy Kerrigan didn't cry, did she?" The first time Coach mentioned the former Olympic medalist, Sadie had to Google her on her phone. In the YouTube video she found, Nancy Kerrigan was crying like a baby and screaming, "Why? Why? Why?" so Sadie wasn't sure what Coach was talking about. If Sadie got whacked with a police baton, she wouldn't be ashamed to cry.

She pulled her boot warmers over her skates and followed Emma to the rink. Most of the team was already warming up, some skating around the edge of the ice, others doing back crossovers or simple spins. Sadie stood by the boards and watched the other girls, trying to clear her mind so she could focus on practice.

"Will you be joining us today, Kaplan?" Coach Volkov yelled from the other side of the rink. She was wearing the long puffy coat with the fur collar. Sadie hated that coat. Anytime she saw someone wearing a similar one, it brought to mind Coach's unsmiling face and harsh voice. She hated the way Coach insisted on calling them by their last names and wouldn't let them talk during practice.

"Yes, Coach." Sadie skated out onto the ice, did a few laps to loosen her muscles, and then started her warm-up routine. While she was doing her alternating back crossovers, she looked over and saw Emma in the middle of the rink, always the center of attention here, like she had a spotlight following her at all times. Sadie watched Emma skate backwards on her right leg and then turn her head over her left shoulder and step forward into an effortless double axel jump, landing smoothly on her right leg. Her blade carved a smooth edge into the ice and Sadie was close enough to hear the crunching sound of a perfectly landed jump.

Sadie tried to catch her eye, but Emma moved right into a

gorgeous layback spin, her back arched, arms intertwined up in the air. When they had first started skating together in third grade, Coach had paired them up because they were at a similar level, but as the years passed, Emma had progressed more quickly, mastering jumps and spins much more easily. Sadie had tried to catch up for years, but recently she'd realized it was no use. Some people were just born with more talent, and no amount of practice would close that gap. Sadie wasn't even close to mastering the double axel and her layback spin was clumsy and travelled too far. Sometimes she wondered why she even continued skating. She clearly wasn't going to the Olympics, so what was the point of spending so many hours in this frigid rink? But she knew her mother wouldn't let her quit. Her mother would say something about the importance of commitment or stick-to-it-iveness and then change the subject to make it clear the conversation was over.

Coach blew her whistle. "Time to work on pairs. Wright and Kaplan, you go first."

Emma skated over and took Sadie's hand. They skated together to the end of the rink so they could go through their routine and make sure they both had the choreography memorized. Normally, Emma's grip would be firm, but today it felt looser, less committed, like Sadie wasn't worth her energy. They took their place side by side, their hand on their hips, waiting for the instrumental version of "My Favorite Things" to come through the speaker system.

When the music started playing, Emma skated forward on the eighth beat and launched into an intricate footwork series, her feet moving too fast for Sadie's eyes to keep up. Though Sadie knew the routine, she couldn't make herself do it. Her feet felt like they were frozen to the ice.

"Kaplan, Go." Coach motioned with her hand.

Sadie sat down on the ice and buried her face in her knees. The tears started flowing down her cheeks, wetting her practice dress, and Coach Volkov's voice and the music faded away. All she could hear was the sound of her own sobs.

CHAPTER EIGHTEEN

Grant

March 15, 2019

AFTER ALISON'S SURGERY, Grant stopped in the locker room to make himself look presentable before talking to Michael. If he showed up in the family waiting room all sweaty and disheveled, he definitely wouldn't inspire confidence. He wasn't sure how, but he'd turned the surgery around. When he had closed the dura and fit the bone flap back in place, the bleeding was well controlled and everything seemed okay. The nurses and techs had even given him an ovation, calling him a hero. Lucky bastard was more like it.

Standing at the sink, he splashed water on his face and washed his hands, drying them with a paper towel. You can do this, he told himself. This wasn't the first time he would speak with a family member after a challenging surgery, but it was the first time the patient was his own family member.

When he got to the family waiting room, Michael was alone; all the other operations had finished hours ago. Michael looked up, his eyes bloodshot and a day's stubble shadowing his cheeks.

"Grant," he said, standing up. "What's going on? I was starting to worry."

"Everything's fine," Grant reached for Michael's shoulder, guiding him to sit back down.

"She's okay? What happened?" With the look of fear in Michael's eyes, Grant felt his heart speeding up. Keep it together, he told himself. After salvaging the surgery, he could make it through this conversation.

"It took a little longer than expected," he said. "The malformation was quite large, but I was able to take a good portion out."

"That's good?"

"Yes. She did have a bit of bleeding which prolonged the surgery time." It was more than a bit of bleeding, more like a fucking tsunami, but Michael didn't need to know that. Nothing good would come from sharing that information.

"And now it's stopped?"

"Yes. She's on her way to the ICU. The nurses will come and get you when she's ready for visitors."

"Can I go now? I need to see her."

"In a half hour or so," Grant said. "But she'll remain unconscious tonight. I need to give her brain some rest, so she'll be getting sedatives to keep her comfortable." He put his hand over Michael's for a moment, trying to reassure him that everything was under control, but then he wondered if Michael would notice the clamminess of his palm. He took his hand back and stood up.

"I'll come back in a few hours and check on her," he said, turning and walking back to the locker room.

He opened his locker and checked his phone. He'd missed a call from Sadie's skating coach. That was odd. She usually contacted Cynthia about the logistics of skating practice. He texted Cynthia that everything went fine, saying he would fill her in over dinner. He had suggested she would be more comfortable waiting at home rather than sitting amongst all the other anxious family members in the surgical waiting room. Really, he needed her out of his hair. He peeled off his scrubs and threw on his street clothes.

On the drive home, he couldn't help thinking about the day's events. While he knew the rapid heart rate, sweating, and panicky feeling were probably related to the extra Adderall he'd taken this morning, he couldn't understand what had happened in the locker room. Wendy said she had paged him over the intercom, but he hadn't heard a thing. Could he have actually passed out? Syncope wasn't a side effect of Adderall as far as he knew, but he would have to take a closer look at the package insert. He couldn't make a habit of blacking out during operations. That would certainly earn him an interrogation by the screwed-up doctor committee, the one Vik was currently chairing. That interview would prove awkward, to say the least.

Turning the car off the Mass Pike at exit sixteen, he got another call from Coach Volkov. What did this woman want? He decided to answer so she wouldn't keep calling him.

"Dr. Kaplan?"

"What's going on, Coach?"

"I tried Mrs. Kaplan first, but I couldn't get her."

"What can I do for you?"

"I wanted to let you know about something that happened at practice today."

"Is Sadie okay?" Grant didn't have the mental reserve to deal with any more crises. One near miss with a family member was enough for one day.

"I think so," Coach said. "She had a bit of a breakdown at practice. She and Emma were about to start their routine and Sadie sat down on the ice and started crying."

"That's strange."

"I got her into my office and tried to figure out what was bothering her. She just kept saying she was fine. I couldn't get her to share anything else."

"Maybe she's stressed out about the upcoming competition."

"I don't know. I want to make sure everything is okay at home."

"Fine," Grant said. He wasn't about to tell the coach more than she needed to know. "Absolutely fine. I'll sit down with Sadie when I get home."

He hung up. He didn't know what was going on with Sadie, but there had to be a logical explanation. When he entered the house, the smell of cooked onions made his stomach grumble. On days when he had long surgeries, he ate a small breakfast and then waited to eat again until he got home. If he stopped to snack in the middle, it threw off his rhythm.

"What's cooking?" he yelled as he took off his jacket.

"Brisket," Cynthia came into the mudroom, a wild look in her eyes. "What happened? Is everything okay?"

"It's not Passover," Grant said. "Is it some other obscure holiday I forgot about?" He'd never known Cynthia to make a brisket just for the hell of it. She barely cooked at all anymore. "It smells delicious."

"Enough about the food, Grant. Tell me about my sister."

"Everything went as planned." His heart sped up as he told this lie. "Couldn't have gone better."

"Really?" Could she tell he was hiding something? She was an expert at reading him after all these years together.

"Yes, really." He tried to say the words with as much confidence as possible. "She's on her way to the ICU."

Cynthia released a long breath. "You don't know what I've gone through sitting here all day by myself. I thought I would go insane."

"Where's Sadie?" Grant followed Cynthia into the kitchen.

"She wanted to shower before dinner." Cynthia made a face as he came closer. "Something you could use right about now."

Grant lifted his armpit and took a whiff. He *was* smelling a bit rank after all those hours sweating it out under the OR lights. He'd have to take a quick shower before heading back to the hospital. Cynthia dished out three helpings of meat, potatoes, and carrots and brought the plates to the table.

"I just got a strange call from the skating coach." Grant sat down. "She said that Sadie cried at practice."

"She didn't mention anything to me."

"Why didn't you take the coach's call?"

Cynthia picked up her phone. "I must have been in the bathroom." She checked to see if she had any other missed calls and then started scrolling through her emails.

"Put the phone down Cynthia. We need to figure this out."

Cynthia placed it face down on the table. "What else did Coach say?"

"Not much, just that Sadie lost her shit at practice and that she wouldn't explain why."

"Maybe she's taking this all harder than we think. We'll talk to her when she comes down."

"I don't want her to get lost in all this," Grant said. "No matter how mature she is, she's still a teenager."

"I'm sure she's fine," Cynthia said. "Tell me more about the surgery."

"I was able to resect more than I'd thought I could." When Grant brought a bite to his mouth, he felt a sudden wave of nausea. The food had smelled good at first, but now the thought of putting anything in his stomach made him ill.

"Can I see her?"

"Tomorrow," Grant said. He didn't want Cynthia to see Alison until he knew she had woken up with all of her faculties intact. Plus, he hadn't had a chance to speak with Wendy yet. The last thing he needed was for Wendy to say something in front of Cynthia about his episode in the OR. "She's still intubated and groggy from the anesthesia."

"Are you going back tonight?"

"After dinner." Grant put his fork down on his plate.

"I'm coming, too," she said. "You make me stay home while you cut my sister open and then you expect me to sit here watching *Naked and Afraid* while you go back to see her? No way."

"I never said you had to stay home."

"No, not exactly. You said the operation would take a long time and that I might be better off waiting at home."

"The decision was yours. You can't blame everything on me."

"I'm not, Grant. I'm just scared." Grant felt sweat starting to bead up at his temples. The Adderall was wearing off by now and he would definitely have to take a few Oxy to chill him out before he headed back to the hospital.

"I know this is stressful," Grant said softly, hoping his gentle tone might convince her to stay put. "She's getting the best care possible, I promise."

"I won't be able to sleep until I see her."

"I'm not sure seeing her now is a good idea, Cyn. After major surgery people don't look like their normal selves." He had to think of a way to convince her to stay home. He felt confident that he'd salvaged the surgery—stopped the bleeding and resected as much of the AVM as possible— but there was always the chance of an unexpected complication. What if she woke up with slurred speech or weakness in her fingers? The last thing he needed was Cynthia breathing down his neck while he performed the exam.

"Please," she said. "I need to go. I can handle it."

"I'm not sure you can."

"I'm not an idiot, Grant. I'm an adult and I can make my own decisions." This wasn't looking good. He wasn't sure what other roadblocks he could put in her way.

"I'm the surgeon of record," he said, trying the only other tactic he could think of. "I decide who can and can't see my patient."

"Like hell you can," Cynthia stood up. "I can't sit here anymore. I need to see her with my own eyes."

Grant knew by Cynthia's tone that he had to give in. He was tired of fighting with her. It seemed like every conversation they had these days quickly turned into an argument.

"Fine," he said. "But Sadie doesn't come. I'll go up and check on her before we go." He wanted to make sure she was okay, and it would give him a chance to take his pills before they left.

Cynthia cleared the dishes from the table, covering Sadie's plate with foil. Grant noticed Cynthia's portion hadn't been touched either. She scraped the food into the garbage and piled the dishes in the sink.

As Grant climbed the stairs, he didn't hear the shower running. The light in Sadie's room was off. When he opened the door, Sadie was in her bed, bundled under her purple comforter. Stepping closer to the bed, he could see the rise and fall with her breath. She was okay. The discussion about what had happened at practice would have to wait until later.

❀

"I want to make sure you know what to expect," Grant said in the elevator on the way to the ICU. "She still has a breathing tube and—"

"I know Grant," Cynthia said. "You already told me several times in the car. I know."

"I just want to make sure you understand." The elevator doors opened and Grant stepped out first. He had to figure out a way to check out the situation in advance. He walked down the hallway with Cynthia following behind him, waved to the clerk and stopped at the family waiting room.

"You can wait in here while I check to make sure everything's good."

"Like hell I will." She stormed ahead of him through the automatic sliding doors of the ICU. He should have expected it wouldn't be so easy to brush her aside.

After he passed through the doors, Wendy made eye contact with him from behind the nurses' station. "Dr. Kaplan, can we speak for a minute?" she asked.

"Not a good time." Grant picked up his pace to reach Alison's room before Cynthia. When he got to her assigned room, he was pleased the ICU staff had been efficient getting her settled. Alison rested peacefully on the bed with her eyes closed, the monitor beeping regularly, the EKG on the monitor at the bedside in normal sinus rhythm. He heard Cynthia gasp behind him.

"She looks so swollen," Cynthia said. "And her hair." Grant knew the swelling of the left side of Alison's face and the bandaging wrapped around her head would come as a shock, but she hadn't wanted to listen. Also, the whoosh and click of the ventilator reassured Grant, but he knew it sounded scary to most people.

"I know." Michael came over to hug them both. "I had the same reaction."

How are you holding up?" Grant asked.

"I'm okay," Michael said. "I want to thank you for what you've done, Grant."

"It's too early to thank me," Grant said. "Let's make sure she's out of the woods before I accept any thanks." He stepped up to the bed and took his penlight out of his pocket. Lifting Alison's eyelids with his fingers, first one and then the other, he shined the light to make sure her pupils were equal and reactive to light. The rest of the neurologic exam would have to wait until she woke up and could follow commands.

"When will we know she's okay?" Michael asked.

"Tomorrow. After such a long surgery, we need to let her brain recover. When we take out the breathing tube and she wakes up, we'll get a better sense of what's going on.

"The surgery went well?" Michael asked, again.

"As well as I could have hoped." Grant felt guilty repeating the same lies, but he had no choice. There was no way he could come clean with Michael or Cynthia about the complications during surgery. "It wasn't easy, but I removed a lot of the AVM, as much as I could. Now, we'll use stereotactic radiation to treat the remaining parts."

Cynthia kneeled down at the bedside and laid her face down on Alison's chest. Grant watched Cynthia's head rise and fall with each whir of the ventilator.

"What are you doing, Cyn?"

"Praying," she said without raising her head.

"You don't pray," he said. Grant couldn't remember Cynthia ever praying before. Even at Sadie's bat mitzvah, she had been obsessed with planning the party, the meaning of the religious ceremony completely lost on her.

She ignored him.

"I'm sure her prayers will be heard," Michael said. "It can't hurt. Right now, Alison can use whatever help she can get."

CHAPTER NINETEEN

Alison

September 17, 2019

IN BECCA'S CAR, Alison closed her eyes and inhaled the smell of sweat mixed with the scent from the vanilla air freshener hanging from the rearview mirror, the familiar combination immediately calming her. Michael stood at the bottom of the ramp right next to the car, but she couldn't look at him. She deserved to feel elated right now and the hang-dog look on his face would ruin the moment for her.

Becca sat down in the driver's seat and turned to talk. Alison shook her head. "Go," she said. She couldn't have a conversation with Michael staring her down.

"He looks pretty dejected," Becca said, pulling away down the street. "How did it happen?"

"I just ... I said it," Alison said.

"You just came right out with it?"

"Yes."

"What did he say? Is he angry?" Becca turned off Alison's street and stopped in a quiet cul-de-sac well past a row of houses, the bushes outside the window wild and overgrown.

"Sort of," Alison said. His reaction had been mixed, but it had seemed more sad than angry. Wounded. Like a deer who had no idea it was being hunted until the bullet pierced its chest, a look of shock in its eyes.

"Do you think he's going to fight for you?" she asked.

Alison paused to think about her question. Michael had never been a fighter, though he certainly had been standing up against Grant and Cynthia. He'd coasted through life, always opting for the path of least resistance, and she knew that tendency would never change. She couldn't allow her life to slip idly past anymore. Even if he did fight for her, Alison knew she'd said yes for the wrong reasons. He was looking for someone to play the part of doting wife, and she couldn't pretend to be someone she wasn't any longer.

"No," Alison said.

"He'll just let you slip away?" Becca reached over to take her hand. "He doesn't appreciate what he's losing. I can't believe you did it." A squirrel ran across the road into the bushes.

"I know." Alison couldn't believe it either. She had been thinking about getting out of this marriage for so long, and now that it was happening, it felt surreal. When she leaned over to kiss Becca's cheek, her skin tasted salty and familiar, like when they used to rush to Becca's bed after the gym. On the treadmill, Alison had felt herself getting turned on and she could tell by the look in Becca's eyes she was feeling the same way. Stopping to shower was out of the question. They would run from the car and make a beeline for Becca's bed, all tongues and fingers and open legs. Remembering that now, Alison thought about the early days with Michael and how sex had never been as urgent and undeniable with him.

Becca reached her hand around the back of Alison's neck, the tickle of her fingertips sending shivers up her scalp. Alison's heart pounded as her own fingers itched to reach out and touch.

"You're free," Becca whispered, her breath hot in Alison's ear.

Alison's heart stuttered for a moment. Was she? Her head filled with questions again, the blissful silence when she walked out of the house suddenly gone. She felt like she still had a mountain to climb. When she'd imagined this day, her mind had never allowed her to get beyond the divorce conversation. Now, when she heard the word "free" she felt the weight of all the unknowns. She'd told Michael it was over, but what came next? Should she stay with Becca? How did divorce work? She'd never thought about lawyers and mediation and the logistics of untangling their lives. Now that she was on the other side, she needed to figure out her next move. She felt her shoulders tense with the weight of these decisions. When Becca leaned in, her kiss was soft and gentle, filling Alison with relief. Maybe the questions and decisions could wait. Something Cynthia had said came to her mind. She couldn't change the past. But Alison had just changed her future and that was a major step. She allowed herself to push her concerns aside and relish the moment.

CHAPTER TWENTY

Grant

March 16, 2019

"TO VIK," GRANT SAID, raising his wine glass for a toast. "Happy birthday man, and welcome to the mid-forties." The two couples clinked their glasses together. Grant took a healthy sip of wine and leaned back against the cushy banquet.

"Happy birthday," Cynthia said. "I'm so glad we made this work."

"Yes," Meera said, leaning over to give her husband a kiss. "It's an important tradition."

The four of them always made it a priority to celebrate birthdays together, but with Alison's situation, he hadn't been sure it would happen this time. Grant had checked on her this afternoon, and she was doing even better than he'd expected for the day after surgery. The respiratory therapist had removed her endotracheal tube, her labs looked good, and the intensive care team was keeping a close eye on her. He'd decided a night out was exactly what he needed.

"You're getting up there, old friend," Grant said with a smile.

"Uh, pot—meet kettle." Vik pointed his thumb at Grant and then back at himself. "And I beg to differ. Forty-four is not mid-forties. I'm clinging to my early forties as long as humanly possible."

"That's your prerogative," Cynthia said. She actually looked almost hot tonight in a black dress that camouflaged the rolls of fat on her back. When it was just the two of them, she put in minimum effort—no make-up, old jeans and a baggy sweater—but when they had plans with another couple, she put on lipstick and a sexy dress. He wondered if all married couples stopped trying after twenty years, or if maybe it was the sign of an unhealthy marriage. He hoped not. Cynthia could be annoying at times, but most days he still loved her, and he couldn't imagine his life without her.

"Before you know it, we'll be collecting social security," Meera said.

"We can reserve adjacent rooms in assisted living," Cynthia said.

"And neighboring cemetery plots," Vik added.

They all laughed, and Grant noticed the cute crinkles at the corners of Cynthia's eyes. They only appeared when she thought something was truly funny. He couldn't remember the last time he'd said something that brought them out.

"Now we're getting morbid," Grant said. "This is supposed to be a celebration."

Vik raised his glass again. "And to Grant for a successful surgery. To thinking on your feet and putting your knowledge to the test."

Grant looked over to see if Cynthia had picked up the comment, but she seemed pleasantly oblivious, having a side conversation with Meera. When he took a sip of his wine, he could feel the warmth travel down his esophagus into his stomach. He was so relieved that Alison was doing well that he'd only taken one Oxy tonight. He leaned back in his seat and sighed. This was going to be a good night.

"There aren't many people in the world who could have done what you did yesterday, Grant," Vik said. "Your surgical skills are a wonder to behold."

What the hell? You'd never guess from this conversation that Vik was one of the smartest guys Grant knew. His intelligence certainly wasn't on display right now.

Cynthia broke from her conversation with Meera. "What are you talking about, Vik?"

"You really came back from behind on that one," Vik added.

"Came from behind?" Cynthia said. "What does that mean?"

"Nothing," Grant said. "He just means that the surgery was more difficult than expected."

"You told me everything went well." Cynthia said. Grant could tell she sensed she wasn't being told the whole story, and knowing her, she wouldn't let the topic go until she'd beat the dead horse to a second gruesome death.

"Okay, enough with the toasts already." Meera said. "With the size of your egos, there won't be room left for us at the table."

"What are you two talking about?" Cynthia looked at Grant and Vik who both remained silent.

Grant shrugged his shoulders, pretending not to understand the question. "We're celebrating, Cyn. Try to enjoy this one night."

"To be continued," she said, giving Grant a stern look. He'd have to figure out how to explain himself later.

"Absolutely." Grant was glad Cynthia had already downed her glass of wine or she wouldn't have let him off the hook so easily.

"What are the twins up to these days?" Cynthia asked. "Did they enjoy Mexico?"

The waitress arrived with their appetizers and Grant dug into his grilled octopus over arugula.

"They never wanted to leave," Meera said. "Rohan spent the whole time on the flying trapeze and Risha had a crush on one of the counselors at the kids club."

"You better watch that girl," Cynthia said. "She might be trouble."

"Don't remind me," Meera said. "I like to pretend the teen years will never come."

Grant reached for the bread basket and put a piece on his plate. "We had a rude awakening a few weeks ago."

"Not Sadie," Meera said. "She's such a good girl."

"That's what we thought," Grant said. "But you have to stay on top of them. Just a little freedom and they go down the wrong path."

"What happened?" Vik asked.

"Nothing," Cynthia said.

"She went and got a tattoo," Grant said.

She shot him a look. He knew she hated airing their dirty laundry, but he'd decided to do it anyway. If they couldn't be honest with their best friends, then who could they be honest with?

"Really?" Vik said. "That's so unlike her."

"I told you she was becoming a real teenager," Grant said. "The black clothes and makeup was one thing, but the tattoo takes her rebellion to a whole different level."

The hostess tapped Grant on the shoulder and said there was a phone call for him at the desk. He found his phone in his jacket and noticed a missed call from Cal, along with a text from him that said, CALL ME ASAP. He hadn't heard the ringtone in the noisy restaurant. Since Cal was on call for the practice, Grant had told him where they were eating in case something came up with Alison, but he'd never expected Cal to actually call.

Grant started over to the hostess stand.

"What's going on?" Cynthia asked.

"Is everything okay?" Meera said.

Vik stood up to follow, but Grant motioned for everyone to sit down and stay calm. His heart was threatening to escape his chest, but he didn't want everyone else to get alarmed. As Grant walked across the crowded restaurant to the hostess stand, the din of multiple conversations sounded louder than it had a few moments earlier, and the smell of garlic wafting from the kitchen made his stomach churn.

He reached the stand and accepted the receiver from the hostess.

"Hello?"

"Grant, we need you here, pronto," Cal said. "You picked a great time to ignore your cell phone."

"What's going on?"

"It's Alison. She was doing great. Sitting up, talking, and even drinking clear liquids—"

"What happened, Cal?"

"All of a sudden she said she had the worst headache of her life. Started slurring her words."

"Fuck," Grant said. He felt his stomach drop. In neurosurgery, when a patient reported the "worst headache of their life," it was never a good sign, inevitably a huge brain bleed of some sort.

"We rushed her down for a stat head CT. It's bad, Grant. There's a bleed in the operative cavity."

"How bad is it?"

"The whole cavity is filled with blood. There's some midline shift."

Grant thought he had cauterized all of the visible vessels really well. If the bleed was so big that it was causing the brain to get pushed across to the other side, he might need to take her back to the OR to drain the hemorrhage and prevent the pressure from damaging her normal brain tissue.

"How fast can you get your ass in here?" Cal asked.

Grant played the night back in his head. He would have no problem functioning on just one tablet of Oxy and a glass of wine. Had the waitress refilled his wine glass while he was downing his appetizer? He couldn't remember.

"I'll be there in twenty minutes."

"I can bring her back to the OR now if you want."

Grant wondered if Cal could hear something in his voice that made him concerned, something that told him Grant wasn't fit to perform surgery right now.

"Not necessary," he said. "You know I finish what I start." There was an unspoken understanding in the group that each guy took care of their own patients. The only time he'd let Cal deal with an epidural abscess on one of his post-operative patients had been when he and Cynthia were on a cruise in the Greek islands.

He hung up and stood at the desk for a moment, trying to figure out how to excuse himself from the birthday dinner without sending Cynthia into panic mode. As he walked back, the tables in the restaurant felt much closer together, and everyone seemed to be staring at him. Was he not walking straight? He tried to focus his thoughts and erase the worsening sense of paranoia. He had to get himself together to take care of Alison. Nothing else mattered right now. When he arrived at the table, Grant decided to sit back down for a second so Cynthia would be less likely to jump to conclusions.

"What's going on, Grant?" Cynthia asked as soon as he took his seat.

"Was it Cal?" Vik asked.

"Yes. It seems Alison's hit a bit of a speed bump. I'm going to run over and check on her." So many thoughts raced through his head, but the one he couldn't dismiss was that this must be his fault. He'd been so relieved to finish the operation, he must have gotten careless with bleeding control. He definitely could have spent more time making sure none of the vessels would give way after he'd closed up.

"Do you want me to go with you?" Vik held up his glass of wine. "I've only had a few sips."

"I'm really fine. I don't want to completely ruin your birthday celebration. At least you and Meera can still enjoy your meal."

Cynthia stood up and put on her jacket. Grant would rather Vik and Meera drive her home after dinner, but he couldn't think of how to make her stay, especially after the argument they'd had yesterday.

※

"I don't understand what's going on," Cynthia said as they walked to the car. "You said the surgery went well. Is this normal? What are you planning to do now?" Her rambling continued as they got in the car and started driving. Grant wished she would just shut up so he could concentrate on the road and plan how he would evacuate the hematoma. He hoped he'd get there in time so the slurred speech wouldn't become a permanent deficit.

Fuzzy haloes around the streetlights and the headlights of the oncoming cars sent off streaky starbursts. He shut his eyes tight, trying to clear the lingering spots from his retinas. When he opened his eyes, he noticed flashes of red and blue in his rearview mirror. Someone must be in trouble tonight, Grant thought. He pulled his car over to the right shoulder to let the police car pass, but the cruiser came to a stop behind him.

Cynthia closed her mouth and looked over her shoulder. "What did you do, Grant?"

"Nothing," he said. "Maybe my tail light is out."

The officer approached Grant's door and made a motion for him to roll down the window. Grant could tell by his uniform—the blue button-down shirt and wide-brimmed navy hat—that this was a state trooper instead of a local Boston cop. These guys were known to be particularly tough. Fumbling with the buttons on the door, Grant finally found the one that lowered the window.

"Were you aware you were swerving?" the officer asked.

"No, sir," Grant said. "If I was, I apologize. We're in a bit of a rush." He'd been distracted by the lights and Cynthia's incessant chattering, but Grant didn't think he'd been swerving. Maybe the officer was trying to reach his quota of traffic stops for the night, make a little money for the state budget.

"Where are you rushing to?" the officer asked.

"To the hospital," Cynthia said. "There's been a complication."

"Which hospital?"

"I'm on the medical staff." Grant opened the storage compartment between the front seats, took out his hospital ID, and showed it to the officer.

The officer took the ID and examined it. "Dr. Kaplan, Neurosurgery," the office said. "Impressive. Are you going on official business or as a visitor?"

"Business, sir. I need to take a patient back to the operating room." As Grant spoke, his cell phone rang and he saw Cal's name on the screen. He wanted to pick up, but he didn't think he could answer with the officer standing over him.

"You need to take that?" the officer asked.

"Thank you," Grant said and pressed Accept. "Cal? What's going on."

"Where are you? It's been more than twenty minutes."

"I've been delayed." Grant could feel the officer's eyes on him.

"What do you mean delayed? That isn't funny."

"It's not a joke."

"She's worse. Her speech is harder to understand, and she's getting weak on her right side. Get here quick."

Grant's skin felt flushed, probably from the combination of the Oxy and red wine, and he could feel the warmth of the officer's breath on his face. He told himself to calm down. If he started getting worked up, he'd never make it to the hospital.

"I'll do my best." Grant pressed End and put his phone in the cup holder between the seats.

"Is there something you need to take care of, Dr. Kaplan?" the officer asked.

"My patient is in trouble. She's bleeding into her brain."

"Sounds serious. We'll just do a quick field sobriety test, and I'll send you on your way."

Grant had hoped the officer would take pity on him and forgo the breathalyzer and walking in a straight-line crap, that he would sense the gravity of the situation and give him a pass. No such luck.

When Grant stepped out of the car, the cars whizzing by felt much too close to the shoulder. The officer told Grant to stand on the white line along the side of the road behind the car.

"I'd like you to walk heel to toe for me, like this," the officer said, demonstrating the way he wanted Grant to walk.

Grant wasn't sure he would be able to walk this way. When they'd left the restaurant, he'd been sure he was sober, but now he wasn't feeling so well. The octopus appetizer and red wine swirled around in his stomach, and he felt acid rising in his throat. As he stepped on to the line and began to walk, the officer watching his every move, Grant heard a painful keening noise, like the sound of a dying animal. What the hell was that? Maybe they'd run something over as they were pulling over? He looked back at the car and saw Cynthia opening the passenger door, her mouth wide open, the horrible sound coming from her.

"Ma'am, stay in the car please." The officer walked toward her.

"Officer, you don't understand," she said, stepping out of the car.

"If you stay in the car, I'll get you on your way soon."

"My husband is the only one who can save her," she said between gasps. "He's one of the best neurosurgeons in the country. He's a *Boston Magazine* best doctor every year."

Grant could see the look on the officer's face softening with each of Cynthia's pleas. At first, he thought she would only delay them further, but now it looked like it might work. If Cynthia got them out of this mess, it would be the first time her hysterics were in any way productive.

The officer turned back to Grant. "We'll just do a quick breathalyzer and you'll be out of here."

Cynthia wailed again, even louder than the first time. "If we don't get there soon, my sister could die!"

The officer abandoned Grant and walked over to deal with Cynthia. He took her hand and helped her back into the passenger seat. "This sounds more serious than I thought," he said. "Your sister is the patient?"

"My only sister." Cynthia took a gasping breath. "She's bleeding, and it doesn't look good. My husband needs to get there to help her."

"It'll only take a few minutes and I'll get you right back on the road." He turned his attention back to the field sobriety test.

"Officer," Cynthia said, "My sister may not have a few minutes."

The officer looked at Grant. "Is that true, Dr. Kaplan?"

"Yes, sir." Grant nodded.

The officer sighed. "Well, Ma'am, I certainly couldn't live with that on my head." He motioned for Grant to get back in the car. "Dr. Kaplan, consider yourself warned. You're free to go."

CHAPTER TWENTY-ONE

Alison

September 25, 2019

THE SPEECH THERAPY ROOM was much brighter today, sunlight streaming through the windows and reflecting off the desks. For the first time she could remember, Alison was excited to be here. She smiled when she saw her therapist, Paul, at his regular seat waiting for her.

"Well, you're in a good mood," he said, "Did you wake up on the right side of the bed?"

"Yes, I did." Alison took her seat across from him. Since Michael had moved out last week, she felt so much lighter, as if she'd finished a long training session with the heavy barbells, finally leaving the weight of them behind on the rack. Today, unlike every other day she'd come here, she was ready to face the challenge. Bring it on, Paul, she thought.

"I thought we'd start with some flashcards." Paul tapped the cards into a neat pile.

"Alright." She hated the flashcards. Looking at pictures of fruits and vehicles and animals seemed like a complete waste of time.

Paul held up a cartoon picture of a vacuum cleaner. "What is this?" he asked.

Alison knew exactly what the damn thing was, but shuttling the word "vacuum" from her brain to her mouth was a different story.

"A va ... um. Vaaaaa."

"Very good," he said. "A vacuum cleaner. And do you use this to cook dinner or clean the floor?"

"Clean floor," she said with a smile.

"Excellent." He held up another card showing a turtle with a dark green shell. "Who's this guy?"

"Toot ... tootle." It wasn't quite right but she knew it was close.

"Turtle. Can you say turt-le?" He separated the word into two distinct syllables.

"Turt-le," she repeated slowly.

"You're doing great. One more and we'll quit while we're ahead, huh?" This card featured a piece of pizza covered with round slices of pepperoni.

Her mouth watered. "Peeee ... Peeeezaa." she said.

"Wonderful. And do you have pizza for dinner or put it in your mailbox?" Paul said with a wink.

"For ... dinner." All the long hours here may not have been a waste after all.

"Wonderful work, Alison." Paul swept the cards into his desk drawer. "Now we're going to do some conversational therapy. Just think of it as having a little chat."

This part was the worst. They'd tried it before and it never worked. Paul would ask a question which Alison knew the answer to, but her response stalled before it even turned over.

"Don't make faces," he said. "You can do this. Just pretend we're two friends talking over a cup of coffee. I'll start easy. So, where do you live?"

"In New ... In New ..." She grunted with frustration.

"Okay, do you live in Newton or in Brookline?"

"New ... Newton," she said.

"What a lovely town. So leafy and green. And do you have any children?"

"No ... none." Alison shifted, waiting for the usual stomach cramping that accompanied this painful question, but nothing clenched. Her body remained quiet even as her mind raced. Had she made peace with being childless? Was this question not so loaded anymore?

"Very good. And are you married or single?" Paul continued, unaware of Alison's distraction. She shifted again, pulling her thoughts back to the conversation. He thought he was asking an easy one.

"I'm … married." It was easier to keep it simple. Alison was still married, but not in the same way she was just a week ago. She'd taken the first step to extricate herself from the marriage, but she was hardly single yet. Becca's face came to her mind, and Alison's thoughts floated back to Paul's previous question. Did Becca want children? She couldn't remember ever discussing it. Alison wasn't sure she could picture having children with Becca, not because she couldn't imagine two moms, but more because of the inherent complications and responsibilities. From deep inside her, the word "no" came to the surface and Alison's breath caught with the realization.

"I'm really impressed with your progress, Alison," Paul said and Alison snapped back to the moment. Questions of parenting would have to wait. "Usually improvements come gradually over time, but sometimes recovery comes in fits and starts. You should be very proud of yourself and all your hard work."

Alison smiled back, her mind still swirling. She was proud of committing herself to her recovery, proud of the improvements she'd made, and most of all, proud she'd decided to prioritize her own happiness for once. She pushed her thoughts aside. One step at a time.

❀

The doorbell rand and Rhea crossed the room to answer it.

"Mr. Jacobs, you don't have to ring the bell," she said, opening the door.

"Someone's made it clear I no longer live here." Michael stepped past Rhea. "I figured I'd announce myself." Alison wasn't surprised he'd chosen to play the passive aggressive card. It was one of his favorites.

"Welcome home," Rhea said, returning to the kitchen.

When Becca had dropped her back at home the day she'd told Michael she wanted a divorce, the alarm clock was missing from his nightstand and he had emptied most of the clothes from his closet. She didn't seek him out in the guest room, and when they spoke the next day, it was only about the details of where he would be staying. It was a relief not to have to face him again, to have some time to process all that had happened.

Now, the house seemed so quiet without the sound of Michael talking to clients, the beeping of the microwave, the sound of the shower running. Accustomed to having someone else around all the time, she felt uncomfortable on her own. Becca had been coming over almost every night for a few hours to keep her company.

"I'm just here to pick up a few things," he said.

"How is the hotel?" Alison asked. When Michael had booked a room at the Extended Stay America in Waltham, Alison found the choice a bit odd. It wasn't like they had child custody or visitation schedules to worry about, so a hotel closer to work would have made more sense.

"Well, you've certainly made progress in just a week." he said.

"My speech?" His exit had done more for her recovery than all the hours of therapy combined: her walking was more coordinated, the drooling nearly gone, and her speech much more fluid. Though it didn't make biological sense, when Michael walked out the door, Alison made a major breakthrough in her recovery. She couldn't help smiling while thinking about it.

"Amazing," he said. "We've been working toward this for so long."

"Thanks."

Something changed in his face, his smile suddenly fading. "Was it a miracle recovery or where you bullshitting the whole time? Playing the martyr to garner sympathy? I wouldn't think you were capable of such a disgusting charade."

"Not ... charade," she said firmly. Even though their relationship had seen better days, she was shocked he would accuse her of such a thing.

"Then what was it?"

"I don't know," she said. "May ... maybe stress."

"The old ball and chain were too heavy for you?" Michael said.

Alison stiffened. "No, too much ... too much thinking."

"Oh, so dumping your husband with no warning whatsoever helped you regain your faculties?" he yelled. Alison was sure Rhea could hear every word from the other room. "The guy who's been by your side through this whole fiasco? How nice for you."

"That's not fair," Alison said, taking a deep breath, trying to remain calm. "Not about you." It was no coincidence that she'd made all these improvements right after Michael left, but she didn't want him to think he'd been holding her back. There was no need to be cruel.

"Now you're trying to spare my feelings? You didn't seem to be thinking about them when you threw me out."

"Maybe ... hhh ... hard, but it's right," she said, looking at the floor.

"Maybe for you."

"For both," she said. "Not happy."

"Funny, I never knew I wasn't happy."

She hobbled to the bedroom, hoping he'd take the hint and follow her. The situation was complicated enough already without worrying about Rhea overhearing their argument.

"Not that simple," she said, closing the bedroom door. She'd been trying to be reasonable, but now she couldn't hide the venom in her voice.

"Our whole marriage was a sham? Is that what you're saying?"

"We were young." Alison paused to gather her words." We haven't ... ggg ... grown together."

"I'm just a stupid numbers guy who doesn't use big words. Is that it?" He went to the closet and started collecting the few things left hanging, throwing shirts, shoes, and belts into a pile on the bed.

"That's not it."

"Then what are you saying? I need to stop crying over spilt milk and get over you?" His use of a stupid cliché at this moment made her even more confident in her decision.

"Spent too long hiding," she said.

"Hiding what?"

"Everything."

"Would you care to give me an example?"

"I'm ... I'm with Becca, okay?" She hadn't planned to bring Becca into the conversation. It felt strange to say it out loud, but maybe telling him about Becca would make this whole thing easier, less about what was wrong with him and more about her.

Michael paced back and forth in front of the closet, his eyes wide with shock. Alison wasn't sure of what to say to calm him down, how to make the wild look in his eyes go away. She'd never seen him so worked up.

"Are you serious?" he asked.

Alison nodded.

Michael sat down on the bed with a groan. "Okay, let's slow down a minute here. This is all moving too fast. Maybe this is just a passing phase."

"Not a phase."

When he stood and tried to hug her, she held her cane out in front of her. "Alison, I think we can fix this. I'm not ready to give up."

She sighed. Seeing the pathetic look on his face, she felt the urge to apologize. She couldn't think of anything else to say to him. "I'm sorry."

"So, you just go sailing off into the sunset with your new girl-friend? Where does that leave me?"

Michael wanted her to change her mind, to tell him she'd made a mistake and they should give their marriage one more chance. Images flashed through Alison's mind—the happiness that had filled her on their wedding day, the security she'd felt when they moved into this house, the predictability of their week-end routines—but they quickly dissolved. The time for second chances had passed. Alison needed more than this now. She needed to stand on her own two feet, as unsteady as they may be, and figure out what would bring her passion and joy.

Michael grabbed a shoe and hurled it at the floor. "You're breaking up our family, just like your blasted brother-in-law. He's the one with the addiction, you know. It's common knowledge now." He turned and stormed out of the bedroom, slamming the door behind him. She sat down on the bed and picked up one of the belts, sliding the smooth leather between her fingers. Michael's anger was making him lash out at anyone and everyone. Though she felt badly for hurting him, he needed to hear the truth so he would give up on saving their marriage and start to rebuild his life.

Rhea's voice from the kitchen snapped Alison back to reality. Alison made her way to the kitchen table where she found a bowl of her favorite comfort food, the neon orange macaroni and cheese from the box. She looked at Rhea, wondering if she'd heard the whole conversation. Her mouth was smiling but her eyes weren't. As Alison sat down and chewed a bite of pasta, she felt comforted by the familiar, salty taste, a constant in her life when everything else was shifting and uncertain. Rhea looked at her and said nothing, the awkward silence stretching on.

The day Michael left, Rhea had noticed Michael's toothbrush and deodorant missing from the bathroom counter. She'd asked if he was on business trip and whether she should work longer hours while he was away. Alison shook her head, somehow communicating that he was never coming back.

"How could he walk out at a time like this?" Rhea had said, her tone angry. "What kind of man leaves his wife when she's struggling?"

"No," Alison said. "Not his idea. Mine."

Rhea went quiet. Alison had never felt so much judgment in simple silence.

"It was nice of Mr. Jacobs to come by," Rhea said now.

"Yeah," Alison said.

"He's a good man."

"Yes, he is."

"He's still in love. There's no mistaking the way he looks at you. Maybe you should give him another chance."

Alison took a sip of water, not sure how to respond. She and Rhea had grown quite close in the past few months, but with this comment, Rhea had overstepped her bounds. Alison decided to let it slide.

"Good," Alison said, taking another bite of macaroni. "Thank you."

"You're welcome," Rhea said, without meeting her eyes.

CHAPTER TWENTY-TWO

Sadie

March 16, 2019

"WHERE DID YOUR PARENTS GO for dinner tonight?" Emma asked, sprawled on her bed.

"That Italian place in Cleveland Circle, the same one they always go to," Sadie said, flipping through the latest *People Magazine* on the trundle bed. She loved looking through this magazine when she was at Emma's house, especially the real people stories at the end, the ones about normal people whose lives have gone awfully wrong in some way or another.

Emma scrolled through her Instagram feed. "Is it good?"

"A little stuffy," Sadie said. "My dad likes it because they fawn all over him. They keep his wine glass full." Sadie didn't like the idea of her father driving home after these birthday dinners, but she certainly couldn't bring that up with him.

"Better to be here instead."

"Totally. And at least they didn't ask me to babysit the twins." Sadie used to watch Vik and Meera's kids, but lately she'd done everything she could to avoid it. A few months ago, Risha, the girl with the angel face, had disappeared during a game of hide and seek. Sadie had called her name over and over and searched every corner of the house, starting to panic when there was no reply. The boy was of no use, sitting on the couch playing video games the entire time. When Sadie picked up the phone to call the police, Risha materialized as if nothing had happened, asking if she could have some ice cream, the little brat. Sadie would pay *them* to avoid going through that again.

"How'd you get out of it?"

"I told them I raised my rates." Sadie played with the hem of the pink bed skirt, the same one Emma'd had since she was eight.

"Uh excuse me, what is this?" Emma held up her phone, showing the shot Piper had taken of the guy on the train when they'd gone to Boston last month.

"How'd you find that?"

"It was on Piper's Insta feed. Train hottie? Who is this guy?"

"He was sitting across from us. Piper flirted with him."

"He looks ancient," Emma said. "And what's with the chest hair? It's like a forest."

"I don't know. Why were you looking at Piper's stuff anyway?" Sadie had slept on this trundle bed for years, but suddenly it felt much less comfortable than usual. Several inches lower than Emma's bed, if made her feel small, like Emma was more important than her, on higher ground.

"I don't know," Emma said. "I want to make sure you're okay. Something's not right about that girl."

"I'm fine. You don't need to take care of me."

"Why are you getting mad?"

"I'm not mad." Sadie didn't want to get into a fight with Emma.

"What were you doing in Boston anyway?"

"I don't know. Hanging out."

"Hanging out where?"

"Why do you have to stick your nose in it?" Sadie said. "I have a new friend, okay? People are allowed to make new friends. It's not such a big deal." She closed the magazine and tossed it on the ground.

Emma scrunched her eyes together like she might cry. Sadie couldn't stomach her good girl act right now. She grabbed her toiletry kit and went to the bathroom.

Gathering her hair into a ponytail, she secured it with a hair tie and squeezed soap into her hand. She rubbed her hands together and covered her face with the thick foam. When she looked in the mirror, her face was completely hidden, all imperfections concealed behind a coating of white. She waited a moment before splashing warm water on her face, watching the bubbles circle down the drain.

When she returned to the bedroom, Emma was watching a video on her phone with her earbuds. Sadie was relieved they wouldn't have to continue their conversation. Emma had no right to choose her friends. She lay down on the trundle and pulled the covers up over her shoulders. Knowing Emma, everything would be back to normal in the morning.

As she started to drift, she felt Emma touch the back of her neck.

"What?" Sadie played dumb but she knew exactly what was going on. She'd forgotten to take her hair out of the ponytail and Emma had seen the tattoo. It was bound to happen at some point—they always wore their hair up for competitions—but Sadie had been avoiding the confrontation for as long as possible.

"When did you get this?" Emma asked, removing her earbuds.

"I don't know. A while ago." Sadie couldn't bring herself to turn over and face her friend.

"And you didn't show me?"

There was a soft knock on the door. "Girls," Mrs. Wright said. "It's time to turn off the light. Early practice tomorrow."

Emma clicked off the light clipped on the headboard of her bed. Sadie felt thankful for the sudden darkness, the only light from the streetlight sneaking through the crack between the blinds and the window frame.

"Why did you get it?" Emma asked, her voice quiet.

"I'm not sure. It just seemed right."

"The ice skate?"

"Yeah. When I saw it, I knew it was the one."

"What do you think Coach will say?"

"I'm trying not to think about it."

"Do you want to know what I think?" Emma asked.

"I don't know." Sadie wasn't at all sure she wanted to hear what Emma thought.

"You thought I would be judgy, didn't you?" Emma said. "I'm not always that predictable."

"No, I ... I guess I wasn't sure," Sadie said. Something about the tone of Emma's voice told her it was okay.

"Well, I'm not. I think it's beautiful," Emma said. "It's just right."

CHAPTER TWENTY-THREE

Grant

March 16, 2019

AS THEY FINALLY ARRIVED at the hospital, Grant got a call from Matt, his chief resident. "Just got here," Grant said, walking as fast as he could to the elevator.

"You can slow it down," Matt said. "Dr. Shin couldn't wait any longer. He scrubbed in a half hour ago."

Grant wanted to scream profanities. Who the hell did Cal think he was making an important decision about his patient without him? But ensnaring a resident in this drama would only serve to complicate things even further.

He hung up and got in the elevator, Cynthia following behind.

Grant pushed the elevator button several times, willing the elevator doors to close before anyone else got on. He needed to get to the OR as quickly as possible. As the elevator went up, he felt a little light-headed, wondering again how many glasses of wine he'd had at the restaurant.

"What's going on?" Cynthia asked. "Is she in danger?"

"She'll be fine," he said, speaking as clearly as he could. "Just a little complication."

"You'll take care of her, right?" she asked, her brow furrowed.

"Of course," he said. After getting Cynthia situated in the family waiting room, Grant quickly changed in the locker room, scrubbed up and entered the OR. From this side of the drape, Grant could see Alison's face. At first glance, she looked just as she had this afternoon, peaceful and quiet, her eyes closed and the left side of her face swollen and puffy. But when Grant looked more carefully, her mouth looked slightly asymmetric, the right side lower than the left. A plastic drain exited the left side of her scalp and snaked down along her neck. Cal stood at her head with instruments in both hands, one of the senior residents at his side.

"How are you feeling, Dr. Kaplan?" Wendy asked. "I hope you got some rest after yesterday."

"Yes, thank you." He was feeling completely off his game after the encounter with the trooper, but he wasn't about to tell her that.

Grant walked over to Alison's head to assess the situation, but Cal had already fit the bone flap into place and was replacing the staple line.

"You're done already?" Grant asked. "I thought you just started."

"It didn't take too long. I evacuated as much of the hematoma as I could."

"I told you I was on my way. You could have stalled."

"I waited as long as I could," Cal said.

"Do you think there's more blood left? If there is, we should try to clear it out. Maybe I can do better." He didn't mean to be rude, but he felt the need to take over. If he left blood in the operative bed, it could cause problems with brain function and serve as a site for infection. Neither of those things would happen on his watch. Grant grabbed the stapler from Cal's hand and edged him out of the way with his shoulder. He took the staple remover from the sterile tray and started removing the staples Cal had just placed. Alison's scalp oozed as he jimmied the metal teeth under each one.

"What do you think you're doing?" Cal said. "I just closed up."

"This is my patient," Grant said, removing the bone flap to expose the dura. The throbbing pain in his temples told him his blood pressure was up, but he tried to ignore it. He had to focus. This was too important a moment to lose his cool.

"Dr. Kaplan, I'm not sure this is a good idea," Wendy said. "Maybe you need to take a moment."

"This is my case, Cal. You have no right to interfere." Grant knew he was being unreasonable, but he couldn't contain himself. He felt very possessive of Alison. If something went wrong, he wanted to be able to say he had done everything he could, that he went above and beyond.

"You gave me no choice," Cal said. "You said twenty minutes, and I waited for almost an hour," Cal said. Intellectually, Grant understood exactly what Cal was saying. One of the main tenets of brain surgery, "Time is brain," guided all of their clinical decisions. He probably would have made the same call.

"I can fix her, Cal. I need to make this right." All Grant wanted to do was slice through the dura and use every technique he knew to make Alison well, but something told him he couldn't do that right now, that he wasn't in the frame of mind to operate. He felt the sobs coming, his nose stinging and eyes burning, before the noise escaped his mouth. He dropped his instruments and escaped into the hallway.

Grant wanted to hide in the locker room but he couldn't make himself go any farther. Leaning against the wall, he used the cold cement for support. He could hear Cal tell the senior resident to close up the wound and get Alison back to intensive care. When the OR door opened, Grant tried to tell Cal to go away, but he couldn't make any intelligible words come out between sobs. He knew he wasn't really angry at Cal but at himself: for failing to get here in time, for getting delayed by the trooper, for agreeing to take on Alison's surgery in the first place. With the mistakes piling up, he wasn't sure he'd ever be able to dig himself out.

"You've done everything you can for her," Cal said. "You can't beat yourself up because of a complication."

"I'm ... not sure," Grant managed to say.

"I never operate on anyone I know for just that reason."

Grant couldn't tell if Cal was judging him or simply stating a fact, but he felt the need to defend his choice. "I didn't want to do it. I tried to convince her to go with Richman in Columbus, but they wouldn't go for it. And Cynthia basically threatened me with divorce if I wouldn't agree."

"Sounds intense. I don't envy you, bud."

"Do you think she'll turn around?" Grant asked. He couldn't

talk any more about his bad choices. What's done was done, and now he had to deal with the consequences.

"We can only hope," Cal said. "There was even more hemorrhage than I thought. She must have continued to bleed while we waited."

"I didn't mean to drag you into this."

"I had no choice. She was about to herniate." Grant knew Cal couldn't just stand by as Alison's brain was pushed down out of her skull by the massive bleed, but he still resented what he'd done. Grant was used to being the hero, the one who saved the day and accepted the accolades, not the loser who took the fall. "What was the hold up?" Cal asked.

Grant's stomach burned. "Do you think she has a right facial droop?" he asked, avoiding the question. Cal didn't need to know about his close call with the state trooper.

"I wouldn't be surprised. She had significant weakness on that side before we took her back. We'll have to keep a close eye on her tonight, and see how she is tomorrow."

"Cal?" Grant said, after a moment of quiet.

"What, bud?"

"I don't know if I can do this anymore."

"Do what?"

"Take care of her." Grant said. "I thought I could stay above it all, but now, I'm not so sure."

"What are you saying?"

"The lines are getting blurry."

"If you're asking my opinion, the lines were blurred the second you decided to take on the case. But that's done now."

"This must be my fault. I should have cauterized more before closing."

"That's crazy," Cal said. "We all have complications and you know it. You can't let it all rest on your head."

"I can't help it."

They sat for a minute, neither of them sure what to say next. Grant felt another stomach pang, the red wine lapping at his esophagus.

"I don't know how to ask this," Grant said.

"What?"

"Since your name's now in the chart," Grant said, "you could just take over the case from here."

"And inherit your complication?"

"I've never asked you before," Grant said.

"You're right. It's not like you." Cal sighed and took off his blue cap, running a hand through his hair. "Okay, I'll take one for the team."

Grant nodded, a sense of relief washing over him. He usually felt most at ease in the driver's seat, all successes and the occasional failure attributed to him and him alone. That's the way he liked it, but in this situation, he knew it was time to relinquish his authority. Now, Grant could focus solely on being a brother-in-law and husband. Though he hadn't been there when Alison needed him most, he would stay next to her in the ICU for as long as it took, watching her every breath until she woke up. He wished he's brought some Oxy with him to take the edge off. This was going to be a long night.

CHAPTER TWENTY-FOUR

Alison

October 2, 2019

"ONLY ONE MORE MONTH of rehearsal and there's so much more to do." Nate took a bite of his cheese stick. "Some people aren't even off book. Ms. Logan keeps yelling at them but it doesn't help. We're not allowed to call for lines, but Cooper still does. We're never gonna be ready." Nate was supposed to be doing his homework, but he was doing more snacking and chatting than work.

"I'm sure you'll be ready," Alison said, trying not to grin as the full sentence rolled off her tongue.

"It's been quite an experience for you," Rhea said. "Putting on a show is far different than training for soccer or baseball."

"And a lot more fun," Nate said. "I've got the bug."

"The bug?" Rhea said.

"The acting bug. Elise Cohen said that's what it's called. When you do one show and then you just have to keep doing more."

"At least it's not life threatening," Rhea said.

"It's contag ... it's contagious." Alison couldn't help but smile this time. A few weeks ago, she wouldn't have fathomed saying a big word like that so soon.

"Totally. We all have it. Even the kids whose parents forced them to try out. Now you're officially a stage mom," he patted Rhea on the back. "Like, you have to obsess about what part I get and what song I sing for auditions and stuff like that."

"You'd think things would be quieter around here," Rhea said. "You can always count on Nate to keep things lively."

"Full of energy," Alison said.

Rhea pointed to his blank homework sheet. "How about fractions?"

"Okay, fine," Nate said, picking up his pencil.

"Mr. Jacobs called earlier while you were napping," Rhea said. "I told him you're doing much better."

"Much better," Alison said.

"Is Mr. Jacobs coming home?" Nate asked.

"Nathaniel." Rhea said sharply.

"It's okay." Alison knew Rhea didn't approve of her divorce and she didn't want to go into the details with her, but she also didn't want Nate to feel badly for asking about Michael.

Rhea took Nate's face in her hands and planted a kiss on his forehead. "My silly boy."

"Don't treat me like a baby," he said.

"Now you're going to get Mrs. Jacobs upset," Rhea said. "Why don't you finish your homework?"

"Is Ms. Corrie coming over?" Nate ignored his mother. Alison's heart sped up. She didn't mind Nate mentioning Michael, but bringing up Becca was trickier. Since he'd seen them on the deck, he hadn't said anything, but in the back of Alison's mind she wondered if Becca had let anything slip at school or if Nate had seen more than he'd let on.

When Rhea went silent, Alison panicked. Had Rhea seen or heard something when Becca had come over? Did she know how often Becca had been visiting? She wasn't sure why she didn't want Rhea to know about Becca, but her stomach clenched at the thought of her finding out.

"I think it's time for you to finish up your math sheet," Rhea told Nate. She walked over to the sink to load the dishwasher.

"Maybe they're in love," he said. And now Alison really thought her heart would stop.

"Who?" Rhea asked, her attention seemingly on the dishes.

"Ms. Corrie and Mrs. Jacobs."

"Nate, why would you say that? They're friends. Besides, love is for a man and a woman." Rhea pointed a fork toward Nate. "Didn't you listen to Pastor Franklin's sermon last month? I don't know why I even bring you to that church if you're just going to sit there and daydream."

Alison's heart sank even farther. She had known Rhea wouldn't approve, but she'd still held out hope she would respond with grace. Because Rhea had fed her and wiped her mouth and helped her shower with the utmost patience and care, her resolute judgment felt harsh.

"Did you hear me, Nathaniel?"

Nate walked over to the coffee table and picked up a framed photo of Alison and Becca taken at the PTA holiday lunch a few months before her life imploded. Becca had brought it over when she'd visited on Monday. Alison's first instinct had been to stick it in a drawer after she left, but that wouldn't have been fair to either of them. In the photo, Becca's arm was around her shoulder, both of them beaming at the camera. In her photos with Michael, even the ones from their wedding day, Alison's smile was never so broad.

"I think they look nice together," Nate said. "Like they belong."

❀

At the sound of the front door opening, Alison grabbed the remote control and tried to turn off the TV, but she was too slow.

Becca collapsed onto the couch and lifted Alison's feet up onto her lap. "What's happening, sexy?"

"Not much."

Becca looked over at the TV. "The L word? That's so last decade."

"I have to figure it out."

"It's a show, Alison. Being a lesbian doesn't mean you have to pierce your nose, chain smoke, and work at vegan cafes. But Jennifer Beals is exceptionally hot. I'll give you that."

"Starting somewhere."

"Why don't you start with me?" she asked. "Ask me anything you want. I'm a real flesh and blood lesbian. I don't just play one on TV."

"Still thinking," Alison said. "Trying to sort it out."

A look of disappointment crossed Becca's face. Alison knew Becca was hoping she would open up, spill her feelings about her newfound sexuality and what it meant for their future.

"I'll wait for you," Becca said. "As long as it takes."

Alison squirmed at the thought of Becca waiting for her. She didn't want her to waste her life waiting for something that may never be right.

"So, what did you do today?" Becca asked.

"This," Alison said. "Days all the same."

"Mine, too. We started the decimals unit today. I swear it feels like I just did it, but the carousel keeps coming around again, ready or not."

"Getting diz ... dizzy?" Hearing Becca talk about school, about what she was teaching in Alison's classroom gave Alison a twinge of sadness. She missed the energy of the classroom: the noise of the kids chattering, the look on their faces when they suddenly understand how to multiply fractions, even the boys' endless bathroom jokes.

"Don't get me wrong," Becca continued. "I love the kids. They can be supremely annoying, but they're mostly silly and delightful. I can't think of any other career that would inspire me as much."

"Yeah." The problem was, neither could Alison. There was probably something else she could do—answer phones or enter data—but those jobs sounded incredibly dull.

"Enough about school. What else is going on with you?" She massaged the bottom of Alison's feet, using her thumbs to work the pressure points.

Alison sighed with pleasure, her fingers releasing the tension from her body. "Rhea's been strange."

"What do you mean?"

"Nate told her." Alison filled her in on the rest of what happened earlier in the day, finishing with Nate's comment about the photo.

"I knew I liked that kid," she said. "We do look good together."

"And Michael wasn't happy either."

"You told Michael about us?"

"I had to," Alison said.

"I am so proud of you." Becca took her hand. "That couldn't have been easy."

"It had to be done."

"Coming out is a big moment, no matter your age or circumstance." Becca leaned across the couch to give her a hug, but Alison pulled away sharply. Alison had told her husband that their marriage was over and that she was dating a woman, but that didn't mean she was ready to plant a rainbow flag on her front lawn. She needed to take it one step at a time.

Becca's face clouded over. "What's wrong? This should be your proudest moment. You can start living your best life now."

"I don't know."

"What do you mean you don't know? You're a lesbian, Alison. Whether you like labels or not, that's what you are. The sooner you accept that, the sooner we can move on with our life together."

A lesbian? Strangely enough, even after spending time with Becca all those months—the workouts at the gym, the shower, hours in bed together at her apartment—Alison hadn't thought much about labels. She enjoyed being with Becca. She loved her infectious laugh, and her clever intelligence and the way she could always keep a conversation going with anyone, anywhere. She desired her body—her gap-toothed smile, her muscular legs, and her musky smell—but she'd never thought of herself as a lesbian. She wasn't ready for a coming out party. She had enough trouble making words come out of her mouth.

On the screen, Jennifer Beals and the other ladies were at a nightclub dressed in sexy outfits. Nothing about them seemed familiar.

"I don't feel like a lesbian," Alison said.

"What do you mean?" Becca said. "You're still the same person. Just uncovering who you've always been."

Becca had been supremely patient, more patient than Alison could expect anyone to be. Was she right? Was this who Alison had been all along and she just hadn't realized? Maybe Alison had put off asking for a divorce because she was afraid of coming to terms with her sexuality, of having to announce to friends and family and coworkers the real reason she'd left Michael. How would she answer the questions from Michael's parents, Cynthia, the other teachers at school? What happened? Did Michael cheat? Was it the stress of trying to conceive?

Warm tears ran down Alison's cheek.

"I didn't mean to upset you," Becca said, grabbing a tissue from the coffee table and wiping Alison's face.

"I'll be okay," Alison said. She felt overwhelmed with emotions, questions about the divorce, and her sexuality and her future all roiling in her head.

"You're better than okay," Becca said. "You're exquisite. Maybe we should go out and celebrate."

"A date?"

"Yes. A proper one. We could even get dressed up and order all three courses."

"I'm not sure." Tears threatened again and Alison tried to hold them back. Becca was trying to encourage her to step out of the darkness, but Alison wasn't ready for that yet. People were already talking about her, whispering about the poor lady whose brother-in-law messed up her brain. She didn't want to add more fuel to the fire, as Michael would have said.

Becca took Alison's face in her hands. "You are an incredible woman, Alison Jacobs, and I don't care what Rhea or the cashier at the grocery store or the UPS delivery guy has to say. I love you." She leaned in for a soft kiss, the kind that said I love you rather than I want you.

Alison relaxed into Becca's arms. She knew Becca was frustrated, that she wanted them to be together without having to hide behind closed doors. Alison hoped she would be patient enough to wait until she was ready, if that day ever came.

"Should I make a reservation? Maybe at that seafood place by the harbor?"

"Maybe," Alison said.

Squeals and moans came from the TV, a scene with the butch hairstylist and one of her many one-night stands. They watched in silence for a few minutes.

"There's something about her," Becca said. "She embodies sex, animal magnetism."

Alison's eyes were fixed to the screen as Shane and her partner went at it in every position imaginable. When Shane spread her partner's legs and buried her face in between, Becca turned to her. Without a word, she knelt down on the floor and pulled Alison's sweatpants and underwear down over her hips. She slid her hand underneath Alison's hips and brought her up to her face, her breath hot on her skin. All Alison wanted at this moment was to feel Becca's tongue sliding in between her legs, the delicious sensation as she started in slow teasing circles and then moved ever more quickly back and forth. She groaned in anticipation.

"You like this?" Becca whispered. "It's been way too long."

Alison recalled the last time Becca went down on her. It was the day she would never forget, the day she first bled into her brain and had to be taken to the hospital by ambulance. In the faculty bathroom during their break, Alison's heart pounded as Becca pulled up her skirt. As Becca's tongue coaxed Alison to climax, waves of pleasure coursing through her body, a blood vessel burst in her brain. Maybe if she'd kept her pants on, she would have lived the rest of her life never knowing anything was wrong. Her irrepressible desire for Becca had played a part in this disaster, and keeping the affair secret from Michael, desecrating the vows they'd made to each other, couldn't have helped either.

Now, Alison sighed and closed her legs, pulling her pants back up.

"What's wrong?" Becca asked. She got up and sat back on the couch.

"Not right now."

"Is everything okay?"

"Too much on my mind." Alison would never tell her why she'd turned off. The last thing she wanted was for Becca to feel guilty. There was already more than enough guilt to go around.

CHAPTER TWENTY-FIVE

Sadie

March 23, 2019

WHEN SADIE AND EMMA EXITED the T station, they saw the Museum of Science on the other side of the bridge. It was almost six o'clock and the sun was starting to set behind the museum, the blue sky giving way to pinks and purples over the Cambridge skyline.

Emma had talked incessantly on the train about her calculus grades and whether she would be inducted into the music honor society, and how much practice they needed before the Bay State Games, while Sadie had spent the entire train ride thinking about Aunt Alison. Her surgery had been a week ago and all Sadie knew was that there'd been some sort of complication and that the road to recovery would be long. There was something they weren't sharing, babying her as always.

They started walking onto the bridge toward the museum.

"You're thinking about your aunt?" Emma asked, breaking the silence.

"I can't think about anything else. Maybe this show will take my mind off things." When Piper asked Sadie to meet her at the Justin Timberlake light show at the planetarium, Sadie's first reaction had been to say no. There was no way her mom would let her go downtown on a Saturday night without an adult, but after she hung up, she thought of a way she could make it work. She'd say she was going with Emma. The only problem with her plan was that Emma had no idea Piper would be meeting them there.

"Definitely," Emma said. "You've had so much stress. It'll be good not to focus on it for one night."

"What do you think they're hiding?"

"What do you mean?"

"My parents won't tell me what's going on."

"I'm sure they'll share what you need to know," Emma said.

"My mom won't let me visit. I don't understand why they keep shutting me out."

"I'm sure your aunt will be fine," Emma said. "Meanwhile, the sleepovers have been fun."

"Yeah."

"Where's the planetarium?" Emma asked when they had nearly reached the museum.

"You can't see it from the street." Sadie remembered when her father took her to the planetarium when she was in kindergarten. She could still recall every detail of the daddy-daughter day: how fast he drove on the highway to get there, the sunlight glistening on the surface of the river, how excited she felt while they waited in line for tickets. "It's in the back."

They crossed the street and continued walking.

"Look at the T-rex!" Emma said. "It's so cute." They stopped to look at the statue by the museum entrance.

"Tyrannosaurus Rex was one of the most vicious and deadly dinosaurs to walk the earth," Sadie still remembered some of the facts she'd learned from researching the infamous carnivore for her fourth-grade science project. "They were anything but cute."

"Look at the teeny tiny arms."

"They were used to hold its prey in place."

"This was a great idea." Emma ignored Sadie's corrections and started walking to the ticket line. "It's going to be fun."

Sadie hadn't told Emma that Piper would be meeting them because she knew it would cause a scene. Emma hated Piper without ever giving her a chance. Planning to break the news gently on the train ride here, she'd gotten distracted by her thoughts about Alison.

"My mom said she'd pay for this." Emma's parents had been more than generous over the past week—driving Sadie to and from skating practice, taking her out to dinner, even letting her stay over several nights—while her parents were basically living in Aunt Alison's hospital room.

Emma dug in her bag to find her wallet. The sounds of a moving sculpture in the corner, balls plinking and gears turning, caught Sadie's attention. People moved in all directions through the cavernous entry hall, children's laughter and yells echoing off the walls and glass ceiling.

After Emma bought the tickets, she gave them to the employee at the museum entrance and they stepped through the turnstile.

"We have an hour until the show," Emma said. "Let's go learn some science."

She pointed to a sign for a special exhibit, and Sadie trailed her down the hall. A sign above the exhibit entrance read, "Welcome to the Mirror Maze: The Many Facets of You."

A girl with a lower lip piercing sat at the desk near the maze entrance. "You girls ready to face the maze?" she asked.

"Totally," Emma said.

"If you notice the light flickering or the colors changing, that's just me playing around out here," the girl said. "No reason to freak out."

"We won't," Emma said.

"Em, let's head over to the planetarium," Sadie said. Things like this made Sadie feel claustrophobic.

"We have plenty of time." Emma led the way into the maze. "Don't worry."

As soon as they stepped inside, they were surrounded by mirrors. Hundreds of Sadies and Emmas glared at her from the ceiling and walls and floor, making her feel disoriented and a little bit queasy. When she managed to focus on one of her own reflections, she made eye contact. You have to tell Emma about Piper, she thought. Whatever her reaction, better to tell her now than face her anger later.

When she caught a reflection of the top of her head, she noticed that her hair had started growing out, the natural light brown color of her hair fighting its way out from her part. With the mess she'd made last time—droplets of inky black on the marble countertops and white tile floor, which her mom had had to scrub with bleach— she wasn't sure she was up for dyeing it again. She squeezed her eyes shut and took a deep breath.

"I'm not sure about this," she said.

"Come on, it's fun." Emma started walking deeper into the maze.

If Emma was willing to keep going, Sadie had to follow. Stop being such a baby, she told herself. When she put her hands out to the side, she was relieved to feel the cool glass. She ran her fingers up and down the smooth surface, imagining the prints she was leaving behind. It felt satisfying to leave behind evidence that she'd been here. Her mom never let her touch the mirror in their entryway for fear of dirtying the spotless surface, revealing the Kaplans were anything less than perfect.

Sadie took a few steps to try to catch up to Emma. When she reached a bridge, Emma was standing and looking down over the edge, the floor covered completely in mirrors.

Sadie used the railing to steady herself.

"It looks like you could fall for forever," Emma said.

Emma's voice sounded too loud. Sadie gripped the metal of the railing, staring straight across at one of her reflections on the opposite wall.

"You have to look down," Emma said. "It's really cool."

"I don't want to." Sadie was afraid that if she looked down, she would completely lose it. News would get around school that she had barfed in the mirror maze and the story would circulate for eternity. Like the one about Brianna Levitt, who'd gotten a hot dog stuck inside her and had to go to the hospital to get it removed.

The lights flickered for a second and then dimmed.

"I'm not sure I can do this," Sadie said.

"What's wrong?"

"I'm feeling a little sick."

"I'll help you." Emma took Sadie's hand and started pulling her through the maze. After all the hours practicing their pairs routine together, Emma's hand felt familiar and comforting. Sadie closed her eyes, shutting out the hundreds of disorienting reflections surrounding her, and allowed her oldest friend to lead the way.

❁

When they finally found the exit, Sadie took a deep breath, a sense of relief washing over her. They made their way to the planetarium lobby where a crowd was gathered. Piper was standing by the wall with two guys Sadie had never seen before. They looked a lot older; one had a goatee and the other a patchy mustache. They weren't the kind of boys Sadie usually hung out with. And she still hadn't warned Emma.

"Hey there," Piper said.

"I didn't know you were coming," Emma said, looking directly at Piper without a hint of a smile.

"Happy to see you too, Emma," Piper said.

"I brought my brother and his friend," Piper said. "Brian, this is Sadie and her friend, Emma."

Emma grabbed Sadie's hand behind her back and gave it a firm squeeze. Sadie wanted to tell Emma she was sorry for keeping her in the dark, but all she could do was squeeze back.

"Hi, Brian," Sadie said. "I've heard a lot about you." She wanted to kick herself for saying such a stupid thing.

"This is Axel," he said, nodding to his scruffy friend.

"We have a few minutes until the show. How about some fresh air?" Piper pointed to the double doors that led to the street.

"I think we should go get seats," Emma said.

"Relax, Emma," Piper said. "We won't miss anything."

Piper led the way, Sadie and Emma lagging behind.

"What's going on?" Emma whispered. "I can't believe you didn't tell me they were coming."

"You would have bailed."

"You still should have told me."

"Don't worry. It'll be fun." Sadie wanted to reassure Emma even though she wasn't feeling so comfortable herself.

When they got outside, it was still warm, but the sky had darkened to a charcoal gray. Sadie took a deep breath and looked to see if any stars were visible. With the lights downtown, it was always hard to see any stars, but she felt like she needed something to ground her. She longed to see real stars, not the fake ones twinkling from the ceiling of the planetarium before the light show began.

Axel took a baggy from the pocket of his jeans. He removed a joint and handed it to Piper, who smiled and placed it between her lips. Axel lit the end with a red lighter.

Piper took a long drag, held her breath, and exhaled, a look of peace coming over her face. She seemed to be a very experienced smoker, making Sadie wonder when she'd first tried it.

She handed the joint to Brian. "This'll make the show that much more enjoyable," she said.

"Yeah," Brian said in a croaky voice, smoke wafting through his lips. "You can't listen to Justin Timberlake without medicinal assistance."

"Totally," Piper said.

After Axel took a hit, Piper grabbed the joint back from him and came over to stand next to Sadie. She put her arm around Sadie's shoulders and brought the joint to Sadie's lips. "It's your turn," Piper said. "Just suck in and hold your breath a few seconds."

Emma had a shocked look on her face, but with everyone watching, Sadie knew there was no way she could refuse. She pulled on the end of the joint and felt the hot smoke travel into her lungs, searing her insides and forcing her to cough.

Piper smiled. "Everyone coughs the first time."

Piper turned to Emma. "Do you want to try?" Piper knew full well that Emma wouldn't do it, but making fun of Emma and her prudish ways was one of Piper's favorite pastimes.

Emma shook her head. "I'm okay for now."

"Oh, come on, Emma. It won't scar you for life."

Blotchy redness crawled up Emma's neck. "I'm really fine."

"You'll still ace the SATs and get into an Ivy League college." Piper held the joint out to Emma.

"Yeah," Axel said with a chuckle. "Just like us." Sadie was pretty sure they didn't go to college. She seemed to remember Piper saying something about Brian apprenticing with a local electrician.

"I'll take it." Sadie grabbed the joint from Piper. She had to do something to let Emma off the hook. This time, the smoke went down smoother and didn't feel quite as hot.

She passed the joint to Piper, who took another drag and handed the joint back to the boys.

"I think we're sufficiently relaxed to tolerate JT," Brian said, putting the joint in his pocket.

As they walked back inside, Sadie felt like walking took less effort than usual. She also felt a bit light headed, but if this was all weed did, she wasn't very impressed. When they entered the planetarium, Sadie was overcome with nostalgia. She remembered sitting next to her father, her face tilted to the ceiling while a man with a deep voice talked about supernovas and constellations and black holes. She found herself wishing she was here with her father now instead of her friends. This crisis with Aunt Alison wasn't the only reason they'd drifted apart. Between high school and Piper, and her dad's busy operating schedule, it seemed like she barely saw him anymore.

Piper chose seats in the back row, and everyone followed without question, even though Sadie would have preferred to sit up front. When they first started hanging out, Sadie had liked that Piper always called the shots, her confidence and decisiveness new and exciting, but now it was starting to get old. Why did everything always have to be her way? Maybe she should take other people's feelings into consideration once in a while.

When they filed into the row, Emma ended up sitting between her and Piper, leaving Sadie to sit next to Brian. Emma shot Sadie a panicked look.

"This is going to be cool." Sadie hoped Piper wouldn't give her grief about using that word again.

"Sure," Emma said. Sadie could tell by the way she was sitting up straight in her chair that she was uncomfortable.

"Yeah, cool," Piper said, as if she used the word all the time.

A family filed into the row in front of them: a mother, father, and two middle school aged kids. They sat down next to a group of college students wearing Boston University baseball hats and sweatshirts.

"It's filling up," Emma said.

"Yeah," Sadie said.

Piper pressed the button on the armrest to make the chair recline. "Let's make ourselves comfortable."

Sadie and Emma followed her lead. As her legs lifted and her head tilted backwards, Sadie felt her head start to spin. Whether the feeling was because of the pot or she'd just reclined too fast, she wasn't sure. She tried to relax and let it pass. This was supposed to be a great show and she should try to enjoy herself.

"I hope they play the songs from Trolls," Emma said. "'Can't stop the Feeling' is one of his best songs!" Sadie couldn't believe Emma was talking about a cartoon.

"Yeah, trolls. I know a few of those," Piper said loudly in Brian's direction. "They're sitting right over there."

"Shut up, Piper," Brian said. He turned to Sadie. "The curse of having a sister."

"I wouldn't know," Sadie said. "I'm an only child."

"Sounds so peaceful," he said.

"Or lonely."

"I could deal with lonely once in a while." His breath smelled funky. She wondered if smoking marijuana gave you bad breath. "She's always in my business."

Sadie noticed that Brian didn't mention anything about their mother. She wanted to ask him whether she was really in prison, but she knew she couldn't. They'd known each other less than an hour, so that would definitely cross a line.

"Sometimes I wish my house wasn't so quiet," she said. "My dad's always at work and my mom ... I don't know what the fuck she's doing half the time." She wasn't sure why she felt the need to swear. Even though she found Brian faintly repulsive, for some reason she still wanted to impress him. "I've always wanted a big sister. Someone to show me the way."

"Don't follow *my* sister. She'll definitely lead you in the wrong direction."

The lights dimmed, and Sadie reclined her chair even farther so she was looking straight up at the domed planetarium ceiling. The catchy beat of "Rock Your Body" came through the oversized speakers lining the walls, and Sadie couldn't help but get excited. She reached over to grab Emma's hand to make sure she was doing okay. As streaks of color strobed across the ceiling, and purple and green bubbles floated upwards, Sadie didn't know where to look first. With every beat of the music, there were new colors and dazzling effects. Just when she got used to a pattern, it changed to something completely new, the streak and bubbles morphing into a pulsating checkerboard and then into haphazard diagonals of shooting stars. Glancing over at Brian and Axel, she saw their eyes were also fixed on the ceiling.

The song switched to a quiet one and Sadie heard a rattling sound coming from Emma's direction. When she turned she saw Piper taking a pill bottle out of her pocket, the one she'd stolen from Sadie's dad's nightstand a few months ago.

"What the hell?" Sadie whispered across Emma.

Piper twisted off the safety cap and spilled a few pills into her hand. "Emma has a headache," Piper said. She offered two pills to Emma.

"What is it?" Emma asked.

"It's a pain pill," Piper said. "For your head."

Sadie tried to grab the pills, but Piper closed her fist. "No, no," Piper said. "Emma's head hurts, not yours."

Piper opened her palm again.

"Okay," Emma said, popping the pills into her mouth.

"She doesn't do drugs," Sadie said. When Piper had taken the bottle from her dad's drawer, Sadie had freaked out, but her fear was that her father would notice the bottle was missing and she would get in trouble. She hadn't really thought about when Piper would take them, and whether she would share them with anyone else. Now she wanted to kick herself for being so stupid. Sadie watched Emma wash the pills down with a sip from her water bottle.

"This isn't a good idea," Sadie said.

"If we only did what you thought was a good idea, life would be pretty boring," Piper said, putting two pills into her mouth and handing the bottle of pills across her to Brian.

When the speakers started blasting a louder song, it became impossible to talk, and Sadie couldn't think of what to say anyway. A very small part of her wanted to stand up to Piper—to tell her she was being pushy and obnoxious and inappropriate—but she knew she would never have the nerve to do that.

The lights from the show projected onto Emma's face, tinting her skin red, then blue and green. Emma didn't turn back to look at her. She seemed peaceful and relaxed, the black light giving Emma's white t-shirt an otherworldly glow against the black leather seat. Sadie wished it would all stop: the loud music and the colored lights and the sound of Brian and his friend laughing about some stupid joke. Closing her eyes, she hoped her sense of uneasiness would pass before the show ended.

After several more songs that seemed much longer than they did on the radio, the show finally ended, and the lights came on. Sadie opened her eyes and looked around. In the light, she felt much more in control. There was no need for panic. Everything would be fine.

Brian and Axel stood up and started walking toward the exit and Sadie followed.

"Wake up," Sadie heard Piper say.

She looked back and saw Emma lying back in the chair, her eyes closed. Piper was sitting next to her and shaking her by the arm. How had she fallen asleep with all of that noise? Sadie walked back and sat down next to Emma.

"Em," Sadie said. "It's time to go."

When Emma didn't respond, Sadie leaned over and started patting her on the cheeks, hoping to startle her awake. "Wake up, Emma," she said in a louder voice.

"This is just what I need," Piper said.

"Let me sleep," Emma moaned. When she spoke, her face looked slack, not at all like the normal Emma. "Leave me alone."

"We can't stay here. The show is over," Sadie said.

The mom from the family in the next row stood up to leave. "Is everything okay?" she asked.

"Fine," Piper said.

The woman walked to the aisle and came into their row. "I'm a nurse," she said. She took Emma's wrist in her hand for a moment. "She's got a nice strong pulse."

"Great," Sadie said. "Thank you." She knew this woman was well meaning, but she just wanted her to go away. With her father's hospital a few blocks from the museum, this nurse probably knew him.

"She seems a bit sedated," the nurse said. "Was she drinking?"

"Not at all," Sadie said.

"Did she take anything?"

"No," Piper said. "I think she's just tired."

"It's been a long week at school," Sadie added. "Mid-terms."

"Right, well, let's see if we can get her up." The nurse mo-

tioned for Piper to stand up so she could sit down next to Emma.
She draped one of Emma's arms around her neck and placed her
arm on Emma's back. "Let's go, sweetheart," she said, using her
strength to get Emma to stand. She must have had a lot of practice
doing this with her patients.

"Where ... we going?" Emma leaned on the chair in front of
her to keep from falling.

"Home," Sadie said. "Before our parents start to worry." When
she said this, she really meant Emma's mom, since her own parents barely noticed she existed these days, their focus only on
Aunt Alison.

"Do you want me to call an ambulance?" the nurse asked.

"No, thank you." That was the last thing Sadie needed. Her
parents had enough going on right now without her adding more
stress.

"Mom, how much longer?" one of the nurse's kids asked from
the aisle.

"I'm fine," Emma spoke up, her voice stronger. "Really."

The nurse held up a wait-one-minute finger to her family
and looked back to Emma. "How do you feel?" she asked.

"Much better."

"Your color is coming back," she said. "Take her home and
put her to bed," she said before rejoining her family.

Sadie was relieved that Emma had pulled herself together
enough to stop the nurse from calling 911, but her relief soon
changed to fear. She wasn't sure how they'd get Emma home in
this state.

Sadie coaxed Emma into the aisle and tried to drape her arm
around her shoulder like the nurse had done, but it kept flopping
off. "Come on, Emma. Help me out here."

"What help?" Emma said, leaning her entire body weight on
Sadie. If Emma wasn't so tiny, they would have no chance to get
her home tonight.

"Try to walk," Sadie said.

"I'm trying," Emma said.

"She only had two," Piper said. "Such a lightweight."

"I tried to tell you this wasn't a good idea. It was too much for
her." Sadie wanted to focus on Emma, but she also felt like Piper
deserved a piece of her mind.

"This is all your fault," she said. It was the closest she could get to telling Piper off.

Sadie gave up trying to keep Emma's arm on her shoulder and tried to support her under her arm, motioning Piper to do the same on the other side.

"My fault?" Piper said. "You're the one who decided to bring her. I'm doing you a favor here."

"A favor?"

"I never signed on to take care of your lame friend."

"Are you kidding?" Sadie said angrily, a few drops of spit escaping with her words.

They finally reached the now empty lobby where the guys were waiting for them.

"What took you so long?" Brian asked and then noticed Emma. "Whoa, she's not looking so good."

"Not feeling good," Emma said and wobbled a few steps into the lobby, where she bent forward and retched. After depositing the entire contents of her stomach onto the red carpeting, she wiped her mouth with her hand and sat down.

"Let's get her out of here before anyone sees that," Axel said, turning to go.

"Wait a minute," Brian said. "We can't leave her there like this." He helped Emma up and draped her arm around his neck, securing it with his hand. He made it look so easy. Sadie went to Emma's other side, holding Emma's arm for support.

"Let's go," Piper said.

"Shut up, Piper," Brian said.

Piper rolled her eyes and followed behind with Axel. They managed to make it to the street and moved slowly in the direction of the T-station. Holding Emma's free arm seemed unnecessary, but Sadie felt like she had to do something to help. She also needed something to distract her from Piper who was whispering to Axel, something about Sadie being lame and a prude.

When they were almost at the train station, Emma walked to the railing along the side of the bridge and vomited again into the river. When she turned back to the group, she took a few tottering steps and then tripped on the uneven sidewalk, her ankle twisting as she pitched forward. Brian's attempt to catch her failed, and she ended up in a heap in the street. Sadie stepped behind her into the traffic lane and waved her arms at an oncoming bus, the driver honking as he careened into the adjacent lane.

"Oh, come on. I've really lost interest in the dramatics," Piper said. "Let's go."

"I think she's hurt," Brian said. He bent down to help Emma up. "Ax, we need to carry her. Her ankle's busted."

He motioned for Axel to help him lift Emma off the pavement. The guys formed a chair with their arms and started carrying her down the sidewalk. Emma's right foot hung at an unnatural angle and her lower leg was noticeably swollen.

"It hurts," Emma screamed. "Owwww." Sadie froze in horror, unsure what she could do to help. This night just kept getting worse

"We have to bring her to the hospital," Brian said. "She can't go home like this."

"We should go there." Axel pointed to the towering building a few blocks ahead, just on the other side of the bridge. "It's not too far."

The group made it back to the sidewalk and moved in the direction of the hospital, Sadie and Piper falling in line behind the boys and Emma.

"I'm not sure that's a good idea," Sadie said. "My father works there."

"Then your father can look out for her," Piper said.

"He's already exhausted by everything going on with my aunt. This won't make him happy."

Piper unzipped her bag and took out the bottle of pills. "Thanks for these by the way," she said, slipping the bottle into Sadie's jacket pocket.

Sadie took it out and tried to hand it back to Piper. "What do you mean? I don't want this."

"They're yours," Piper said, walking ahead. "I'm done with them."

Sadie sighed and put the bottle back into her pocket. She couldn't allow Piper to prevent her from making sure Emma was okay.

CHAPTER TWENTY-SIX

Grant

March 23, 2019

THE SOUND OF HIS CELL PHONE woke Grant from a nightmare, the same one he'd had several times this week while attempting to sleep in a chair at Alison's bedside. Blood cascaded from the operating table onto the floor, a raging torrent of red rushing out the door and down the hallway. The other times he'd had this recurring dream, he'd been swept away in the river, only waking up as he was being pulled under by the current, struggling to keep his head from going under.

He squeezed his eyes shut, trying to blink away the color red. He could feel the effects of the Oxy tablets he'd taken a few hours ago to help him sleep in this god-forsaken place, his thoughts still pleasantly blurry. Taking his phone from his pocket, he saw Sadie's name on the screen. She should have been fast asleep at Emma's house. Why would she be calling him at one in the morning?

"Sadie, is everything okay?"

"I'm fine, Dad," she said. "But I'm in the ER. Emma fell and broke her ankle."

"Broke her ankle? How'd that happen?" He didn't have the energy to deal with this right now. At least it wasn't Sadie who'd fallen. That would really put him over the edge. "Where are you?"

"At your hospital," she said.

"What are you doing here?"

"We went to see a show at the Museum of Science. Mom said it was okay, remember?" No, Grant didn't remember. Taking care of himself was proving enough of a challenge this week without trying to keep track of Sadie as well.

"You're downstairs?" he asked.

"Yeah," she said. Grant could hear a note of hesitation in her voice.

"Stay where you are. I'll be down in a minute."

Grant stood up and twisted from side to side to try to loosen up the muscles in his lower back. Sleeping here for almost a week wasn't doing his body any favors, he and Cynthia taking turns going home to shower and put on new clothes. He'd had Wendy put all his surgeries and appointments on hold.

He looked over at Cynthia, snoring away in the other chair, and decided to let her rest.

When he arrived in the ER, he found Sadie and Emma in a private room, Emma lying on the gurney with her swollen leg elevated on a bed of pillows.

"Dad, I'm so glad you're here," Sadie said, throwing her arms around him "I didn't know what to do."

He closed his arms around Sadie. "Don't worry," he said. "I'm here now." He felt badly his daughter was going through this, but it also felt good to be needed for once. "Are Emma's parents on the way?"

"Her dad should be here soon," Sadie said.

"What happened?"

"We were walking back to the T from the museum and Emma just tripped."

"The sidewalk was ... weird," Emma said. Sadie shot Emma a look. It seemed like Sadie was trying to tell Emma to shut up, but Grant wasn't sure why.

"And before I knew it, she was on the ground," Sadie said. "Her ankle blew up. I knew it was bad."

"How did you get here?" Grant asked.

"We were with other friends," Sadie said. "They helped carry her."

"Where are they now?"

"They left once Emma got checked in." Sadie refused to look at him, making Grant think Piper must have been involved. After the tattoo debacle, Sadie knew he wasn't her biggest fan. He was about to ask more questions about who exactly these so-called friends were and why they took off so quickly, but before he could say anything else, he heard a knock on the doorframe.

Grant turned and saw Vanessa Hidalgo, one of the ER doctors. "Dr. Kaplan, could I have a word with you outside for a moment?" Vanessa had consulted him about countless neurosurgical emergencies over the years, so he wasn't sure why she chose to address him so formally tonight. Also, whatever she had to say, she could say it in front of the girls. A broken ankle didn't seem like sensitive subject matter.

"Sure," he said. "Girls, give me minute to speak with the doctor."

He followed Vanessa through the packed emergency room. They'd always had a good working relationship in the past and he'd even done her some favors. When her younger daughter had fallen off the balance beam a few years ago during a gymnastics competition, cracking her skull on the way down, Grant had left Cynthia and Sadie at the movie theater on a Sunday afternoon to see her. When they reached a quiet alcove in the corner of the ER, Vanessa stopped and turned around.

"Is Emma going to need internal fixation to stabilize the fracture?" Grant asked. "Troy Womack is the best guy for foot and ankle. He fixed my cousin's compound ankle fracture last year with great results." Maybe if he talked enough, the serious look on Vanessa's face would soften.

She crossed her arms over her chest. "I wouldn't normally share any information with you since Emma is not your daughter, but this isn't a straightforward case."

"No fracture is too complicated to fix. It's not brain surgery." He hoped the joke would bring a smile to her face.

Vanessa refused to budge. "When Emma was brought in, she was quite altered. She wasn't oriented to place or time, and she was unable to follow simple commands."

"That's odd," Grant said. "Doesn't sound like her."

"I thought it was strange, too, which is why I decided to send a tox screen."

"I'm not sure that was necessary." What a waste. Emma had always been a good girl, the ultimate rule follower.

"Unfortunately, it was completely necessary."

"What do you mean?"

"It came back positive for opiates."

"Holy shit,' he said. "Should we wait until Derrick gets here to discuss this further?" Grant didn't know how Emma got her hands on drugs, but he knew her father would want to be here for this conversation.

"I didn't pull you aside to discuss Emma's care," Vanessa said. "That I will reserve for her family. I wanted to talk to you about the pills."

Grant could feel his pulse quicken. He didn't like the accusative look on Vanessa's face and the way she'd kept her arms crossed for the entire conversation.

"I don't understand."

She pulled an orange pill bottle out of the pocket of her white coat. "Sadie had this in her pocket. She owned up when I gave them the blood results."

"Where the hell did she get that?"

"Why don't you take a closer look at the label." Vanessa held the bottle up. He scanned the print on the label and found exactly what he'd dreaded, his own name listed under prescriber information. Usually, he peeled off the labels from the bottles he collected, but he must have forgotten this time. If he hadn't been so lazy, he could have avoided this predicament. Grant reached out to take the bottle, but Vanessa stashed it back in her pocket before he could grab it.

"I assume you must have an explanation for how your daughter got this bottle," Vanessa said. "It seems to have been prescribed to a patient you performed surgery on a few months ago. Robert Ward? I looked him up in the system."

"What are you trying to say?" Grant honestly wasn't sure how Sadie had gotten ahold of that bottle. There was no way he had been careless enough to leave it in a drawer in the kitchen or in the cabinet in her bathroom, and he couldn't imagine Sadie snooping in his nightstand.

"I'm just trying to figure out how your daughter ended up with this bottle."

"I don't like where this conversation is going." Grant took a deep breath, trying to clear the Oxy from his system. He needed all his wits about him for this conversation. "You know me. We've worked together forever." Maybe appealing to her sense of loyalty would get him off the hook.

"I do know you, which is why I found this so surprising," Vanessa said. "Do you have any idea where she got the bottle? If you can't illuminate me, then I'll have to ask the girls."

"Is that a threat?"

"Call it whatever you want. I'm just trying to take care of my patient."

"And taking care of your patient includes threatening a senior surgeon on staff? I bring so much fucking money into this place. Much more than you ever will." He hoped Vanessa wouldn't notice the slight slurring of his words.

"I don't think that's relevant right now. Do you have an explanation or not?

"What was the question?" Grant stalled. Pulling rank didn't seem like it was working, so he had to take a different tack.

"Maybe I'm not being direct enough with you, Grant. Let me make my question perfectly clear. How did your daughter get ahold of a bottle of pain pills prescribed for your patient?"

"Sadie shadowed me at the office for her school's career day a few weeks ago," Grant lied.

"And on career day, you give out samples?"

After this sarcastic jab, he knew he had to come up with something better fast. "She must have found the pills in the disposal bin." He knew the explanation sounded lame, but it was the only thing that came to mind. He hoped Vanessa would cut him some slack and move on.

"You expect me to believe that you leave bottles of controlled substances lying around your office in open bins?"

"Not in bins exactly. I meant to say that maybe Mr. Ward left his bottle in the exam room and Sadie picked it up."

"Now you're changing your story altogether."

"No, I'm just trying to explain—"

"Grant, I have an ER full of patients to see."

"I know. I'm trying to tell you how this happened." He could feel his armpits getting damp.

"Well, you're not doing a very good job," she said. "Is there anything else you'd like to say?"

Grant was out of ideas. He couldn't think of anything believable to get her off his back.

Vanessa gave up waiting for a response. "Fine, if you don't want to give me the straight story, I'll leave it to the administration to sort out." She turned and walked out.

Watching Vanessa disappear down the hallway, Grant prayed she was just blowing smoke. Once she calmed down, she'd realize that reporting him to the administration would only cause them both unnecessary aggravation. Meanwhile, it was time to have a talk with his daughter.

CHAPTER TWENTY-SEVEN

Alison

October 12, 2019

AS ALISON SMOOTHED THE FRONT of her black jersey dress and chose a pair of silver ballet flats, she noticed she hadn't shaved her legs in weeks. Oh, well. Rhea had already gone home and it took too long to do it herself. Becca had called an hour ago to say she'd planned a surprise date for tonight and Alison had been turning in circles ever since. It had taken Becca over a week to make good on her promise. Alison had sort of hoped Becca would let it go so she wouldn't have to deal with it, but maybe it would be fun after all.

When she heard Becca's car pull into the driveway, Alison grabbed her purse. Becca came to the door and offered her arm, opened the car door and helped her inside. Alison couldn't recall the last time Michael had been so attentive. In their marriage, chivalry had kicked the bucket ages ago.

"Where are we going?" Alison asked.

Becca turned the car toward town. "It's a surprise. I have a whole evening planned."

"Nowhere too crowded, I hope." Alison should be proud to have Becca by her side, but it wasn't so easy. Everything she thought she knew about herself, about her identity and her place in the world, had changed. It was like the tectonic plates she taught the kids about in the science unit were shifting over each other. She wasn't sure she was prepared for the aftershocks.

Becca parallel parked in front of Alison's favorite bookstore. Golden light emanated through the large windows, the display tables in front stacked with colorful hardcover books. "Don't

185

worry so much and try to enjoy yourself," Becca said.

Alison used to come here all the time, but since the surgery, she'd been ordering her books online. The store was nearly empty, only a few people in the front browsing the new release tables. Lorraine, the owner, came over to greet them.

"Alison, it's so good to see you," Lorraine said. "I've heard you haven't been well."

"On the mend," Alison said. Becca introduced herself and shook Lorraine's hand. While the two of them made small talk, Alison meandered into the stacks, breathing in the smell of books and running her hand over the rows of spines.

Becca caught up to her. "Are you happy?" she asked.

"I've missed this place," Alison said. "The feeling it gives me."

"I know. There's something I want to show you." Becca led Alison to a display table in the middle of the store, full of books wrapped in brown paper, some on display stands, others stacked on top of each other in piles. Each book had a few clues written in black marker on the cover.

"What's this?" Alison asked.

"Blind date with a book," she said.

"You buy the book without knowing?"

"Isn't that fabulous?"

Alison wasn't sure how she felt about it. On one hand, the mystery was enticing. Maybe it would be a book she'd always wanted to read or one she'd never even known was right up her alley. But what if it was one she'd already read or the type of story that just wasn't for her? Not knowing what was inside seemed unnecessarily risky.

Becca grabbed a few of the wrapped books and flopped down on the large beanbag chair in the corner, patting the spot next to her. Once Alison got down there, she'd need help getting up, but she decided to go for it.

"Close your eyes and choose," Becca said, holding three books in front of her.

Alison closed her eyes and pointed to one.

"Okay," Becca said. "I'll read the clues and then we take turns guessing what book it is. You ready?"

"I'm not sure."

"Just relax and enjoy it. Okay here they are. Clue number one, young love. Clue number two, tragic end. And clue number three, different family backgrounds."

"That's easy," Alison said. "Romeo and Jul ... Juliet."

"But maybe it's a trick. You're supposed to think that, but there's lots of other books that fit that description."

"Like what?"

"There are so many. You just have to open your mind a little. *Me Before You* fits this description." She stopped to think for a few seconds. "Oh, what about *The Notebook*? That works, too."

"*The Notebook*?" Alison tickled Becca's side. "Take that back."

"No way."

"I'll go home."

"You don't have a car," Becca said, her eyes twinkling.

"I'll hitchhike," Alison said. "I know another one. *Love Story*. That fits, too."

"Should we buy it so we can see what's inside?" Becca handed Alison the book.

"I like the mystery," Alison said, warming up to the idea. "You can imagine anything."

"I know what I'm imagining right now." Becca leaned over for a kiss. All Alison could think about was Becca's soft lips, and her warm breath and the way Becca made her feel so alive. The sound of Lorraine answering the phone, the weight of the book in her hand, and the crunching of the beanbag chair all faded away.

A familiar voice jolted her back to reality. She pulled away and saw Michael standing at the display table looking straight at them.

"Make out session in a bookstore?" he said with a sneer. "Really classy, Alison."

"Uh ... what ... you doing here?" In all their time together, she and Michael had never gone to a bookstore or a library together. His idea of reading was scrolling through the ESPN app on his phone.

He held up a book, a photo of a guy wearing a Red Sox uniform on the cover. "Kyle from the firm said it's a must read. I've got a lot of time on my hands now, thanks to you." Alison had

had enough of sad sack Michael. She wished he would quit feeling sorry for himself already.

Becca extricated herself from the beanbag chair and helped Alison up. "Glad to see you're using the time to improve yourself," Becca said with a smile.

"Not only do you leave me for a woman, but now I have to deal with her sarcasm, too? Spare me." He directed his response to Alison, refusing to look at Becca.

"Please," Alison pleaded. "This won't help anything."

"I'm sorry I'm such a burden on you," he said. "You didn't seem to feel that way when I was taking care of you for all those months."

Becca put her arm around Alison. Whether she was trying to protect her or claim possession, Alison wasn't sure.

"Michael," Alison said. "Maybe you should leave."

"Get out while the going is good." Becca would never say something so trite, so Alison knew she was heckling Michael, poking fun at his fondness for clichés.

Lorraine walked over. "Can I help anyone find anything?" she asked.

"All set." Michael held up his book. He headed for the register without saying goodbye, Lorraine following behind him.

When they'd gone, Alison and Becca started giggling. It felt good to release the bubbles of nerves from the confrontation with Michael.

"This is the last place," Alison said.

"I know," Becca said. "Small world."

They pretended to peruse the display table, waiting for Michael to pay and leave the store. He stepped away from the register, then looked back at Alison with a pained look in his eyes.

"One minute," Alison said. As she walked toward Michael, the thumping of her cane on the hardwood floor pierced the stillness.

"Let him go," Becca said.

Alison continued walking, Lorraine and Michael both watching her slow progress.

"Can I speak with you outside?" Alison whispered once she'd reached Michael's side.

He grunted and followed her out the door.

"What do you want, Alison?" he said, facing her on the sidewalk. "You're the one who just told me to leave."

"I know." She never expected their separation to be this hard. Michael was no longer the right partner for her, but she hated to watch him suffer. "I'm sorry."

"Bullshit," he said. "I don't believe you for one second. You tell me you want a divorce and the next thing I know, you're making out with your girlfriend in public. Enough with the innocent act, Alison."

This was a new side of Michael, so full of venom and vitriol. He had always been so passive and agreeable. She tightened her grip on her cane. There had to be a way to separate from each other without hostility, to work things out civilly. "Don't be angry," she said. "We'll figure this out."

"Looks like you've already figured it out. Dump the chump and take up with the hot chick. I've got your number."

"No." She felt her pulse quickening. "That's not what happened."

"Sure looks that way to me." Michael took a breath. "Listen," he said, his voice calmer, "I've been thinking about something and I want to run it by you."

"What?"

"I think we should sue Grant," he said. "He clearly has a problem. Maybe he was under the influence when he operated on you. Plus, he's the reason our marriage fell apart. He deserves to pay for that."

"I don't think—" She didn't know why Michael insisted on harping on the drug use allegation when it was all based on hearsay. He had no proof that rumor was true.

"Hear me out. We're going to need the money to pay for your care. Physical therapy, speech therapy, and who knows what else. Why should we be strapped while he's rolling in dough?"

"I don't know." As bad as things were, Alison couldn't picture bringing a lawsuit against Grant. Such a drastic step would ensure they would never repair the rift in their family. "I'm not sure it will solve anything."

"Just think about it, okay?" Michael took his car keys from

his pocket and unlocked his car with a beep. "For me."

Alison watched him get into the car and drive away, leaving the conversation unfinished. When she went back inside, Alison felt jittery and uneasy, like she'd been spun around in one of those zero gravity rides at the carnival where the floor drops out suddenly and just when you think you can't stomach the spinning anymore, the floor rises back under your feet.

Should we head to the restaurant?" Becca rose from the bean-bag and checked her watch.

"You'll never believe what Michael suggested," Alison said.

"I can't wait to hear."

"He wants to sue Grant. For malpractice."

"Oh," Becca said. "I wasn't expecting that."

"What do you think?"

"I'm not sure I want to take sides in your family feud. Can we just focus on us? Our reservation is in twenty minutes."

"I don't think I can go," Alison knew Becca had planned a whole night out, but all she wanted to do was go home, get into her pajamas and watch TV. When she desperately needed Becca's opinion and support, Becca had excused herself. Alison couldn't sit at a restaurant and pretend everything was fine.

"What do you mean?" Becca said. "You don't want to have dinner?"

"I'll have to take a raincheck," Alison said. Tonight, she needed some time to herself.

CHAPTER TWENTY-EIGHT

Sadie

March 23, 2019

AFTER EMMA'S FATHER ARRIVED in the ER, Sadie followed her dad into the hospital elevator and he told her to press the button for the fifth floor. When she was little, she'd always loved coming with him on weekend rounds because he would let her press the buttons. The elevator doors opened up again and a couple stepped in. The man gripped the woman's hand so tight it had to hurt, but the woman looked calm, like she was the one guiding her husband through the medical crisis.

"What's the fifth floor?" Sadie asked.

"ICU," he said. "Intensive care unit."

"I know what ICU means, Dad." Sadie knew this unit was for the sickest of the sick, the patients who couldn't walk to the bathroom, couldn't breathe on their own, couldn't tell their family they loved them. Sadie hadn't pictured Aunt Alison that sick.

"Of course, you do," he said.

"Will I be allowed to see Aunt Alison?"

"Yes."

It was pathetic that she had to show up in the emergency room in order to see her aunt, but she'd take it. It's not like her parents would send her home alone in a cab in the middle of the night. Piper and the guys were probably already fast asleep by now.

"Will Emma get better?" Sadie asked. Fractures weren't her dad's thing, but he must have some idea of how well Emma's ankle would heal. This mess was all her fault. She had convinced Emma to come downtown; her friend's typical Saturday night usually involved a bag of microwave popcorn and binge watching *The Gilmore Girls.*

"She'll be fine," her father said. He had been very short with her since he'd spoken with Dr. Hidalgo. When he'd left the room, he seemed his normal self, but when he returned, he looked different, more serious and reserved. She had a sinking feeling she knew what they had talked about. The pills. She'd been so focused on making sure Emma was okay, she hadn't thought through the consequences of handing them over.

"I'm really worried about her." Sadie couldn't help thinking about whether Emma would be able to compete in a few weeks.

The elevator stopped at the fifth floor. Her father stepped out and turned toward the ICU. The other couple walked the opposite way, toward the pediatric ICU, making Sadie wonder what was wrong with their child. That was why the man seemed so nervous.

Before they reached the pneumatic doors sealing the unit off from the rest of the hospital, her father pulled Sadie into an empty waiting room and shut the door behind them.

"I think you owe me an explanation, young lady," he said.

"An explanation for what?" She didn't want to offer more information than necessary.

"For what really happened tonight," he said. "You haven't told me the whole story."

When Sadie had gotten in trouble in the past—stolen the Bratz doll from Lauren Fleming's house in third grade, plagiarized her essay about Harriet Tubman for her sixth-grade social studies class, skipped skating practice last year to go to the mall to buy hair dye—his eyes always narrowed and the skin between them bunched together. Today, his eyes were wide open and his pupils looked like big black holes, red lines creeping across the white parts.

"I told you what happened. Emma tripped and fell."

"Is there anything else you want to share?"

"I'm not sure." Usually, when Sadie made mistakes, she fessed up long before her parents figured anything out. The secret always started as a tiny spark, but over time, the flames increased in intensity, heating up her insides and threatening to engulf her if she didn't set it free.

"Where did you get those pills?"

"It's not what you think."

"I'll decide what I think."

Sadie had two choices. She could cover for Piper, tell her dad that she'd been the one to take the pills, or she could tell him the truth. It was an easy decision. This night was already a disaster without piling lies on top of everything else.

"It was Piper," Sadie said. "I invited her over after school and she wanted to go through your things. I told her it wasn't a good idea, but she wouldn't listen. She kept opening drawers and taking stuff." A tear slid down her cheek. "I didn't mean for anyone to get hurt."

"You let your sleazy friend have the run of my bedroom?"

"She's not sleazy, Dad."

Her father paced the room and ran his hands through his hair. "This is completely unacceptable. I don't know what's gotten into you lately."

"I couldn't stop her. There was nothing I could do."

"You had no right to invade my privacy," he said.

"I didn't mean to. I didn't know what to do."

"That girl is no good," he said. "I absolutely forbid you to see her again."

"That's not fair," Sadie said. Even though she was angry with Piper, she wasn't about to let her father choose her friends.

"I can't think of anything more fair," he said in a stern voice. "And by the way, you're grounded. For real this time."

Sadie's tears now turned to sobs. She wasn't sure if she was crying because of her father's tone of voice or because of what happened to Emma, but once she started she couldn't make herself stop.

"Don't worry." His face relaxed a bit. He'd always hated seeing her cry. "We'll figure things out."

"Okay," she said, trying to get herself under control.

"Listen, your mom is already wound up about everything. She doesn't need to know about this, okay?"

"About Emma?"

"We can tell her about the broken ankle, but that's all she needs to know."

❀

When they reached Aunt Alison's room, Sadie's mom was asleep in a chair next to the bed.

Her father nudged her mom, and she opened her eyes, her dark hair a tangled mess.

"Sadie? What's going on?" Her mom squeezed her eyes together. "What time is it?"

"Everything's fine," Grant said.

Her mom picked up her phone to look at the time. "It's the middle of the night."

"Emma had a little accident on the way home from the museum. Sadie came in with her."

"What kind of accident? Is she okay?"

"She'll be fine. Just a broken ankle."

Sadie approached the side of the bed, tuning out the sound of her parents' voices. Aunt Alison looked like she was asleep, her eyes closed and her arms resting by her sides, but Sadie knew they were probably giving her medicine to knock her out. Bandages covered her head, a few strands of hair escaping out the bottom, and multiple tubes went into both arms and crossed her chest. A plastic tube came out of her mouth and attached to a noisy machine at the bedside.

The Aunt Alison Sadie knew would never be so still. No matter how many times this week her parents had told her how bad things were—that Alison had a major complication, that the road to recovery would be very long, that she may never be the same person she once was—Sadie didn't really get it until now.

"Did you leave Emma alone down there?" Her mother's voice interrupted Sadie's thoughts.

"Is that what you think of me?"

"It was a simple question. Why do you insist on answering a question with a question?"

"It's the middle of the night. Can you give me a break for once?"

Her mother stood up. "She can't be by herself. I'm going down there."

"It's fine, Cynthia," her dad said. "We waited for Derrick to arrive before we came upstairs."

Sadie wished she had her earbuds so she wouldn't have to listen to her parents arguing again. She pulled one of the chairs up to the bed and sat down. All she wanted to do was reach out and touch her aunt's hand, to make sure it was warm and soft, but she couldn't make herself do it. What if her hand felt cold? What if it was rough and scaly? The thing she was most afraid of was that she would grasp Alison's hand and her aunt wouldn't respond.

"Derrick must be so upset." Her mom sat back down. "I hope he doesn't blame us for this mess."

"Why would he blame us?" Her father's voice sounded unnecessarily loud.

"Emma was with Sadie." Her mom's voice got louder, too. "How did it happen anyway?"

"She tripped on the sidewalk."

"I feel like we can't catch a break."

"It was a freak thing, Cynthia," he said. "Don't go getting all worked up about karma or some other shit. She twisted her ankle and it broke. Period. End of story."

"It was an accident, Mom." Sadie wished her mother would drop the subject. The last thing Sadie needed was for her mother to find out about the pills.

One of the nurses came in. "Everything okay in here?"

"Sorry about that," Cynthia said. "I know you like to keep it quiet."

The nurse hung a bag of fluid on the pole and pressed a few buttons on the monitor. "It's time for her antibiotics."

Sadie took her phone out of her pocket to check the time. 4:14. Always in bed by eleven at the latest, Sadie couldn't recall ever seeing 4 AM. After the nurse hooked the tubing up to Alison's IV and used her thumb to start the antibiotic drip, she announced that she had one more test to do: an arterial blood gas. She remembered her father saying that it was one of the most painful of all medical tests. The nurse took a needle out of the pocket of her scrubs and peeled off the plastic wrapping. The crinkling of the plastic hurt Sadie's ears.

"Will she be able to feel this?" Sadie asked as the nurse swiped the pale skin of Alison's wrist with an alcohol pad and felt for her pulse.

"She shouldn't feel anything," she said. "The sedation keeps them in a nice twilight."

Sadie watched the needle plunge straight down into Alison's flesh and wondered how it wasn't doing some sort of permanent damage. She knew the wrist had all sorts of vessels and ligaments and stuff, but when she looked at Alison's face, she still looked calm, her eyes taped shut and her mouth relaxed. Sadie wondered if, somewhere behind the wall of sedation, her aunt was screaming in pain, begging for mercy. Bright red blood filled the tubing connected to the needle, pulsing up and down with every beep of the monitor.

Sadie reached out and took Alison's other hand. It felt warm and familiar and when she squeezed, she felt something. It was faint, but Sadie desperately needed it to be real, not a figment of her imagination. Aunt Alison definitely squeezed back.

CHAPTER TWENTY-NINE

Grant

March 25, 2019

GRANT OPENED HIS EYES and tried to orient himself. Everything in Alison's hospital room felt the same—the beeping of the cardiac monitor, the whoosh of the ventilator and the chatter of the nurses changing shifts—but Grant now remembered today was different. Today, ten days after her surgery, Alison was scheduled to wake up.

Cal entered the room for morning rounds, a team of residents and medical students following behind. "Let's talk about the plan for Mrs. Jacobs," he said, looking to the chief resident. "Matt, why don't you do the honors."

Grant stood up and shook Cynthia awake. She sat up in the chair and ran a hand through her hair.

Matt tracked his finger down his patient list. "This is hospital day number ten for Alison Jacobs, age thirty-eight. She presented for resection of a large left parietal AVM with a postoperative hemorrhage requiring repeat operation and evacuation of the hematoma."

Grant squeezed his eyes closed. It was bad enough that he had caused the complication, but now he was forced to relive his mistake every single day on rounds. Sometimes he imagined the interns and medical students giving him accusing looks but maybe that was just his paranoia and exhaustion playing tricks on him. Now, a cute med student with a ponytail looked at him and quickly averted her eyes.

"And what's the current plan?" Cal asked.

"The plan is to extubate today. And now that the brain has

had time to rest, we can dial down the sedatives so we can assess her neurologic status."

Cynthia stood up. "What does that mean?"

"Today's the day we'll really get a sense of how Alison's doing," Cal said. "We've kept her sedated to make sure she doesn't bleed again. But now that it's been over a week, it's safe to bring her out of the coma and see how she really is."

Cynthia's eyes welled with tears. "Today? Will she be able to talk to us?"

"I'm not making any promises, but I certainly hope so," Cal said. "We'll start tapering the sedatives with a goal to take out the breathing tube in an hour or so. I hope she'll be fully alert soon."

"I can't believe it." Cynthia wiped tears from her face. "I feel like it's been forever since we've heard her voice. Right, Grant?"

Grant nodded. With the whole team looking on, he tried to say as little as possible.

"I think it's better if you step out while we remove the breathing tube," Cal said to Cynthia. "Many patients have a violent reaction to the procedure. This tends to make family members upset."

"Of course," Grant said. "We'll go downstairs for a bite to eat."

Grant waited for all of the team members to clear out before stopping Cal in the doorway. "I can't thank you enough for doing this," Grant said.

"No need to thank me," Cal said. "We have to watch each other's backs in this crazy business."

After Cal left, Grant looked over at Cynthia, her eyes still shiny. He wrapped his arms around her and cradled her head to his chest. Dwelling on the mistakes he had made, things he should have done, how he could have prevented this mess, wasn't going to help anyone now, himself included. He needed to be present for Alison right here and right now, to hold her hand and help her move forward from here, from their current reality.

"What if she doesn't wake up?" Cynthia asked, her voice muffled by the fabric of his shirt.

"She will." Memories of his patients who hadn't done as well as he'd hoped, the ones who'd woken up altered in ways he hadn't expected—their speech not quite as clear, their fingers clumsier, their gait not quite straight— came to his mind, but he pushed them away.

Grant stepped back and tipped Cynthia's chin up toward him. "We have to remain optimistic. Her scans look good and she's so strong. She needs our positive thoughts."

"She's coming back to us today," Cynthia said.

"Let's go down to the cafeteria. Give Cal some space to do his job." Grant said. All of a sudden, Grant was ravenous and he couldn't bear talking in circles about hypotheticals any longer. He'd barely eaten all week, subsisting on coffee and the occasional snack from the vending machine in the family waiting room. "Michael will be here soon anyway."

Grant wasn't sure why, but Michael had refused to stay over at the hospital. For whatever reason, he preferred to spend the night in his own bed, arriving back at the hospital around eight every morning.

In the elevator, Grant noticed a picture of Vanessa Hidalgo, the ER doctor, beaming and holding a wood plaque over her chest, her name etched into a gold plate. The hospital president and chairman of the board stood on either side of her. "Congratulations to our physician of the month honoree," the caption under the photo read. Grant wondered if she had really reported him to the administration or if that had been an empty threat.

"Figures," Grant mumbled.

"I don't remember you receiving that award," Cynthia said.

"No," Grant said. "It should be called the kiss-ass awards. Always goes to the most effective brown-nosers, not the best doctors."

"Really? Didn't Vik receive that one a few years ago?"

"Did he? I don't remember." Grant remembered all too well that Vik had indeed been given the same award. Grant had attended the ceremony in the hospital auditorium and put on his best smile, shaking Vik's hand and spewing some canned words of congratulations, but he remembered thinking what a load of crap it was that Vik had received the award before him. Though Vik was by far the best anesthesiologist on staff, all he really did was stare at a computer screen and press a few buttons once in a while. Grant was the one who did the hard work that took practice, and skill, and mastery of technique.

"I'm sure he did," Cynthia said. "I remember Meera talking about it."

"It's really not a big deal. Just an excuse for the hospital to spew out more bullshit on social media."

I'm sure you'll get it one day," Cynthia said, squeezing his arm. "It's just a matter of time."

CHAPTER THIRTY

Alison

October 27, 2019

ALISON AWOKE with her pulse pounding in her ears. She wiped the sweat from her face with her pajama top and used her left arm to help her sit, her muscles quivering with the effort. Despite just waking up, she felt exhausted. The nightmare always robbed her of the feeling of rejuvenation from a night's sleep.

Since Michael had moved out, she'd been plagued by the same nightmare almost every night. In the dream, Calvin Shin stood over her and pulled out the breathing tube in one swift motion. As Alison watched him, there was always a delay before she felt the pain, a searing burn deep in her throat, as if she'd swallowed a big gulp of boiling water. The pain was just as intense as it had been in real life. All she wanted to do was reach her hands to her throat to make it stop. She always woke up drenched in sweat, her heart racing in her chest. When she had the dream, she experienced that same horrific day over again, like Bill Murray in that annoying movie about Groundhog Day, every time just as vivid as when it had happened in real life.

She remembered Cal urging her to take a breath. Was she not breathing? And where the hell was Grant? Shouldn't a surgeon be there when his patient woke up from anesthesia? The room seemed so quiet. The white-coated minions around the bed stared at her as Cal rubbed his knuckles back and forth over her breast bone, pain burrowing into the center of her chest. He kept rubbing, but when she tried to reach her right arm to make him stop, it wouldn't follow her command. She heard a gurgled intake of air.

When Cal said, "She's breathing," Alison realized the wet sound had come from her, the air flow broken up by trapped phlegm. Cal called for suction and a nurse put a clear tube in her mouth and moved it around. The tube made an aggressive burble and when she stuck it farther down her throat, Alison gagged, a rush of vomit spilling onto her chest, the warm pool collecting around her neck and dripping down her upper back. It smelled vile and strangely reassuring at the same time—an affirmation that she was still alive, still able to breathe, and gag and puke. The nurse lifted her head to put a dry pad behind her.

"Welcome back," Cal said, looking into Alison's eyes. "We've missed your smile."

That was a strange thing to say. She remembered being wheeled into the operating room, Vik putting the oxygen mask over her face, the sting as he pierced the vein in her hand to put in the IV, a sour taste in her mouth as the milky medicine travelled up her arm. It seemed like only a few minutes ago, but she knew the surgery was supposed to take several hours.

"You've been in a coma for over a week," the nurse said, unsnapping the wet gown and replacing it with a dry one.

What the hell was this woman talking about? Her surgery had been today. Alison tried to reach her right hand to feel her head, but she couldn't make it move.

"Today you were finally ready for the tube to come out," Cal said. "How are you feeling?"

If he really wanted to know, her body was listless, her eyelids were sticking to her eyeballs, and her throat felt like it had been run over by a lawn mower. Everyone in the room was staring at her and waiting for her to say something, but when Alison opened her mouth to speak, nothing came out. She wanted to say, "Okay," a word she'd said so many times without a second thought, but the more she tried to say it, the less happened. With every ounce of her being focused on forming those two syllables, she managed a long moan that sounded vaguely like the letter O.

Cal's expression changed from guarded hope to grave concern, his friendly smile vanished. He reached into his pocket to retrieve a small black leather pouch, and took out a penlight, shining the painfully bright light into one of her eyes and then the other.

"Her pupils are equal, round, and reactive to light and ac-commodation," he said. "I know you all write the acronym in your notes every day, but you better damn well be examining your patients' eyes before writing it down." Something in Cal's voice told Alison something was off, an undercurrent of tension in his tone.

"The next thing to do is check the tracking of the eyes, looking for fluidity and nystagmus," he said, holding his finger over her left temple and moving it slowly to the right. "Any hitching or beating of the eye movements could indicate an injury."

What kind of injury was he talking about? Grant had assured her the AVM was treatable, that he had done this surgery hundreds of times and that he was confident he would be successful. Was he referring to the problem with her arm or the fact that she couldn't make the words come out? Maybe both. She wished Cal would stop with the doctor speak and tell her what the hell was going on. And that's when Grant and Cynthia walked in.

CHAPTER THIRTY-ONE

Grant

March 25, 2019

WHEN GRANT AND CYNTHIA RETURNED from the cafeteria, Cal was at the bedside doing a neurologic exam, the whole team looking on. Alison's eyes were wide open in panic. Cynthia hurried to the other side of the bed and grabbed her hand.

"I can't believe you're awake," she said. Grant was relieved to see Alison breathing on her own.

"Yes," Cal said. "I just need a few minutes to conduct a thorough exam. Would you mind waiting outside? I'm sure Michael could use some company in the waiting area." Grant knew Cal would never ask family to wait outside unless there was a major problem, but he held his tongue. He didn't want Cynthia's anxiety level to skyrocket.

The nurse guided Cynthia toward the door. "Can I get you a cup of coffee while you wait?" she asked.

"We just had breakfast," Cynthia said. "I want to stay with my sister."

The nurse continued speaking to Cynthia in a soothing voice, successfully leading her down to the hall and out of earshot.

"What's happening?" Grant asked. The ponytailed med student eyed him again. "Any chance you can do this exam without an entourage?"

"Yes, of course," Cal said, turning to the group. "Team, let's reconvene in fifteen."

When they all cleared out, Grant turned back to Cal. "What the hell is going on, Cal?"

"She woke up quicker than I thought." Cal tracked his finger in front of Alison's face, focusing his attention on her eye movements. "I was trying to get the exam done before you came back, so I would have a complete update."

"Well, I'm here now, so I'll watch you do it."

Cal asked Alison to squeeze his hands first on one side and then the other. He then tested the strength in each leg by asking her to push against him as hard as she could in different directions. Next, he used a sharp pin and a feather to test her sensation.

The panicked look on Alison's face was getting worse. One of them needed to say something to calm her down.

"Everything's fine," Grant said, even though he had a sinking feeling this was far from the truth. He couldn't think of anything else to say.

Cal lifted the sheet from Alison's feet and took a reflex hammer from the pocket of his white coat. Using the pointed end of the metal handle, he scraped the bottom of her left foot and her toes curled downward, a normal response. Grant breathed a small sigh of relief, before he realized her other foot would be the one affected. Injury of the left side of the brain affected the right side of the body and vice versa.

The omelet he'd had in the cafeteria swirled in his stomach. When Cal brought the handle of the hammer to Alison's right foot and dragged the sharp end from the heel upwards, Alison's big toe pointed backwards and the other toes splayed. Textbook positive Babinski sign, a telltale indication of brain injury.

"Fuck," Grant said, forgetting that Alison was awake and listening to every word they said.

"Do I need to ask you to step out, too?" Cal asked. "I don't want you upsetting my patient."

Alison's eyebrows raised in question. Grant noticed that her left eyebrow was slightly higher than the right.

"We'll explain everything in a minute, okay?" Grant said. When he took her hand, her smile made his stomach drop. The right side of her mouth remained neutral, the nasal labial fold flat, while the left side turned up normally.

"I'm almost done," Cal said. "Then we'll talk."

Hearing the word "talk" made Grant realize that he hadn't

heard Alison say anything. The whole time Cal had been conducting the exam, Alison hadn't said a single word.

Grant leaned down over the bed. "Alison, how are you feeling?"

She looked back at him and nodded.

"How are you feeling? I need you to tell me." He brought his hand to her cheek and turned her face toward him. "Tell me how you feel."

Her eyes darted around the room. Her mouth gaped open and the only thing that came out was a thin line of saliva trailing down the right side of her chin onto her neck.

"Dr. Shin, can we speak in private, please?" Grant said.

Cal assured Alison they would return soon and met Grant in the hallway outside the room.

"Is she aphasic? Because I can't get her to say a fucking word." One of the residents at the nurses' station looked up at them.

"Keep your voice down. You're yelling."

"I think I have the right to be yelling right now."

"Listen, you know better than I do that aphasia is not always permanent. With effective therapy, the patient can regain some or all of the speech they had before."

"Cut to the chase, Cal. What else did you find?" Grant asked "She has some sensory loss. Any weakness?"

"Definitely some in the right leg and right arm, and you saw the facial asymmetry. We won't know how much the weakness affects her until we can get her up and walking."

"Well let's do that now. I need to know what we're dealing with."

Cal made a quiet down motion with both hands.

"The sooner I know what we're dealing with, the sooner we can all wrap our heads around it," Grant said.

"What's going on?" Cynthia asked. Grant had been so upset he hadn't noticed her coming down the hall, Michael at her side.

"There are some complications," Cal said. "Why don't we sit down so we can talk things through?"

"I don't need to sit," Cynthia said. "Tell me right now."

"What kind of complications?" Michael asked.

"Sometimes with brain surgery, we don't know the full story

until the person wakes up. Patients with large tumors or big bleeds can wake up totally intact and those with smaller lesions end up with big deficits. We always hope for the best, and cross our fingers for good measure."

"And?" Cynthia looked from Cal to Grant, trying to glean information from their faces.

"And the outcome for Alison doesn't seem to be as positive as we had hoped," Cal said.

"What do you mean?" Michael said.

"She's got some weakness on her right side," Grant said, trying to take some of the pressure off Cal.

"Okay, that's doesn't seem so bad," Cynthia said. "There's that great physical therapy place right in Newton Centre. Lisa Newmark took her mother there after her stroke last year. I'm sure there's a therapist there who specializes in patients with brain injury."

"There's more," Grant said, placing a hand on Cynthia's arm. "She also has some speech deficits."

"Deficits?"

"She's not able to speak right now."

You're joking." She tried to break away. "I'm going to see my sister."

Grant pulled her back. "It's not a joke. The bleed damaged the speech part of her brain. She can't talk." Grant couldn't bear to look at Cynthia.

CHAPTER THIRTY-TWO

Alison

October 30, 2019

ALISON SETTLED IN AT THE CONFERENCE TABLE, resting her cane against her chair. The blinds were raised, sunlight pouring through the windows overlooking Boston Common. The swan boats had stopped running for the season, but the park was filled with people: tourists with baseball hats and sneakers, business-people eating their lunch on benches, kids riding scooters and chasing soccer balls. The idyllic scene gave Alison hope that one day she'd be able to enjoy a hot dog in the park. Swallowing a hot dog was still out of the question, but the thought of the salty meat smothered with sweet ketchup made her mouth water anyway.

Over a month since Michael had moved out, Alison hoped he would come to this meeting with a good attitude. So far, he was still fighting her every step of the way, making everything more difficult than it needed to be. The glass door opened and a tall woman entered.

"Good morning," she said, reaching her hand across the table. "Shelly Green. You must be Mrs. Jacobs."

"Alison." There was no chance she could stand on such short notice. Like a child learning to ride a bike, she needed a good push to get going. "Nice to meet you," she said, returning the handshake from her seat.

"Likewise." Shelly took a seat across from Alison. "I'd like to thank you for sending me all the information I requested. The more I have, the easier this process will be for everyone."

Alison couldn't imagine this would be easy, especially with Michael involved. She was surprised Michael had agreed to mediation at all, and accepted her choice of mediator to boot. Becca's neighbor had used Shelly Green for her divorce a few years back.

"No problem," Alison said. In reality, it had been quite a problem. Gathering all of her financial information—pay stubs, car titles, insurance policies—hadn't been an easy undertaking. You don't realize how much you owned until someone asks you to make an exhaustive list of your possessions. There was nothing like a divorce to make you want to simplify your life. Plus, with Rhea constantly insisting she give Michael another chance, Alison had to do it all on her own. When Rhea said Michael was a good man, what she was really saying was that Alison's relationship with Becca was unnatural and immoral. Alison couldn't deal with her judgment on top of everything else.

Shelly rubbed her lips together to smooth her lipstick. "We'll get started as soon as Mr. Jacobs arrives."

"Michael," Alison said, trying to keep this meeting as casual as possible. When they'd looked Shelly up online, Becca had said she looked like Rose Byrne from that movie about the bridesmaids and Alison saw the resemblance now, the same slim nose and sleek hair. Michael knocked and came in. He looked worn, dark stubble on his cheeks and his hair tucked under a Red Sox cap. He introduced himself to Shelly and then starting pulling out a chair beside her.

"If you don't mind," Shelly said. "I'd like you two to sit side by side. It's better for negotiation. Less adversarial."

Michael nodded and came around the table. When he got closer, Alison smelled a familiar unwashed odor, like after he'd gone for a long jog. She wondered if he was taking care of himself.

"Before we get started, let me tell you a little about myself," Shelly said. While she went into detail about her college career, law degree from an Ivy League law school, position as vice-president of law review, and who knows what else, Michael made a show of moving his chair farther away from Alison before taking a seat. "I'd like to thank you both for reaching out to me," Shelly continued. "You've taken an important first step. It says a lot that you've decided to use a mediator instead of lawyering up."

"You *are* a lawyer," Michael said.

"By training," Shelly ignored his attitude. "But I've chosen to serve as a mediator instead of divorce attorney. I like to keep things amicable rather than pitting one team against the other."

"So, I have a question for you," Michael said. "What if we decided to sue the doctor who did this to Alison? How would we do that?"

"Well, that's outside of my area of expertise and also not the reason we're meeting today. Why don't we focus on mediation for now?"

"That sounds like a good idea," Alison said, shooting Michael a stern look.

"We've got some work to do," Shelly said. "Why don't we talk things through. See if we can come up with solutions that meet both of your needs."

"Seems pie in the sky to me," Michael said. "You're going to convince me that Alison deserves my money. This isn't cocktail hour."

"It sounds like you're bringing some anger to the table," Shelly said. "That's quite common and understandable."

"Damn straight, I'm angry." Michael stood up and started pacing in front of the window. "My wife, who pledged to love me forever, has all of a sudden decided she bats for the other team. I think I have the right to be angry, Shelly."

"It's not about you," Alison said. "You didn't do anything wrong."

"Well, I can't help but take it personally, Alison." A spray of spit flew out of Michael's mouth.

"Very good," Shelly said. "Airing your grievances at the outset is healthy. We can't begin negotiation until both parties have agreed to participate."

"This whole thing came out of nowhere," Michael said to Alison, "and you're acting like I should get over it already. It's going to take me a while. I can't just turn on a dime like that."

"I know."

"I thought we would be together forever," Michael said. "I can't picture myself without you."

"I never wanted to hurt you," Alison said. "I mean that."

Michael looked at her, and she caught a glimpse of the old

Michael, the one who made her laugh with his stupid sayings and silly jokes, the one who had who sat by her side all those months in the hospital, the one who would do anything and everything for her.

"Why don't you sit down?" she said.

Michael collapsed into his seat with a groan.

"Well, that was a productive conversation," Shelly said. "Shall we get started with the details?"

❀

The following afternoon, Alison sat by the window at Starbucks watching people passing outside, mothers pushing strollers, men in business suits, teenagers texting while they walked. Two women at the table next to hers discussed the pros and cons of hot yoga. She breathed in the earthy smell of roasted coffee and sighed. It felt indescribably good to be out in the world.

Alison had told Rhea she was meeting a colleague from work, conveniently forgetting to mention a name, and Rhea agreed to drop her off. When Becca picked her up, she was literally in the driver's seat and Alison wanted to meet on her own terms today. She was here to tell Becca they needed to slow things down. After the scene in the bookstore, she'd been doing a lot of thinking. Rushing right into another relationship wouldn't be fair to either of them. Alison needed time to breathe, to figure out the details of the divorce and what her life would look like going forward.

She looked up and noticed Robin Weintraub, Cynthia's annoying tennis partner who was always on some diet or other. As Robin claimed her Frappuccino from the counter, Alison saw she was wearing one of those ugly rubber bracelets. She wondered if Cynthia made them for all of her friends and if any of them found it as odd as she did. Turning to the window, she hoped Robin would pass without recognizing her.

"Alison, is that you?"

"Robin, "Alison said, as if she had no idea Robin was there. "How are you?" She hoped Robin wouldn't take the opportunity to tell her about the ups and downs of her latest diet. Given the five-hundred-calorie milkshake in her hand, Alison figured she was on a downswing at the moment.

"Can't complain," Robin said. "I haven't seen you in forever. Maybe since you were in the hospital. You really look great."

"Nowhere to go but up," Alison said.

"I guess so."

Alison looked out the window, hoping Robin would take the hint and leave.

"Have you spoken with Cynthia lately?" she asked.

"No."

"Maybe you should give her a ring."

"Thanks for the advice." Sarcasm crept into Alison's voice. It had been almost two months since their fight in the craft store, but with everything going on with Michael and Becca, Alison hadn't had much time to dwell on it. Plus, the ball was in her court, as Michael would say. Cynthia had essentially called Alison a prissy bitch and stormed out the door, so Alison wasn't about to go crawling back to her. She still had her pride. Out of the corner of her eye, Alison saw the door open. Becca wore a full peasant skirt and a white tank top, her hair draped over one shoulder.

"I hope I'm not overstepping my bounds," Robin said. "It's just that Cynthia's been so upset about your fight. And since Grant moved out, she keeps rehashing it and asking me what she should do. She feels like she lost her whole family all at once."

What was she talking about? Sadie had mentioned they were fighting, but she hadn't said anything about Grant moving out. Alison decided to pretend she was in the know.

"And what did you tell her?" Alison asked.

"I told her that a sincere apology goes a long way, but she's afraid."

Becca was placing her order at the counter. Alison hoped she would wait for Robin to leave before coming over.

"Did you hear what I said?" Robin asked.

"Yes. I'll call her." Alison had no intention of calling Cynthia, especially when she hadn't even had the courtesy to tell her about Grant moving out, but she'd say anything to make Robin go away.

"That's amazing," Robin said. "I'm so glad I ran into you today."

"Me, too," Alison said.

Becca walked over and placed her coffee on the table, leaning down to give Alison a hug. She hung her tote on the back of the empty chair and sat down.

Now Alison had no choice but to introduce them. "Robin, do you know Becca? We used to teach together." She prayed that Robin wouldn't pick up on the energy between them.

"Nice to meet you," Robin said, turning her attention back to Alison. "Are you going back to work, soon? You seem like you might be ready."

"Maybe soon." Since her speech had improved, people seemed to think she was completely recovered. Though her sentences were more fluid, it still took a lot of effort to find words and string them together. And no matter how hard she tried, some words still eluded her.

"I hope so." Robin waved goodbye. "It was great to see you today and nice to meet you, Becca."

"This seems so formal," Becca said, once Robin was gone.

"I know," Alison said. She didn't know how to look Becca in the eyes and say what she needed to say, that their relationship had to slide over to the back burner for a bit.

"I could have picked you up," Becca said.

Alison took a sip of iced coffee, thankful to the person who had invented the straw. When she used one, she almost never dribbled. They may be terrible for the environment, but that was the least of her concerns.

"I want to start doing things on my own."

"Should we pretend this is a Tinder date?" Becca said. "Ask each other get to know you questions? It'll be fun."

"Shhh ..." Alison made a quiet down motion with her hand, looking around to see if anyone else looked familiar: parents from school, Michael's coworkers, more of Cynthia's annoying friends. News of her divorce was probably spreading around town, so she didn't want to create more fodder for gossip. Maybe meeting at Starbuck's hadn't been a good idea.

"Now you're making me nervous," Becca said. "I feel like I never really know what's going on in your head."

"I want to be honest," Alison said "This isn't easy."

"What's not easy? Stop talking in code. Just tell me what you're trying to say."

"I'm feeling ... overwhelmed." Alison wanted to say more, but the words were slow to come.

"Overwhelmed with what?" Becca said, a look of concern on her face. "The divorce?"

"Sort of. I don't ... know."

"I need you to be more specific."

"Money for one. Not enough."

"I manage it. You'll just have to be more frugal."

"I'm not used to it."

"To not having Michael's big bucks? We'll figure it out. Maybe we can move in together." She looked so sexy, the strap of her tank falling off her shoulder.

"Not just the money," Alison said. "It's everything at once."

"You are so much better than you were," Becca said. "You've really come a long way."

Alison gathered herself. She needed to make Becca understand her. "A lot farther to go. I need to feel good about myself before ... someone else." It was less than eloquent, but she'd gotten the point across.

"I can help you recover. You don't need to push me away."

"One more thing," Alison said. "I'm not ready for rainbow flag." She'd been doing a lot of thinking about labels. Becca wanted her to stick a LESBIAN sign on her forehead for all the world to see. Alison wasn't there yet and may never be.

"Coming out isn't as big a deal as you're making it," Becca said. "People will accept you, and if they don't, you don't need them anyway. It helps you figure out who your true friends are."

"It's too much."

"What are you trying to say?" Becca's eyes were glossy. "Are you breaking up with me?" That wasn't it. Alison didn't want to break up. She just needed to put on the brakes until her life was more settled. The dejected look on Becca's face made Alison want to take her in her arms and kiss the tears away.

"No," Alison whispered.

"Then what?"

"I need some time. Can you can be patient?"

"I'm doing my best." Becca wiped the tears from her cheeks

with a brown paper napkin. "I'm not trying to be pushy. I just know this is right, and I don't want to waste any more time."

"I know."

"So where do we go from here?" Becca asked.

"One step at a time."

"I'll follow your lead."

"Alright," Alison said. "Not ready for big ann ... announce-ment."

"So, keep it on the down low?" Becca said.

"Yeah," Alison smiled. "On the down low."

CHAPTER THIRTY-THREE

Sadie

March 25, 2019

TWO DAYS AFTER EMMA'S ACCIDENT, Sadie pulled her leg warmers over her tights, wishing she could pull them up over her whole body and hide inside. She hadn't wanted to come to practice today, but her parents had insisted Sadie keep to her regular schedule. She finished lacing up her skates and stood up, centering her weight over her feet. No matter how many years she'd been skating, it still took a moment to get her equilibrium on the thin silver blades. Today, she wasn't sure anything was going to feel right. Emma wasn't here.

When she reached the rink, Coach Volkov called the girls over to the boards.

"You all need to be aware of something that happened this weekend," Coach said.

Sadie saw the looks of concern on the other girls' faces. Though she knew exactly what Coach was about to say, her teammates had no idea.

"Emma had an accident on Saturday night." There was a gasp followed by whispers. Sadie stepped onto the ice and joined the others. "She'll be okay, but her ankle is pretty banged up. She made it through a long surgery and just came home this morning."

"Surgery?" Natalie said. "It was that bad?" The second-best skater on the team, Natalie must have been thinking about how Emma's absence would affect her chances to go to the Olympic trials.

"They needed to line the bones up to help them heal," Coach said.

"What does that mean?" Natalie asked. She hadn't asked it outright, but what Natalie wanted to know was whether Emma would be back.

"Will she be back?" Sadie asked. She figured she'd save everyone the trouble and ask the question out loud.

"Not for a while," Coach said. "She'll start physical therapy in a few weeks and then we'll play it by ear."

When Coach said "play it by ear" it meant there was no way it would happen. Emma was never going to skate again. Maybe she'd put on a pair of crappy rental skates with her kids in twenty-five years at some stupid pop-up rink on her local golf course, but her competition days were over. The second her toe caught the curb and she landed in the street, all of her hard work had evaporated. Sadie would never forget that moment, Emma's body in a heap, the blinding glare of headlights, the screeching of brakes as the bus veered out of the way. Sadie tried to wipe the memory away so she could focus on what Coach was saying.

"I've made a plan to fill in the gaps," Coach said.

"But the Bay State Games are twelve days away." Natalie's voice squeaked with nerves. "How will we compete without her?"

"We'll make it work," Coach said. "Today's practice will be dedicated to changing the choreography of the precision line routine to account for her absence."

The whispering had turned to loud murmurs, anxiety levels clearly raised by Coach's surprise announcement.

"And Sadie?" Natalie asked.

"Sadie will have to sit out the pairs competition. With so little time, it's too late to sub in someone else."

❀

As soon as Sadie exited the rink, she saw Piper standing off to the side, smoking a cigarette. What was she doing here? She didn't skate and would have no reason to be hanging out here. Emma's mom's SUV was parked by the curb and Sadie didn't want to keep her waiting. Sadie already felt bad that Mrs. Wright had offered to pick Sadie up despite Emma's injury.

"Oh hey," Piper said, flicking her cigarette onto the ground.

"I was waiting for you." She sounded so nonchalant, like nothing had happened between them.

"What are you doing here?"

"I'm not allowed to come say hello to my friend?"

"I guess," Sadie didn't know what Piper wanted from her.

"I have something to say," Piper said.

"What?"

"I shouldn't have given your little friend those pills. She wasn't ready."

Sadie waited to see if there was anything more. If this was Piper's idea of an apology it was pathetic. The way she said "little friend" was so condescending, like Emma was a toddler in pre-school.

"Is that all?" Sadie asked. "Because my ride is here."

"No, there's more. I have four tickets for the P!NK concert next week. There's one for you if you want it."

Sadie had seen awesome videos of her concerts on YouTube with all sorts of crazy acrobatics and trapeze tricks. She would have loved to see the spectacle for herself, but she knew she couldn't accept. It would send Piper the wrong message, that her friendship could be bought.

"How did you get them?"

"My mom scored them," Piper said.

"Your mom?"

"Yeah. She has her ways," Piper said. Sadie realized she didn't care to hear anything more about Piper's mom or her ways. She didn't care if she was in jail, at home baking brownies and packing lunches, or in Zimbabwe. It was none of Sadie's business, and the less involvement she had with Piper and her family, the better.

"I'm sure she does," Sadie said. "Anyway, I have to go."

"We can give you a lift." Piper pointed to a black pick-up truck parked in the circle, Brian at the wheel.

"I'm all set." Sadie hoisted her skate bag onto her shoulder and started walking toward Mrs. Wright's car.

"Do you want the ticket or not?" Piper asked.

"No," Sadie said. "I'm good, thanks."

"You're serious?" Piper said. "It's your loss."

Sadie ignored her and opened the car door. It would be awkward sitting in the back with no one else in the car, so Sadie sat in the front, fitting her skate bag at her feet.

"Is that the Morris girl?" Mrs. Wright asked.

"Yeah," Sadie said.

"I read something about her mother in the Newton Reporter the other day. Something about a restraining order."

"Oh." Sadie didn't want to talk about Piper or her stupid mother.

"How was practice?"

"Fine, I guess," Sadie said.

"Did you girls work on the precision line?"

"Uh-huh."

"How's it looking?"

"Okay." They were having the same conversation they would have had if Emma was in the car and everything was normal, but things were far from normal. After Coach's announcement, practice had not gone well. All the skaters felt a sense of imbalance, their spins not as centered, their jumps not as high, their footwork messy and imprecise.

Mrs. Wright turned onto the main road. "Did Coach say anything about Emma?"

"Yeah." Was that really a serious question? Did she think no one would notice when their star skater failed to show up less than two weeks before the biggest competition of the year?

"What did she say?"

"Just that Emma broke her ankle and we would play it by ear." The more she thought about that phrase the less sense it made.

"Yes," Mrs. Wright said. "That's just what we'll do." She clicked on the radio and "Happy" by Pharrell Williams came through the speakers. Sadie had found it catchy when it first came out, but now it sounded repetitive and irritating. She wasn't feeling particularly happy and she knew Mrs. Wright wasn't either.

When they pulled into the driveway and Mrs. Wright turned off the car, the silence felt jarring. Now, Sadie missed that song, anything to fill the void. Sadie was supposed to have dinner here and hang out until her mom picked her up on the way home from the hospital. Sadie hadn't seen Emma since she'd left her in the ER Saturday night and she felt nervous, her stomach making weird noises.

"Well," Mrs. Wright said. "Emma will certainly be glad to see you. She's been bored out of her mind."

Mrs. Wright opened the front door and went upstairs, leaving Sadie in the entryway. Emma was lying on the couch, her leg elevated on two pillows, watching an episode of *Gilmore Girls*. Sadie used to watch that show, too, but when Piper made fun of her for watching it, she stopped. She'd forgotten how much she loved it: the quaintness of Stars Hollow, the sweet relationship between Rory and Lorelai, Rory's obsession with books and reading. Watching it felt like putting on a cozy old sweatshirt she would wear around the house, but never in public.

Sadie sat down in the armchair next to the couch. On screen, Rory was at the dance wearing a satiny dress, her arms wrapped around a guy's neck.

"Dean is the cutest," Emma said.

"Yeah." He wasn't actually Sadie's type. She usually liked the geekier guys, but now was not the time to disagree with Emma. "Totally hot."

Sadie looked down at Emma's leg, her ankle imprisoned by a thick white cast, several thick metal pins piercing the plaster at right angles and attaching to a large scary looking metal contraption. It made Sadie think of Frankenstein with those metal bolts coming out of his neck.

"Crazy looking, isn't it?" Emma said. "It's called an external fixator."

"An external what?"

"Fix-at-or," Emma said, pronouncing each syllable separately.

"Does that mean it's going to fix things?"

"One can only hope," Emma said. "How's Alison doing?"

"I know she's awake, but not much else," Sadie said. "My mom said she's going to need physical therapy."

"So will I," Emma said. "It's all the rage."

"I guess. When do you start?" A few years ago, Sadie's mom had torn a tendon in her thumb playing tennis. She'd worn a splint and gone to physical therapy twice a week. Sadie wasn't sure what happened at therapy, but she remembered her father complaining that the sessions were expensive, something about having to pay the deductible, whatever that meant.

"I need another surgery to get this thing taken out first."

"Did your surgeon say anything about skating?"

Emma shook her head. "My mom asked, but he wouldn't say anything definite. He said everyone heals differently and he can't make any promises one way or the other."

Sadie could hear the wobble in Emma's voice. Emma had been skating since she was four, her whole life dedicated to practicing routines, reviewing choreography in her head, fantasizing about standing on the Olympic podium with a medal around her neck. Up until Saturday night, that fantasy had a chance of becoming reality.

"He wouldn't make any predictions?"

"No." Emma started to cry, her brave facade gone. "Why did this happen? I knew it was a mistake to go with you. Nothing good happens around that girl."

Blaming everything on Piper would be an easy thing to do, but Sadie didn't think that would be fair. Sadie had been the one who'd invited Emma, encouraged her to hang out with Piper and the guys, failed to stop Piper from giving Emma the pills. The pills were her fault, too. She'd looked on as Piper rummaged through her dad's nightstand and taken them. If she'd stood up to Piper that day, focused less on impressing her and more on doing what was right, this whole disaster could have been prevented.

"I know," Sadie said. She wanted to apologize but she couldn't figure out how. She didn't think a simple "I'm sorry" would suffice when Emma's lifelong dream had disappeared before their eyes. She stood up and moved to the couch, gently lifting Emma's leg and the pile of pillows, then sitting back down with her friend's injured leg on her lap. "Em, I don't know what to say."

"There's nothing you can say. My ankle is totally busted up and I'll probably never skate again." She wiped her face with the back of her hand.

"There's more," Sadie said, her heart pounding.

"What do you mean?"

"There's something I haven't told you." Sadie put her hand on Emma's knee above the cast. She needed to tell her before she lost her nerve, but she couldn't make herself do it.

"What's going on?" Emma asked. "You got so serious all of a sudden."

"This is serious."

"What is it?"

Sadie took a deep breath. "The pills ...."

Emma was looking her with a look of complete trust. She'd been such a loyal friend for so many years and look what Sadie had done to repay her loyalty.

"I made the decision to take them," Emma said. "That had nothing to do with you."

"But you don't know where Piper got them."

"I wouldn't put anything past that girl. I told you about her mom, and her brother and that gross friend of his didn't seem much better—"

"This isn't about Piper. It's about me." Sadie couldn't let Emma continue badmouthing Piper and her family. Everything she said may be true, but that was irrelevant. She had to own up to her involvement, to be honest instead of continuing to hide behind lies.

"What are you talking about?"

"Piper stole the pills from my father's drawer, and I stood by and watched her do it."

Emma's mouth dropped open. "What do you mean?"

"It was my fault," Sadie said. "I let her steal them."

Emma's eyes widened, and then she looked away. Without a word, she turned up the volume on the TV and immersed herself once again in the pleasant world of Stars Hollow.

CHAPTER THIRTY-FOUR

Alison

November 1, 2019

"MY UBER DRIVER WAS SO WEIRD," Sadie said after Rhea let her in. "He kept offering me food."

"That is odd." Alison felt badly that Sadie had to Uber here. She wished she could pick her up at school and take her to the mall, but she wasn't there yet.

Sadie took off her jacket and sat down on the couch. "How are you?" she asked.

"I have news for you," Alison said. Sadie had never been particularly close with Michael, but Alison needed to tell her what was going on. "Uncle Michael and I have decided to get divorced."

"Really?" Sadie asked, her face scrunched. "I can't believe this. First my dad moved out and now this. Our family really is falling apart." She wiped tears from her face with her sleeve.

"What?" Alison said. She'd been trying to forget what Robin had said, but now she couldn't pretend any longer. "When did your dad move out?"

"Right after he came back from rehab. Mom found him a place in Newton Centre."

"Rehab?"

"Yeah. He went there in the spring. To get off the pills. Mom said he's been taking them for five years."

Michael's horrible accusation had been true. Alison had been hoping it was just a vicious rumor. Had Cynthia known about Grant's addiction when she'd begged him to take on Alison's case? If Grant had really been addicted for that long, there must have been some signs: mood swings, unpredictable behavior, pill bottles around the house. Cynthia must have known how quickly things would fall apart if his secret came to light, so she'd wrapped herself in a comfortable blanket of denial.

"How will you manage on your own?" Sadie asked with a sniffle.

Alison pulled herself away from her thoughts. She had to be present for Sadie. "I'm doing just fine. I'm much stronger than I thought."

"You absolutely are. I'm so proud of you," Sadie said.

"And I have lots of people who love me."

"I sometimes wondered if Uncle Michael was right for you." Sadie took a deep breath. "Like you didn't always click." She leaned over to give Alison a hug.

"Enough about this," Alison said. "What's happening with you?"

"Skate America was last week. I can't stop thinking about it."

"Why?" Alison asked. "Were you supposed to skate there?" Sadie was a good skater, but Alison knew she couldn't compete at the national level.

"No, Emma was."

"What happened to Emma?"

"Oh my gosh," Sadie's expression turned serious. "I can't believe you don't know. She broke her ankle and it was all my fault."

"What do you mean?" Alison had missed a lot when she was out of commission, but surely Sadie was exaggerating. How could a broken ankle be her fault? Sadie launched into a dramatic story about a planetarium show, Emma taking pills that came from Grant's nightstand, and falling down in the street. Her voice wavered as she finished. Alison put her arm around Sadie and pulled her in again.

"You're being too hard on yourself," Alison said.

"Emma will never skate again because of me," Sadie said.

"That is so sad. But no one person is responsible. You could also blame your father or Piper or Emma. Life is com ... complicated."

"I guess."

"Learning to forgive is important. Even yourself." As Alison spoke, she thought about taking her own words to heart. Before you can forgive anyone else, you have to learn to forgive yourself. She couldn't blame herself for everything, just like she couldn't allow the blame to lie only with others. Her marriage didn't fail because of her or Michael alone. Maybe if she hadn't entered the marriage with her eyes closed, things might have turned out differently. Her AVM would have bled at some point, even if it hadn't happened while fooling around with Becca. Her surgery may have turned out the same even if she'd chosen a different surgeon. And when it came to Grant and Cynthia, she'd been standing on principle, but maybe she needed to stop being so defensive, take off her blinders so she could see other sides of the story.

"It's been months," Sadie said. "I'm not sure Emma will ever really forgive me. Things will never be the same as they were."

"It will take time," Alison said. "You need to be patient with her."

"I'm trying," she said.

"You'll have to prove yourself worthy of her trust. You're a very special person, Sadie Kaplan. Don't you ever forget that."

Sadie nodded, her eyes clouded with thought. Alison hoped at least some of what she'd said had struck a chord with her.

"There's something else ..." Sadie said. "I heard my parents arguing a couple nights ago. It sounded like therapy assignment, like he had to be honest about everything as part of his treatment. My father was telling my mom about what happened during your surgery. My dad mentioned a panic attack and leaving the room. Then he said something about a lot of bleeding."

Alison's mouth dropped open. She couldn't believe it, but she knew Sadie would never lie. Not to her. How could Grant leave the operating room with her on the table? Was Grant high when he'd sawed open her skull and removed chunks of her brain? Is that why things had gone so disastrously wrong? Had Grant and Cynthia been trying to hide this from her? So many questions flew through her mind, but she did her best to control her anger and listen.

"Then my mom said something about being pulled over by the police when you started bleeding the next day. I'm not sure what that's about."

What? Why wasn't Grant at the hospital watching over her?

Why would he get pulled over? The questions screaming through her brain had no acceptable answers. She took a breath, trying to prevent the fear and confusion from showing on her face.

"I'm sorry you heard that," Alison said. The last thing she wanted to do was put Sadie in the middle of the family feud. Though she acted mature, she was still a child. Alison knew now she could never sue Grant. It would destroy Sadie. Alison had always protected Sadie and she wasn't about to stop now. No matter how bad things were, she'd have to find another way to work them out.

After Sadie left, her words played over and over in Alison's mind. She had trusted Grant with everything, and he had betrayed her trust in the most horrifying ways. Anger and hurt surged through her all over again. She'd been duped, convinced by Cynthia and Michael that Grant would be her savior, when in reality, he'd been the worst possible choice.

CHAPTER THIRTY-FIVE

Grant

March 27, 2019

OUTSIDE THE ADMINISTRATIVE CONFERENCE ROOM, Grant's necktie threatened to cut off the blood flow in his carotid arteries. Maybe that was why he had weird tingling in his scalp and pounding in his temples. He loosened the knot and took a deep breath. What was taking them so long? They'd asked him to be here at 8 AM and it was almost 9:00. The only other times he'd been called to the conference room had been for accolades: five-star reviews on the hospital surveys, glowing patient letters sent to the CEO, focus groups on how to bring in more surgical volume.

At least he didn't have to wear a monkey suit on a regular workday. On the rare day he escaped for lunch, he saw financial guys on the streets around the hospital wearing identical gray suits, phones glued to their ears while they walked. How could they focus on work while wearing such constricting clothing? In his usual scrubs, his body felt comfortable, freeing his mind to focus on the surgical field and his hands to work their magic.

His suit jacket stretched tight across his back. He really should get back to his schedule of going to the gym on Tuesdays and Thursdays after office hours, but nothing about his daily routine had been normal in the two weeks since Alison's surgery.

"Dr. Kaplan has had a family emergency," he had heard Laura in his office saying on the phone when he'd stopped in to pick up an extra bottle of Oxy. Though the explanation was entirely true, it was incomplete, like one of those beautiful Russian dolls that looks so perfect on the surface but is completely hollow inside, all form and no substance. Of course, his staff couldn't tell his patients that he'd caused the family emergency, that he was taking time off to try and clean up the mess he'd made. Grant could feel the collar of his shirt getting damp. He wondered how much longer they'd make him wait. The sooner he got this misunderstanding cleared up, the more quickly he could put it behind him.

The conference room door opened and Vanessa Hidalgo stepped out. Instead of scrubs and a white coat, she was wearing a black dress and heels, a necklace of silver beads around her neck. Her fancy dress ramped up his anxiety level even more. When he'd come home Monday night after Alison had woken up, all he'd wanted to do was take a few Oxy, have a glass of wine, and forget about the day. He needed a break from the hospital, an hour without talking about complications, and percentages, and therapy options. As soon as he took his pills and sat down at the kitchen table to go through his emails, he'd noticed one from Vik's hospital email account, the red and navy shield-shaped hospital logo emblazoned at the top. Why would Vik have sent him an official hospital email? He scrolled down past the heading to the body of the email.

To Dr. Grant Kaplan,

A fellow staff remember has reported an incident to this committee in good faith. The professional assistance committee is obligated to investigate all reports received in a timely and thorough manner. This correspondence should not be cause for alarm. The goal of the investigation is to ensure the highest level of safety and compliance at our institution. Please report to the seventh-floor administrative conference room on Wednesday March 27th at 8 AM.

Sincerely,
Vikram Chawla, MD
Chairman of the Professional Assistance Committee

Vik had been known to kid around, but it was too early for an April fool's prank. Grant's stomach dropped. This was no joke.

Now, Vanessa walked by him without making eye contact. How could she act like he was invisible, like he wasn't sitting right in front of her?

Grant stood up and followed her.

"Vanessa," he called when he'd almost caught up. When she refused to turn around, Grant grabbed her by the arm. He wouldn't let this stupid misunderstanding ruin their working relationship.

"Don't touch me," Vanessa said, shaking her arm free.

"This is getting a little out of hand," Grant said. "We're friends and you're acting like I'm some sort of monster."

"I never said that."

"The look on your face certainly did. I'm an excellent surgeon. You know that."

"I never said you weren't," Vanessa said. "Patient safety is my number one priority. When I see anything that threatens that, I have an obligation to speak up."

"I didn't hurt anyone."

"A young girl with a promising ice-skating career may never skate again because of you. I would classify that as hurting someone."

Grant's breath caught. With all of the craziness of the past few days, the repercussions of Emma's injury hadn't even crossed his mind. After he'd made sure she was plugged in with the best orthopedic surgeon, he'd moved on. He made a mental note to text Derrick later and see how she was doing.

"What did you say in there?" he asked.

"I told them the truth," Vanessa said.

"The truth about what?"

"Oh, come on, Grant. You know as well as I do exactly what happened and who was at fault. Don't play games with me."

"Grant?" Vik stood in the doorway of the conference room. "We're ready for you."

Before Grant could respond, Vanessa turned and walked away.

He walked back to the conference room door, trying to assess the situation by the look on Vik's face, but he looked like the same guy who'd been by his side for years. And now, Vik was tasked with investigating him. They were supposed to be on the same side, not on opposing teams.

"Everything okay?" Vik asked.

"Well, let's see. My sister-in-law may never walk or talk again, my daughter has befriended the devil, and my best friend is accusing me of God knows what. Never been better."

"Listen, I know this isn't the best situation," Vik said. "I'd much rather talk with you over dinner and a few drinks, but this is part of my job. Can we try to make this as smooth as possible?"

"You tell me, Dr. Chawla. You're the one in charge."

"Enough with the sarcasm," Vik said. "We have to take this seriously. Between the alleged drug use and the pending legal action, there's a lot to unpack. I trust we can all cooperate on this."

Grant adjusted his collar.

"I hope we can put this all behind us." Vik motioned for Grant to enter the conference room and pointed to an empty chair at one end of the long oval-shaped table. He then made his way to the head and sat down so that he was looking directly at Grant.

About ten other people sat around the table, some of whom Grant recognized from his years working here. A heavy woman seated to Vik's left used to be a nurse in the ICU for many years. She'd been promoted to nursing administration, but Grant recalled she was always a stickler for protocol. He would never forget the time she yelled at him for forgetting to put on one of those stupid yellow gowns to see a patient on contact precautions. A lanky man wearing thick black glasses along the side of the table had been the head pharmacist for as long as Grant could remember. Joel Hitchens, the obstetrician who had delivered Sadie, was seated to his left. In the complete silence of the room, Grant couldn't exactly start up a conversation with Joel and he didn't know what he would say anyway. He decided to nod and Joel nodded back.

"I'd like to welcome Dr. Kaplan to our monthly meeting of the professional assistance committee," Vik said. "Some of you may know that Dr. Kaplan and I have been friends since our residencies right here at the mother ship." While a few people smiled at Vik's attempt to lighten the mood, the nurse remained serious. Sadie would have said she had a bad case of RBF, resting bitch face. Grant was sure Sadie had learned this expression from Piper. "Despite our relationship, I assure you that our friendship will remain separate from the matter before our committee today. I've asked Nancy Kovatch to take the lead on questioning to make sure we don't introduce bias."

Grant wasn't sure which one was Nancy until he saw the fat nurse put on a pair of reading glasses. She looked down at a paper on the table and cleared her throat.

"Dr. Kaplan, this committee is going to put your malpractice suit aside for now. We'll leave that for legal to sort out. In an effort to get straight to the point, I would like to ask you some questions about what happened on the night of March 23rd." Nancy stopped talking and looked at him.

Grant wasn't about to say anything until there was an actual question at hand. He couldn't help but think about all of those legal TV shows he'd watched over the years. Did he have the right to remain silent like all those people on *Law and Order* who were arrested and brought into one of those windowless interrogation rooms for questioning? For a second, he thought that maybe he should have contacted an attorney in preparation for this meeting, but that would have been ridiculous. This wasn't a legal proceeding. No one was threatening to arrest him.

"Dr. Kaplan, do you have an answer to that question?"

"I'm not sure what the question is." Grant knew what she was asking, but he chose to play dumb rather than offer up information.

"Would you kindly explain what happened to your daughter and her friend, Emma Wright, last Saturday night?"

"Emma broke her ankle," Grant said.

"Could you elaborate for the committee?"

"I'm not sure what you want to know," he said, his pulse throbbing in his temple.

"From what I can glean from the medical record, Emma Wright fell and broke her ankle and was brought to the emergency department by your daughter, Sadie Kaplan. Is that correct?"

"Yes."

"When a tox screen was sent by the ER doctor, it came back positive for opiates. Am I doing a good job summarizing so far?"

"I wasn't there at that point. Everything you've said I've heard from Vanessa, so it's really hearsay." Grant wished he could take back that word. Using legal terms was certainly not going to him help him here.

"Fair enough," Vik said. "Let's ask Dr. Kaplan about things he has direct knowledge of."

"I'm trying to make sure all of the facts are straight." Nancy flipped her page over. "So, Dr. Kaplan, what the committee would really like to know is, how did Emma Wright get access to opiates?"

"I wouldn't know," Grant said. He certainly wasn't going to admit that his daughter stole the pills from his bedside table and then gave them to her friend. That would be akin to signing the death certificate of his surgical career. "She's not my daughter."

"Are you trying to evade the question?" Nancy took off her glasses and stared at Grant, her eyes narrowed.

"Let's not get hostile," Vik said. "We're all colleagues here."

"Yes, we should maintain respect for Dr. Kaplan," Joel Hitchens said.

"I'm sorry," Nancy said. Grant knew she only apologized because two doctors had cut her down to size. "Let me backtrack for a minute. Everyone in this room knows that you are a skilled neurosurgeon as well as a world-renowned expert on the treatment of vascular malformations. We know that you have written numerous scholarly articles, treated thousands of grateful patients, and trained scores of residents to become master surgeons themselves. However, that is not why we are here today. Our sole purpose today is to figure out what happened on Saturday night in the hope of maintaining patient safety at our institution."

"Very well said," Vik said. "Let's continue with the questioning."

Nancy put her glasses back on and looked at her paper, pausing for a moment to review her notes. "Okay, what this committee would like to know, Dr. Kaplan, is how your daughter ended up in possession of a bottle of Oxycontin prescribed to one of your patients."

The room went silent. All rustling of papers, clearing of throats and clicking of pens seemed to cease. He was cornered and there was no way out but through.

"I had them in my bedside table." He looked down at the table. "Sadie must have found them there."

"So, to be clear, you brought your patient's pain pills home with you?"

"Yes."

"And how often do you use them?" Nancy asked.

"Once in a while," he said. In anticipation of this meeting, he'd cut back on the Adderall. That hadn't proven difficult since he wasn't operating, but the Oxy was harder to taper. He'd really wanted to stop taking it as soon as he got Vik's email, but he just couldn't do it. Without the evening pills, his mind wouldn't shut off. Thoughts sprinted around in his head and the harder he tried to shut them off, the faster they ran.

"When you say once in a while, does that mean once a month or once a day? I think the committee could use a bit more specificity on this," Nancy pushed.

Grant cleared his throat. Not sure how to answer this question without lying, Grant was starting to wish he could plead the fifth.

"I think we've gone far enough with this interview," Vik said, rescuing Grant. "The next step in the protocol is to send Dr. Kaplan to employee health for a drug test. Once those results come back, we'll figure out where to go from there."

CHAPTER THIRTY-SIX

Alison

November 12, 2019

AT PHYSICAL THERAPY, Alison walked back and forth across the floor using the cane. After more than two months of practice, Svetlana had swapped out the bulky cane for a simpler one a few weeks ago. The bottom made a satisfying thump on the wood floor, as Alison stepped forward with her right leg. She was now able to lift her foot off the ground and swing her right leg forward, her toes no longer dragging. There was a new crop of patients here, but Thomas, the man with the advanced Parkinson's, would never leave. His disease only moved in the wrong direction.

"We're looking good." Svetlana stood off to the side.

"We are, aren't we?" Alison smiled.

"So good that it's time to lose the cane," Svetlana said.

Alison stopped walking. Was she serious? Alison couldn't fathom walking without something to support her, without the cane to bear her weight and propel her forward. The idea thrilled and terrified her the same time.

"Today?" Alison asked.

"It's as good a time as any. We knew this day would come," Svetlana said this as if it was a foregone conclusion that Alison would walk on her own. "Your right leg is so much stronger than you think. I'll demonstrate." Svetlana turned and took a few slow steps, bending her knees in an exaggerated way and planting her feet, the opposite arm bent forward in front of her chest as each leg moved forward. It looked like a slow version of a military march, precise and regimented.

"Can we practice a little more with the cane first?" Alison

wasn't sure why Svetlana had so much confidence in Alison's right leg. In her experience, it wasn't to be trusted. Some days it felt strong and ready for a challenge and other days it gave way without warning.

"No stalling," Svetlana said, reaching for the cane. "You're ready for this."

When Svetlana tried to take the cane from her hand, Alison held on for moment, her hand refusing to release the handle.

"I'll try." Alison stood in the middle of the floor for a moment, the wood under her feet firmer than before Svetlana had announced today's assignment. Transferring her weight from one foot to the other, she took a breath and gathered her courage.

Svetlana snapped her fingers. "No wallowing today. Every new challenge requires focus and hard work."

"I've gotten so used to it."

"Go ahead," Svetlana said. "I believe in you."

"Now?"

"Now or never."

"Never sounds good." Alison knew the joke wouldn't work, but it was worth a shot. She would love to make her body do what Svetlana had demonstrated, but she wasn't sure it was possible.

"We can do this," Svetlana said.

"We?"

"*You* can do this." She backed up a few steps, motioning for Alison to come to her.

Alison took a deep breath and let it out. Though Svetlana was only a few steps away, the distance seemed so much greater. She couldn't imagine how her feet would take her there. She decided to lead with her right foot because her balance was better with her left. She bent her left knee and advanced her right leg, but when she planted it on the floor, she felt unsteady.

"Make sure to bend your knees," Svetlana said. "Engaging your thigh muscles helps with stability."

Svetlana loved to talk about stability. First, she claimed the walker would give her stability, then the cane, and now she expected it to come from within Alison, from the same body that had been so fickle and unpredictable. Alison longed to feel steady. She was still reeling from her realization about Grant's duplicity and Cynthia's nearsightedness about his behavior.

"I thought I was bending them," Alison said.

"Even more. Bend to the point that it feels ridiculous." This whole situation did feel ridiculous to Alison, so far-fetched that no one could make it up. Suddenly, she felt like she could almost laugh it was so ridiculous. Feeling a little lighter, she turned her attention back to her knees.

When Alison bent her right knee more, she noticed the difference. Her right leg now seemed stronger and ready to hold her weight. She clenched her fists to focus her energy, and when her left foot contacted the floor, she entered the zone. All of a sudden, something clicked. She kept going, one foot and then the other, everything else fading away: Svetlana's voice and the burble of the water cooler and the clinking of the weights against the rack. It was just Alison and her body, walking across the floor without assistance. Endorphins flooded through her. She hadn't realized how much she'd missed this natural high until now. A barbell thudded to the floor, and everything came back into focus. When Alison looked up, Svetlana grabbed Alison by the shoulders and shook her with excitement.

"I knew you were ready! You're a rock star." She gave Alison her usual fist bump, and then threw her arms around her for a hug. Looking over Svetlana's shoulder, Alison noticed the photograph on the wall again, the one of the runner crossing the finish line in triumph, and thought of Becca. Since their talk at Starbuck's two weeks ago, Becca had only been coming over twice a week instead of every night. At first, Alison had enjoyed the alone time, space to collect her thoughts and plan for her future, but now she was really starting to miss her. She couldn't wait to show Becca her new trick.

❀

On the ride home from physical therapy, Alison wanted to tell Rhea about her progress, but Rhea didn't seem to be in the mood to talk. At home, Rhea got Alison a large glass of ice water as always, but then she invited Alison to sit in the living room instead the kitchen. It felt strangely formal, the chair Alison sat on too stiff and straight backed.

"What's going on?" Alison asked.

Rhea cleared her throat. "I would like to thank you and Mr. Jacobs for everything. You've truly been wonderful employers."

"Okay." Alison could tell by the look on Rhea's face that she was about to quit, but she wanted those words to remain unsaid for a few more moments. She wasn't ready to hear them. "You've been such a big help."

"You are so strong," Rhea said. "One determined woman."

"I guess.

"Truly an inspiration."

"What are you trying to say?" Alison asked. Enough beating around the bush, as Michael would have said.

"I'm giving you my notice," Rhea said. "I've taken another job closer to home." Rhea lived right here in Newton, so Alison knew her decision had nothing to do with proximity.

"What do you mean?"

"I've been assigned to an elderly lady with Parkinson's. She needs me."

"But I still need you." Even with her recent strides, Alison wasn't yet independent. It was going to take a lot of work to walk smoothly without the cane, she still dribbled when she ate, and Svetlana had yet to clear her to drive.

"You think you do, but I know better," Rhea said. "You are strong and fearless."

"I don't feel fearless."

The room fell silent.

"Is this because of Becca?" Alison said quietly.

"Not at all." Rhea's quick denial confirmed she was right.

"Are you sure?"

"You're doing so well," Rhea said. "You don't need me anymore."

"I still have a long way to go."

"If you want someone here, the agency can send another aide."

"I don't want another aide," Alison said.

"I'm so sorry. I've already made the commitment."

"What about Nate? Will he come to visit?" Nate's incessant talking had become the background noise of her home. Without him, Alison's world would be eerily quiet.

"He's been getting really busy with school." Rhea picked at one of her cuticles. "I don't think there will be time to visit."

"I'd like to come to his play. I promised him I would."

Rhea pulled an envelope from her pocket and handed it to Alison. "When I told him about my new job, he was heartbroken. He's really taken a liking to you."

Alison opened the envelope and removed a piece of lined paper ripped from a spiral notebook, the words written in blue marker.

Dear Mrs. Jacobs,

I would be honored if you would come to my play on Saturday night. It might actually be good. I got you two tickets in case you want to bring someone. LOL.

Hakuna Matata,
Nate

The envelope also held two tickets to Nate's show.

"Thank you," Alison said, her eyes filling with tears.

"Don't thank me," Rhea said. "It was all Nathaniel. He wouldn't let me see read the note."

"He's such a good kid."

"He really is," Rhea said.

Alison would miss Rhea's kind words and gentle touch, but maybe the time had come for her to leave. Like Mary Poppins, she stayed only until the wind changed. The wind had definitely shifted, but Alison could handle whatever blew her way. Now, there were two people she needed to reach out to, Michael and Cynthia.

CHAPTER THIRTY-SEVEN

Grant

March 27, 2019

AFTER GRANT LEFT THE CONFERENCE ROOM, he could have taken the blue elevators straight down to Alison's room, but he needed a few minutes to collect his thoughts. He decided to swing by the lobby for a coffee. As he crossed the lobby, a walk he'd done thousands of times in the seventeen years he'd been at this hospital, the floor felt different under his feet. His hospital clogs usually gripped the carpeting, while the loafers he now wore slid over the surface, making him unsure of his footing.

The sound of the water in the fountain seemed louder and more aggressive today, closer to a rush than a gurgle. Grant felt a sense of rising panic and a sour taste in his mouth. He swallowed and did his best to clear his mind. If he stayed calm and focused, he'd find a way out of this mess.

When he stepped up to place his order, Grant noticed a new employee behind the counter, a twenty-something guy with a face full of acne.

"What can I get for you today?" the boy asked.

On a normal day, Grant would ask the regular barista, Millie, for the usual and she would know to make him a large skim latte with a triple shot of espresso, but today was not a normal day. He sighed and gave his order.

Once he got his coffee, he took a seat at one of the tables next to the counter and took off his suit jacket. He thought freeing himself from the tight blazer would allow him to breathe a bit more easily, but he didn't notice much of a difference. Removing the cover of his cup, he inhaled the familiar aroma of roasted espresso before taking a sip. A sappy Barry Manilow song, "Looks Like We Made It," played through the sound system. Grant didn't feel like he'd made it. He felt like everyone on that damned committee had already presumed him guilty.

Clarise Bates, one of the urologists, sped across the lobby toward the blue elevators in her scrubs with Cal close behind. Neither of them noticed him sitting here in this stupid suit. Wednesday was usually his long OR day, so he'd usually be scrubbed in from dawn until late afternoon. No one would expect to see him sitting in the lobby wasting time. It had only been twelve days since he'd scrubbed in, but it seemed like forever. He missed the weight of the scalpel in his hand, the calm that came over him when Wendy turned on a great jazz album, even the smell of bone dust as he sawed through the skull to expose the operative field.

He turned and saw Joel Hitchens approaching him, now wearing scrubs instead of the shirt and tie he'd had on in the conference room. Joel didn't usually operate om Wednesdays. Maybe the scheduler had given him Grant's OR time, his sacred time slot used now for bullshit uterine fibroids and ovarian cysts that were never going to cause a problem anyway. Grant took pride in performing operations that made a difference. If he didn't remove the astrocytoma, coil the aneurysm, debulk the meningioma, his patients could have disastrous deficits: paralysis, personality changes, aphasia. He tried not to think about Alison, that these deficits could also be a result of surgery, that if he wasn't careful, his knife could harm instead of heal.

Grant hoped Joel wouldn't notice him, but it was too late.

"May I join you?" Joel said.

"Of course," he said, taking his bag off the other chair.

Joel went to the counter to order, giving Grant a minute to think about what to say. How could he possibly explain this situation? Was there any way this could all make sense? Maybe it would be better to avoid the topic altogether.

Joel returned and put his cup on the table. "Quite a morning, huh?"

Grant nodded. This had been one of the worst days of his life and it wasn't even lunchtime. Everything about this day felt all wrong, like one of those terrible Lifetime movies about a doctor who falls from grace, forcing him onto the straight and narrow.

That wasn't him. Sure, he took pills to help him function at his best, but he wasn't an addict. He was doing just fine, thank you very much.

"I want to make sure you know that the committee is never about punishment," Joel said. "It's about making sure our doctors are healthy and working in the best interests of patients at all times."

"Right," Grant said. "You all say the same thing. You sound like a broken record."

"Get the test done and we'll move on from there. One step at a time. I've been on this committee for over twenty years. I've seen lots of docs come out the other end."

"Out the other end?"

"Rehab and recovery. Addiction is a disease. Just like diabetes and hypertension and cancer. It's nothing to be ashamed of."

"I don't like what you're implying, Joel." The last thing Grant needed was rehab. Hundreds of patients were alive and functioning because of him. Addicts were those meth heads he saw begging in Boston Common, those pitiful specimens with their clumpy hair and rotting teeth. If they were addicts, he couldn't be. No way.

"It's normal to get defensive," Joel said. "You worked very hard to get where you are today. It's only natural to get your back up."

Grant stood up. He'd had enough of Joel's holier than thou speech. They were colleagues and Joel was acting like he was superior, when in reality Grant was the superstar and Joel was a run of the mill crease monkey.

"Sorry, I've got to run." Grant grabbed his coffee cup and headed to the blue elevators.

⚘

On the way up upstairs, Grant took a detour to the locker room to change into a pair of scrubs. He piled his shirt and suit onto the metal shelf. He'd left his clogs at home, so he'd be stuck wearing loafers for the rest of the day. The clang of the locker door jarred his nerves, the sound of metal-on-metal grating and abrasive.

When Grant arrived in Alison's room, she was sitting up in a chair, pillows propped around her to keep her from listing to the side. The physical therapist was doing passive range of motion exercises, bending her arms at the elbow and then extending them fully. Sitting up, her facial asymmetry looked even more prominent, the right side of her mouth sagging down toward her chin. Cynthia sat in a chair next to Alison.

"Where have you been?" Cynthia asked.

"I've been around."

"What do you mean you've been around? You said you would be here two hours ago. It's not like it took you forever to get dressed." She made a face at his scrubs, her eyes trailing down to his feet. "What's with the shoes? Where are your clogs?"

"They're getting a little worn out. The foot bed isn't giving me the support I need."

Cynthia gave him a questioning look. "They were fine yesterday, and all of sudden today they're no good?"

"That's right."

"What's going on, Grant? I'm not an idiot."

"Let me give my sister-in-law a kiss." The last thing he wanted to do was argue in front of Alison. She had more than her share of stress. "How you feeling, Blondie?"

She gave him a weak smile.

"I know," he said. "This is a lot to handle. Every day will get a little bit easier." He gave her a kiss on the forehead and followed Cynthia into the hall.

With one look at her face, Grant knew he owed her the truth. If he lied to her, she'd smell his bullshit right away and call him on it.

"Okay, this is it," he said. "I'm wearing these shoes because I came in wearing a suit. I had a meeting upstairs this morning." One of the interns rolled a cart of blood draw supplies past the door, the wheels squeaking on the linoleum.

"Upstairs?"

"In the executive conference room. The professional assistance committee."

"Doesn't Vik chair that one?"

"Yes."

"Since when are you on that committee?"

"I'm not." He took a breath. He had to tell her the truth, but he hoped she wouldn't cause a scene in the middle of the ICU. "I was called in for an interview."

"You? What do you need assistance with?"

"I'm not sure I do," he said.

"So why did they call you in?"

"They had some questions for me," Grant paused and took a deep breath. "About the pills." He could feel his pulse galloping is his neck as he spoke. Admitting weakness wasn't easy for him.

"The ones Adam gives you?" she asked. "You said that wasn't a problem."

"Everything is under control." Grant said.

"What did they ask you?"

"The usual," he said. "It's really not a big deal."

"It sounds like a big deal to me. Does this have anything to do with the lawsuit you're dealing with?"

"No, not at all," Grant said quickly. "Totally separate issue."

"How did they leave it?"

"They want me to get a blood test at employee health this afternoon."

"What if it's positive? What happens then?"

"I'm sure it'll be fine." If he was being honest, he would tell Cynthia that the test was almost certainly going to be positive, but he just couldn't do it. After facing the firing squad this morning, he didn't have the energy to deal with Cynthia's hysterics. He'd figure out how to tell her when the results came in.

Cynthia looked at him, studying his face for a moment. "Maybe this is a wake-up call, Grant. They called you in for a reason."

"I told you, I'm fine."

"This doesn't seem fine at all," she said, her voice wavering. "Maybe you need help."

"There's no reason to worry," he said. "I promise."

"You can tell me that all you want, but I am worried. I think you need to take this seriously, if not for yourself, then for me. And for Sadie."

CHAPTER THIRTY-EIGHT

Alison

November 13, 2019

IN THE SHOWER, Alison relished the feeling of the water streaming down her body. She'd always loved a hot shower, but today, because she was doing it on her own, the water felt even more luxurious.

She turned off the water and opened the door, steadying herself against the wall. Usually, Rhea would help her step over the ledge onto the bathmat, her steady arm bolstering her and giving her strength. For a moment, Alison wished she were still here, but she pushed that thought away. I've got this, she told herself. Leaning the right side of her body against the shower frame, she lifted her left leg over the ledge, then pushed against the wall, the momentum allowing her to bring her right leg over. With that small win, she dried off and took an embarrassingly long amount of time getting dressed into a pair of sweatpants and a t-shirt.

In the kitchen, she poured a bowl of granola and topped it with almond milk, giving the cereal a few minutes to soften. As she took her first bite, her thoughts drifted back to yesterday, the triumph of walking on her own followed quickly by Rhea's disappointing announcement. So used to the background noise of Rhea cooking, doing laundry, watching daytime talk shows, she found the quiet unsettling. She hadn't been alone for eight months. Now, Alison was left with the chirping of birds outside the window and the occasional swish of a car passing on the street. Today, she could do anything she wanted: binge on Netflix shows for hours, eat macaroni and cheese straight out of the pot, walk, or should she say limp, around naked.

After stacking her dishes in the dishwasher, Alison sat down on the living room couch. She slid open the drawer inside the coffee table which housed plastic bags full of photos and a few empty albums. There never seemed to be a good time to sit down and organize the photos. Maybe she was afraid to confront images of the way she used to look, the person she used to be, but today she felt ready to look in the mirror and accept the woman reflected back at her.

Emptying the drawer, Alison placed the bags of photos on one side of the couch and the photo albums on the other. At the bottom, she found an old album with a red felt cover, the last one her mother had made before she died. The fabric was nubby with age, the word "Memories" embroidered across the front in white thread. She opened the book and ran her fingers over the plastic sheet covering the photos. If she could face these happy memories, maybe it would help her imagine her future, however different it may be from what she'd envisioned.

On the first page, there was a photo of her and Cynthia, side by side on the swings in their backyard. Alison wore her favorite jean overalls, the ones her mom called dungarees, and Cynthia had on a pink, flowered dress, both of them smiling wide. Her mother was always behind the camera, saying funny things and telling silly knock-knock jokes to get their eyes to twinkle. After the accident, the photos dwindled, her father leaving the camera at home or forgetting to charge the batteries.

Removing the plastic covering, she lifted the photo, the back tacky with adhesive. Her mother had probably shooed them outside when they declared themselves bored. The swing set was their favorite place, she and Cynthia swinging their feet to the sky, coming up with funny ways to go down the slide, playing pretend in the shady area underneath. Alison followed Cynthia everywhere, longing to be just like her confident big sister. After their mom died, Cynthia became Alison's keeper, bossy and shrill, the girl Alison had idolized crushed alongside their mother in the car. Now, Alison felt Cynthia's absence more acutely than ever. Maybe she'd been too rigid and unyielding. Maybe her months of silence were punishment enough and it was time to open the door a crack, to let her sister back in.

She turned to the next page, a Halloween photo catching her eye, the last time they'd worn their mom's homemade costumes. Cynthia was dressed as a cowboy in a tan hat, chaps made of brown and white cow-print fabric, and a red bandana around her neck. Her little cowgirl sidekick, Alison stood at her side with her hands on her hips, proud in a red-fringe vest, jean skirt, and leather boots. In later years, their father would forget all about Halloween until they reminded him a few days before, their costumes purchased in a frenetic trip to the mall on a school night. Alison wiped tears from her cheek. There were no photos of her mother on this page, but she felt her presence in every one: in the hand sewn costumes, their childhood innocence, the way they both beamed straight at the camera.

On the next page, there was a picture from Alison's second grade Thanksgiving play. Dressed as a pilgrim in a black dress with a white apron, she was delivering a line, classmates on stage dressed as fellow pilgrims and turkeys with rainbow feathers. Her thoughts turned to the Thanksgiving dinner that followed, all of them crammed around the dining room table, her mother in and out of the kitchen with serving dishes, her little cousin, Josh, sticky from apple pie, her grandmother suggesting they go around the table and announce what they were each thankful for.

In recent years, they'd always gathered at Cynthia and Grant's for Thanksgiving. Maybe Alison would go to the movies or something, anything to take her mind off the idea of happy families sitting around tables together, smiling and basking in their love for each other. She wanted to call Cynthia, but she couldn't make herself pick up the phone just yet. After all this time, their rift seemed too wide to bridge with a phone call. What would she say anyway? Alison closed the album and placed it back in the drawer. It was time to contact Michael. She opened her laptop and signed into her email account. It might take her an hour to peck out an email on the keyboard, but it had to be done.

From: aljacobs12@gmail.com
November 13th, 2019
To: michaeltjacobs@gmail.com

Dear Michael,

I hope you are doing well and that you've calmed down since our meeting with Shelly. I really think she's very good. She can help us both get through this tough time. I've been thinking about your suggestion. About suing Grant. I could spend the rest of my life blaming him for his mistakes, but I can't do that. It doesn't feel right. He's not perfect, but neither am I. None of us are. I need to repair my relationship with my sister and move toward forgiveness. I hope you understand.

Best,

Alison

After she finally pressed send, Alison felt a renewed sense of energy. She *would* call Cynthia. It was long overdue. Picking up her cell phone, she navigated to favorites and found Cynthia's name. With each ring, she felt her breakfast swirling in her stomach, and then the call went to voicemail. As she listened to her sister's recorded voice, the photos from the albums flashed through her mind.

She waited for the beep and then tried to speak. "Uh, hi Cyn. It's been ... a while." Even if her speech were perfectly fluent, Alison still wouldn't have the right words for this moment. "Call me, I guess ... okay ... talk soon." Alison pressed the red button to end the call, exhausted by the effort, like she'd struggled up a steep mountain, but now that she'd done it she was overcome with relief. She hoped it would be all downhill from here.

CHAPTER THIRTY-NINE

Grant

March 29, 2019

AS GRANT DROVE ACROSS the Longfellow bridge and merged onto Cambridge Street, he noticed the trees on the sidewalk starting to bud. The endless Boston winter would soon come to an end. Yesterday, the day after the committee interview and blood test, he'd sat on the couch all day pretending to watch TV. He'd managed to convince Cynthia he was developing a man cold, making his voice sound nasal and faking a cough, and she'd seemed to believe his act, spending the whole day at the hospital without him. He couldn't face another day of wallowing, so he'd decided to go with her today, anything to prevent him from thinking about the results.

He was about to turn into the hospital garage when he heard a text come through on his phone.

Glancing quickly, he saw Vik's name.

"Stop looking at your phone when you drive," Cynthia said. "You know I hate that."

"Lay off me today, okay?"

"The last thing you need right now is to get pulled over again right in front of the hospital," she said. Getting pulled over would be nothing compared with the heat he would face when the blood results came back. He had a sinking feeling that's why Vik was texting him.

He pulled into a spot in the garage and looked at the text.

"Have a minute to stop by?"

Shit. He knew Vik wasn't inviting him for a social visit. He pocketed his phone and walked with Cynthia to the lobby.

"I've got to go fill out some charts in medical records," he said. The hospital records had been completely electronic for several years, but Cynthia wouldn't pick up on the white lie. "I'll be up in a few."

He watched Cynthia head down the hall to the blue elevator, waiting for her to turn the corner before going in the opposite direction. When he got to the anesthesia department, Vik was sitting at his desk, his face nearly hidden by a massive pile of papers and journals. Usually, Grant would walk right in and make himself comfortable, often bringing snacks from the vending machine or two cups of coffee from the lobby, but today he felt like he had to knock. This wasn't a normal visit with one of his closest friends, but instead a staff physician reporting to the chairman of the professional assistance committee.

"Grant," Vik said. "I wasn't sure if you were around. I know you have a lot going on."

Grant took a seat in the chair opposite the desk.

Vik pushed the piles aside so he could make eye contact. "I don't want to prolong the inevitable. This is just as awkward for me as it is for you."

Grant somehow doubted that, but he nodded anyway. He wanted to get this over with as quickly as possible. He was used to be being the one making the important decisions, not the one squirming while someone else called the shots.

"Give me a minute to pull up the lab results." Vik turned to his computer and clicked the mouse, biting his lower lip with his front teeth. Grant had seen him do that in the OR when the shit was hitting the fan—when he lost airway access and couldn't navigate the tube past the true cords, when a patient's blood pressure was dropping or oxygen saturation plummeting—so Grant knew the news wasn't good.

"Here it is." Vik said. "I received the results of your drug test a few hours ago. It came back positive for both amphetamines and opioids."

"Oh," Grant said. He'd known this would be the case, but he'd allowed himself to hope for a miracle.

"Do you have anything to say about the results?" Vik asked.

"I've been taking Adderall for a few years. It helps me con-

centrate. Improves my focus in the OR. I thought you knew that."
Maybe if he distracted Vik with an explanation about the first result, he might forget about the other one.

"I think you may have mentioned that at some point."

"So that explains that." Grant stood up. "I'm going to go check
on my sister-in-law."

"Sit down, Grant," Vik said. "Please don't make this harder
for me than it has to be."

Grant could tell by Vik's tone that he meant business. This
discussion was not going to end well.

"On behalf of the committee, I'm requesting a letter from
your physician attesting to the prescribed dose and reason for
the prescription."

"I'm sure Adam would be happy to do that."

Vik bit his lip again. "And what about the Oxy? Did Adam
prescribe that, too?"

"No, not exactly." Grant couldn't think of an explanation Vik
would buy. Vik knew he didn't have a medical condition requiring
its use, no history of cancer or anxiety or chronic pain. He stared
up at the ceiling, wishing he was anywhere but in this office, a
no-nonsense look on his best friend's face.

"What's going on?" Vik asked. "If I don't know the truth, I
can't help you."

"Everything's fine," Grant said.

"Grant, everything is far from fine. Allow me to summarize
the situation. You are being investigated by professional assistance, your drug test came back positive, and your sister-in-law,
on whom you performed a craniotomy, remains in the ICU after
a difficult surgery and—"

"Wait a minute!" Grant interrupted. Vik's voice sounded jarring and much too loud. He needed him to stop talking.

"I'm not finished," Vik said. "This one's the cherry on the sun-
dae. The pills your daughter's friend took to get high happened
to have been prescribed with your DEA number to one of your
surgical patients. And to make matters even worse, that's the
same drug that showed up on your test. I sure hope you have a
reasonable explanation because the committee isn't going to look
favorably on all of this." Grant wished he could stop Vik's voice

from grinding into his eardrums.

"There's a reason that I had those pills ..." Grant trailed off. He knew Vik would see through his lies in a second.

"And that would be what?"

"Nothing." Grant stared at the floor.

"There's another important piece you need to know," Vik said.

Grant couldn't imagine how anything could be worse than the dirty laundry Vik had just hung out to dry.

"Nancy Kovatch has referred you to the ethics committee."

"That bitch." The second Grant said the word he wished he could take it back. Insulting the head of nursing was not going to help him here.

"Honestly, I think it's a fair question. If Alison had an ideal outcome, you probably would have gotten away with it, but the protracted recovery she faces calls your choices into question. It puts everything you did under a microscope."

"An ethics investigation on top of everything else?"

"I'm afraid so," Vik said. "If I try to pull strings, it will only raise a red flag. Everyone knows we're friends."

"Seriously? Honestly, I feel like the whole fucking world is against me right now. If you can't count on your friends at time like this, I don't know when you can."

"I wish I could give you another answer," Vik said, "but my hands are tied."

"Whose side are you on anyway?"

"I'm always on your side, but I still have a job to do."

Grant knew this was true, but he still couldn't help feeling betrayed. Vik had been faced with a difficult choice and he'd chosen his job over his best friend.

❁

After the meeting, Grant decided to stop by his office, give his blood pressure a few minutes to normalize. Wendy had texted him earlier to say there were some checks to sign. Usually a micromanager, he'd put his office business on the back burner the past few weeks, assuming Wendy would keep everything under control. He sent her a quick text saying he was on the way.

When he stepped into the elevator, he noticed Nancy Kovatch, the last person he wanted to see right now, or ever. She refused to acknowledge him; her eyes remained fixed to the panel of buttons at the front.

"How you been, Grant?" Someone clapped Grant on the back. Grant turned to see Roland Butler, one of Vik's partners.

"Can't complain," Grant said, trying to sound casual. He couldn't help wondering if Roland was just making small talk or if he'd heard something from Vik or, even worse, through the OR rumor mill. He looked over at Nancy, but she gave no indication she was listening.

"How are the kids?" Grant knew he might be opening a can of worms—Roland's daughter had placed second in the national spelling bee a few years ago, and he never missed an invitation to talk about it—but Grant wanted to seem as natural as possible.

The elevator dinged and the doors opened on the second floor. Nancy stepped out without a second look, the cloying smell of rose perfume trailing in her wake.

"Hilary is taking seven AP classes, and her mock trial team is moving on to the state finals, and of course you know about the spelling bee. And Landon just made varsity volleyball ...."

The elevator finally opened on the first floor, allowing Grant to escape with a wave over his shoulder. He walked quickly down the corridor, trying to get Nancy Kovatch out of his mind. He didn't understand why she'd to be so nasty about this whole thing. So he took a few pills to help optimize his performance. That wasn't the end of the world. She acted like that made him less than human, not even worthy of acknowledgement.

He stopped for a minute to look out the window, cars double parked in front of the main entrance of the hospital. One of the valets was helping an elderly man transfer from a wheelchair into the passenger seat of a car, his head wrapped in a thick swath of bandages. Grant couldn't help wondering when he would be able to operate again, how he would navigate his way through this mess in order to clear his name. Nancy Kovatch certainly wasn't going to make it easy for him. After his family, he loved his job more than anything else in the world: the feeling of separating a malignant tumor from the healthy brain tissue, the gratification of draining a hematoma, the satisfaction of giving someone their life back. He couldn't fathom how he would go on if he was stripped of his career.

The waiting room was empty. Grant wondered why Laura wasn't at the front desk. He hoped the staff hadn't taken advantage of his absence by slipping out early. When he got to his office, Wendy and Laura were sitting in the two chairs facing his desk. Maybe Wendy wanted to fit in quick performance review while he was there.

"I sent everyone else home," Wendy said.

"No problem," he said, trying to sound easygoing. Really, he hated the idea of paying people to do nothing, but he wasn't in any position to argue today. "I'll sign everything and get out of your way."

He took a seat in his chair, and Wendy passed the checks and a few forms across the desk. After scribbling his signature a few times and quickly filling in the forms, Grant stood to leave.

"There's another reason I called you in today," Wendy said.

After working with Wendy for so long, Grant could tell this had nothing to do with Laura's job performance. He sat back down, bracing himself for whatever she was about to say.

"First of all, you know I love working for you and that I always have your best interests in mind," she said.

"Of course," he said. "And this practice wouldn't run half as smoothly as it does without you. We're never going to let you retire," he said, trying to ease the tension with a shameless compliment. Laura sat with her hands clasped on her lap and her eyes fixed on the window behind him. He thought of throwing a compliment her way too, but he didn't want to overdo it.

"Right," Wendy said, her eyes roaming. "So, I wanted to speak with you about some things I've noticed lately. I was concerned with your demeanor in the OR during Mrs. Jacobs' surgery. You seemed altered. Something wasn't quite right—"

"It's been a high stress situation for everyone. I think the pressure got to me."

"It seemed like more than that to me," she said. "Yesterday, I took the opportunity to organize your office, and I found the pills in the bottom drawer."

"Oh, that's what your worried about?" he gave a tense laugh, trying his best to brush off her discovery. "I collect them from patients when they're pain free. It's not a big deal."

"It seems pretty important to me."

"What are you saying?" He'd tried to stay calm, but now he couldn't keep his anger below the surface. "Is this some sort of intervention?"

"I think you need help, Dr. Kaplan," Wendy said.

"I don't know what you're talking about." He couldn't believe Wendy had the nerve to stage this ridiculous conversation. Had she heard about the committee firing squad through the hospital rumor mill? "Laura, could you excuse us for a minute?"

Laura didn't have to be asked twice, escaping the room in a flash.

"I can't believe your fucking nerve Wendy," Grant said, once Laura had gone and closed the door behind her. "And in the presence of another employee to boot."

"You have to know I'm trying to do what's best for you. We've worked together for a long time."

"I came in to sign checks and meanwhile you planned a staged attack."

"It's not an attack," she said. "You know I care about you. I want to make sure you get the help you need."

Grant met Wendy's eyes, looking for some sign of spite or ulterior motive, but he saw only tenderness and allegiance. By his side since he'd begun practicing, Wendy would have no reason to broach this topic other than concern for his health and the well-being of his patients. The look on her face made Grant realize it was time to come out from behind the facade of false bravado. He let his shoulders drop from around his ears and took a deep breath.

"I understand," he said. His thoughts turned to what Cynthia had said in the ICU when he'd told her about the committee meeting. Perhaps she was right. Maybe it was time to take this seriously, to prioritize his marriage and his family over the operating room for once in his life.

CHAPTER FORTY

Alison

November 15, 2019

THE AUDITORIUM BUZZED with excitement, parents chattering and little kids running up and down the aisles. Alison had decided to leave her cane at home in an attempt to look as healthy as possible for her first visit to school since her surgery. Tonight, she wanted the spotlight to remain on Nate and his show, but she still couldn't stomach looks of pity from the other teachers. Becca held her by the right arm while she fished the tickets from her purse with her other hand.

"C12 and 13," Alison said. She felt a flutter in her chest at the thought of them sitting together right up front. Using Becca's arm to steady her, she made her way down the ramp toward the stage. Because Becca adored Nate, Alison had decided to invite her to the play, but now she felt torn. She was excited to be there with her, but also anxious that they might draw attention away from Nate on his big day. As they found their seats in the third row, Priscilla Weaver, the principal, crossed the front of the auditorium waving at them.

"Alison, it's so nice to see you out and about," Priscilla said as she came up the aisle. "I had to bounce over and welcome you back." At faculty meetings, they used to count how many times Priscilla used the word "bounce," keeping tallies in their notebooks and comparing totals at the end.

"Nice to see you, too," Alison said.

"Rave reviews of our play brought you in?"

"I couldn't miss Nate's big debut." As Alison spoke, she felt people's eyes on her. They must have noticed Priscilla's excitement and looked over to see what was going on. A warm flush crept up her face.

"I'm sure Becca has been keeping you apprised of the goings on here at Newton Elementary, hasn't she?" Priscilla said.

"That's Alison Jacobs," Alison heard a woman behind her say in a loud whisper. "The teacher who had the stroke." Alison used to like being the center of attention, but that had been for positive things—debate team in high school, welcoming parents on back-to-school night, teaching a spin class at the gym—but now people were looking at her because she was weak, wounded, an unfortunate victim.

"Of course," Becca said. "We talk about school all the time."

"When can we expect you back in the classroom?" Priscilla asked. "We've missed you here."

"I'm not sure."

"She doesn't seem sick," the woman behind her said.

"You've really bounced back," Priscilla said. "I remember when I visited you in the hospital. I wasn't sure you'd ever be able to rejoin our staff."

"She's really doing well," Becca said. "Maybe soon, right?"

"I ..." Alison didn't know how to answer. Even though she'd made great progress, she didn't feel ready to manage a classroom of ten-year-olds. Dealing with the girls' catty drama and the boys' discussion of farts and video games was beyond her current abilities. She had enough trouble getting herself out of bed and eating breakfast without dribbling food on her shirt.

"Let's talk this week," Priscilla said.

As she walked away, Becca held her hand up to her ear, her thumb and pinky making a telephone receiver, and mouthed the words "Call me" with a devious smile. Alison stifled a laugh, glad that Becca was making light of the conversation. The focus today should be on Nate's show, not on if, or when, she would return to work.

Alison turned around to survey the room and noticed Michael seated towards the back. He gave her a nod and she smiled back. Robin Weintraub, Cynthia's annoying tennis partner, glanced from him to Alison with a questioning look.

Alison ignored Robin and turned around.

The light dimmed, quieting the chatter in the auditorium. When the curtain parted, the children filled the stage wearing straw skirts and colorful face make-up, a large orange sun glowing from the backdrop. As they started singing "The Circle of Life," Alison scanned the stage for Nate and found him on the left, beaming into the audience. Following his gaze, Alison saw Rhea sitting at the other end of the row in front of them, her face bursting with pride.

When the song ended and Nate walked off stage, Alison found it harder to focus, distracted by the warmth of Becca's arm next to her, the way her legs were crossed, the smell of her spearmint gum.

"He's the best one up there," Becca said.

"Wait until you see his song." He'd performed his part of the duet for Alison countless times in her kitchen, but she was excited to see him sing with his partner under the lights. They sat through a few more scenes and songs, some better than others, until Nate's big moment finally arrived. He had changed into a brown striped onesie and a fur cap. The girl playing Pumba wore a hat shaped like a warthog.

They begin singing and when they reached the familiar chorus, the audience began to sing along. Nate and his partner did some cute choreography, linking arms and swinging in circles around each other. Halfway through the song, the other kids returned to the stage and joined in while the audience continued singing and clapping to the beat. Even the women behind them joined in. It felt good to forget her problems for a few minutes.

When Becca sang, the air whistled ever so slightly as it passed through the gap in her front teeth. Her singing voice was barely even in tune, but Alison couldn't imagine a sweeter sound. When Becca reached over to take her hand, Alison's first instinct was to pull hers back, for fear of who might see or what they might think. Instead, she left it there and allowed Becca's finger to intertwine with hers. At that moment, she didn't care who saw them—Robin Weintraub or Priscilla Weaver or the nosy women behind them. She wanted to hold Becca's hand and to hell with anyone who had a problem with that.

❀

The crowd filled the lobby, waiting to congratulate the little actors on a job well done. The mother of the kid who played Simba stood by the door holding a bouquet of flowers. The villain lion weaved his way through the crowd trailed by a few of the hyenas. Becca took Alison's hand again as they walked through the crowded space. They passed Priscilla Weaver, Liza Diaz, one of the kindergarten teachers, and Kyle Sampson, the office secretary. Their stares made the blood rush to Alison's head.

Alison saw Nate at the other side of the lobby, surrounded by adoring fans.

"Let's go congratulate the star," Becca said. They passed a group of cast members belting Hakuna Matata and a bunch of others jumping around cheering.

Nate held a cookie bouquet wrapped in clear plastic, tied in a festoon of green ribbons. A smile covered his face as several people complimented him on his singing and comic timing. Adele Logan, the music teacher and director of the show, stood in a nearby group, but Alison didn't see Rhea anywhere. When Nate saw Alison, his eyes lit up.

"Mrs. Jacobs, you came!" He wrapped his arms around Alison's waist. "I didn't know if you would."

"Amazing." Alison returned his hug, relishing the unconditional love emanating from his small body. "We're so proud of you."

"We wouldn't miss it for anything," Becca said. "You were terrific."

"Now I know why they say being onstage is an adrenaline rush." Nate said.

"Isn't he a little star?" Adele Logan said, turning around and putting her arm around Nate's shoulder. "Next stop, Broadway."

Alison smiled. "On the express train."

"How are you, Alison?" Adele asked. "I heard you've had a tough recovery."

"Yes. But I'm in a good place now."

"That's great to hear," she said. "And Michael? How's he been?"

"We're no longer together." Alison glanced at Becca, wondering how she felt about this line of questioning.

"It's okay," Nate jumped in. "Mrs. Jacobs and Ms. Corrie are a couple now."

Alison's heart sank. One of the things she loved about Nate was his open-mindedness and willingness to accept everyone for who they were, but this wasn't the right time or place for this discussion.

"I had no idea," Adele said, a look of confusion on her face.

"They're good together," Nate said.

"Oh," Adele said. "I didn't know."

"Um ..." Alison desperately wanted to change the topic, but she couldn't think of what to say.

"Yes, we are," Becca said, raised their clasped hands in the air.

"No ... I," Alison's cheeks flushed with anger. It wasn't Becca's place to insert herself here.

"Better late than never," Nate said.

"Absolutely," Becca said.

Alison let go of Becca's hand and buried hers in the pockets of her jeans.

When they turned to leave, Alison noticed Michael standing by the door, a woman she didn't recognize at his side. She tried to pivot, but it was too late. He called out her name.

"What's he doing here?" Becca asked.

"I guess Nate asked him to come," Alison said, as they reached Michael.

"Nate was awesome," Michael said.

"Yes," Alison said. "He really was."

"With all his talk about the show," Michael said, "I wasn't sure what to expect. It was really cute."

"So cute." She looked over at Becca, hoping she would find a way to extricate them from this conversation.

"He's a great kid," Becca said. "One of the school leaders."

"Hello, Becca," Michael said. "Nice to see you again." The pleasantries seemed odd. This certainly wasn't the guy who'd lashed out at the bookstore or the one who'd had a hard time sitting down at mediation. "This is Sarah." He placed his hand on the woman's back.

"Nice to meet you," Sarah said.

Alison gave Michael a look. Sarah was disgustingly adorable with her upturned nose and wavy dark hair. What was he trying to pull? He could have at least given her a heads up. Was this his announcement that he was over her and ready to move on? Or maybe he was just using Sarah to make her jealous. Either way, it felt like a punch to the gut. She wasn't expecting another woman to appear on the scene so soon. Her eyes started to burn, but she willed herself not to cry in front of Sarah.

"There's been a lot of change," he said, "but I'm starting to wrap my head around it. I got your email by the way. I understand."

"Really?" Alison knew there was no way he'd come to a place of acceptance so quickly, but she had to play along with his act. "I'm so glad."

"It's an ongoing process," he said, putting his arm around Sarah's shoulders. "But there's light at the end of the tunnel."

"Wow." Now he was really laying it on thick. Alison didn't think she could stomach any more of his platitudes.

"Mrs. Jacobs," Nate came up behind her. "We're all going to the diner. Do you wanna come?"

"Maybe," Alison said. The last thing she wanted to do was sit at the diner with Becca, Rhea, and Adele, but she was thankful for Nate's well-timed interruption. She'd figure out how to get out of it once they were in the car.

CHAPTER FORTY-ONE

Sadie

April 2, 2019

SADIE WALKED BEHIND EMMA, her own backpack on one shoulder and Emma's on the other, trying not to bump anyone along the way. The hallway seemed even busier than usual today. It was Emma's first day back at school, and Sadie was doing her best to help her navigate on crutches, making sure Emma wouldn't get hurt again on her watch. Though Emma was barely speaking to her, she did allow Sadie to carry her things between classes.

"What happened to you?" Tyler Blundell yelled as Emma hobbled past.

"Stupid accident," Emma said.

Stupid accident was right. The events of that night had played over and over in Sadie's head for the past week. If only she'd decided to leave when Piper pulled out the joint, if only she'd grabbed the bottle of pills before Emma took them, if only she had accepted help from that nurse after the show, but there was no way to go back and change any of that now. What's done was done.

"No more spinning in circles?" Tyler said.

Mason Brock, captain of the football team stood next to him. "What about the Olympics?" he asked.

"If this is wrong, I don't wanna be Wright," Tyler said.

"Good one, man," Mason said.

Emma ignored their dumb comments and kept going. Sadie had expected the kids at school would talk about Emma's accident, but the reality proved even worse than she'd imagined. Sadie knew it may take a while to earn back Emma's trust, but she was willing to do whatever it took to prove herself worthy.

When they'd almost made it to Emma's calculus class, Sadie spotted Piper standing by a locker talking to Kylie Miller. Piper hadn't wasted time finding a replacement friend.

"Well, looks who's back," Piper said. "I heard you had surgery."

Emma nodded. "I don't mess around."

"What happened?" Kylie asked. She looked so innocent in high-waisted jeans and a lace-up sweatshirt. Sadie wondered how long it would take for her to see through Piper's bullshit.

"I just tripped," Emma said. "No big story."

"She tripped all right," Piper said with a smile. "I watched it happen."

"That must have been scary," Kylie said.

"I helped get her to hospital," Piper said. "The bones were sticking out of her ankle."

"That's not the way I remember it," Sadie said.

Piper shot Sadie a nasty look. "Maybe you should check your memory."

"It's time for class." All Sadie wanted to do was get away from Piper. Talking to her gave her a hollow feeling in her chest.

"Why do you let her talk to you that way?" Emma asked, making her way down the hall away from Piper.

"I don't know."

"She's a bitch," Emma said.

"I know," Sadie said, following Emma into math class. "I'm sorry." The words hung in the air, sounding trite and meaningless the second she said them. There was so much more she wanted to express, that she missed the closeness between them, that she would do anything to repair their friendship, that thinking about the way she'd destroyed Emma's skating career made her want to vomit. Maybe if she worked super hard to prove to Emma how much their friendship meant to her, one day they could be a pair again—if not on the ice, then everywhere else.

Emma maneuvered herself into her chair and leaned her crutches on the desk. Sadie hung Emma's backpack on the chair, hoping her friend would say something, anything to give Sadie hope that things would eventually be okay, but she didn't. Emma unzipped her backpack and took out her laptop. She didn't even bother turning around to say goodbye.

❁

When Sadie got home from school, she was surprised to see both of her parents sitting at the kitchen table. Whatever was going on, it couldn't be good. Was it about Aunt Alison? Sadie knew she'd been moved from the ICU to a regular hospital room a few days ago, and from everything her mom said, she was getting better. Sadie had stopped asking to visit because her parents always came up with some reason to postpone. Initially, they said she should wait until Alison was moved to a regular floor, but now that she was there, her dad said it would be better to wait until she was transferred to the physical rehabilitation place. It could be a while before that happened. Sadie missed her so much. She missed their text conversations, and their shopping trips, and just having her around.

"Hi Sadie," her mom called in a perky voice. "How was school?"

"Fine." Sadie got the sense her parents didn't really want to hear about school right now. She dropped her backpack in the front hall and walked into the kitchen.

"Can you sit with us for a minute?" her mom said. "There's a few things we need to talk about."

"What's going on?" Sadie looked at her father. He was slouched forward, his elbows on the table and his forehead resting on his palms. "Dad, are you okay?"

"He will be," her mom said. "We'll get through this as a family, but right now we need you to sit down."

Sadie didn't want to sit down. "Is it Aunt Alison?"

"Alison is fine," her mom said. "She's moving in the right direction which is all we can ask for right now."

"Then what is it? Can you guys just tell me what's happening? Whatever it is, I can handle it. I promise."

"Your father has had some difficulties at the hospital—"

"Cynthia, don't sugarcoat it," Grant said. "I got myself into this. I should be the one to explain."

"I'm trying to help you, Grant. You don't need to snap at me."

"I'm not snapping," he said. "I'm just trying to take responsibility for my actions."

"Can you guys stop arguing and focus?" Sadie said.

Her father rubbed his temples. "Okay, I'm just going to say it. My hospital privileges have been suspended. I'm not allowed to operate until I get some help."

"You were fired?" Sadie asked.

"Not fired," her mom jumped in. "Just put on hold. It's only temporary."

"Why?" Sadie had thought the complications after Alison's surgery were just bad luck, but maybe her father had actually done something wrong.

"I have a problem. This is not something I ever thought I would have to say, not to anyone, and certainly not to you, but it's time for me to be honest. I've been taking pills for a while. For longer than I care to admit."

"Why?" Sadie asked.

"The why isn't important," Cynthia said. "Right now, we need to focus on how to help your father recover and get him back on his feet."

"And those pills you found in my nightstand?" Grant said. "I took them from my patient."

"You did what?" Cynthia said. "You stole pills from your office?"

Up until now, Sadie had gotten the sense her parents were a united front, that they both knew the whole story and were working together to clear the air, but clearly there were some things her mother didn't even know.

"I didn't steal them exactly," he said. "I collected them. To get pills without a prescription."

"Charming," Cynthia muttered before sighing and rubbing her face with her fingers. "Is there anything else you've refrained from telling me?" she asked quietly. "At this point, we might as well get it all out in the open so we can start picking up the pieces."

Her father rested his head back on his hands. When his shoulders started shaking, it took Sadie a minute to realize what was happening. He wasn't making any noise, but he was definitely crying. She couldn't remember having ever seen her father break down like this before, and it made her scared: scared for Alison, scared for her mother, but most of all, scared for him. He wouldn't be the same person without his scalpel, and his patients, and his annual listing in *Boston Magazine*.

He took a napkin from the holder on the table and blew his nose. "I really messed up. It's all my fault."

Cynthia said nothing but raised her eyebrows, before reaching out to rub his arm.

"It's okay, Dad," Sadie said. "What's the next step?"

"The hospital won't let me return until I get treatment," he said.

"And we think inpatient rehab will help your father get better as soon as possible," her mom added, still rubbing her dad's arm. Sadie realized that she hadn't seen her parents this close in months and she couldn't remember the last time she'd seen them touch each other. It was gross, but she couldn't help feeling a little bit hopeful, too.

"I check myself in on Friday."

"How long will you be gone?" Sadie asked, her spirits plunging again.

"It's thirty-day program," Grant said. "Up in Maine."

"A perfect chance to clear your head and get everything straightened out," said Cynthia.

"Wow," Sadie said. Even though Sadie hadn't spent much time with her father lately, she couldn't imagine being away from him for a month. She was so used to hearing his deep voice on the phone, his heavy footsteps on the stairs, the whir of the blender before dawn. What would she and her mom talk about for so many days together? She guessed she'd find out, whether she liked it or not.

CHAPTER FORTY-TWO

Grant

April 15, 2019

IT WAS HIS TENTH DAY OF REHAB at Arden Cottage and Grant was just beginning to feel vaguely human. Tapering off Oxy had been no joke. It had started with sharp abdominal pains, like someone was stabbing him in the intestines with a scalpel, followed by constant nausea and profuse watery diarrhea. He still had a constantly runny nose, ever present low-grade headache and fine tremors in his hands, but the other symptoms were finally starting to subside, his body acclimating to functioning without pills.

Grant looked out the window at Penobscot bay, the sun peeking over the horizon. Cynthia had surely paid extra for the view, but he didn't dare ask how much. The daily yoga classes, perfectly cooked organic meals, and attentive staff made the place feel more like Canyon Ranch than inpatient rehab. Every time Grant went into crow pose or took a bite of spring ramp and morel quiche, his mind immediately turned to finances. If he wasn't operating, he'd be taking a significant hit. His partners would surely float him a salary on leave, but nothing close to his normal take home pay. The next time he spoke with Cynthia, he'd have to remind her to curb the pedicures, massages, and unnecessary shopping.

"Good morning, Dr. Kaplan." His nurse entered the room. "Open, please."

Grant opened his mouth and she placed the Suboxone film under his tongue. At first it had seemed odd to substitute one addiction for another, but apparently, people who took meds had less chance of relapse than those who went cold turkey. It was the mainstay of treatment now, they'd said.

"Group therapy starts in five," she said on her way out.

Grant groaned. He hated group. Even on a good day, talking about feelings seemed like a complete waste of time. Doing it with a bunch of strangers while fighting symptoms of withdrawal was even worse, but it was a requirement of the program, so he'd have to show up. The last thing he wanted to do was flunk out of rehab after failing in so many other unthinkable ways.

When Grant dragged himself to the dayroom, the staff was arranging the seats in a circle. The white linoleum floors and institutional windows screamed hospital, but a multicolored throw rug, a couch, and a few upholstered chairs warmed up the room a bit. Grant chose a seat and nodded to those who had already gathered. Finn, the social worker who led the group, sat in a straight-backed chair, a pile of folders in his lap, while Xander, a twenty-something graduate student in a black knit cap slouched on a loveseat, arms crossed over his chest. A few others straggled in and sat down.

"Welcome back," Finn said. "I know this isn't easy. The last thing you want to do is talk about your failures, but trust me, that's the best way to free yourself from your addiction and start your life over. If I got through it, so can you."

Finn talked about his own recovery at nearly every session. He seemed so put together—dressed in pressed khakis and a button-down shirt, his hair neatly parted to the side, stylish blue plastic glasses perched on his nose—it was hard to believe he'd once battled addiction, too. Then again, Grant had been fooling people for years, getting dressed for work, seeing patients in the office, and performing hundreds of successful surgeries without raising suspicion. Addiction could be incredibly sneaky, an evil-eyed monster hiding in the most unsuspected of places.

"We had a good discussion yesterday on the topic of isolation," Finn said. "No matter how isolated you feel through the process of recovery, you are never alone. Not only do you have all of the wonderful staff at this facility, you also have each other."

Grant looked around the room, avoiding eye contact. He couldn't imagine leaning on Xander, the go-to source for prescription pills at Boston University, or sharing his secrets with Tori, a housewife from Wellesley; Kevin, a plumber who'd become addicted after knee surgery, certainly wasn't the kind of guy Grant would confide in.

"Today, we're going to discuss another feeling that often arises in the recovery setting. Shame. It's a common emotion during this time and it's nothing to be ashamed of." Finn smiled. "Let's start with a show of hands, and don't be shy. Who has felt shame about their addiction?"

Tori slowly raised her hand to waist height. No one else dared.

"Tori, thank you for your honesty. Can you elaborate on that thought?"

"I guess." Tori put her hand down and gathered her blond hair over one shoulder. A several-carat diamond ring projected dots of sunlight onto the wall, making it hard for Grant to focus on what she was saying. "I mean, I've always felt like I needed to be perfect, have a spotless home, the newest car, the most accomplished children. All that pressure got to me. If anyone knew I was using pills to keep me going, I'd be mortified."

"A common feeling for sure. And for everyone else, if you can't be honest in this room, then you're making recovery even more difficult than it needs to be." Finn looked around for his next volunteer, nodding at Kevin to go ahead.

"I don't know." Kevin adjusted his Patriots cap. "I'm not the first one in my family to deal with addiction, but somehow it seems worse. All the rest were run of the mill drunks: my pop, my grandfather, my uncle. Always sauced. It's almost like I'm rejecting the tried-and-true Donnelly tradition. Like I couldn't even get my addiction right." Listening to Kevin's Boston accent made Grant think about patients he'd cared for over the years, blue collar types from Charlestown or Jamaica Plain who were always grateful for his surgical treatment. They would often send tokens of appreciation to the office: homemade shepherd's pies, boxes filled with Mike's connolis, or carrot cakes from Modern Pastry. He missed being in the operating room, the gnawing emptiness growing larger with each day away from the hospital.

Finn nodded. "Shame often centers around family in one way or another. That's an important point. Xander, how about you?"

"Can I take a pass?" Xander pulled his cap over his eyes.

"Let's not make it a habit, please." Finn flipped through the folders on his lap. "Grant, you've been quiet so far. What do you have to say about shame?"

"I'm not sure what to say." Grant squirmed in his seat, his head starting to pound. The chair, which had seemed so cushy a few moments ago, now felt firm and unforgiving.

"There are no right answers in group. It's about validating and accepting each other, no matter what feelings come to the surface."

"Alright ..." Sweat collected under the waistband of Grant's sweatpants. Shame was an emotion he could definitely identify with right now. He felt ashamed that he'd fallen prone to addiction, ashamed that he'd let the problem fester for so long, and most of all, ashamed that he'd disappointed his family, colleagues, and patients, but admitting those things out loud was a different story.

"It's okay to let it out, Grant." Finn said.

"Yeah, no judgment, man," said Kevin.

"Like we have grounds to judge," Tori placed her hand on his. Her hand felt cool and dry. She was probably disgusted by the dampness of his skin, but he felt comforted by her touch anyway, by the unexpected human connection. Tori was more made-up than Alison usually was, but her straight blond hair and clear eyes brought his sister-in-law to mind. He took a deep breath and looked around at the random people in the circle, all of them trying to make addiction a painful part of their past, and realized he had to make the most of this program. He had to give it his all, if not for himself, then for Cynthia and for Sadie, and most of all, for Alison. He owed it to Alison to beat this thing and come out the other side a better man. No more half-assing it.

"You can't make progress until you own up to how you're feeling," Finn said.

"Okay." Grant's right eye throbbed and watery snot dripped into his mouth. "This is really hard for me."

"You can do this, Grant," Tori said.

"Okay ... I'm ashamed. I admit it. I've let everyone down. More people than I can count." He took a ragged breath. "I'm not the man people think I am."

"Thank you for sharing, Grant," Finn said. "Shame is completely natural. It's real and raw and important to face. One you come to terms with your shame and allow others in, that's when the real work begins."

Finn passed a box of tissues around the circle. The room fell silent for a moment, pierced only by the sound of Grant blowing his nose. When Finn moved on to other topics, Grant was aware of voices, but he couldn't focus on words, much less their meaning. This was the first time he'd shared something real in group, the first time he'd made himself vulnerable, and he had to reclaim his dignity. Like a turtle flipped upside down, his soft underbelly had been exposed and he needed to retreat back into his shell to protect himself.

CHAPTER FORTY-THREE

Alison

November 18, 2019

ALISON DROVE PAST MINUTEMAN PARK and put on her turn signal at the sign for Walden Pond. Last week, Svetlana had given her the go ahead to start driving. Being behind the wheel again felt exhilarating. For her first drive, she'd gone less than a mile to Whole Foods, her heart racing and hands shaking, but now it felt more natural. She steered mostly with her left hand. Her right foot wasn't agile enough to switch between the pedals, so she made it work by keeping one foot on the gas and one on the brake.

After she parked, she grabbed her purse and cane. Her walking had been improving a little every day, but with sand and dirt paths, she'd need the cane to help her balance. Becca stood by the entrance to the trail leading to the beach, looking flawless in jeans and a fleece pullover. By the look on her face, Alison could tell Becca had no clue why they were here today. Since Nate's show a few days ago, they'd only talked on the phone once. Alison had needed time to process everything that had happened there.

When Becca leaned in for a kiss hello, Alison turned her head, offering her cheek.

"Nice day for a drive," Becca said.

"So nice," Alison said.

On the trail to the beach, Alison led the way, her cane crunching in the fallen leaves. They were both quiet as they walked. Alison wondered if Becca had realized yet what she was about to say. The small beach was empty except for a woman walking her retriever by the water's edge. Alison sat on a bench at the tree line and patted the seat next to her.

"Now you're making me nervous," Becca said, taking a seat.

"I've been thinking a lot," Alison said. With Rhea gone, Alison had all the time in the world to think and reflect.

"Thinking is never healthy," Becca's chuckle was timid, not her usual tumbling laugh.

"I've made a decision," Alison said.

"About what?" Becca asked, her voice quivering.

"I'm going back to school."

"That's wonderful." Becca took her hand. "I thought you were ready, but I didn't want to push. When will you start?"

Becca's skin felt smooth, her nails painted a bright teal shade. "January, after break."

"So soon," Becca said. "That's wonderful. You were convinced you'd never teach again, and now look at you. I'm so happy for you."

"I'm still in shock. I never expected to be where I am now."

"You spoke with Priscilla? Bounced the idea off her?" Becca smiled at her use of Priscilla's favorite word.

"Yester ... yesterday." Priscilla had been true to her word, calling to discuss a plan for Alison to return to work. She'd been unsure at first, but the more Priscilla talked about modified schedules and adding another aide to her classroom, the more Alison warmed up to the idea. By the end of the call, they'd ironed out most of the details, except for one. Priscilla wouldn't give Alison a straight answer about Becca, about whether she would remain at school or be out of a job. "Priscilla said she'd call you," Alison said.

"Oh, I'll look forward to that," Becca said sarcastically. "So, I guess we may not be working together anymore."

"I'm not sure." Alison looked out at the now empty beach, the trees along the edge of the pond partly bare, crimson and yellow leaves scattered on the sand. As a cloud passed over the late afternoon sun, a chilly breeze came in off the water, lifting some of the leaves into the air. "I don't know how to say this," Alison said, her voice shaky.

Becca pulled her hand back, her eyes unsure. "What is it? Now you're making me nervous."

"I want to return with a clean slate." Alison's pulse quickened.

She was sure this was the right move, both for her and for Becca, but it didn't make this conversation any easier. "I need to be on my own now."

"Where did this come from?" Becca said, her eyes shiny with tears. "Everything is going so well."

"It's too much. With the divorce and my family and therapy—"

"But I can help you through all of that," Becca said. "That's what partners are supposed to do."

"There's more," Alison said. "After Nate's play, I felt weird. It's just too much."

"We can slow things down." A tear ran down Becca's cheek and dripped onto her jacket. "I know we can make this work."

"I'm not ready," Alison said. "I need to love myself again before I can give my heart to someone else."

"But we're so good together. There has to be a way."

"No," Alison said firmly. "For now, I need to be on my own."

Alison looked back out at the pond. An orange leaf tumbled in the breeze before coming to rest on the surface of the black water.

CHAPTER FORTY-FOUR

Grant

May 4, 2019

GRANT STRETCHED HIS LEGS onto the soft grass, the wood of the Adirondack chair firm against his back. A white sailboat glided across the bay, the sun glinting off the dark water. Thick-needled pines lined the rocky coast along the water's edge. Grant looked forward to the hour after lunch, a much needed respite from the busy schedule. Today, Cynthia and Sadie were slated to visit sometime before afternoon group, so his break would be cut short.

Grant saw Finn, his group leader, standing by the water on his cell phone. After he finished his call, Grant waved him over.

"Hey, Grant." Finn took a seat. "Ready to fly the coop? Monday's the day, right?"

"Are you saying I'm a chicken?" Grant smiled. Finn had grown on him. He was certainly one of the reasons Grant had come as far as he had.

"Never," Finn said. "You're one of the bravest people I know. You've been working really hard and it shows."

"Do you think I'm ready?"

"I do. But, when you're home, you'll certainly encounter triggers you don't have here."

"I'm starting to get nervous about that."

"Which strategies do you think you'll use?"

Grant reached into his pocket, palming the painted rock Sadie had sent in the mail. When Finn told them to find an object to serve as a touchstone, Grant knew it had to be connected to Sadie in some way. It was time to find his way back to her, to become a proper father again.

"Definitely visualization," Grant said, stroking his thumb over the stone. "When I get the urge, I'll picture myself in a relaxing place. Maybe right here, looking out at the water."

"Where doesn't matter, just as long as it centers you."

"Right." Grant couldn't believe the thirty-day program was nearly over. There had certainly been challenging moments—tough questions in group, intense sessions with his psychiatrist, sudden overwhelming urges—but overall, the month had gone by in a flash. "Also, I'm going to practice self-care." Before this month, Grant never would have imagined using this woo-hoo phrase, more apropos for Buddhists or yogis than for a world-class neurosurgeon.

"Exactly," Finn said. "And what does that mean for you?"

"Eating healthy, no more vending machine lunches. And avoiding the morning shakes for sure."

"Yes, that could definitely set you off."

"I've been thinking about a hobby, too," Grant said. "When you first suggested it, I pictured knitting or scrapbooking and that was a no-go. But how about fitness? Working out qualifies as both self-care and a hobby, right?"

"Leave it to a surgeon to prioritize efficiency." Finn smiled.

"There's something else I'm worried about," Grant said. "Something I didn't fully address in the program."

"I thought we really got into your motivations," Finn said. "We've done a lot of good work this month."

"Yes, but there's something I didn't share. I think I was afraid of opening a can of worms." Grant went on to tell Finn about Alison, about how he'd taken on her case against his better judgment, finishing with her surgery and the subsequent complications.

"Wow, that's a lot to deal with," Finn said.

"I know," Grant said. "And when I go home, I'll have to face up to what happened."

"You will," Finn said, "and I'm confident that you can."

"Seriously, thank you for everything, Finn. I couldn't have gotten through this without you."

Finn clapped Grant on the back. "You've got this."

"He's over here, Mom." Sadie's voice travelled across the manicured lawn. Sadie looked more mature every time he saw her, the shape of her face and set of her mouth that of an adult rather than a child. Grant's stomach rolled with shame as he thought back to the group discussion about that topic. His addiction had put so many people at risk, but endangering Sadie was one of his biggest regrets. He shuddered to think about the stolen pills and what else could have happened because of them. A father is supposed to protect his child and Grant had done the exact opposite.

When they reached him, Grant stood up to kiss Sadie's cheek and give Cynthia a hug. Finn introduced himself before going back to work.

"How was the drive up?" Grant asked, as they all sat down.

"Long," Cynthia said. "It's so easy to forget how far away this place is. It's a really a long state." Something looked different about Cynthia, too. Her haircut was shorter and it seemed like she'd lost a few pounds.

"We did listen to a good podcast," Sadie said. "It's about a psychiatrist who takes advantage of his patients, starts controlling their lives and shit."

The old Grant would have reprimanded her for her language, but he held back. He had to earn back her trust before she would respect his authority.

"It was disturbing," Cynthia said. "But it passed the time."

"How's your summer program going?" he asked. "Mom said you've signed up for some interesting courses."

"It's okay." Sadie turned her body to face the bay. "I'd rather be at camp." After the business with Piper and the pills, they hadn't felt comfortable sending her back to Camp Wanaka this summer. Sadie was still holding a grudge.

"We've been through this already," Cynthia said.

Sadie stood up and stormed to the water's edge. She picked up a handful of rocks and started pelting them into the water.

"This is what I'm dealing with. One minute we're listening to podcasts and the next she hates me." Cynthia rolled her eyes in Sadie's direction. "I think she's afraid you won't get better."

"I'm doing the best I can," Grant said.

"You're looking much healthier. I'm glad to see that. We should talk about plans." The sun slipped behind a cloud.

"I can't believe I'm coming home."

"About that ..." Cynthia paused, pushing her sunglasses up onto her head, "there's something you should know."

Grant didn't like the serious look on her face.

"I got a call from Vik. He wanted to visit you here, but I told him only immediate family was allowed."

"Okay ... I'm not sure I want to hear this."

"He said they're extending your suspension through November."

"Fuck them." Grant stood up and started pacing back and forth. He looked to see if Sadie heard him yelling, but she wasn't standing by the water anymore. "I'm busting my ass to get better and this is the thanks I get?"

"He said they're assigning you to the medical school. Something about teaching neuroanatomy. It sounded like a fair compromise to me."

"Oh yeah? Well it sounds like a crock of shit to me."

"We should look at the bright side." Cynthia reached out to touch his arm, but he pulled away. "Isn't that what they teach you here? Maybe you'll learn some new skills."

"Yeah, whatever."

"Also, I almost hate to bring this up, but I'm not sure coming home is the best idea."

"What are you saying?"

"It's better for you to be on your own, to focus on your recovery. And I could use the space to figure things out, too."

"Are you divorcing me?" Grant asked. "I can't believe this."

"No, nothing like that," Cynthia said. "It's just a break. I've signed a lease on a nice apartment in Newton Centre. Very close to home, so you can be near Sadie."

"You've got to be fucking kidding me," Grant said. "This is really the icing on the cake."

"It's not only about you," Cynthia said. "I've got a lot to sort through as well. Being apart will allow us to regroup."

"What's going on?" Sadie appeared behind them, three cans of soda in her hands. "You're kicking Dad out?" She narrowed her eyes at Cynthia.

"Don't worry. I'll be very close by." Grant sat down again. The last thing Grant wanted was to make Sadie more anxious than she already was about his recovery. As angry as he was at Cynthia, he needed to smooth things over for Sadie's sake. "We'll see each other every day."

"Why?" Sadie dropped into her chair, letting the soda cans fall to the ground. "Why does it have to be this way? I don't know how ..." Her voice trailed off as she began to cry.

"This isn't easy for any of us," Cynthia said, her eyes filling with tears, too. "But we'll figure it out as we go along."

Grant stood up and went over to sit on the arm of Sadie's chair. He pulled her towards him and stroked her soft hair with his hand. "It's going to be okay. Your mom and I will both be there for you."

Sadie wiped tears from under her eyes with her fingertips. "Did Mom tell you about her news?" she asked.

Grant hadn't even thought to ask Cynthia how she was doing. Looking at her again, he was now sure she'd lost weight, and she looked happier, more self-assured.

"You're not going to believe this." Cynthia said, a grin spreading across her face. "I got a job. I went on one of those legal job boards on a whim, and before I knew it, I got hired. It's all a bit surreal."

"I didn't know you wanted to work," Grant said. He wondered if she really wanted to go back or if she was doing it to cover for him. Another wave of shame washed over him at the thought of not being able to provide for his family.

"I didn't either, but I'm excited for the challenge."

"Lots of changes in the Kaplan household." Sadie picked up the sodas and handed one to each of them.

"Here's to good changes." Cynthia raised her soda in the air.

Grant cracked his open and took a generous gulp. He couldn't remember the last time he'd had a soda. It tasted surprisingly sweet and refreshing. Being punished with med student duty was annoying and demoralizing, but the board had thrown down the gauntlet and Grant had no choice but to accept. And Grant hadn't expected Cynthia to evict him from his own house. Living on his own was going to feel strange, but he'd do whatever it took to mend the rift in his family and earn his way back into the operating room.

CHAPTER FORTY-FIVE

Sadie

May 10, 2019

SADIE CARRIED HER LUNCH TRAY out to the courtyard, following Emma to a table. Nearly two months since the accident, Emma was off crutches and her right ankle was only slightly stiffer than the other. Sadie had been doing everything she could to rebuild their friendship. She went with Emma to physical therapy, brought her takeout food from The Grape Leaf and Jake's Falafel, and watched countless, sappy *Gilmore Girls* episodes. They still danced around certain topics—Sadie knew not to talk about skating practice, and Emma avoided getting on Sadie's case about Piper—but things were definitely moving in the right direction.

"This looks extra gross today." Emma pushed the Sloppy Joe meat around her plate.

"Mystery meat at its finest," Sadie said. "Only the best for the students of Newton North."

"I don't think I can do it." Emma dropped her fork.

Sadie gave up, too, opening her chocolate pudding cup instead. On the other side of the courtyard, Piper shared a table with Kylie Miller, her replacement sidekick, and some new girl whose name was Mia or Mara, Sadie thought.

"How's your dad doing?"

"Okay, I guess," Sadie said. "He's not living with us right now."

"What do you mean?"

"My mom got him an apartment. She said it's better for us to have some space or something like that."

"That must be weird."

"Yeah, but I guess I have to deal with it."

"Holy crap." Emma picked up her phone. "I forgot to show you something. You're not going to believe this."

"What? Newton North decides to revamp menu and serve edible food? Details at eleven—"

"You have to see this for yourself." Emma held up her phone. It was a newspaper headline someone had posted to Instagram.

NEWTON WOMAN, GENA MORRIS, SENTENCED TO 8 YEARS IN
PRISON FOR SECOND DEGREE ATTEMPTED MURDER

"Who's that?" Sadie asked. "Do you know her?"

"That's Piper's mom, dummy."

"Let me see that." Sadie grabbed Emma's phone and clicked on the link in the bio.

Gena Morris, 47, of Newton was sentenced on Tuesday May 7th in Newton Superior Court to eight years in federal prison for second degree attempted murder of her ex-husband, Timothy Morris. She will serve her time at the Northeast Correctional Center.

"No way," Sadie said. She couldn't believe she'd been so naive. "I'm so stupid. I fell for her act."

Sadie looked back over at Piper. She was holding court, probably feeding the other girls the same exact lies she'd told her. Enough was enough. Sadie wasn't going to be taken advantage of anymore. The chaotic events of the last several months played back through her mind, like a movie on fast forward: Emma working her butt off at physical therapy, Aunt Alison struggling with her disabilities, and her dad battling to overcome his addiction. If they could all be so brave and strong up against these incredible obstacles, then so could Sadie. Holding Emma's phone, she stood up and started walking toward Piper's table.

"Clearly, she's had it rough," Emma said, following a few steps behind. "Maybe now's not the time."

"It's long overdue. I should have done this a long time ago." Sadie's heart pounded in her chest as she reached Piper's table.

"Well, look who's here." Piper looked up. "I thought you were both done with me. You and Little Miss Perfect."

"I am." Sadie held the phone up so Piper could see the headline. "You lied to me. Our whole friendship was one big lie."

"Old news." Piper rolled her eyes at her new underlings. "Took you a while to catch on."

"You're right. It did, but now that I have, I'm through. I don't want your tickets or your charity and I certainly don't want to hear about your mother. I don't want anything to do with you."

"Boo-hoo," Piper said. "I'm devastated, can't you tell?"

"No matter what you have going on, you can't treat people like they don't matter." Sadie knew Piper couldn't care less what she thought about anything, but it still felt good to speak her mind. She may have made some bad choices, but she was still a good person and deserved to be treated with respect.

"That's fine," Piper said. "I have my real friends right here."

"They're welcome to you," Sadie said.

"Let's go," Emma whispered.

"Are you done?" Piper asked.

"Yes, completely." Sadie hooked her arm through Emma's and turned around. As they walked together back across the courtyard, she could feel everyone's eyes on her and it felt surprisingly exhilarating. Sadie held her head high, proud of herself for taking a stand and content to be walking arm in arm with her best friend.

CHAPTER FORTY-SIX

Grant

May 28, 2019

"THE PLACE WHERE THE MOTOR FIBERS cross over in the medulla is called the pyramidal decussation," Grant said, using the cursor to point to the cartoon drawing of the brain on the screen. In the illustration, the motor fibers were represented by a bright red line traveling from the frontal lobe down through the internal capsule, midbrain, and finally crossing over in the medulla. In the OR, the brain was all the same fleshy pink, the vital structures impossible to discern.

"Is this all clear?" Grant looked out at the sea of medical students. Though the students' questions were occasionally annoying, teaching hadn't been as bad as Grant had expected. Their enthusiasm reminded Grant why he'd chosen medicine and how crucial his career was to him. Being in his own apartment still felt odd, but he was getting used to it. He missed Cynthia more than he'd expected to, but he'd been picking Sadie up from school almost every day, to get in face time with her. The cravings were slowly lessening and the lectures gave him somewhere to be. Listening to hours of bullshit at daily NA meetings—drivel about triggers and higher powers and cultivating an atmosphere of recovery—was driving him insane and the weekly urine tests at employee health were a nuisance; but if these were the hoops he needed to jump through to prove himself, so be it.

A student raised her hand. "I don't understand why everything crosses sides," she said. "It doesn't make sense." Grant knew neuroanatomy wasn't easy to comprehend. The digestive system was simple plumbing, the esophagus leading to the duodenum to the jejunum, just a series of tubes through which the food passed, while the brain, a mass of soft flesh at first glance, was the most complex organ of all, millions of neurons crossing in every direction. A slight slip of the knife could cause irreversible damage. Grant supposed that's why it took seven years of neurosurgery residency to learn the dizzying anatomy inside and out.

"Why is philosophical," he answered. "I can only explain the how. Let's say a patient has a lesion in their left frontal or parietal lobe, a stroke or bleed, for example, the right side of the body will be affected. This is a very important point to remember." As Grant described this scenario, his thoughts turned to Alison. Her AVM had been located in an unfortunate spot, centered on the motor strip controlling the right side of her body. With such a difficult case, any other surgeon would likely have had the same outcome.

"And depending on the exact location of the lesion, other functions may also be affected. Like speech for example. These patients can develop both expressive and receptive aphasias."

"What's aphasia?" The same girl asked, this time without raising her hand. "We already had so many new words to learn, and now you're piling on even more." This girl was starting to get on Grant's nerves. If she stopped whining and started studying, maybe it would all make more sense.

"Aphasia is difficulty with speech," he said. "It can present as a problem with finding and forming words or as a problem with understanding them." When she'd first woken up, Alison had been nearly mute, her aphasia quite dense. Grant hoped she'd been able to regain at least some speech with intensive therapy. He was happy to learn she'd been transferred to Spaulding. They hired the best speech therapists in the business.

A student in the back raised his hand. "Can those patients recover or are the deficits permanent?" Now this class was becoming a free for all, veering off course from the topic at hand. Grant looked at his watch. With two minutes left, he decided to indulge their questions rather than trying to redirect.

"Yes, sometimes they can, if they get the best therapy available. But recovery can be unpredictable." Grant felt an unexpected hitch in his breath. Even with the best possible care, Alison may never make a full recovery. She would live the rest of her life re-minded of the damage he'd inflicted, the mistakes he'd made. No matter how many times he told himself he'd done a good job, that was just a lie he'd been telling himself, not the honest truth. When Alison had needed him most, when she'd literally put her life in his hands, he'd allowed his addiction to run the show.

"Are you okay, Dr. Kaplan?" the first girl asked.

Grant tuned back in to reality and look out at the auditorium, the students staring back at him with concern. "Yes," he said, tears starting to collect in his eyes. "Class dismissed."

While the students filed out of the lecture hall, chatting about anatomy lab and upcoming final exams, Grant turned away from the door, quickly wiping his face with his shirt. He slipped his laptop back in to its case and checked his pocket for Sadie's stone. Running his thumb over the smooth surface, Grant wondered what Alison was doing right now. He still couldn't bring himself to pay her a visit. He wasn't ready to witness her disabilities first hand, knowing they might have been prevented if he'd been at his best.

Grant waited for the students to clear the hall, then headed toward the garage, his head down. The last thing he wanted to do was make small talk.

"Dr. Kaplan?" A young woman fell in step beside him. "Do you have a minute?"

"Uh, not really," he said.

"Sorry to take you by surprise. Your office staff told me I could find you here."

"I'm not taking appointments right now," he said.

"No, nothing like that. I'm Julia Barker from the Newton Re-porter. I interviewed you last year for the meningioma article?"

"Oh, Julia, yes." Grant now remembered sitting with Julia on a bench in the hospital courtyard, her dark eyes sparkling with interest as Grant described new and improved ways to cut the brain apart and piece it back together. He wasn't in any mood to speak with her today. After almost losing his shit in front of the class, he needed to get to the gym and work out his frustrations.

"I was just on my way out," he said, picking up his pace. "This isn't a good time."

"Dr. Kaplan, at least hear me out. This is an important topic."

"And that would be?"

"Could we sit for a few minutes?" she asked. "I'd love to explain more."

Grant kept walking towards the main entrance. If he reached his car, he could make a clean getaway from Julia and her damn article. "I have someplace to be, so you'll have to walk and talk."

Julia tried to keep up, her heels clicking on the tile floor. "I'm writing a piece about your ongoing malpractice litigation. I would love to hear your take on the case."

"How did you—"

"I'm sorry. I can't reveal my sources." Though malpractice suits were in the public record, they weren't usually of major interest to the press. Grant wondered if Nancy Kovatch had slipped her some intel, or maybe it was the hospital pharmacist from the committee, the one who never talked. He didn't think Joel Hitchens would have snitched.

"I've already spoken to the victim," Julia said. "But I'd really like to get your side of the story."

"What did he say?" Grant's head pounded. He couldn't believe Jeff Stone would malign him to a reporter. "He knew full well about the risks of surgery." Grant stopped himself. Talking to a reporter about an open case would only get him into hot water.

"What did you tell him about the risks?" she asked.

"I'm sorry. I can't comment any further." As they walked through the lobby, the smell of espresso shot to his olfactory cortex. Grant saw Millie, the regular barista, back at her usual post. "I'm still focused on helping myself."

"There's nothing to be ashamed of," she said. "Everyone makes mistakes."

Julia's mention of shame brought Grant back to the group session with Finn at Arden Cottage. He recalled what Finn had said about shame being a natural reaction and how important it was to let others in, to make peace with the emotion in order to progress through recovery. Once this lawsuit was settled, he'd have to think about going public about his addiction. Maybe sharing the truth would help his family heal and let others know they weren't alone in their battle. He filed that thought away for the future.

"It's okay to admit you're not perfect," she insisted. As they neared the main entrance, Grant saw Vik and Cal descending the garage stairs together, both wearing scrubs and laughing about something. He stopped and turned around.

"I think we're done here. I can't discuss this case," Grant said firmly. "Why don't you take it up with legal." He pointed her to the blue elevator and took off in the other direction. He'd take a roundabout route to his car to avoid his friends. Grant owed them each a call, but he wasn't ready to face them yet. He needed to get his shit together, make sure his recovery had sticking power before he tried to making amends with anyone else.

CHAPTER FORTY-SEVEN

Grant

November 20, 2019

GRANT TURNED OFF THE BURNER and transferred the scrambled egg whites to his plate. Six months since rehab, Grant had been doing his best to eat healthy breakfasts instead of shakes, as Finn had suggested. Most days, he forced the tasteless food down his throat, but once in a while, he stopped at the Dunkin' Donuts drive-through and ordered a muffin the size of his head or two sausage and egg sandwiches. Six months since rehab, the cravings still nagged at him, but the Arden Cottage program had given him a foundation. Sometimes, it seemed quite sturdy; on other days, he wasn't sure it was strong enough to build upon. Finn had warned him there would be ups and downs, good days and bad, and he'd been right on target.

He poured himself a cup of coffee and sat down at the counter to eat before Sadie arrived. She had a day off from school and Cynthia needed to go to work. Even though Sadie would be doing homework most of the day, it would be nice to spend some time with her.

There was a knock at his apartment door and Grant went to answer it. Cynthia was dressed for work in a navy cardigan and skirt. She had continued to lose weight, bidding the extra thirty pounds goodbye along with Grant's addiction. She'd found some sort of weight loss plan that actually worked, communing with other devotees online about fueling hacks and staying in fat burn, and speaking with her health coach once a week for encouragement and moral support.

At first, Grant hadn't been thrilled about moving out or about

287

her new job, but they'd finally settled into a new routine. The apartment was still sparse, but it allowed Grant the space he needed to acclimate back into his life free from pills and the distance to appreciate his wife again, to remember the Cynthia he'd fallen in love with.

"Good morning." Cynthia and Sadie stepped inside. "How are you?"

Sadie took off her jacket and hung it in the hall closet.

"Making it through another day," he said. "What's the plan?

"Sadie needs to finish her English term paper," Cynthia said. "If I left her home alone, she'd be on Netflix all day."

"Mooooommmm," Sadie rolled her eyes.

"Just make sure she buckles down and gets it done," Cynthia said. "I'll swing by after work."

"I might pop over to the gym, but otherwise I'm free all day." Since Grant had returned from rehab, he'd become a gym rat, consciously replacing his toxic addiction with a healthy one. To distract himself from cravings, he'd head over to the gym and do an obscene number of bench presses, cable rows, and hardcore sprint intervals on the treadmill until he shone with sweat. Even though he hadn't spoken to Alison since returning from rehab, the gym made him feel connected with her in some way, working out his form of atonement.

"I'm glad you're getting healthy," Cynthia said. "Don't forget couples therapy tomorrow at four."

"I'll be there," he said.

"Did Sadie tell you she's speaking at the Thanksgiving assembly?"

"That's amazing." Grant tousled Sadie's hair.

"Thanks, Dad. I'm going to go get started." She headed to her bedroom with her backpack slung on her shoulder.

Cynthia waited for Sadie to close the door. "You know, Alison called me last week. I think it's time." Her voice trembled.

"Time for what?" Grant's heart rate picked up.

"Time to apologize. This craziness has been going on long enough. She's struggling and we need to be there for her in whatever way we can."

"I thought she was doing well," Grant said. Cynthia had told him about their run-in at the craft store, and Grant had been happy to hear she was walking and able to say a few words. In his imagination, he'd pictured the worst, his sister-in-law completely mute and confined to a wheelchair for the rest of her life.

"I heard a rumor at tennis the other day that she and Michael are getting divorced," Cynthia said.

"I don't believe it." Grant said. After all they'd been through together, he couldn't imagine them splitting up.

"I have to find out what's going on," Cynthia said. "My sister might need us. We have to put aside our pride."

"I don't know," Grant said.

"Well, I do. Enough pretending we're on higher ground, because we're not."

"I'm not pretending anything, Cynthia. It takes every ounce of energy I have to ignore the call of the pills and stay clean. I've got nothing left for pretending."

"You're not the only one with problems," Cynthia said. "Did you every stop to consider that? I had to go back to work, Sadie went off the rails, and we've left Alison to fend for herself. Sometimes, you have to think about other people for once."

"You're acting like I hurt Alison on purpose. I tried my best to help her, I swear."

Cynthia's face softened. "I know that. But I think it's time you told her that, too. She needs to hear you say it."

"How do you know?"

"She's my sister," Cynthia said. "I know. I'm going to stop over there after I leave here."

Grant paused for a moment. He'd come so far in the past year, coming to terms with his addiction, making strides in his recovery, and accepting responsibility for his mistakes, but he wasn't sure he was ready to face Alison. It was an enormous step. Sometimes, his recovery felt tenuous, like a seesaw on the playground, even the slightest pressure on one side or the other causing the balance to tip.

"I know it's scary, Grant, but it's a step we need to take," she said. "A step *you* need to take."

"I'm not sure," he said.

"I might invite her for Thanksgiving," Cynthia said. "It isn't appropriate for you to be there, but maybe Sadie could spend the morning with you. Then you could drop her home in time for dinner."

Grant reached into his pocket for Sadie's stone, the coolness of it centering him and reminding him to stay on track.

❀

After the gym, Grant decided to stop at the hospital to see Vik. It was time to take Cynthia's cue and start making amends. He parked in the hospital garage and headed through the main doors. It was Vik's administrative day, so Grant knew he would find his friend at his desk. Vik reached for the phone receiver as Grant knocked on the door.

"Grant," Vik said, placing the phone back down.

"Is it a bad time?" Grant avoided his eyes. He felt guilty it had taken him so long to get here.

"I have a lot going on right now," Vik said.

"I can come back another time. I didn't mean to barge in."

"No." Vik stood up and started clearing a pile of binders and papers off his guest chair. "I have a few minutes."

"I don't want to bother you if you're in the middle of some-thing." Grant put his hand in his pocket, cupping his palm around Sadie's rock.

Vik stopped clearing and looked at Grant. "How about a walk? I could use a coffee."

"Yes," Grant said, "as long as I'm buying."

There was an awkward silence in the elevator and on the walk to the lobby. Vik had always been there for him, but this time, Grant may have asked too much, more than any friend ever should.

When they reached the kiosk, Vik stepped up to the counter. "Well, hello doctors." Millie said. "I haven't seen you two together in a long time."

"It's been a while," Vik said.

Millie told them to have a seat, that she would bring out their usual drinks in a few.

"Put it on my account, Millie," Grant said, following Vik to a table in the corner.

Vik used a napkin to scoot crumbs off the table. "So, to what do I owe the honor?"

"You're not going to make this easy for me, are you?" Grant said. "I guess I deserve that."

"Hold on a minute. You haven't made things easy for me," Vik said. "I've spent the last several months defending your honor, convincing people they should give you another shot. You put me in a tough spot."

"That's why you haven't called?"

"I've needed time to digest," Vik said. "Plus, Cynthia's been calling us with updates. There's no such thing as privacy between friends."

"About that." Grant said. "I haven't been a very good friend to you for a long time. I know it's taken me awhile, but I'm ready to change that."

"Whatever do you mean, Dr. Kaplan? That interviewing your best friend in the professional assistance committee was a bit awkward to say the least? That really sucked."

"It was horrible. I know."

Millie placed their coffees on the table.

"Why didn't you tell me?" Vik asked. "If you'd reached out, I could have helped you. We could have figured it out together."

"I'm stubborn, I guess. I thought I was okay."

"But you weren't." Vik took a sip of coffee. "Far from it. If you'd let me in, it could have turned out differently."

"I know that now," Grant said. "And I'm here to apologize."

"That's all you have to say?"

"I never meant to drag you into this," Grant said. "Now that I'm coming out the other side, I'm see how much pain I've caused everyone I love."

"That's all you've got?" Vik smiled.

"I bought you the fucking cappuccino," Grant smiled. "What else do you want from me?"

"Why don't we try my birthday dinner again? And this time, you're paying."

"Medical student purgatory isn't payment enough?"

Vik took out his phone. "Hey Siri, what's the most expensive restaurant in Boston?" He scrolled through the results. "Sorellina it is."

"Whatever you say, boss."

"Is the teaching gig that bad?" Vik asked. "I thought it might be a good way to ease back in."

"It's actually not bad at all, believe it or not. But I'm ready to go back. I miss using my hands to make people better. I need to get back to the operating room."

"The committee meets the week after Thanksgiving."

"I know." Grant sighed. "I may not have any patients after this whole fiasco and that stupid article only made matters worse. But I have to give it a shot."

"If we give you the go ahead, you'll be under supervision for at least a year. That's the way it usually plays out."

"I'll do whatever it takes to climb my way back. I'm not ready to give up my career."

"Maybe I'll put in a good word for you," Vik said.

"That means a lot."

"Are there any other stops on the apology tour?"

"It took me a while to work up to this one. You know this isn't easy for me."

"I know," Vik said. "How's Alison doing?"

Grant took a sip of coffee. He wasn't sure how to tell Vik he'd been avoiding Alison since he'd come back from rehab.

"You haven't seen her?" Vik asked, an incredulous look on his face.

"No," Grant said, "not since March. I haven't been able to face her."

"Wow, I think you've found your next stop."

CHAPTER FORTY-EIGHT

Alison

November 20, 2019

THE SOUND OF THE DOORBELL startled Alison. When she opened the door, she was surprised to see Cynthia on her doorstep, wearing a skirt and a long cloth coat with a belt. Now that she was standing in front of her, Alison was glad to see her, all of the bitterness and resentment she'd been harboring since their argument at the craft store melting away.

"I wasn't expecting you," Alison said. "Come in."

"I got your voicemail. It's so good to see you." Cynthia stepped inside and took off her coat. "It's been way too long."

"You look nice," Alison, said, indicating Cynthia's skirt and nude patent heels.

"Oh, thanks. I got a job, if you can believe it." Now that was a shocker. Alison hadn't thought Cynthia would ever return to the work force.

"Where?"

"Finkelstein and Berg. They had a good opening and I couldn't pass it up."

"Very nice."

"You're speaking so well," Cynthia said. "How did that happen?"

"When I told Michael I wanted a divorce, I made a huge leap forward. Go figure." Alison limped over to the couch.

"Robin Weintraub told me about you and Michael," Cynthia said, taking a seat in the chair across from Alison, "and Sadie did, too. I've been worried about you. How are you doing with the change?"

"Not so bad."

"Did he already move out?" Cynthia asked.

"Yes," Alison said. "He's staying at a hotel in Waltham."

"You've been all alone?"

Alison wasn't sure if Cynthia was asking about Rhea or digging for information. Maybe Robin Weintraub had also mentioned seeing her and Becca together at Starbucks. Neither of those things were her business, so she ignored the question. She missed Becca, but the more days passed, the more confident she was in her decision. Her life was complicated enough without being pressured to label herself.

"I've been meaning to call you," Cynthia said. "But I didn't know what to say. Your call came at the perfect time. I never thought we'd be here."

"Me neither." Alison wondered if they'd ever thought about calling each other at the same time, each sitting on their respective couches, receivers in hand, wondering whether there was any way to salvage their relationship. Maybe it was time to let go of their grudges, to stop being so stubborn. Yes, Cynthia should have recognized that her husband had a problem with pills and gotten him help earlier, but that didn't mean all the blame should rest on her shoulders. At this point, Alison wanted to figure out ways to repair relationships and move forward, rather than standing her ground and remaining estranged. "What made you come today?"

"Grant and I have been going to therapy. We should've started years go. Anyway, my homework assignment this week is to apologize. I'm supposed to brainstorm a list of the people I've hurt and try to make peace with each of them. You were the first person I thought of."

"I'm flattered, I guess."

"I should have seen what was going on with Grant. He'd been spiraling for a while and I chose to ignore it." Alison recalled the conversation she'd had with Sadie about the importance of forgiveness. Cynthia was doing her best to meet her halfway, so it was up to Alison to bridge the distance.

"You aren't your husband's keeper," Alison said.

"I know, but I was sort of his accomplice. I enabled him to

keep taking the pills which led to what happened to you. With Thanksgiving next week, I've been thinking about how thankful I am to have a sister like you. Our relationship isn't perfect, but I love you and I always will."

Alison raised her eyebrows. "I feel like we're in a Hallmark movie." This didn't seem like the Cynthia she knew. Alison had never expected Cynthia to make their relationship a priority, to own up to her mistakes and try to make amends.

Cynthia smiled. "And there's one more thing."

"I can't imagine what."

"I'd like to invite you to join us for Thanksgiving dinner," Cynthia said. "I think it would do us all some good."

"Are you serious?" Alison couldn't picture herself showing up to Thanksgiving dinner alone. "Will Grant be there?"

"You know he moved out?"

Alison nodded.

"I figured as much." Cynthia sighed. "No, he's not invited. Sadie will be with him earlier and then he'll bring her home."

"Okay." Alison hesitated. "I'm ... not sure."

"Our table won't feel complete without you."

"Are you making the sweet potato casserole with the marsh-mallows on top?"

"Just like always."

"The green beans with the crunchy fried onions?"

"Of course." Cynthia's face filled with hope.

Alison took a deep breath and forced herself to smile. "Then I wouldn't miss it." This wasn't going to be easy, but Alison knew she had to say yes. If there was any chance of salvaging their relationship, they needed to start somewhere. Cynthia had strayed way out of her comfort zone, so the least Alison could do was accept her invitation.

CHAPTER FORTY-NINE

Grant

November 28, 2019

GRANT WHISKED THE EGGS and added the milk, sugar, and a splash of vanilla. If he couldn't make Thanksgiving dinner this year, he was going to prepare the greatest brunch his daughter had ever tasted, make the best of the situation. It felt good to have a few days off from work. The medical students were home for the holiday and Grant was waiting for the committee to decide his fate. He knew it was a long shot, but he couldn't give up hope. If they reinstated his privileges next week, he'd do everything in his power to prove them right.

"Can I help with anything?" Sadie came into the kitchen wearing a green wrap dress and ankle boots. She was clearly excited to be seeing her aunt later today. Grant's emotions were more mixed, mostly anxiety about what he would say and how she would react to him, sprinkled with a bit of relief to finally be putting the dreaded reunion behind him. Just because Alison had accepted Cynthia's invitation didn't mean she would see clear to forgive him. Plenty of people, including several members of the professional assistance committee, considered what he'd done unforgivable. He prayed Alison wasn't one of them.

"Sure." He slid her the bowl. "Why don't you pour the eggs into the casserole?"

Grant watched as the yellow liquid spilled over the cubed bread pieces, filling in the spaces in the casserole dish.

"What else?" Sadie asked.

"A little sprinkle on top." He handed her a spoon. "How about you do the sugar and I'll do the cinnamon? But hurry up, or we'll miss the beginning of the parade."

Once the casserole was in the oven, they settled in on the couch. It wasn't nearly as comfortable as his sectional at home and Cynthia wasn't sitting on his other side, but this would have to be enough, for now.

On the screen, Tom Turkey rolled down Fifth Avenue, a prim Pilgrim couple sitting on his back.

"His eyes are creepy," Sadie said. Grant knew she hated this float, but he found the mascot comforting, like no matter how things changed, some would always stay the same.

"Gobble, gobble," Grant teased, tickling Sadie's side. "Tom's out to get you."

"Daaaad," Sadie protested, before leaning into him.

Grant put his arm around her and kissed the top of her head. A balloon floated across the screen, an enormous Snoopy in a red astronaut suit and helmet.

"This is a new one," Sadie said with excitement.

"Do you remember when you were obsessed with 'Peanuts'?" Grant said. "We had to watch the Thanksgiving special every single year."

"With all of them sitting around the table together," Sadie said, her eyes glistening.

"Don't worry," he said, smoothing her hair with his hand. "I'm going to do everything in my power to make sure we're all together around the table again next year."

"Do you promise?" Sadie asked.

"I promise I'll do my absolute best."

The camera switched to Herald Square. Savannah Guthrie said, "And now Broadway star, Idina Menzel, with a jazzy rendition of the classic Christmas standard, Sleigh Ride."

The singer sang and danced in a fur-trimmed coat and cream-colored hat.

"I still love her," Sadie said.

"For a few years, you and Aunt Alison used to watch Frozen every time you visited her," Grant said. "Sometimes several times in a row."

"I know," Sadie said. "I never get sick of that movie. Are you excited to see her?"

"Yeah, of course." Grant tried to make his voice sound convincing. "You must be as well. You haven't seen her in forever."

"Forever," Sadie answered quickly.

His phone rang and he sat up to answer it.

"Hi, Cal," Grant said.

"Hey, bud. You're not going to believe this one."

"What's going on?" Grant could hear the hum of the OR in the background. "Why aren't you home basting the turkey?"

"Duty called. When Javier Peguero comes in with a ruptured MCA aneurysm, you leave the turkey on autopilot."

"Are you serious?" Grant couldn't help feeling jealous of Cal. In normal times, he would have been called to operate on the Red Sox center fielder, the go-to man for high profile cases, but with his trip to rehab and pending lawsuit, it would take him ages to climb back to the top of the list, if he ever made it there.

"As a heart attack," Cal said. "Coiled it up and the angiogram looks pristine. He should be ship-shape in time for spring training."

"Nice job," Grant said. "Now you can go home and dig in to some stuffing and turkey."

They were both quiet for a moment.

"You'll be back," Cal said. "You know that, right?"

"From your mouth to the committee's ears." Grant hoped he'd done enough to prove his commitment to recovery. There'd definitely been some ups and downs, but he felt confident he could go the distance. He hadn't missed an NA meeting in months.

"Happy Thanksgiving, bud."

"Seriously, Cal. You really saved my ass."

"I'd say anytime, but let's avoid a repeat performance."

"Agreed." Grant said, finishing the call.

"Who was that?" Sadie asked. "Is everything okay?"

"Just Cal, calling to wish us a happy holiday."

"Oh," she said. "The casserole is starting to smell good."

Grant had been so focused on the phone call, he hadn't noticed the aroma of warm cinnamon and sugar filling the apartment. "Sure is," he said. "Let's eat."

He took a bowl of fruit salad and a bottle of freshly squeezed orange juice out of the fridge and the maple syrup from the pantry. Using potholders, Sadie removed the casserole from the oven and they brought everything to the small kitchen table together. After Grant served them generous portions, they each tried a bite of the French toast casserole.

"It's delicious," Sadie said.

"Your sprinkle was the finishing touch. Wouldn't be the same without it."

They ate in silence for a few minutes.

"Do you want to know what I'm thankful for?" Grant asked.

"What, Dad?" Sadie said.

"I'm thankful for you. I know these past few months have been hard, but you've taken it all in stride. I couldn't ask for a better daughter."

Sadie looked up from her plate and raised her eyebrow.

"It's true," he said. "Can't I tell my daughter I love her once in a while?"

"I love you, too, Dad," Sadie said, pouring an extra turn of syrup onto her French toast.

CHAPTER FIFTY

Alison

November 28, 2019

AS ALISON TURNED ONTO LANGLEY ROAD and approached Grant and Cynthia's house, her hands started to tremble. She pulled into their driveway and put the car in park, taking a minute to gather her thoughts. It would have been so much easier if Becca had come with her tonight, to have someone in her corner. She wondered if she had flown home to Texas for the holiday.

When Alison looked up at the house, Cynthia pulled aside the curtains to peek through the window. The longer Alison stalled, the more awkward this whole thing would become.

She got out of the car and walked to the front door, using the railing to help her navigate the stairs.

When she reached the stoop, Cynthia propped open the front door to make it easier for Alison to make her way inside.

"I'm so glad you're here," Cynthia said.

The house smelled like roast turkey, onions, and sweet potatoes. The familiar aromas reminded Alison of all the Thanksgiving dinners they'd shared, making her realize how much she'd truly missed Cynthia, and Sadie, and even Grant. She wasn't sure if the gaping hole in her life would ever be filled, if their family would ever truly reconcile after all that had happened.

"It smells good," Alison said, unsure of what to say.

Cynthia led the way to the kitchen. "You know Grant usually makes the turkey, so we'll have to cross our fingers. I hope it cooks all the way through."

Alison thought back to all the years they'd celebrated the holiday together in this house, Grant manning both the oven and the stove simultaneously. Otherwise, he rarely cooked, but he laid claim on Thanksgiving. It was hard to believe Alison hadn't seen him since March. On one hand, she felt ready to look him in the eye and tell him how angry she was, but another part of her wanted to hear his side of the complicated story.

"I bought the ingredients for Dad's cranberry brie bites," Cynthia said, opening the fridge. "Are you up for it?"

"Okay," Alison said. The mention of the appetizer brought Alison back to their Thanksgiving celebrations as children, first with all four of them, and then how lonely the table felt once their mother was gone. "I like that idea."

Cynthia set up two cutting boards on the counter. She opened the package of Crescent rolls and handed Alison the triangle of brie. "A little nostalgia goes a long way, right?"

They worked for a few minutes. Cynthia fit small squares of dough into the mini muffin tins while Alison added small pieces of brie on top of each one. She had expected this holiday to feel strange, but Alison felt surprisingly comfortable standing side by side with her sister.

"I love these." Alison's mouth watered. "Really brings me back."

Cynthia handed her a teaspoon and took one for herself. "We'll do the garnish together."

They both spooned perfect dollops of cranberry sauce onto each appetizer. Once they added the final sprigs of rosemary, Cynthia slid the tray into the oven.

As Cynthia put the finishing touches on an apple crumb pie, the doorbell rang.

Sadie burst into the kitchen and threw her arms around Alison's neck, crying and hugging her with all her strength.

"I can't believe you're here," Sadie said between gasps.

"I know."

When Sadie finally let go, she wiped her eyes with the back of her hand.

Grant appeared behind her in the kitchen doorway. It felt surreal to see him walking towards her. Even after all this time, he still looked like the same old Grant.

"It's so good to see you," he said. His words were pleasant, but he looked like he might throw up. Maybe this situation was as nerve racking for him as it was for her. "I've missed you, Blondie."

"No." The nickname made her bristle. She wouldn't make it that easy for him to slip back into old patterns. "Not yet."

"Fair enough," he said. "Before I leave, there's something I need to say."

Cynthia whispered something to Sadie, then led her to the living room. Watching them go, Alison wished they wouldn't leave her alone with him. All of sudden, the kitchen felt stifling. She unwrapped her scarf and fanned her neck with her hand.

"This is really hard for me," Grant said. "I've rehearsed this conversation so many times in my head, but now that it's real, it feels different."

"Okay," she said, giving him room to speak.

"I'm just going to come out with it." He took a deep breath. "Until now, I've blamed everything on the pills, like it had nothing to do with me, but that's not the truth. It's a cop-out, an easy way out. It was me who made the mistakes. Me, Grant Kaplan, not the pills."

"Wow … I …" This was the man who took drugs before he cut open her brain and mucked around, the man who deserted her when she needed him most, the man responsible for this whole disaster. Alison had every right to hate him forever, and now he expected her to let him off the hook just like that? She wasn't sure what to say. She knew he was trying to mend their damaged relationship, to place them on the path to healing, but maybe they were damaged beyond repair.

"Wait a minute," he said. "I'm not done. If I don't finish what I need to say, I'll lose my nerve." He started to get choked up. Alison's gut instinct was to stop him so she wouldn't have to witness him squirming, but that would make it too easy for him. She'd waited a long time to hear the words he was trying to say. She deserved to hear every single one.

"Alison, I am truly sorry. I'm sorry I agreed to do your surgery. I'm sorry my performance was altered. And most of all, I'm sorry I haven't been there to help you recover."

"I don't know," Alison said. "It may take more time. I'm not sure I'm ready." She certainly wasn't about to forgive him outright, but she couldn't imagine severing their relationship forever. For now, maybe they'd all have to settle for something in between. If Becca were here, she would have helped her navigate this conversation. It wasn't easy, but being apart was the best thing for both of them. Becca deserved to find someone who truly loved her, and Alison needed to speak for herself and find her own way.

"This is a lot to take in," Grant said. "You don't need to say anything else."

"I'll think about it," Alison said.

Grant nodded and turned to the front door. "I understand. I'll see you tomorrow, Sadie," he called and closed the door behind him.

Through the window, Alison watched him walk down the front walkway, his shoulders hunched and head bowed. She waited until he got into his car and his taillights disappeared down the street.

Cynthia and Sadie joined her in the entryway. "You okay?" Cynthia asked.

"Yes," Alison said. "It's just a lot."

"I know," Cynthia said. "Let's try to forget about all that and just be together. You and Sadie can have a seat in the living room. I'll be there in a minute."

Alison sat down next to Sadie on the couch. She relished the feeling of Sadie's warm body next to hers. Being with family, however flawed or imperfect, made Alison aware of how lucky she was to be alive. She may always talk with a stutter and walk with a limp, but for the moment, she was content to be in the moment, breathing in the aromas of stuffing and apple pie.

Cynthia carried in the platter of cranberry brie bites and placed it on the coffee table. "Appetizers are served," she said.

"Yes," Alison said, taking Sadie's hand in hers. "Let's take this meal one step at a time."

THE END

ACKNOWLEDGMENTS

ONE MIGHT THINK that writing a novel would be easier the second time around. For me, that was true in some ways, and in others, not so much. By choosing to feature three points of view and a dual timeline, I certainly created a difficult challenge for myself. As I was editing, I swore I would never do either of these things again, but like the pain of childbirth, my difficult memories will surely fade with time, leaving behind only the joy of bringing something meaningful into the world.

Nancy Cleary and the entire staff of Wyatt-MacKenzie Publishing, I am so glad you fell in love with this story. I am thrilled to partner with you to deliver this book to readers. Ann-Marie Nieves and the staff of Get Red PR, thank you for lending your incredible talent to spread the word about my book.

There's a reason why people often say writing a novel takes a village. I couldn't have written this story without the support of the wonderful teachers and writers at the Westport Writers' Workshop. A special shout out goes to Chris Belden, Chris Friden and Loretto Leary. I know I will be both nurtured and challenged to step out of my comfort zone when I write alongside all of you. Sally Allen, my first instructor there, thank you for encouraging me to embark on this crazy journey in the first place.

Revisions are really hard. I would never have gotten through them without Michele Montgomery and all of the Women's Fiction Writers Association members at the daily write-ins and Amy Nathan and her early bird writing group. Thank you so much for encouraging me to keep going to get the story just right and Michele, I even had fun (most of the time). Allison Dickens, a talented editor is a wonder to behold. You helped me take a lump of clay and mold it into something special and for this, I am forever in your debt.

I am truly grateful to my early readers: Corey Dockswell, Michele Even, Joan Frimmer, Ivy Gosseen, Judith Marks-White, Jody Rudin, and Marisa Sosinsky. your reactions and comments helped shape this story. Naureen Attiullah, Barbara Stark-Nemon,

Lauren Cerullo, Leonard Cerullo, and Elizabeth Winter, your expertise in brain surgery, aphasia, addiction and disability helped me make the medical details accurate and believable.

One of the most rewarding things about my second career is the amazing friendships I've built with other writers around the country and even around the globe. I couldn't possibly list all of the authors who have generously helped me along the way. Special thanks to Sandra Block, Sarahlyn Bruck, Alisyn Camerota, Julie Clark, Maureen Joyce Connolly, Saumya Dave, Fiona Davis, Leah DeCesare, Camille Di Maio, Rea Frey, Galia Gichon, Emily Liebert, Stephanie Jimenez, Angie Kim, Lynda Cohen Loigman, Judith Marks-White, Kimmery Martin, Daniela Petrova, Nina Sankovitch, Susie Orman Schnall, Suanne Schafer, Meghan MacLean Weir, Molly Wizenberg, and Kitty Zeldis.

Authors would be nowhere without the bloggers and bookstagrammers who tirelessly post about books that have touched their hearts. Again, naming them all would be impossible, but I'd like to give credit to those who've been especially kind to me: Melissa Amster, Kristy Barrett, Jennifer Blankfein, Athena Kaye, Elizabeth Petrovich, Susan Peterson, Kayleigh Wilkes, and Linda Zagon. And last, but never least, Suzy Leopold: blogger, book tour organizer extraordinaire, and cherished friend. I hope our bookish adventures with KC Davis, Sheryl Kane and Nadine Tanen will resume someday soon.

Finally, the Frimmer clan deserves a standing ovation. Benjamin, Shea, and Ari, you have faith in me every step of the way, even when I'm having a hard time believing in myself. The three of you light up my life.

BOOK CLUB QUESTIONS

1. The story is told through three alternating perspectives of Alison, Grant and Sadie. What do you think about this choice? Does one character draw you in more than the others? How would this novel have been different if it were told only from Grant's or Alison's viewpoint?

2. How do you feel about the use of two different timelines for Alison and Grant? Does this add to the dramatic tension or detract from it?

3. What do you think about Grant's choice to perform Alison's surgery? What role do other characters play in this decision? How do the opinions of Alison, Michael, Cynthia and Sadie affect Grant's decision?

4. When asked about Grant taking on Alison as a patient, Cal says, "It's a tricky situation. He certainly could lose his objectivity if he chose to treat Alison. It's not looked upon favorably." Talk about the ethics of Grant's choice. Is there ever a time when treating a family member would be acceptable? If so, when?

5. How does Sadie's story add to the family drama? Why do you think she is given her own voice in the novel? How do you feel about Piper? Does the revelation about her mother explain the way she acts? Does it change the way you feel about her?

6. What role does Sadie's competitive ice skating play in her life? Is this physical challenge symbolic in some way?

7. What feelings did you have about Grant's addiction? Do you think his struggle is portrayed realistically? What do you imagine will happen to Grant after Thanksgiving?

8. Grant's group therapy session at rehab focuses on the topic of shame. The group leader says, "Shame is completely natural. It's real and raw and important to face. Once you come to terms with your shame and allow others in, that's when the real work

begins." How does Grant deal with his shame? And how does this apply to the other characters as well? Alison? Sadie? Cynthia?

9. What are your thoughts on Alison's infidelity? Do you feel differently about it because her affair is with a woman? How do Alison's surgery and her resulting disabilities change the way she looks at her marriage? Do you think she would have left Michael if she'd never had the surgery?

10. How do you feel about Michael? What do you imagine for his future?

11. How do you feel about Cynthia? How does she change over the course of the novel? Do you think she will give Grant another chance?

12. What role do some of the minor characters play in the story? How do these characters deepen the story? Vik? Cal? Rhea? Nate?

13. What did you learn while reading? Did you learn anything about prescription drug addiction, neurosurgery, aphasia or disability? Did reading this inspire you to read further about any of these topics?

14. Did you expect Alison and Becca to break up? How do you feel about Alison's choice to be on her own for a while? What does Alison's discomfort with labelling her sexuality say about her or about our society?

15. In many ways, this is a story about loss. What do each of the main characters lose and what steps do they take to heal from these losses?

16. The novel concludes at Thanksgiving dinner. What do you think about the symbolism of this setting? How do you feel about the ending? Is the ending too messy? Too neatly tied up?

17. If this novel were adapted for film or TV, who would you cast in the lead roles? Who do you picture as Grant, Allison, and Sadie?